J. D. ROBB

CELEBRITY IN DEATH

piatkus

PIATKUS

First published in the United States in 2011 by G.P. Putnam's Sons,
a division of Penguin Group (USA) Inc.
First published in Great Britain in 2012 by Piatkus
This paperback edition published in 2012 by Piatkus
Reprinted 2012 (twice)

A CIP catalogue record for this book
is available from the British Library.

ISBN 978-0-7499-5502-1

Typeset in Bembo by M Rules
Printed and bound by CPI Group (UK) Ltd, Croydon, CR0 4YY

Papers used by Piatkus are from well-managed forests
and other responsible sources.

MIX
Paper from
responsible sources
FSC® C104740

Piatkus Books
An imprint of
Little, Brown Book Group
100 Victoria Embankment
London EC4Y 0DY

An Hachette UK Company
www.hachette.co.uk

www.piatkus.co.uk

Have you read them all?

Go back to the beginning with the first three In Death novels.

For a full list of J.D. Robb titles, turn to the back of this book

Book One
NAKED IN DEATH

Introducing Lieutenant Eve Dallas and billionaire Roarke. When a Senator's granddaughter is found shot to death in her own bed, all the evidence points to Roarke – but Eve senses a set-up.

Book Two
GLORY IN DEATH

High-profile women are being murdered by a knife-wielding attacker. Roarke has a connection to all the victims, but Eve needs his help if she's going to track down the real killer.

Book Three
IMMORTAL IN DEATH

With a new 'immortality' drug about to hit the market, Eve and Roarke must stop a vicious and evil drug dealer and killer – before it's too late.

Head to the end of this book for an exclusive extract from the **NEW J.D. Robb** thriller,
DELUSION IN DEATH

From fame to infamy is a beaten road.

THOMAS FULLER

The lust for power, for dominating others,
inflames the heart more than any other passion.

TACITUS

1

With frustration and some regret, she studied murder. It lay in the quiet room on a sofa the color of good merlot, with heart blood staining a pale gray shirt beneath the silver bolt of a scalpel. Her eyes, flat and grim, tracked the body, the room, the tray of artfully arranged fruit and cheese on the low table.

'In close again.' Her voice, like her eyes, was all cop as she straightened her long, lean frame. 'He's lying down. He's deactivated the droid, leaving it and the house security programmed for DO NOT DISTURB. But he's lying here and he doesn't worry about somebody coming in, leaning over him. Tranqs maybe. We'll check the tox screen but I don't think so. He knew her. He didn't fear for his life when she came into the room.'

She stepped to the door. In the corridor outside the pretty blonde sat on the floor, head in her hands, with the sturdily built, newly minted detective smirking beside her.

And she stood, framed in the doorway with murder at her back.

'And cut! That's the money shot.'

At the director's signal, the area – dressed as the late

Wilford B. Icove Junior's home office – became a hive of sound and movement.

Lieutenant Eve Dallas, who'd once stood in that home office over a body that did not – as this one did – sit up and scratch his ass, felt the weird sense of déjà vu shatter.

'Is this iced or what?' Beside her, Peabody did a restrained little dance by lifting and lowering the heels of her pink cowboy boots. 'We're on an actual vid set watching ourselves. And we look good.'

'It's weird.'

And weirder yet, Eve thought, to watch herself – or a reasonable facsimile – coming toward her with a big, happy smile.

She didn't smile like that, did she? That would be yet another weird.

'Lieutenant Dallas. It's so great you made it on set. I've been dying to meet you.' The actress held out a hand.

Eve had seen Marlo Durn before, but as a sun-kissed blonde with dark green eyes. The short, choppy brown hair, the brown eyes, even the shallow dent in the chin that matched her own gave Eve a little bit of the wigs.

'And Detective Peabody.' Marlo passed the long leather coat she'd worn for the scene – a twin of the one Eve's husband had given her during the Icove investigation – to a wardrobe person.

'I'm a huge fan, Ms Durn. I've seen everything you've been in.'

'Marlo,' she told Peabody. 'We're partners, after all. Well,

2

what do you think?' She gestured at the set, and a twin of the wedding ring on Eve's finger flashed on Marlo's. 'Are we close?'

'It looks good,' Eve said. Like a freaking crime scene still with people tromping around.

'Roundtree – the director – wants authentic.' Marlo nodded toward the burly man hunched over a monitor. 'And what he wants, he gets. It's just one of the reasons he insisted we shoot everything in New York. I hope you've had time to look around, really get a sense of things. I wanted this part the minute I heard about the project, even before I read Nadine Furst's book. And you, both of you, lived it. Now I'm babbling.'

She let out a quick, easy laugh. 'Talk about a huge fan. I've steeped myself in all things Eve Dallas for months now. I even did a few ride-alongs with a couple of detectives when even Roundtree couldn't budge you or your commander to let me and K.T. ride with the two of you. And,' she continued before Eve could respond, 'having steeped myself, I completely understand why you put up the block.'

'Okay.'

'And babbling again. K.T.! Come over and meet the real Detective Peabody.'

The actress, deep in discussion with Roundtree, glanced over. Annoyance showed in her eyes before she put on what Eve assumed was her meet-the-public smile.

'What a treat.' K.T. shook hands, gave Peabody the once-over. 'You're letting your hair grow.'

'Yeah. Kind of. I just saw you in *Teardrop*. You were totally mag.'

'I'm going to steal Dallas for a few minutes.' Marlo hooked an arm through Eve's. 'Let's grab some coffee,' she said, drawing Eve out of the crime scene set and through the mock-up of the Icove home's second story. 'The producers arranged for me to have the brand you drink, and now I'm hooked. I asked my assistant to set us up in my trailer.'

'Aren't you working?'

'A lot of the work is waiting. I guess that's a similarity to police work.' Moving quickly in boots and rough trousers, her prop weapon – Eve assumed – in a shoulder harness, Marlo led the way through the studio, past sets, equipment, huddles of people.

Eve stopped at the reproduction of her own bullpen. Desks – cluttered – the case board that took her back to the previous fall, the cubes, the scuffed floor.

The only thing missing was the cops – and the smell of processed sugar, bad coffee, and sweat.

'Is it right?'

'Yeah – some bigger, I guess.'

'It won't look it on-screen. They reproduced your office, in the same layout, so they can shoot me or one of the others going through this area and in, or out. Would you like to see it?'

They walked through, past the false wall and an open area Eve assumed wouldn't show on-screen either, and into a near-perfect model of her office at Cop Central, right down to the narrow window. Though this one looked out on the studio instead of New York.

'They'll CGI in the view – buildings, air traffic,' Marlo said when Eve walked over to look out. 'I've already shot some scenes in here, and we did the conference room scene where you lay out the conspiracy – Icove, Unilab, Brookhollow Academy. That was intense. The dialogue was straight from the book, which we're told stuck very close to the actual record. Nadine did a brilliant job of merging the reality with a page-turning story line. Though I guess the reality was page-turning. I admire you so much.'

Surprised, mildly uncomfortable, Eve turned.

'What you do, every day,' Marlo continued, 'is so important. I'm good at my work. I'm damn good at it, and I feel strongly what I do is important. It's not uncovering-a-global-cloning-ring important, but without art, stories, and the people who bring those stories to life, the world would be a sadder, smaller place.'

'Sure it would.'

'When I started researching this part, I realized I've never had another role I wanted so much to do justice to. Not just because of the Oscar potential – though the shiny gold man would look great on my mantel – but because it's important. I know you only watched the one scene, but I hope if there was anything that didn't ring true, didn't feel right to you, you'll tell me.'

'It seemed right to me.' Eve shrugged. 'The thing is, it's strange, I guess a little disorienting, to watch somebody being

5

you, doing what you did, saying what you said. So since it felt strange and disorienting, it must be right.'

Marlo's smile exploded. And no, Eve thought, she absolutely did not smile that way.

'That's good then.'

'And this.' Eve did a turn around the office set. 'I feel like I need to sit down and knock out some paperwork.'

'Carmandy would be thrilled to hear that. She's the head set designer. Let's get that coffee. They'll need me back on set soon.'

Marlo gestured as they went out into the sun–blasted October of 2060. 'If we go this way, you'll see some of the Roarke/Dallas house set. It's spectacular. Preston, our AD, told you they were going to want some publicity shots while you and Peabody are on set? Valerie Xaviar, that's the publicist, is handling it. She's on top of everything.'

'It was mentioned.'

Marlo smiled again, gave Eve's arm a quick, light rub. 'I know it's not something you'd choose to do, but it'll be great publicity for the vid – and it'll make the cast and crew happy. You're going to make the dinner tonight, I hope. You and Roarke.'

'We're planning on it.' Couldn't get out of it, Eve thought.

Marlo let out a laugh, shot Eve a look. 'And you're wishing you had a hot case so you could skip it.'

'I guess you are good at your work.'

'It'll be more fun than you think. Which won't be hard, because you think it'll be torture.'

'Have you got my office wired?'

'No, but I like to think I'm wired into you.' Marlo tapped her temple. 'So I know you'll enjoy yourself a lot more than you think. And you'll love Julian. He's nailed Roarke – the accent, the body language, that indefinable sense of power and sex. Plus, he's gorgeous, funny, charming. I've loved working with him. Are you on an investigation now?'

'We just closed one a few days ago.'

'The Whitwood Center case, at least that's what the media calls it. As I said, I'm steeped. Still, even when you're not working something active, you're supervising other investigations, testifying in court, consulting with the officers and detectives in your division. It's a full plate. Dealing with—'

Marlo broke off when Eve's communicator signaled.

'Dallas.'

Dispatch, Dallas, Lieutenant Eve. See the officer at Twelve West Third. Possible homicide.

'Acknowledged. Dallas and Peabody, Detective Delia, en route.' She clicked off, signaled Peabody. 'We caught one. Meet me at the vehicle.'

Pocketing the communicator, she glanced at Marlo. 'Sorry.'

'No, of course. You caught a case, right when we're standing here. It's probably a stupid question, but how does it feel when you're contacted, told someone's dead?'

'Like it's time to go to work. Listen, thanks for showing me around.'

'There's so much more. Big Bang Productions basically built Dallas World here at Chelsea Piers. We'll be shooting for at least two more weeks – probably three. Maybe you can make it back.'

'Maybe. I've got to go. I'll see you tonight, work permitting.'

'Good luck.'

Eve wound her way around to the VIP lot and her vehicle. She wasn't happy somebody was dead – but if they were going to be dead anyway, she wasn't *un*happy to have picked up the case *before* the stupid photo shoot thing. She'd found Marlo Durn personable, maybe a little intense, but personable, smart, and not an asshole. But she had to admit it got to be a little unnerving to keep looking at somebody who looked so much like you. And to do it in surroundings that looked like your surroundings.

Dallas World.

Huh.

'Wouldn't you know we'd catch one.' Peabody hustled up. 'That was fun! And Preston – Preston Stykes, the assistant director – said I could do a cameo! They're going to be shooting some street scenes next weekend, and I get to be a pedestrian – with a closeup, and maybe even a line. I bet I get a zit.' She patted a hand around her face, checking. 'You always get a zit when you have a closeup.'

'Had many – closeups, not zits. I don't want to know about your zits.'

'It'll be my first.' She settled into the passenger seat while Eve got behind the wheel. 'And tonight we get to hob with the nob at dinner. I'm having dinner with vid stars, with celebrities, at the swank Park Avenue residence of the hottest director in Hollywood, meeting the most powerful and respected producer – and founder of Big Bang Productions.' Peabody stopped checking for potential zits to press her hand to her belly. 'I feel a little sick.'

'Then you can boot in the swank john of the hottest director in Hollywood.'

'He was looking for you, Roundtree. He was about to send a gofer to find you.'

'I was having the surreal experience of having myself show myself around my office and bullpen.'

'Oh! My desk. I could've sat at my desk. I could've sat at *your* desk.'

'No.'

'It's a vid set.'

'Even then, no.'

'Mean. The other you is nice. I can call her Marlo. The other me is kind of a bitch.'

'There you go. Typecasting.'

'Funny, ha ha. Really, she talked to me for about thirty seconds, then brushed me off. And do you know what she said?'

'How can I know when I wasn't there?'

'So, I'll tell you.' Scowling out the windshield, Peabody stuck on her rainbow-lensed sunshades. 'She said if Nadine's book was an accurate portrayal, she suggests I take an assertive course. Otherwise I'm never going to be anything but an underling, or a sidekick at best. But with my subservient attitude I'd never be in charge.'

Eve felt a claw of annoyance scrape down the back of her

neck. Her *partner* had been assertive enough to springboard the investigation and downfall of an organization of dirty cops.

'She isn't kind of a bitch. She's essentially *a* bitch. And you're not an underling.'

'That's right. I'm your partner, and okay, you're my lieutenant, but that doesn't make me some kiss-ass underling with a subservient attitude.'

'Following orders in the line isn't subservient, it's being a good cop. And you have a smart-ass attitude half the time.'

'Thanks. I didn't like me very much.'

'I don't like you a whole lot. Neither does the other me.'

'Now I'm confused.'

'Marlo and K.T. don't like each other much. It shows when the camera's not on them. Once the director called "Cut," they went separate ways, didn't speak or look at each other until Marlo called K.T. over to you.'

'I guess I had Hollywood stars in my eyes because I didn't notice. But you're right. It must be rough to work with somebody so closely, have to pretend you like and respect each other, and you really don't.'

'That's why they call it acting.'

'Still. Oh, and I think the other me has a bigger ass.'

'No question about it.'

'Really?'

'Peabody, I didn't actually look at her ass, and I rarely have occasion to look at yours. But I'm willing to say her ass is bigger if it makes you happy and we can stop talking about the Hollywood people.'

'Okay, but just one more thing. The other me is also a lying sack. She told me she had to go prep for her next scene, but when I cut across where the trailers are to get to the VIP lot, I saw her – and boy, I heard her. Banging on one of the trailer doors, yelling, "I know you're in there, you bastard, and open the fucking door." Like that.'

'Whose trailer?'

'I don't know, but she was pissed, and didn't care who heard because there was crew milling around.'

'It's like I've always said. You're a bitch with a nasty temper and no class.'

Peabody sighed, smiled. 'But not an underling.'

'With that settled,' Eve said as she pulled behind a black-and-white, 'maybe we can check out this DB.'

'A visit to a vid set, a DB, and dinner with celebrities. It's a really good day.'

Not for Cecil Silcock.

His day had ended early on the leopard-print tiles of his elaborate kitchen. He lay there, blood from the head wound running river to lake over the black-spotted gold. It made the floor look a little too much like a terminally wounded animal, in Eve's opinion.

Cecil was definitely terminally wounded. Blood also soaked into the tissue-thin white cashmere robe he'd put on sometime before his head had made contact with a blunt object of some weight, then the unfortunately patterned tiles. From the gash down his forehead, Eve figured Cecil also made contact with the edge of the gold-topped black cooking island.

The rest of the kitchen, the dining and living areas, master bedroom, guest bed and bath were as spotless, accessorized and *arranged* as an upscale home decor showroom.

'No sign of forced entry,' the officer on the door told Eve. 'We got the vic's spouse in the bedroom there. He says he was out of town the last two days, got home – early, wasn't supposed to come in until this afternoon – and found the body.'

'Where's his suitcase?'

'In the bedroom.'

'Let's get the security discs.'

'The spouse said the security was off when he arrived. He claims the vic often forgot to set it.'

'Find their security station, check anyway.' Eve tossed her Seal-It back in her field kit and crouched by the body. 'Let's confirm ID, get TOD, Peabody. He took a hard blow here, left side of the head, across the temple, eye socket. Something wide, heavy, and flat.'

'Vic is confirmed as Cecil Silcock, age fifty-six, of this address. Married to Paul Havertoe, four years. He's the owner/operator of Good Times – party planning company.'

'No more good times for him.' Sitting back on her heels, Eve looked around. 'No forced entry. And the place looks like it's been cleaned and fluffed by magic fairies. He's wearing a – bet it's platinum – wedding band with a big fat diamond. Robbery unlikely as a motive here. The jewelry, plus I can see plenty of easily carried top-scale electronics.'

'TOD ten-thirty-six. Dressed like this, no forced entry, he had to know the killer. He let the killer in, walked back here, maybe to make coffee or something. Whack, and Good Times Cecil is no more.'

'Could be just like that. Or could be, dressed like this, Cecil had company while his spouse was out of town, which out-of-towning we will confirm. Comes out to make a nice breakfast, company whacks him. Or spouse returns, realizes Cecil has not been a good boy, whacks him.'

The uniform came back in. 'The security's been off for twenty-eight hours, Lieutenant. We've got nothing for last night or this morning.'

'Okay. Start the knock-on-doors. Let's see if anyone saw anything.'

Fitting on microgoggles, Eve took a careful study of the body. 'Cecil's as clean as the house. Smells like lemons.' She leaned her face to the face of the dead, took another sniff. 'But there's a little coffee here, too. Had himself a shower and a cup before the whack. No visible defensive wounds or other trauma. Takes the hit, goes down, smacking the edge of the island here, then takes another hit, other temple, on the tiles. It's odd, isn't it?'

'It is?'

'Everything's so clean, so tidy.'

'The vic was neat?'

'Maybe. Probably.' Eve took off the goggles, stood. 'There's no AutoChef. What kind of place is this?' She poked in the fridge. 'Everything very fresh here, and also sparkly clean.' She began opening cupboards, drawers. 'Lots of pots, pans, gadgets, matching dishes, wineglasses, blah, blah.' She pulled out a large, heavy skillet. Wide and flat-bottomed. 'Got weight.'

'Oh, my gran's got one of those. Cast iron. She swears by it, came down from her gran.'

Eve studied the skillet, crouched again, goggles on, to study the wound on the side of Cecil's head. Pulling out another tool from the kit, she took a quick measure. Nodded.

'Betcha. Seal and tag for the sweepers. Let's see if there's any of Cecil on here. So, Cecil has company – or gets it – then they come in here, behind the cooking island. But there's no sign of cooking – and since there's no AutoChef like any other civilized kitchen in the known world, he'd have to use a pan, tools. And what about coffee?'

'That's an espresso-type machine there. You put the whole beans in, water, and it grinds and brews.'

'But it's clean and empty.'

'Maybe he didn't have time before the whack to prep.'

'Uh-uh. He's got a touch of coffee breath. He didn't just come in here with the killer, and get smacked with a heavy object. I'm betting the cast-iron deal is the murder weapon. If he got that out, where's the other stuff, whatever he was going to put in it to cook? If he's arguing with somebody, is he thinking about making breakfast? Why doesn't the killer leave the murder weapon out or take it with him? Instead he cleans it up, stores it – and in what appears to be its proper place.

'If you're getting breakfast, what's the first thing you do?'

14

'Get the coffee,' Peabody said.

'Everybody gets the coffee, and Cecil tells me he did just that. But there's no coffee made, no cup or mug.'

Lips pursed, eyes scanning, Peabody tried to see it as Eve did. 'Maybe he or they had already eaten, cleaned up. Then had the argument.'

'Could be, but if so, was this pan still out handy for the whack? Everything's put away all perfect, but this is within handy reach. Because this?' She lifted the now-sealed skillet. 'It's a weapon of opportunity. Get pissed, grab, whack. You wouldn't open the drawer, take it out of the stack, select the weapon, then whack.'

Peabody followed the dots. 'You think the spouse did it, then cleaned up, then called the cops.'

'I wonder how Havertoe got home. It's time to have a chat.'

Eve released the uniform sitting with Havertoe to join the canvass. Like the kitchen, the master bedroom could have stood as an ad for Stylish Urban Home. From the sleek silver posts and zebra-print spread – with its carefully arranged mound of black and white pillows – the mirror gleam of bureaus, the strange angled lines of the art to the sinuous vase holding a single, spiky red flower that looked to Eve's eye as if it might hide sharp, needle-thin teeth under its petals.

In the sitting area in front of the wide terrace doors, Paul Havertoe huddled on a silver-backed sofa with red cushions, and clutched a soggy handkerchief.

Eve judged him about twenty years his dead spouse's

junior. His smooth, handsome face carried a pale gold tan that showed off well against the luxurious sweep of his caramel-colored hair. He wore trim, pressed jeans and a spotless white shirt over a body that Eve assumed put in solid health-club time.

His eyes when they lifted to Eve's were the color of plums and puffy from weeping.

'I'm Lieutenant Dallas, and this is Detective Peabody. I'm very sorry for your loss, Mr Havertoe.'

'Cecil's dead.'

Under the rawness of the tears, Eve caught hints of molasses and magnolia.

'I know this is a difficult time, but we need to ask you some questions.'

'Because Cecil's dead.'

'Yes. We're recording this, Mr Havertoe, for your protection. And I'm going to read you your rights so you're clear on everything. Okay?'

'Do you have to?'

'It's better if I do. We'll make this as quick as we can. Is there anyone you'd like us to contact for you – a friend, family member – before we start?'

'I . . . I can't think.'

'Well, if you think of someone you want with you, we'll arrange it.' She sat across from him, read off the Revised Miranda. 'Do you understand your rights and obligations?'

'Yes.'

'Okay, good. You were out of town?'

'Chicago. A client. We're event creators. I got back this morning, and ...'

'You returned from Chicago this morning. At what time?'

'I think, about eleven. I wasn't due until four, but I was able to finish early. I wanted to surprise Cecil.'

'So you switched your flight and your car service?'

'Yes, yes, that's right. I was able to take an earlier shuttle, arrange an earlier pickup. To surprise Cecil.' Choking on a sob, he pressed the damp handkerchief to his face.

'You've had a terrible shock, I know. What car service was that, Mr Havertoe? Just for the record.'

'We always use Delux.'

'Okay. And when you got home,' Eve continued as Peabody stepped quietly out of the room, 'what happened?'

'I came in, and I brought my bag in here, but Cecil wasn't in the bedroom.'

'Should he have been home at that time of the day?'

'He was scheduled to work from home today. He has a client coming in this afternoon. I should contact them.' He looked blankly around the room with streaming eyes. 'I should—'

'We'll help you with that. What did you do next?'

'I ... I called out for him – um – the way you do. And I thought he must be in his office. It's off the kitchen, with a view of the courtyard, because he likes looking out at our little garden when he works. And I saw him on the floor. I saw him, and he was dead.'

'Did you touch anything? Anything in the kitchen?'

'I touched Cecil. I took his hand. He was dead.'

'Do you know anyone who'd want to hurt Cecil?'

'No. No. Everybody loves Cecil.' With some drama, he pressed the soggy handkerchief to his heart. 'I love Cecil.'

'Who do you suppose he'd let in, while he was wearing only his robe?'

'I ...' Havertoe struggled to firm his trembling lips. 'I think Cecil was having an affair. I think he'd been seeing someone.'

'Why do you think that?'

'He'd been late getting home a few times, and – there were signs.'

'Did you confront him about it?'

'He denied it.'

'You argued?'

'Every couple argues. We were happy. We made each other happy.'

'But he was having an affair.'

'A fling.' Havertoe dabbed at his eyes. 'It wouldn't last. Whoever he was seeing must have killed him.'

'Who do you think he was seeing?'

'I don't know. A client? Someone he met at one of our events? We meet so many people. There's a constant temptation to stray.'

'You have an impressive home, Mr Havertoe.'

'We're very proud of it. We often entertain. It's what we do. It's good promotion for the business.'

'I guess that's why you cleaned up the kitchen,' Eve said

conversationally as Peabody came back in. 'You didn't want people to see the mess.'

'I . . . what?'

'Was Cecil fixing breakfast when you got in – earlier than he expected? Or had he finished? Were there signs he hadn't been alone? Cheating on you when you were away. He was a very bad boy.'

'He's dead. You shouldn't talk about him that way.'

'What time did you get home again?'

'I said – I think – about eleven.'

'That's odd, Mr Havertoe,' Peabody said. 'Because your shuttle landed at eight-forty-five.'

'I – I had some errands—'

'And the driver from Delux dropped you off at the door here at nine-ten.'

'I . . . took a walk.'

'With your luggage?' Eve angled her head. 'No, you didn't. You came in at nine-ten, and you and Cecil got into it while you – one of you or both – made coffee, fixed breakfast. You wanted to know who he'd been with while you were in Chicago. You wanted him to stop cheating on you. You argued, and you picked up the cast-iron skillet, swung out. You were so mad. All you've done for him and he can't be faithful. Who could blame you for losing your temper. You didn't mean to kill him, did you, Paul? You just lashed out – hurt and angry.'

'I didn't. You have the time wrong. That's all.'

'No, you got it wrong. You got home early. Did you think you might catch him with someone?'

'No, no, it wasn't like that. I wanted to surprise him. I wanted things to be the way they were. I fixed him his favorite brunch! Mandarin orange juice mimosas and hazelnut coffee, eggs Benedict with raspberry French toast.'

'You went to a lot of trouble.'

'Everything made by hand, and I set the table with his favorite china.'

'And he didn't appreciate it. All the time and effort you went to, just to do something special for him, and he didn't appreciate it.'

'I . . . then I went for a walk. I went for a walk, and when I came back he was dead.'

'No, Paul. You argued, you hit him. It was like a reflex. You were so mad, so hurt, you just grabbed the skillet and swung out. And then it was too late. So you cleaned up the kitchen, put everything away.' While he lay there, dead on the floor, Eve thought. 'You scrubbed the cast-iron skillet.' With his blood staining the bottom. 'You made everything neat and tidy again, just the way he liked it.'

'I didn't mean to do it! It was an accident.'

'Okay.'

'He said he wanted a divorce. I did everything for him. I took care of him. He said I was smothering him, and he was tired of me looking through his things, going through his schedule and calling him all the time. He was tired of it. Of me. I made him brunch, and he wanted a divorce.'

'Harsh,' Eve commented.

2

With Havertoe charged and booked, the reports filed, the case closed, Eve couldn't come up with a single excuse to ditch the dinner with the Hollywood types.

And she tried.

She poked her fingers in the active cases of her detectives, hoping to hook an angle that required her immediate and personal attention. When that failed she considered pulling out a cold case at random. But nobody would buy that as an emergency, especially with Peabody breathing down her neck.

'What are you wearing tonight?' Peabody demanded.

'I don't know. Something to cover nakedness.'

'Long or short?'

'Long or short what?'

'The outfit. Short, showing lots of leg. You've got all that leg so you can. Or long and sleek because you're skinny and can pull that off.'

Eve dawdled over a report Detective Baxter had turned in. Reading it three times was just being thorough. 'You're spending too much time thinking about my body.'

'Thoughts of your body haunt me night and day. But

really, Dallas, are you going sexy or restrained, elegant or snap?'

'Maybe the restrained sexy snappy elegant. Whatever the hell any of that is.' Taking her sweet time, Eve signed off on Baxter's report. 'And why the hell do you care what I wear?'

'Because I have two main choices for me, and once I know which direction you're going, I'll have a better handle on it. The one really shows the girls off, but if you're going restrained I don't think I should put the girls on display. So—'

Genuinely stumped, Eve swiveled in her chair. 'You actually think I'm going to help you decide if you should flaunt your tits at dinner?'

'Never mind. I'll ask Mavis.'

'Good. Now why are you and your famous girls in my office?'

'Because it's almost end of shift and you're trying to stall, looking for a reason you can legitimately skip the party.'

'I am so.'

Peabody opened her mouth, then laughed. 'Come on, Dallas, it'll be fun. Nadine will be there, and Mavis and Mira. How often do any of us get to party with celebs?'

'Hopefully this will be the last time. Take your girls and go home.'

'Really? We've still got ten till end of shift.'

And the odds of catching something hot in ten weren't good. 'Who's the boss?' Eve asked her.

'You are, sir. Thanks! See you tonight.'

With little choice once Peabody bolted, Eve signed off on another report. Since staring hard at her 'link didn't cause it to signal that a psycho had just wiped out all the tourists on Fifth Avenue, she gave up and shut it down for the day.

It was just one evening, she reminded herself on the way down to the garage. The food would probably be good, and Peabody was right, there'd be plenty of people there she knew. It wasn't as if she'd have to spend the whole time making small talk with strangers.

But it made her think about the Icoves, the father and son, the respected doctors who had played God in their underground lab. Creating human clones, she thought, dispatching those who weren't perfect, duplicating others. Educating them, training them, enslaving them.

Until they'd both been murdered by their own creations.

After this dinner, she reminded herself, she'd be done. Except she'd already been told she had to go to the New York premiere. But after *that* she'd be done with the whole celebrity thing. And finally she'd be done with the Icove case.

How many of them were out there? she wondered. The clones, the Icove creations? She thought of the little girl and the baby she'd let go – or Roarke had let go – of Avril Icove – the three Avril Icoves, all married to the younger Icove.

Had they read Nadine's book? Wherever they'd gone, were they paying attention to the never-quite-ending interest in how they'd come to be?

And she thought of what she and Roarke had left – no

choice with the facility about to blow – in tubes and hives in the underground lab. The set, the hype, the actress in the long, black coat fixed the lives that had been created in, and had ended in that nightmare facility front and center in her mind.

Yeah, she wanted to be done with the Icove case.

She drove through the gates, rolled her shoulders back. One evening, she reminded herself as she saw the glory of home.

Next time she had a full evening free, and if the weather stayed mild, she and Roarke would have dinner on one of the terraces. Do the whole wine and candlelight thing. Maybe walk around the estate in the starlight.

She'd never thought of doing those things before Roarke, never wanted them. But now there was Roarke, and there was home. And there was a want to cherish both whenever she could.

She parked at the front of the house where it spread, where it rose up in its fanciful towers and turrets. Maybe the party wouldn't last all that long. They could come home, take that walk in the starlight.

Absently she rubbed at the faint twinge in her arm as she got out of the car. The injuries she'd sustained in Dallas had healed – or close enough. But the memory of them ... yes, there was a want to cherish when she could.

As she expected, Summerset – the skinny – and the cat – the fat – waited in the foyer.

'I see you were unable to formulate an excuse to miss tonight's festivities.'

She didn't much care for Roarke's pain-in-her-ass major-domo knowing her that well. 'There's still time for murder. It could even be here and now.'

'There's a message from Trina for you on the house 'link.'

Eve froze on the steps. Freezing was a natural byproduct of blood running cold. 'If you let her into this house, there will be murder. Double homicide when I beat both of you to death with a brick.'

'She's occupied downtown assisting Mavis and Peabody, and will be unable to get here for your hair and makeup before the event. However,' he continued as relief trickled through panic, 'she's left detailed instructions for you.'

'I know how to get ready for some stupid dinner,' Eve muttered as she stomped upstairs. 'I don't need detailed instructions.'

In the bedroom, she stripped off her jacket, her weapon harness. And scowled at the house 'link. 'You think I don't know how to take a damn shower and slap on some face junk?' she demanded of the cat, who'd followed her up. 'I've done it before.'

More in the last couple years, she judged, than in most of the years before combined. But still.

But the cat stared at her with his bicolored eyes. She hissed, stomped to the 'link, and called up the message.

Just do what I tell you and you'll be good to go. I'll know if you screw this up, so don't. Now, start with a long, steamy shower and the pomegranate scrub.

As Trina's voice droned on and on, Eve sat on the side of

the bed. There were a zillion steps, she calculated. Nobody in their right mind took all those steps just to clean up for a party.

And who the hell would know whether or not she scrubbed with pomegranate?

Trina might, she thought.

Anyway, a long, steamy shower sounded fine. No problem.

By the time she'd finished the shower, the scrub, the body lotion, the face brightener, and the hair product that looked and felt a little too much like snot to suit her, she gave murder a more in-depth consideration.

She smeared stuff on her eyes, brushed stuff on her cheeks, smeared dye on her lips, and cursed whoever had invented facial enhancements.

Enough was enough, she decided, and walked back into the bedroom just as Roarke walked in.

How come he didn't need all the fuss and gunk to look so damn pretty? she wondered. Nothing Trina could come up with could improve on that face – that carved-by-benevolent-angels face, and the wickedly blue eyes, the perfectly etched mouth that smiled now as he saw her.

'There you are.'

'How can you tell it's me? I've got so much crap on my face I could be anybody under it.'

'Let's see.' He stepped over, laid his lips on hers. 'There you are,' he said again with that whisper of Ireland in his voice. 'My Eve.'

'I don't feel like your Eve, or mine either. Why can't I just go around with my regular face?'

'Darling, it's very much your face. Just partied up a bit. Sexy. And you smell the same.'

'It's pomegranate, and some other stuff Trina ordered me to use. Why do I let her push me around?'

'I can't say.' And wouldn't. 'How did it go at the studio?'

'It's weird, but Durn's okay. We didn't stay the whole time because we caught a case.'

'Oh?'

'Caught and closed.'

He grinned. 'And I feel I have to say I'm sorry it went so well. Why don't you tell me about Marlo Durn and the others while I shower?'

'You probably know some of them. You've bumped elbows, and more, with the Hollywood crowd.'

'Hmm' was his non-answer as he undressed. 'In any case I haven't bumped anything with Marlo Durn, which should be a relief to all of us as I've seen some of the media coverage of her. She could pass for your sister at this point.'

'I guess. And it's weird.' Hands in the pockets of her robe, she leaned against the door and watched his most excellent ass head for the shower. 'The one playing Peabody's a bitch.'

'Rumor has it,' he called out over the pulse of water. 'And also that there's no love lost between her and Durn. Should be an interesting evening.'

'Maybe they'll punch each other.' Eve felt her enthusiasm click up a notch at the idea. 'That would be fun.'

'We can only hope.'

'The sets are spooky,' she continued. 'All that was missing from the bullpen were crumbs on Jenkinson's desk. That and the smell, but it takes years of cop to get that smell.'

When he stepped out of the shower, wrapped a towel around his waist, she frowned. 'That's it? That's all you have to do? It's not right.'

'Some of it should be offset by the fact you're not required to shave your face.'

'I don't think that's enough.'

She stalked over to the closet, opened it. And scowled again.

'What am I supposed to wear? There are too many choices in here. If you've got one thing, you don't have to think about it. You just take it out, put it on. This is too complicated. Peabody hounded me about this until I wanted to pull her tongue out and wrap it around her neck. Between her and Trina my brain's fried.'

Amused, he walked over, stepped into the closet. 'This.' He lifted a dress off the rod.

Short, she noted, with a kind of drape to the skirt from where it was caught at the side of the waist with a flower of the same material and color as the dress. Not really blue, not really green, with a kind of shimmery overcast. She eyed it, the wide scoop of neck, the thumb-width straps.

'How do you know this one?'

'The little black dress is a classic for a reason, but often expected – especially in New York. So you'll go with color, rich color in a soft sheen. It's feminine without fuss, sexy without trying to be.'

She took it, turned it around, and lifted an eyebrow at the deep plunge in the back. 'Without trying.'

'Very hard. You have shoes to match.'

'I do?'

'You do, yes, and go with diamonds. Leave the color to the dress.'

'Which diamonds? Do you know how many you give me? Why do you do that?'

The aggrieved sound of her voice amused him nearly as much as giving her diamonds. 'It's a sickness. I'll get them for you once you're dressed.'

She said nothing, and stood where she was as he selected a dark suit from his forest of suits, a slate-colored shirt, and a stone-colored tie.

'How come you don't wear color?'

'The better to serve as the backdrop for my beautiful wife.'

She narrowed her eyes. 'You had that one ready.'

'The truth is always ready.'

She jabbed a finger at him. 'That one, too.'

'Such a cynic.' He gave her a pat on the ass as he passed. She could have found more to say, cynic-wise, but decided to save it. By the time she'd dressed, apologized in advance to her feet, and trapped them in the ice-pick heels, transferred her weapon and badge and communicator to one of the useless bags women were forced to carry to evening events, Roarke had the diamonds laid out.

'All of that?'

'All of that, yes,' he said firmly as he finished his tie.

'You could buy New Jersey for all of that.'

'I'd rather see them on my wife than buy New Jersey.'

'They'll see me from space,' she muttered as she plugged in the glittery drop earrings, clamped on the bracelet, the fancy wrist unit.

'No, not like that,' he said as she fought with the clasp on the triple-strand necklace. 'This way.' He adjusted the chains so they draped front and back.

She started to make a comment about shoulder-blade jewelry, but when she turned for a look had to admit it looked damned snappy.

'The evenings are cooling off.' He handed her a short, translucent coat. Over the dress it looked like a thin film of stars.

'Did I already have this?'

'You have it now.'

Her eyes shifted to his in the mirror. She had a smart-ass remark ready, but when he smiled at her, she thought, *Oh what the hell*.

'We look pretty good.'

With his hands on her shoulders, he pressed his cheek to hers. 'I think we'll do.'

'Let's go play Hollywood.'

It felt like a play, the set, the costumes, the lights. Mason Roundtree's primary residence might have been New LA, but he didn't stint on his New York pad.

The Park Avenue townhouse rose three stories and boasted a roof terrace with domed lap pool and garden. He'd gone minimalist contemporary in style with lots of glass, chrome, open space, and blond-toned wood. Here and there a pin light showcased some sinuous sculpture or jewel-toned ball. Art juggled between colorful splashes or dramatic black-and-white photographs.

Off the entryway with its single spear of silver light, the living area spread under high ceilings. A fire simmered low in a silver hearth.

'At last.' Blunt as a thumb in a black suit, Roundtree shot out a hand, gripped Eve's. He sported a goatee, a perfect triangle of blazing red, and a mass of wildly curling hair.

She thought he might look more at home felling a tree with an axe in some mountain forest rather than in a sleekly modern New York drawing room.

'You're a hard woman to wrangle, Lieutenant Dallas.'

'I guess.'

'I missed you on set today. I wanted some time.'

'It was murder.'

'So I heard.' His eyes blazed blue as he studied her face. 'Damn bad timing. I'm hoping you find some time to come down to the studio,' he said to Roarke with another fast grip and grin.

'I'll see what I can do.'

'Damn near wrapped. I don't want to jinx it but so far this project's been smooth as a baby's ass.' He had his sharp blue-bird eyes on Eve again, one hand tugging at his goatee.

'You've been the only wrinkle. Can't get you to consult, take meetings, do lunch, interviews.'

'It's still murder.'

'Ha!'

'Mason, you're hogging our centerpiece.' A curvy brunette wearing lipstick red with glinting sapphires glided up. 'I'm Connie Burkette, Mason's wife. Welcome.'

'I'm an admirer,' Roarke told her.

She purred. 'Nothing lovelier to hear from a gorgeous man. Let me return the compliment to you, and to you,' she said to Eve. 'Mason's been saturated with this project for nearly a year now. And when he's saturated, I get soaked. I feel like I already know both of you. So, champagne, wine? Something stronger?'

At the most subtle of signals one of the staff passing flutes of champagne sidled over.

'This is good. Thanks.' Eve took a glass.

'Your dress is fabulous. You wear Leonardo, don't you?'

'He's a little big for me.'

Connie laughed, an easy, throaty sound that went with her slumberous brown eyes. 'That he is. I loved meeting him and Mavis. She's a true and unique delight. And the baby! What a beauty. Now come along with me, see your old friends, your new ones.'

'Dallas!' Marlo, sleek in a sheath of dull bronze, rushed forward. 'I'm so glad you made it. Peabody said you'd already closed the case. Isn't that amazing?' she said to Connie. 'They caught a killer within hours.'

'It's not hard when the killer's a moron,' Eve commented.

'Aren't the two of you something?' Connie caught one of Eve's hands, one of Marlo's in turn, and made Eve wonder if everybody in Hollywood felt compelled to touch.

'I've known Marlo for years,' Connie continued, 'but seeing you both side by side is, well, surreal. There are differences, of course.' Angling her head, Connie looked them both up and down. 'Marlo's a bit shorter, and your eyes are longer in shape – and without the makeup Marlo lacks the little chin cleft – but at a quick glance, it's—'

'A little spooky,' Eve finished.

'It is.'

'Joel wanted me to have the cleft done surgically – the producer,' Marlo added.

'You're not kidding.'

'I'm not. Joel tends to go over the top. But it's what makes him the best.'

'I shaved my head for him for *Unreasonable Doubt*,' Connie said. 'But in that case he and Mason were right. And I have the Oscar to prove it.'

'It wasn't the shaved head that netted you the Oscar. It was brilliance.'

'See why I keep this beautiful young thing around?' Connie asked. 'Oh, that must be Charlotte Mira.'

Eve glanced back. 'Yeah. That's Doctor Mira and her husband, Dennis.' God, he was cute, Eve thought, in his spiffy suit and mismatched socks. She felt more relaxed just looking at him.

33

'I need to introduce myself. Take care of our star, Marlo.'

'You know I will. She's magnificent,' Marlo said when Connie walked toward the Miras. 'She's the classiest actor, and woman, I know. She and Roundtree have been married – first time for both – for over twenty-five years. That's a good run for anybody, but a miracle in our business, especially when both are in the business.'

Then she stared over Eve's shoulder, blinked. 'Oh my.'

'Ladies.'

'Roarke,' Eve said by way of introduction.

'It certainly is. They didn't get the eyes. Close, but not quite. Sorry. Julian and I have been working together for months now, and I've gotten used to thinking of him as you. But now here you are.'

'It's a pleasure to meet you. I admire your work.'

'You're here.' Peabody, girls rising proudly over a bodice of stars scattered on midnight, rushed over. 'We were getting the tour of the house, which is seriously uptown.'

'Peabody.' Roarke took a flute off a tray and offered it. 'You look delicious.'

'Oh my God,' Marlo said under her breath as Peabody flushed and beamed.

'Thanks. This is so exciting. We're having the best time.'

Beside her, Ian McNab grinned. His version of fancy dinner wear ran to a pumpkin-colored shirt, a lime green suit, and high-top skids that matched the shirt. His blond hair was pulled back from his thin, attractive face in a long tail, leaving the dangle of gold loops on his ear to glint in the light.

Eve started to speak when a man stepped to Peabody's other side. He wore his blond hair pulled back in a long tail, leaving his thin, attractive face unframed. His suit, shirt, tie were all the color of night fog, and fit his slim frame perfectly.

'McNab, that's what you'd look like – almost – if you dressed like an adult human.'

'Pretty tight, huh?' McNab said and chomped into the canapé he'd snagged from another tray.

'Matthew Zank, in the role of Detective Ian McNab.' He held out a hand to Eve. 'Sir.'

The quick charm made Eve smile. 'Dallas will do.'

'Hey, everybody!'

As Eve turned at the familiar voice, Mavis flashed a camera. 'Mag! I'm making an a-s-s of myself, but I want pictures.'

'The kid's not here,' Eve reminded her. 'You don't have to spell "*ass*".'

'Habit. Ass, ass, shit, fuck. God, that felt good. Anyhow, Leonardo's huddled with Andi about her dress for the premiere. Did you meet her yet?' Like McNab, Mavis snagged a canapé. 'Andrea Smythe aka Doctor Mira. She doesn't look so much like Mira tonight 'cause, wow, I've never seen Mira wear a black skin-suit, or heard her curse in Brit.'

'Andi's got the pottiest of potty mouths,' Marlo explained. 'Part of her charm, which she has in spades. Everybody adores Andi.'

'She makes Leonardo blush. It's so totally cute.' Mavis popped the canapé in her mouth.

'That's a Leonardo, isn't it?'

At Marlo's question, Eve looked blank.

'Yes,' Roarke answered for her.

'It's fabulous. I know from my research clothes aren't your thing, which is where we part ways. I love them. Clothes, shoes, bags, shoes, and more shoes. Just can't get enough.'

'We can never be friends,' Eve said solemnly, and made Marlo laugh.

'I'm not half the clotheshorse Julian is.'

'Something else he and Roarke have in common.' Eve glanced around. 'He's not here? I don't think I'd miss him.'

'Always late. He's bringing Nadine.'

'Really?'

'Who knows,' Marlo said with a shrug. 'K.T.'s not here yet either, so—'

'Both our stars. Valerie, get a picture. Joel Steinburger.' The tall, robust man with steely hair and hard black eyes pumped Eve's hand like a well handle, then turned, gripped her shoulder, bared his teeth at the woman with the camera. 'This is a pleasure, a pleasure.' Baring his teeth again, he hooked his free arm around Marlo's waist, pulled her in. 'How did you enjoy your visit to the set today – better late than never! Preston tells me Detective Peabody is going to do a cameo for us. Delighted. We'll get you in there, too.'

'No,' Eve said.

'It'll be fun. We'll see you get the full glamour treatment. Who doesn't want to be a vid star for a day?'

'Me.'

'We'll talk.' He winked at her, but those black eyes bored in. 'Valerie's handling the public relations and media for the project. The two of you have to set up lunch, discuss promotion.'

'No,' Eve repeated, glanced at the pretty woman with milk chocolate skin and tiger's eyes. 'Sorry, but I don't do lunch or promotion.'

'Valerie will handle everything, make it fun for you. Word is you don't have an agent or manager. Saves some time without the middlemen. We're going to need you for a couple of days for the extras for the home discs, but the cop look. No glamour there. The audience wants the real you.'

'Does the word *no* ring any bells?'

'Now, now, honey, no need to be shy. Valerie will walk you through it. And get those photo ops we missed on set today rescheduled. Asap.'

'Joel.' Smiling easily, Roarke put a hand on Steinburger's arm. 'Why don't we find somewhere to talk?'

'Roarke, of course. Another pleasure. The businessman,' he said with another wink at Eve, 'the husband. The helpmate.'

'Do you think he knows Roarke just saved his life?' Peabody wondered.

'Did he really call me *honey*? I think my ears deceive me.'

'Apologies, Lieutenant.' Valerie offered a coolly professional smile with the apology. 'Mr Steinburger's giving a hundred and ten percent to this project. He expects the same from everyone involved.'

'Where does he get the extra ten?'

Valerie's smile tensed at the corners. 'And promotion is part of the whole. If you find you have any time, any at all, please contact me. I promise I'll vet everything, and only make the best possible use of your time.'

'I wonder if she called him *"Mr Steinburger"* when they used to bang like hydrohammers in his Hollywood office,' Marlo murmured when Valerie walked away.

'No, she called him God,' Matthew said, 'as in, "Oh God, oh God, oh God yes!" I've heard her. Sadly, the office has been quiet since we got to New York.'

'Oh, they ended it months ago, before we left the Coast.'

'Got Publicity Chief on the project out of it. Sorry.' Matthew flashed that quick, charming smile at Eve again. 'We're shallow, overly obsessed about who's doing who.'

'Like high school,' Eve suggested.

He laughed. 'Afraid so. Plus gossip passes the time between takes.'

'Darling Eve!'

The Irish was a bit more ripe in the voice, and no, the eyes not as stunningly blue. But Julian Cross hit the gorgeous mark, and moved well.

In fact he moved straight to Eve, yanked her into a quick, hard kiss, with a hint of tongue.

'Hey!'

'I couldn't help it.' The not-quite-blue-enough eyes twinkled at her. 'I feel like we're close.'

'Think that again and they'll have to write a fat lip into your next scene.' She caught Roarke, eyes narrowed, across the room. 'And possibly a broken jaw.'

'Julian, behave.' Nadine Furst sent Eve a sympathetic eye roll as she latched firmly onto Julian's arm. 'Are we the last ones here?'

'K.T. hasn't showed up,' Marlo told her, and tipped her face up as Julian leaned over to kiss her. 'Julian, you haven't met Detectives Peabody and McNab.'

'Peabody!' With enthusiasm, he reached up, popped her right off her feet. She let out a kind of *woo* before he kissed her. Then she said, 'Um.'

'My girl,' McNab said.

'McNab!' Julian didn't pop McNab off his feet, but he did plant one on him.

Eve wondered if tongues were involved this time.

'Hollywood.' Matthew laughed, lifted his hands. 'We're a bunch of assholes.'

'Some of us more than others,' Marlo murmured as K.T. walked in and scowled at everyone.

3

Dinner turned out to be less formal and more freewheeling than Eve expected. She figured that was Connie's deal – the menu of plenty, the variety of wine, the spikes and rolls of conversation.

Since she was cornered between Roundtree and Julian, Eve noted the pattern of the seating arrangement plugged what she thought of as actual people beside or across from their true and fake connections. Peabody between Matthew and McNab, Dennis between Mira and Andrea Smythe – who had an appealingly dirty laugh she used often.

Roundtree, a man who obviously enjoyed his life and took his position at the helm as a matter of course, owned an endless supply of stories. She'd heard of most of the people he talked about, but wondered if she should have taken a who's-who-in-Hollywood primer before the evening.

'I read that you and Roarke met because he was a suspect in a murder.' Julian smiled at her in a way she imagined made a woman feel she had his entire focus and admiration.

Maybe it was even sincere.

'He was a person of interest.'

'It's romantic.'

'Most people don't find being a person of interest in a homicide investigation romantic.'

'A man would when the interest is coming from a beautiful investigator. He's a lucky man.'

'He's lucky he didn't do the murder,' Eve said and made Julian laugh.

'I'd say you both are.'

'You're right.' And she liked him better for saying it.

'How did you become a cop?'

'I graduated from the Police Academy.'

'But why?' He angled toward her, his mostly untouched glass of wine in his hand. 'And a murder cop – that's the term, right? Did you always want to be one?'

Well, hell, it did seem sincere. She eased off the sarcasm. 'As long as I can remember.'

'That was Marlo's take, and how she's playing you. With that intensity and drive, that cop-to-the-core attitude. I'm trying to bring the same sort of package to Roarke – a man of power, wealth, mystery. Marlo and I agreed, early on, that the two of you are the heart of the story. The center of it.'

'I'd say the Icoves were the center.'

'I think of them more as the guts of it. What was it Marlo said, the cancer in the belly. I think.' He shrugged. 'But your love story is the heart.'

'Our—' She found herself tongue-tied between horror and embarrassment.

'That shouldn't throw you.' Julian laid a hand over hers. 'Real love is beautiful. And . . . elusive, don't you think?'

'Julian has a romantic's soul.' Seated between Roundtree and Roarke across the table, Marlo sent Julian a twinkling smile. 'But he's not wrong.'

Julian twinkled right back at her, shifting that you're-my-world focus on a dime. 'Romance makes everything sweeter.'

'And you've got a serious sweet tooth,' Marlo countered.

'I do. The love story aspects of the script are my favorite scenes to play.'

'Oh God' was all Eve could manage.

'These two have the chemistry,' Roundtree commented. 'They're going to burn up the screens.'

'Oh God,' Eve repeated, and this time Roarke laughed.

'Steady, Lieutenant.'

'See how he says that.' Obviously delighted, Julian squeezed Eve's hand before he leaned forward, his gaze riveted on Roarke now. 'Lieutenant,' he repeated, giving the word Roarke inflection. 'It's loving and hot and intimate all at the same time.'

'It's my rank,' Eve muttered.

'He respects your rank. You respect her rank,' he said to Roarke, wound up now, 'as much as you love her.'

'Not quite,' Roarke corrected.

'No, you're right, you're right, but it's up there. And you *like* each other. And the trust. The two of you going down into that secret lab, risking your lives—'

'Oh for Christ's sake, give the ass-kissing a rest, Julian.' K.T. knocked back a slug of wine, then slapped her glass on the table. She actually snapped her fingers at one of the servers so he would deal with the refill. 'Even your mouth ought to be tired of puckering up by now.'

'We're having a conversation,' Julian began.

'Is that what you call it? You act like you and Marlo are the only ones in this goddamn vid, and the two people you're trying so hard to mimic are the only ones who count. It's insulting. So why don't you give it a fucking rest, set up your threesome with Marlo and Dallas on your own time? Some of us are trying to eat.'

In the beat of horrified silence, Eve studied K.T. down the length of the table. 'Peabody?'

'Yes, sir,' Peabody said, shoulders hunched.

'You know how I occasionally mention the possibility of kicking your ass?'

'I'd term that as regularly, but yes, sir, I do.'

'You may get the chance to watch me kick your fake ass while you sit comfortably on your own. That's an opportunity that doesn't come around every day.'

'You don't worry me.' K.T. sneered at her.

'I ought to. Anybody who shows their ass that big in public's just asking to have it kicked. But maybe it's better to just leave it hanging out there, all pink and shiny, while the grown-ups talk.'

'Well done,' Roarke said when Eve shifted back again, picked up her fork.

Julian grabbed his wineglass, drank deep as conversation circled the table in fits and starts. 'I'm sorry.' The instant the server topped off his glass, he drank deep again. 'I'm sorry,' he repeated. 'I wasn't—'

'It's okay, pal.' Eve tried more of the fancy lobster on her plate. 'If you had been, Roarke would have kicked your ass already.' She gave Roarke a grin across the table. 'Real love's beautiful, elusive, and mean as a snake.'

'I'll deal with her,' Roundtree said, and in a cool, flat tone that told Eve he meant it.

'No big. Actually, all this feels less weird now.'

'Can I ask you something?' Marlo leaned toward Eve, kept her voice low.

'Sure.'

'If you decide to kick instead of hang, can I watch, too?'

'The more the merrier.'

After dinner came a buffet of desserts, brandy, liqueurs, coffee, all set up with style in Roundtree's lower-level theater.

'Hell of a deal here,' Eve commented.

'It is, yes.'

She watched the way Roarke studied the massive screen, the arrangement of thick, cushioned leather chairs, cozy sofas, the lighting, the bar. 'I can see the wheels turning.'

'I've thought of doing one, but hadn't decided on design, layout, or location.'

'You just like the really big screen. It's a man and his dick thing.'

'It may be, and I do enjoy indulging mine.'

'Tell me about it.' Eve glanced around idly. 'So where do

you think Connie pulled K.T. off to, and how scalded will her pink, shiny ass be when she's done?'

'Somewhere private, and very. He was hitting on you, however.'

'Reflex, not targeted.'

'Agreed, which is why he lives.'

Nadine, who'd gone with the little black dress and a half dozen ropes of pearls, walked up to tap her brandy snifter to Eve's coffee cup. 'Roundtree promises us an entertaining screen show shortly, but I'm not sure it could live up to the little scene at dinner.'

'Fake Peabody is rude and a moron. I don't mind rude, but combined with moron makes me want to punch it in the face.'

'You wouldn't be the first, the last, or the only with that sentiment. Roundtree works with her because despite her rep for being difficult, she delivers. And I've seen some of the cuts. She's nailed Peabody.'

'How long did she and Julian do the nasty?'

'Caught that, did you? Once or twice, and some time ago. Julian's pretty, has a genuine sweetness, an innate charm. He does his job very well, and will do the nasty with anyone, anytime. He's a man-slut, but he's so affable about it.'

'Is this from personal experience?'

'Not so far, and not likely ever. It's tempting, but just strikes me as too predictable. And he was surprised, but good-natured about the no, thanks.'

Nadine scanned the room with its conversational groups and pockets. 'Joel's pushing a Durn/Cross affair in the publicity machine. It's classic and never hurts the numbers. Julian, being Julian, would be happy to oblige, plus I think he's talked himself into being in love with her. Part of his process. It really does come off on-screen.'

'Is this a vid about sex or murder?' Eve demanded.

'Both fuel the machine,' Roarke commented. 'It looks like our hostess has finished scolding her rude guest.'

'Fake Peabody doesn't look repentant,' Eve noted as the two women came into the theater. 'She just looks pissed. And adding fuel to that machine,' she added, when K.T. went straight to the bar.

Shrugging, Eve turned away, decided the woman had had enough of her attention.

For the next half hour there was more small talk and schmooze, more food and drink as people circled the room or went out, came in. Eve figured she'd just about hit her limit when Roundtree walked to the front of the room.

'Everybody grab a seat. Dallas and Roarke, right up front here. I've put together a short preview of *The Icove Agenda* for a private screening here tonight. I hope everyone, especially our special guests, enjoy the sampling.'

'Let's see how we do,' Roarke said, taking Eve's hand as Roundtree led them toward the front-row seats.

Eve leaned toward Roarke as people shuffled into seats and sofas behind them. 'Are we supposed to pretend we don't hate it if we do?'

'How do you see through those rose-colored glasses?'

He gave her hand a squeeze as the lights dimmed, and the music came up.

She'd give the music a nod, Eve decided. Strong, kind of pulsing and haunting at the same time. The instant she relaxed, Marlo's face – so like her own – filled the massive screen.

'Record on,' she said. 'Dallas, Lieutenant Eve.'

The camera panned down, drew back until it held on Marlo and the body in a high-backed desk chair.

'Victim is identified as Wilford B. Icove.'

When she started to crouch down, the body let out an explosive sneeze.

'Bless you,' Marlo said without missing a beat. She looked up as people off camera laughed. 'The vic appears to be allergic to death.'

It was silly, Eve thought, but helped her relax again. The screen rolled with gags, flubs, intense moments broken by screwups. Andi, as Mira, blew a line and laughed out a stream of bawdy and inventive curses. Marlo and the actress playing Nadine broke off in mid-dialogue to grab each other in a steamy kiss.

That bit of business got a round of applause from the audience.

Matthew tumbling out of his chair as the comp he worked on as McNab collapsed. Julian mangling a line, switching his accent to Brooklyn.

The audience in the theater responded with laughter, applause, catcalls.

'How do they get anything done if they screw up so much?' Eve wondered.

'That's why they call it "take two,"' Roarke told her.

It looked like plenty of take twos, and threes, and more to Eve. But everybody appeared to have a good time doing it – again and again.

The gag reel ended with the camera once again on Marlo, this time in the long black coat, weapon drawn, a breeze ruffling the short cap of hair. 'I'm a cop,' she said, eyes fixed and fierce. And when she flipped back the coat to holster her weapon, she missed, with the stunner bouncing on the ground at her feet.

'Aw, fuck. Not again.'

Roundtree ordered the lights on and stood grinning and stroking his goatee as the applause rolled.

'It wasn't an easy edit, with the amount of screwups I had to wade through.' He dropped down beside Eve, commanded her attention. 'You have to have some fun with it.'

'I'd say you did.'

'I'll add and edit more. This'll go on the home disc extras. People love seeing actors screw up, blow lines, fall on their asses.'

'I have to admit, I did.'

'We're going to have individual interviews with the main cast. I'm not going to push you – that's Joel's territory – but I want to add my bit here. It would enhance the home package considerably if you'd do an interview. Both of you, even better.

'I'm willing to stay in New York after we wrap if that's

what it takes, or to come back whenever you can work it in. Think about it. You lived this. I'm going to promise you we're doing it justice, and I don't break a promise. But you lived it. Everybody who sees this vid is going to want to hear what you have to say.'

'It's closed for me.'

'No, it's not.' He shook his head, and those bright blue eyes were razor-sharp. 'I've got that much about you. The Icoves were the villains of the piece; the Avrils and the others the victims. And still, victim murdered villain, and you had to pursue that. The victims who survived are out there. There won't be any more because of what you did, and that's important. Immensely. But while you ended it, you couldn't close it. So.' He gave her hand a rough pat. 'Think about it.'

'He's good,' Eve muttered when he pushed up and walked away to sit with Andi.

'And he's right about it not being closed.'

'When I agreed to cooperate – to a degree – with Nadine on the book I knew it would widen that crack. Part of me wanted to seal it shut, but you can't. The rest of me thinks it's good that people know who the real victims were – are – in this. How do I talk about that? It's not my job to decide guilt and innocence.'

'Not legally, no. But it's your job to know. And you do.'

Eve huffed out a breath, turned her head to meet Roarke's eyes. 'You're saying I should do it?'

'I'm saying if you decide to, and have control over what you say, how you say it, it may help you close that internal crack on this for you. It's not just the publicity from the book that's kept it in your mind, Eve. You think of it – of them. So do I.'

'Hell. I'll think about it. Can we get out of here yet?'

'I'd say we could start easing that way.'

Easing was right. Saying good night meant more conversations. She watched, with envy, Mavis and Leonardo escape – the baby as the excuse – even as she and Roarke got snagged again.

Eve calculated another solid twenty minutes before they finally made it to the main floor where Julian sprawled on one of the sofas in the living area.

'I was afraid of that.' Connie sighed. 'He was well on his way to a good drunk by the end of dinner.'

'He hit the wine pretty hard,' Eve confirmed.

'He was embarrassed by K.T. at dinner. Julian tends to drown embarrassment and upset. I'd apologize for her behavior again, but, well, she is what she is.'

'No problem,' Eve assured her.

'We can see that he gets home safely,' Roarke told her.

'Thanks.' Connie gave the sleeping Julian a look of motherly indulgence. 'But I think we'll just leave him there to sleep it off. No point dragging him out to his hotel. Just let me get your fabulous coat.'

'And the resemblance continues to diverge,' Eve said quietly. 'You can hold your liquor better, and I've yet to see you curl up hugging a pillow like it's a teddy bear.'

'And hopefully never will.'

'I absolutely love this,' Connie said as she came back carrying Eve's coat.

Just as Eve saw the first real glimmer of light at the end of the tunnel, Matthew Zank, dripping wet, came bolting out of the elevator. Marlo, pale as wax, stumbled out in his wake.

'On the roof. On the roof. It's K.T. It's – she's on the roof.'

'I think she's dead.' Marlo sat down on the floor, eyes fixed on Eve. 'She's dead. She's dead up there. You have to come.'

'Stay down here.' She rounded on Connie. 'Don't let anyone leave until I check this out.'

'I – no – it must be a mistake,' Connie began.

'Maybe. Just keep everybody here.'

With Roarke, she stepped into the elevator. 'Are you fucking kidding me?' was her first comment.

'Roof level,' Roarke ordered. 'Maybe she passed out drunk like Julian.'

'Let's hope, because it annoys the *shit* out of me to investigate a death at a dinner party where I'm a guest.'

'It doesn't happen often.'

'Once is plenty.'

They stepped out into a lounge – another fire simmering, low sofas plumped with pillows, a mirrored bar with an open bottle of wine sitting on it.

The glass doors to the roof terrace whispered open at their approach. When they stepped across the terrace, through another set of auto-doors, the scent of night and flowers filled the lap pool dome.

She felt a flutter of breeze, glanced up.

'Dome's open a little,' she noted, and wondered if it had been that way all evening.

Drenched, K.T. lay faceup beside the sparkling blue water of the lap pool. The staring eyes were Peabody-brown, and gave Eve a hard moment.

She crouched to check for a pulse. 'Shit. Not only dead, but going cold. He pulled her out. Or he pushed her in, drowned her, then pulled her out. Either way, he moved the damn body. Shit!'

'She looks too much like our girl at the moment.'

'But she's not. You'd better go get our girl, and a field kit if you've got one.'

'In the limo.'

'Good. Tell McNab to secure the house – nobody leaves – and to find out if there's any security running up here. Don't let anybody but Peabody come up.'

'All right.' He looked at the body a moment longer. 'A bad end to the evening.'

'It sure was for her.'

As Roarke went down, Eve took her communicator out of her stupid little purse and called in a suspicious death. Then fixed her recorder on the narrow strap of her party dress.

'Dallas, Lieutenant Eve, on record,' she began.

Broken glass, she noted, and a puddle of red wine, likely from the bottle open on the bar inside.

'The victim is visually ID'd as K.T. Harris.'

She filled in details for the record: the location, the reason for the victim's presence, the names – including her own and Roarke's – of the other people in attendance.

'Broken glass and spilled wine here. I observed an open bottle of wine inside the attached lounge.' She stepped to the side, noted a topless pedestal. 'Six herbal cigarette butts in this receptacle. The victim's purse is on the table here, opened.'

She crouched, careful not to touch until she could seal up. 'I see lip dye, a small black case, an undetermined amount of cash, and a key card. The victim is wearing the dress she had on all evening as well as the jewelry, the wrist unit. Her left shoe is in place, bunged up on the heel. I see the right one at the bottom of the pool.'

She turned, deliberately blocking the body when she heard Peabody come out.

'If you can't handle this, I need to know. It's understandable. It's acceptable.'

'I didn't drink that much. I was too nervous and excited. But I took a Sober-Up anyway.'

'That's not what I mean.'

Peabody moistened her lips, and the girls-on-display quivered a little. 'I can handle it.'

Saying nothing, Eve stepped aside.

'Oh . . . ' Peabody's eyes went wide, a little glassy. ''Kay. Maybe I need a minute.'

'Take what you need. Go inside, tag the bottle of wine on

the bar. Roarke's bringing up a field kit. We need to seal up before we get started. I called it in. We'll have some uniforms to secure the area.'

'Got it.' Peabody stepped back inside.

One scenario, Eve thought, as she studied the scene, the body: Harris comes up to smoke, drink, stew. Slips, thanks to drinking and the mile-high heels, takes a header into the pool and drowns. A simple, stupid accident.

Wouldn't that be nice?

'Could be an accident,' she said when Peabody came out again. 'Too much to drink, risky shoes, oops. The water's only about three feet deep. She goes in hard, hits her head.'

'She was knocking them back steady during dinner.'

'So, maybe an accident. Take a look around outside the pool dome, see if you can find anything that indicates she had company up here.'

'Okay, but I'm fine now.'

'Good.' She nodded as Roarke walked out with the field kit. 'Seal up, see what you can find.'

Eve opened the field kit. 'What's the temperature down below?' she asked Roarke.

'McNab's got it under control. He has everyone, including staff, in the living area. He said unless you wanted it otherwise, he'd shift the staff to the kitchen once the uniforms arrive.'

'That works. Vic is confirmed as K.T. Harris,' she said for the record when she pressed the woman's thumb to her print pad. 'Caucasian female, age twenty-seven – got a couple years on Peabody.'

'You're looking for differences.'

Eve shrugged. 'Being dead's a big difference. TOD twenty-three hundred.' She frowned at her wrist unit. 'That would be shortly after the screen show started, I think. People were going in and out before and after. We talked to Roundtree awhile right after, but I wasn't paying attention to the time.'

She closed her eyes a minute, took herself back. 'He put us up front. I don't remember seeing her after we sat down.'

'She was in the back. I noticed because I intended to avoid her, or see that you did.'

'Our backs were to the room. She could've left, come up here after it started. No blood visible.' She ran her sealed hands over the head. 'Feels like a knot back here, a small laceration.'

She reached in the kit for microgoggles just as McNab came out.

'Four uniforms reported, Lieutenant. I had them . . .'

He trailed off with every ounce of color leaking out of his face as his eyes tracked over the body. 'Jesus. Jesus.'

'She's older,' Eve said matter-of-factly. 'Her bottom lip is thinner, her eyes are rounder. Her feet are longer, narrower.'

'What?'

'The victim is K.T. Harris, twenty-seven, actress.'

'There are some glasses, napkins, on a table in a garden alcove,' Peabody began as she strode back. 'I tagged them for the sweepers.'

'Dee.' McNab grabbed her hand.

Peabody gave a little yelp. Eve figured he must have crushed bone against bone before he just pulled her against him, pressed his face to her hair.

'What the – oh. I know. It gave me a major jitter, too. I'm all good. See.' She gave his ass a quick squeeze – something Eve decided, given the circumstances, to ignore.

'McNab, status.' Eve pushed to her feet, and once again angled herself to block the body. 'Detective McNab, give me the status.'

'Sir.' He could have passed for a corpse himself under the moody blue lights.

'Eyes on me,' Eve snapped. 'Look at me when I'm talking to you. Report.'

'We took the staff – household and the outside catering team – into the kitchen. The rest are in the living area. Two uniforms on each group. They're asking a lot of questions. Except for Cross. He's still passed out, and I thought it best to just leave him that way until you advised otherwise.'

'Good enough. Go down, send one of the uniforms on the staff up here to secure this area. You replace him, and start getting names, contacts, and statements. How many have we got?'

'Three household staff on duty tonight, ten catering staff.'

'Okay. Peabody, give him a hand with that. What about security up here?'

'I asked Roundtree. They don't have cams up here. Security cams on the entrances, but nothing internal or here on the roof.'

'That's too bad. We'll want to review what they've got, eliminate any possibility of an intruder. Let's use the dining area for interviewing the owners and guests. Go ahead and get Matthew Zank in there – alone. I'm right behind you.'

Eve waited until they'd gone, with Peabody slipping her hand back in his. 'It's not going to turn out simple.'

'No?'

'It could be an accident. Except the shoe she's still wearing is scraped up on the back of the heel. And a slight bruise on her right cheekbone.'

'You think she was dragged in?'

'I think it's possible she was dragged, then rolled in. Or she could've scraped it up, bruised her face in a fall.'

'You don't think so,' Roarke observed.

'No, it looks like drag marks. It looks like her face bumped against the pool coping on a roll. But even if it was an accident, we've got a corpse that looks uncomfortably like one of the investigators, a houseful of Hollywood – along with a reporter – and a media machine that's going to eat it like gooey chocolate.'

'And the primary investigator is the star of the show.'

Eve shook her head, glanced back at the body. 'Right now I'd say she has top billing.'

Downstairs she asked Roarke to do a quick review of the

security discs, then walked into the living area. Everyone started talking at once.

'Stop. Sit. I'm not going to be able to answer any questions at this time, so don't waste your breath. I can confirm K.T. Harris is dead.'

'Oh God.' Connie put her hands over her face.

'Until the ME examines the body I can't give you any more than that. I'll be talking to each of you individually.'

Andrea held a shot glass. She tossed back the contents, eyed Eve with steady interest. 'We're suspects.'

'I'll be talking to you,' Eve repeated. 'Doctor Mira, if I could have a moment.'

'Of course.'

Mira rose from her position on a sofa, followed Eve out of the room.

'What's your take? Just a quick thumbnail of reactions.'

'Is it homicide?'

'I can't tell you. Really can't. It has earmarks of an accident – or. So until that's determined, we'll proceed as if it's or. What's your take?'

'Individually and as a group, they're upset, nervous. Connie's managed to hold on to her role as hostess. Roundtree had her, and everyone else, half convinced Harris had just passed out like Julian. The producer and the publicist huddled together awhile. He wasn't happy – well, several weren't – when McNab confiscated all 'links. But no one caused any trouble. Matthew and Marlo were the most shaken, but as they found her, that's to be expected.'

'Maybe you could sit in on the interviews, at least for now.'

'If you think I can help.'

'It's a weird, fucked-up situation. You're a shrink. That's your area. Weird and fucked up, right?'

The tension on Mira's face dissolved with her laugh. 'I suppose it is.'

4

She started with Matthew at the dining room table where they'd all shared a meal. A low centerpiece of white lilies and short candles replaced the food and dishes, and a gray T-shirt and sweatpants replaced Matthew's suit.

'Connie gave me a change of clothes. They have a home gym and she keeps some workout gear for guests. McNab said it was okay if I changed. My clothes were wet. Marlo's, too. Wet. She changed, too.'

'No problem. I want to record this, and just to cover everything, I'm going to read you your rights.'

'Been a while.'

'Sorry?'

'I got arrested for drunk and disorderly and underage drinking when I was seventeen. One of those "the parents are away so let's party" deals at a friend's. Too loud, too stupid, and I mouthed off to the cop. A thousand-dollar fine, alcohol school, and three months' community service. I got grounded for three months on top of it.

'Sorry,' he added and scrubbed the heels of his hands over his face. 'That doesn't mean a damn, does it? I've never seen anyone dead before. I've been dead, killed people, held my dying sister in my arms – on-screen. So you think you've got it, but you don't. No matter how good they are with the makeup, the lighting, the angles, it's not the same.'

His breath hitched in and out. 'She was so white. And her eyes ...'

'Would you like some water, Matthew? Some tea?'

He looked at Mira with such gratitude. 'Can I get tea? Is that okay?'

At Eve's nod, Mira rose again. 'I'll see to it.'

'I can't seem to get warm. The water was a little cold, I guess. And the ... Sorry,' he said to Eve again.

'Have you got something to be sorry for?'

'I'm not handling this very well. I thought I was good in a crisis, but I'm not handling it.'

'You're okay.' She set up the recorder, read off the Revised Miranda. 'You got that, Matthew? You understand your rights and obligations?'

'Yeah, sure.'

'What were you and Marlo doing on the roof?'

'We went up for some air, to hang for a few minutes.'

'And what happened?'

'Her feet hurt. Marlo. She said her feet hurt, so I said she should take her shoes off, stick her feet in the pool. We were going to just sit on the edge of the pool awhile. We were laughing about the gag reel when we walked into the dome. We didn't even notice her for a minute. Seconds, I guess, it was just a few seconds.'

Mira came back out with a tray, a short pot of tea, some cups. 'Coffee?' she said to Eve.

'Thanks. What happened then?'

'Marlo yelled. She saw her first, I think, and she yelled. I didn't think. I just jumped in. I didn't think. She was face-down, and I – we got her out.'

'Marlo got in the pool?'

'No. No.' He sipped at the tea. 'I pulled K.T. to the side, and Marlo helped me get her out. She was heavy. I did CPR. I was a lifeguard in high school and college, so I know how to deal with a drowning victim, but she was gone. I couldn't get her back. Marlo was helping me, and crying, but we couldn't get her back. We ran down to get you. We should've called nine-one-one from the roof. But we ran down to get you.'

'Did you see anyone else up there, or on your way up or down?'

'No. Well, we saw Julian passed out on the couch, and Andi was coming out of the powder room off the foyer. Then we took the elevator straight up.'

'Do you know anyone who'd want to hurt K.T.?'

'Jesus.' He squeezed his eyes tight, drank more tea. 'She can be hard to get along with, and when she drinks too much she's harder still. If there's friction on the set, she's usually the reason because the rest of us just get along. But no, none of us would hurt her this way. She's shot most of her scenes so we'd be away from her anyway before much longer. Just have to tolerate her through the media rounds.'

'Did you have any problems with her, specifically?'

He stared down at his tea. 'I don't know what to call you.'

"Dallas' works.'

'Dallas.' He took a long breath. 'We went out a few times. It was months ago, before we started production, before I had the part. And she wasn't drinking when we hooked up. She wasn't drinking when she got the part either, and Roundtree went to bat for her with the money people. She had to audition, and that didn't sit well, but she nailed the character – and she put in a word for me. She helped me get a reading for McNab. They were looking at somebody else, but she helped me get a reading, and I got the part. It's a break for me. Then we stopped going out.'

'Because you got the part?'

'I know it could look that way. And she liked to think that. Liked to think I'd just used her to get a foot in the door.'

'Why else then?'

'Okay.' He rubbed his hands over his thighs, then set them on the table. 'We had fun at first. We only went out for about three weeks, and it was fun. And we worked on the auditions together, and it was good. We were good. Then, when she got the part, she started drinking. Really drinking. And she got, well, possessive and paranoid.'

'How so?'

'She wanted to know where I was every second. Where I was, what I was doing, who I was with. Or if she wasn't tagging or texting me, she'd just show up where I was. If we .

were having dinner and I smiled at the waitress it was because I wanted to fuck her, probably was fucking her. You know how she acted at dinner? She'd do the same sort of thing in public.'

He picked up his teacup, circled it in his hands. 'It was embarrassing, infuriating. She accused me of cheating, lying, using her if I wasn't paying enough attention. We only went out for a few weeks, like I said, and it wasn't serious. Not for me, and I didn't think for her. Then she got scary serious. She'd come by my place in the middle of the night to see if I was with somebody else. She'd start getting physical – shoving, slapping, throwing things. I told her I was done. We were barely into preproduction when she tried to have me fired. I had to go to Roundtree and lay out the whole mess. He backed me up, said it wasn't the first time she'd gone off that way.'

'It couldn't have been easy working with her.'

'It's called acting,' he said with a weak smile. 'If it was easy, everyone would do it. Anyway, she eased off for a while, like none of it ever happened. So, okay with me. It was working, the characters, I mean. Everybody could see we had something going with this project. It's just been recently she started up again. Maybe because we're almost done. Last week, she trashed my trailer. I know it was her. Broke up my stuff, ripped up my clothes. I had to start locking it when I was on set. We don't have any more scenes together,' he added, then winced. 'I mean, before this happened, we'd finished our scenes together.'

He paused for a moment, stared into the empty cup. 'We did good work. Even with all that, we did good work.'

'Okay, Matthew. That's all for now. If you'd ask Marlo to come back, then you can go.'

'You mean home?'

'For now, yeah.'

'I'd rather wait until . . . Is it okay if I stay out there awhile longer?'

'Up to you, but ask Marlo to come back.'

He got up, looked from Mira to Eve, then back again. 'Thanks for getting the tea.'

Eve switched off the recorder. 'Opinion?' she said to Mira.

'He seems younger than he did at dinner. He's still shocked and shaky. Forthcoming, and a little guilty. He can't decide if he used her or not to get the chance at this part, but knows she believed it, so he feels guilty. My read is he'd chosen to give her as little thought as possible, and now he has no choice but to think about her.'

Eve turned the recorder on again when Marlo stepped in. She wore black yoga pants and a tank, and her face was bare of enhancements. 'I guess I'm next.'

'I need to record this,' Eve began, and went through the same routine she had with Matthew while Marlo sat, eyes wide, hands clenched in her lap.

'Why were you and Matthew on the roof?'

She told the same story with little variation.

'It was such a beautiful night. A little chilly. Warmer inside the dome, but still a little cool. Then everything was so cold after Matthew pulled her out. I thought she'd start breathing again. She'd cough and spit out water. But she didn't. He worked and worked to try to make her breathe again, but she didn't.

'It was an accident, wasn't it? I saw the broken glass. She must have slipped and fallen in. Hit her head? She'd been drinking all night.'

'We can't say yet.'

'It had to be. Nobody here would ... we're not murderers.' Her eyes, the same color as Eve's, came back to life, lit with passion.

'You were here for that scene she made at dinner, so there's no point in pretending we were friends. She didn't have friends. She had competitors, assets, possessions, but not friends. But nobody would kill her. We like drama, and we're lying when we say otherwise. We feed on it. But not like this.'

'Do you have specific problems with her? Personally?'

'Oh, let me count.' She shoved at her hair in a way Eve found oddly familiar to her own impatient gesture. 'She hated me.'

'For any particular reason?'

'Again, let me count. I've had an Oscar nomination. I didn't win, but I'm an Academy Award–nominated actor – and that was a pisser for her. She let me know she knew I'd slept my way to that part. I'd dated the screenwriter – before he wrote it, before the casting, before any of it, but we had dated, and we'd stayed friends. She considered that whoring my way to an Oscar nod. I was hogging the screen time in this project, pushing Roundtree to diminish her role and so on and so on. She cornered me tonight, right before the gag reel. She wanted to know how I'd feel when the media got wind I was blowing Roundtree, Matthew, and Julian. She said Connie knew all about it, and Nadine would be leading off with a segment on how I sucked my way to every part on the next installment of *Now*.'

'How did you respond to that?'

'I told her to go fuck herself. That was the last thing I said to her. "Why don't you go fuck yourself, K.T., because nobody else wants to."' She squeezed her eyes shut. 'God.'

'If someone said that to me, I'd want to punch them – at minimum.'

'If I'd been in character, I might've punched her.' After letting out a breath, Marlo stared at Eve, eyes miserable. 'Then I guess I'd feel worse than I do now.'

'Okay, that should do it for the moment. You can go home. Ask Connie to come in before you leave.'

'That's it?'

'For right now.'

'Will you tell us when you know what happened?'

'Yes. I'll be in touch.'

Marlo got up, started for the door. 'We are suspects, aren't we?' she asked Eve.

'You researched the part. What do you think?'

'That you think K.T. was murdered, and one of us did it.' Marlo shuddered. 'I keep waiting for someone to yell "Cut."'

'She doesn't like knowing the last thing she said to a dead woman was ugly,' Mira commented. 'She didn't like her, and quite a bit, but she also felt the victim was beneath her. She found her crude, pathetic, and as ugly as that last comment.'

'And a potential threat to her reputation.'

'You don't believe Marlo's having affairs with Roundtree, Julian, and Matthew?'

'Not with Julian or Roundtree, but she's having one with Matthew.'

Surprised, Mira sat back. 'Why do you think that? I didn't get any sort of indication from either of them of that sort of interest.'

'No, they're good. That's going to be an issue here. Actors, and good ones. They're keeping it quiet. But I have to figure two people aren't leaving a party – the lights, the drinks, the laughs, to go dangle their feet in a lap pool on the roof unless they want a little alone time. And he's out there waiting for her, when he could've gotten the hell out of here.'

She drummed her fingers on the table. 'I could be wrong. But he talks about how she helped him, how she cried; she talks about how he worked and worked to bring the vic back.'

'Because they're in love,' Mira speculated. 'And see each other as heroic.'

'Might be.' Eve reached for the recorder again as Connie came in.

'Before we begin, could I get either of you anything?'

'We're good,' Eve told her.

'Could I ask if I can have more coffee served – maybe some food – to the others? It's hard to wait out there.'

'Sure.'

'Why don't I take care of that?' Mira rose, touched Connie's arm before the hostess could protest. 'Sit down, Connie.'

'I don't know what to do,' Connie said to Eve.

'I'm going to ask you some questions, and I'll keep it as brief as I can. I'm recording, and reading everyone their rights, just to keep it clean.'

The strain showed as Connie nodded her way through the procedure, as she linked and unlinked her fingers on the tabletop.

'Why don't you tell me what went on between you and K.T. when you took her away from the table?'

'I told her, in very clear terms, that she'd watch her mouth and behavior in my home. If she spoke that way again to any one of my guests, I would have her taken out, and she'd never be welcome back.'

Connie looked away, firmed her lips. 'But that wasn't enough.'

'What else?'

'She wouldn't apologize, wouldn't agree to apologize to you or the others, and that just tipped it out for me. So I tossed in, because I was very angry, very embarrassed, that I'd see to it she never worked with my husband again, or with anyone else I have influence with. She should remember I have quite a lot of influence in the business.'

Shuddering a little, she dashed a tear away. 'I would have done it, too. I meant to do it.'

'How did she take it?'

'Initially? Not very well. She went off, telling me she was sick of being told what she could say, what she could do. She had plenty to say, and there was nothing anybody could do about it. Then she told me Marlo was giving Mason blow jobs between scenes.'

'Did you believe her?'

'K.T.'s a talented actor, drunk or sober,' Connie began. 'Sober, she's tolerable as a human being, can even be amusing. Drunk, she's vicious, unreasonable, and occasionally violent. Most of that's been covered up by various agents, managers, publicists, producers, so the public doesn't have the full picture, so to speak.'

'Was that an answer?'

'It was the first part of one. I didn't believe her drunken insults, no, because my husband isn't a cheat, or a man who looks for BJs on the set from an actress he's directing. Added to that, Marlo thinks more of herself than to stoop that way. She thinks more of me, and Mason.

'The second part of the answer is Mason and I have been married a long time. And we have an understanding. If either of us falls out of love, we're to be honest about it. If either of us just needs a break from the other, we take one. If either of us cheats – it's done. No second chance.'

'Sounds like a good policy.'

'It's worked very well for us.'

'What was K.T.'s problem with Marlo, because it's obvious she had one.'

'All too obvious after that ugly remark at dinner. The bottom line?' Connie said, dry-eyed again. 'K.T. was jealous of Marlo, disliked her for many reasons. Her looks, her talent, her charm, her popularity with not only fans but other industry professionals. I think K.T. took a slap at you because you're who Marlo is during this project. So what she feels for Marlo, she feels – felt – for you. I can't get my tenses straight.'

She paused, pressed a hand to her mouth. 'Past, present. It gets mixed up. I don't know how to deal with this.'

'You're doing fine.' Eve wound her through the evening as Mira came back in.

'God. Thank you,' Connie said as Mira set a cup of coffee in front of her.

'Your husband added a splash of brandy.'

'He knows me.'

'Do you remember seeing K.T. leave the theater?' Eve asked her. 'Or anyone else leave during the screen show?'

'I'd seen the gag reel, so I slipped out during the opening credits, went in to talk to the caterers. I was in the kitchen for a little while.' As she sipped the coffee, Connie creased her forehead. 'I came in toward the end, slipped over to the buffet to make sure we had enough out for post-screening. I didn't see anyone go in or come out as I did.'

'What about when the lights came up? Was everyone there?'

'K.T. wasn't. I know that because I'd been keeping an eye on her. She'd been drinking too much, and I didn't want another scene. I'd planned on getting her out, into a car, and gone, but she wasn't in the theater.'

'Was anyone else missing?'

'I'm not sure. My focus was on her because of what happened earlier, and the way she'd been stewing. I wasn't going to risk another scene. I started to go out, see if she'd gone home or was still in the house, but Valerie waylaid me. She wanted a list of the desserts for a story she wanted to pitch on the evening. Then Nadine came up, and we started talking. I let it go.'

Eve caught sight of Roarke, gave him a subtle signal to come in.

'Sorry to interrupt.'

'It's okay. We're good here for now, Connie. I'll send for someone else in just a minute.'

'Your sweepers and the morgue team arrived,' Roarke told Eve when he was alone with her and Mira. 'They went up to the roof.'

'Let's move this along. Tell Peabody I want her to take Roundtree, Dennis Mira, and the publicist, in any order, in some other location. That leaves me with Andrea Smythe and the asshole producer and Nadine. We'll take Julian together last. When we're nearly there,' she said to Mira, 'you could get some Sober-Up in him for me. No point in talking to a drunk.'

*

72

She was a cunt.' Eyes alert, Andrea chugged down coffee. 'It's a term I use for particularly nasty people of either sex, and she was a world–class cunt. I disliked her in the part because I found the character of Peabody so appealing. Water was never wet enough for K.T.'

She paused a moment, smiled. 'And that was a very poor choice of words, considering.' She threw back her head and laughed. 'I don't give a rat's warty ass she's dead. It only means she's a dead cunt.'

'That's a strong opinion.'

'And the only kind worth having. I threatened to shove a stick up her twat and light it on fire just yesterday. Maybe the day before. I lose track as there was rarely a day that went by she didn't make me want to strangle her with my bare hands after I'd beaten her in the face with a rusty shovel.'

Andrea drank some coffee, smiled over the rim. 'She tended to stay out of my way.'

'I bet.'

'I don't mind being a suspect when the corpse is a shit-for-brains fuckwit, but if I'd killed her it would've been bloody and loud. And I'd have enjoyed it too much to keep it to myself.'

For the moment at least, Eve believed her. And cut her loose.

The minute Joel Steinburger strode in, he grabbed for the controls.

'We have to get a few things straight.'

'Do we?'

'Nothing can be released to the media until I, Valerie, or one of my people vets it. This feed has to be carefully massaged. I need my 'link. I can't be out of contact with my people at a time like this. In addition, I need everyone here – that includes the staff, the police, all the guests – to sign a nondisclosure agreement. We can't have some server running to the tabloids selling some twisted version of tonight, or some underpaid cop trying to line his pockets with a 'link vid of K.T. lying up there dead. I'm told you plan to have her taken to the morgue. We can't have that.'

'We can't?'

'I can arrange for a private facility, a private examiner. Jesus Christ, do you know how much one of those Internet hounds would pay for a picture of K.T. Harris, naked on some slab in the morgue?'

'Anything else?'

'Yes. I need—'

'What you need has to wait because you have the right to remain silent. And I suggest you fucking do so until I finish Mirandizing you.'

'What are you talking about?' He looked genuinely shocked. 'What is she talking about?' he demanded of Mira.

'Joel,' Mira began as Eve continued to recite. 'Take a breath. Take a moment. Lieutenant Dallas has to do her job.'

'I have to do mine! Everybody involved in this production requires I give this incident all my attention, and make certain it's handled properly.'

'Do you understand your rights and obligations?' Eve asked him.

'You're not going to treat me like a criminal.' He folded his arms. 'I want my lawyers.'

'Fine. Contact them. We'll go down to Central and wait for them to get there. No problem.'

'You can't—'

'Yes, I can.' Eve slapped her badge on the table. 'I'm in charge here. This and the dead woman on the roof put me in charge. You can give me a statement here or we can go to Central and wait for your lawyers. That part's up to you.'

'You're going to watch your tone or I'll be speaking with your superiors.'

'Whitney, Commander Jack. Have at it.'

Steinburger let out a long breath. The color that had flooded his face cooled a little. 'I want you to understand, this is my project, these are my people. I'm just trying to protect my project, my people.'

'And I'm trying to find out how a woman we all had dinner with a few hours ago ended up facedown in the lap pool. I win. Here or there, Joel. Your choice.'

'Fine. Fine. What do you *want*? None of us did anything to K.T. It's obvious she had an accident. I don't want the media snickering about her being drunk. I don't want Roundtree and Connie suffering because she got drunk and careless in their home.'

'Were you on the roof tonight?'

75

'No.'

'Did you have any problems with the deceased?'

'No.'

'Now that's got to be a lie. Are you the only person in this house who didn't have one?'

He held up his hands, let out a long sigh. 'I'm not saying she wasn't difficult. She was an artist. Actors are children on some level, often on more than one level. K.T. could be somewhat of a problem child. I'm very good at managing people, dealing with the creative temperament and problem children or I wouldn't be where I am today.'

'I hear she was a mean drunk.'

He sighed again. 'That's the kind of gossip I want to prevent. She didn't handle drink well, and she had a temper. She wasn't a very happy woman, but she could and did do fine work. I don't want her smeared.'

'Did you and she have any altercations?'

'I wouldn't call them altercations. She wasn't happy, as I said, she had complaints about the script, the direction, her costars. I'm used to actors coming to me with complaints.'

'How did you handle them?'

'I smoothed them over when possible, was firm when it wasn't. K.T. understood if she didn't cooperate it wouldn't go well for her career. She was good, very good, but not indispensable. I understand she blew off some steam tonight, and it was rude. It was inappropriate.'

He lifted his hands with a rise of shoulders in a what-can-you-do gesture. 'I intended to discuss it with her tomorrow, and urge her to go into rehab, to take some anger management sessions. Otherwise . . . '

'Otherwise?'

The shrugging indulgence shifted smoothly to cold calculation. 'There are plenty of hungry actors waiting for a break. I have another project green lit, and she wanted it. I wanted her for it. But, as I said, she wasn't indispensable, and I would have made that clear.'

Eve released him, glanced at Mira.

'A position of power and politics,' Mira said. 'One he uses and enjoys. He understood her value as a commodity, and would have no problem replacing her – or threatening to – if that commodity devalued.'

'Yeah. Plus, he's pushy and excitable. You have to wonder what any one of these people would do if the vic had something that threatened their career – which equals ego and bank account – or this specific project. So far it's clear nobody liked her, and none of them bothered to pretend otherwise.'

'She was particularly unlikable.'

'No argument. Being unlikable isn't enough to earn you a slab in the morgue.'

'Did she have family?'

'I haven't checked yet. We'll run that down, notify next of kin.'

'Always difficult. Would you like me to start detoxifying Julian?'

Eve had to smile at the term. 'Yeah. I'll talk to Nadine

while he sobers up. I appreciate the help. I imagine you and Mr Mira would like to get the hell out of here.'

'Actually, he's finding it all very interesting. So am I.'

'His socks don't match.'

'I'm sorry?'

'Mr Mira's socks don't match.'

'Damn it.' Mira let out an exasperated laugh. 'I know he doesn't pay attention, but that got by me.'

'It's . . . ' Eve searched for the word. 'Sweet' was the best she could think of, and it made Mira smile.

'His mind's always on something else. He'd live in a ratty cardigan, and he's always worrying holes in the pockets of his pants. He can never seem to find his wallet or anything in the refrigerator. And just when you think he's not paying any attention to what you're saying or doing, he comes up with exactly the right answer or solution.'

Mira got to her feet. 'People who expect perfection in a mate miss a lot of fun – and sweetness. I'll go take care of Julian. Should I ask Nadine to come in?'

'Yeah, thanks.'

She thought of Roarke, imagined a lot of people looked at him and saw perfection. She knew differently, and decided she had a whole bunch of fun and sweetness in her life.

Even as she thought it he walked in with a jumbo mug of coffee.

'Where did you get that? I get these little girlie cups.'

'Which is why I asked the housekeeper for something more formidable.'

When he set it in front of her, Eve crooked her finger so he leaned down. She kissed him. 'You're not perfect,' she said.

'See if I bring you a giant mug of coffee again any time soon.'

'You're not perfect, and that makes you just exactly right.'

'Being just exactly right has it all over perfection.'

'Bet your ass.' She lifted the coffee, took a long, lifesaving swallow. 'Want to sit in on my interview with Nadine?'

'I would if you share that coffee. If you want an update, Peabody and McNab just finished up their end of interviews. Peabody didn't want to interrupt yours, and asked if I'd let you know they've headed back up to the roof to check on the status of the sweepers. The body's been removed.'

'Yeah, I got a text from the morgue guys. Undetermined. We'll need her on a slab before they can rule it accidental or homicide. I'd say self-termination's out, but you've got to keep it in the mix until.'

Nadine carried in her own coffee and a plate of cookies. She plopped the cookies on the table. 'Now, look—'

'No, you sit, and you now look.' Eve grabbed a cookie, just in case Nadine got pissy and snatched them away. 'You're a witness to a suspicious death. I'm required to interview you, get a statement.'

'I'll give you a statement,' Nadine said darkly. 'I want my goddamn 'link, my PPC. You've got no right to—'

'Oh, knock it off.' Eve bit into the cookie – not bad. 'You're not getting either until I clear it because you're damn well not contacting your producer or editor or whatever the hell so Channel 75 can throw up a big special bulletin that K.T. Harris was found facedown in Mason Roundtree's lap pool – details to fucking follow.'

'I'm a reporter, and it's my job to do exactly what you just laid out. I'm on the scene. I had dinner with the corpse.'

Tossing back her streaky hair, Nadine narrowed her cat's eyes to slits.

'If you think for one hot minute I'm letting another reporter, another channel, another *anything* or anybody scoop me on this, then think a-fucking-gain. What are you smiling at?' she snapped at Roarke.

'I'm a man, and I'm sitting here having coffee and cookies while two beautiful women snarl at each other. Being a man I'm required to wonder – perhaps imagine – whether there will soon be physical contact. Clothing may be ripped away. Why wouldn't I smile?'

'Not perfect,' Eve muttered. 'Shut up for five seconds,' she ordered Nadine, 'before we're in his head naked, oiled up, and rolling around on the floor.'

'And my smile grows wider.'

'You'll get your story,' Eve said after baring her teeth at Roarke. 'You'll have the jump on it, and my cooperation – as far as it goes.'

'Which means?'

'What it means. But you did have dinner with the corpse, and when there's a body in the mix my job trumps yours.'

'I want a one-on-one with you, as soon as we're done here.'

'I'll give you what I can give you when we're done here. You're not bringing a camera in, not at this point. The longer you argue or try to negotiate, the bigger the window for one of the staff to get word out to one of your competitors. I need your eye, Nadine. Here's what I know. K.T. Harris is dead. The three people in this room didn't kill her or cause her to die. The Miras didn't. Peabody and McNab didn't. Mavis and Leonardo didn't. Other than that? It's up for grabs. So I need your eye, your impressions, and your catlike ear for gossip, innuendo, and bullshit.

'Now let's get started.'

Nadine slapped her purse on the table, opened it, and pulled out a number of cocktail napkins.

'Look what I'm reduced to. Scribbling with a pen on cocktail napkins. I told McNab I wouldn't use the PPC to contact anyone.'

'And if he'd listened to you, I'd have busted him down to Traffic. Tell me this first – and this time it's official and on record – are you and Julian Cross bumping nasties?'

'You have such a way. No, as I already told you, we're not. He's gorgeous, charming, fun. He's rich, he's famous. I figured we'd give that area a go. But he's also just a bit dim. It's kind of cute, but I like a man with some smarts. Plus, he'd bump nasties with anyone, anytime, anywhere. And I prefer someone more selective. He's not pushy about it, the bumping or the polite refusal to bump. I enjoy him, but I don't want to sleep with him. Unfortunately.

'Added to it,' she went on, 'the promotion machine is pumping out that there's heat between Marlo and Julian on- and off-screen. It's a time-honored publicity angle. It seems to be working well enough, even though there's just warm between them offscreen – as in friendship.'

'And because Marlo and Matthew have the offscreen heat.'

'They what? They do not. Do they?' Nadine shoved at her hair as she stared at Eve. 'Where did you get that? I didn't get that.'

'It's my take.' Eve shrugged. 'You'll have to talk to them about it.'

'Shit. Shit.' Nadine pulled a pen out of the purse, scribbled on one of the napkins.

'Meanwhile,' Eve said mildly, 'you've spent a lot of time on the set. Who'd want to kill K.T.?'

'Is homicide confirmed?'

'No. But.'

'Okay, my answer is who wouldn't? I've been tempted to smash her over the head and drown her myself. Is that what happened?'

'No comment. Why?'

'Fine. Because she's a bitch. Down to the bone, if you ask me. Selfish, whining, rude. She sulks, she explodes, she snaps, she snarks. She considered herself the superior actor on this project, and made that known at every opportunity. She came at me more than once about the Peabody character, wanting changes, more screen time. She wanted a love scene with Matthew, and pushed – hard – to have her character confront Dallas on investigative points. None of what she wanted worked, but Roundtree, Valerie, Steinburger, Preston – or some unfortunate assistant – had to deal with her nearly every day. She slowed production, and that displeases the suits.'

'Anything specific? Did you ever see her go at it with anyone?'

'Dallas, she went at it with everyone at some point or other. Then she'd settle down for a few days, and go at someone else.'

'All right, let's focus on tonight. Besides her pissiness at dinner, did you see her argue with anyone else?'

'She argued with me.' Nadine examined the cookies, carefully selected one, then took a tiny bite.

'About?' Eve prompted.

'She only has a couple short scenes left, and wanted them both expanded. Insisted I need to sit down with Roundtree and work that out, using the changes she'd made to the scenes. I told her, as I had before, that the way she wanted to change it didn't happen. She told me, as she had before, I didn't understand the business or artistic license. I told her to write her own book, her own script, and leave mine alone. But not that politely.'

'Were you up on the roof tonight?'

Nadine smirked. 'No, not tonight.'

'Did she get into it with anyone else?'

'I imagine she and Connie had words when Connie took her out of the room after dinner. And she had a couple with Andi. K.T. was way out of her league there and knew it, so she tended to keep those words short. I noticed she cornered Preston shortly before dinner, and he didn't look happy about it. Otherwise, I admit, I wasn't paying much attention to her.'

'How about during the gag reel thing. Did you notice her leaving the theater?'

'I didn't. She sat in the back, if I remember right, and I sat down next to Andi because she's always got the best things to say. Plus Julian was pretty drunk by that time, and sulking, so I didn't want to sit with him. Then just a few minutes into it I got a tag on the 'link. We're setting up the on-location show in Dallas, the interviews with the Jones twins. I had to take it, so I stepped out, went into the little sitting room down there. I was on with my producer and director for ten minutes or so. When I came back I just sat in the back until . . .'

'She wasn't there. K.T.,' Nadine said, squinting as if trying to see. 'I glanced around before I took a seat, making sure I didn't sit too close to her, and she wasn't back there. I assumed she'd changed seats, but I guess not. She must have gone out. She might've gone out before I did. I didn't notice either way. Sorry.'

'Did you notice anyone else missing?'

'I didn't, and I popped out to use the restroom the minute the lights came up. It seemed like everyone was in there, or around there, when I came back a couple minutes later. Except for K.T., but I only noticed she wasn't there because I wanted to avoid another chat with her.'

'Okay, what was the mood in the other room while everyone's waiting to talk to me or Peabody?'

'Shock, upset, nerves. Everybody's nervous when there's a dead body and a cop in the house, Dallas. Roundtree pacing and brooding, Connie trying to keep everyone calm, Julian passed out drunk, Matthew and Marlo huddled together – which I took as bonding over finding a body – and looking sick. Andi entertaining Dennis Mira or telling Connie to sit down and relax. Steinburger huddled with Valerie – which is SOP – or bitching about McNab taking his electronics – to which I related. Preston talking to Roundtree or me or Steinburger or staring into his beer. It was stilted, awkward, nerve-racking, and difficult. Everyone believes, or wants to believe, it was a terrible accident, and no one's sure.'

Peabody started in, stopped when she saw Nadine. 'Ah. Can I have a minute, Lieutenant?'

'That's all I need for now, Nadine. You can wait in the living area. We'll return your electronics shortly.'

'Come on, Dallas. You said I'd have the story.'

'And you will. But I need a minute with my partner.'

'Fine. I'm taking the cookies.'

Sadly, Peabody watched the cookies leave with Nadine. 'They looked good.'

'They were. Report?'

'We've got all the statements. McNab made a copy for your review and file.' She passed Eve a disc. 'It's got nothing that puts a blinking GUILTY arrow over anybody's head. The only one who seemed genuinely sad was Roundtree. I don't think he liked her, but he didn't not like her as much as everybody else seemed to. The sweepers are wrapping it up. There was blood.'

Eve looked up sharply from her notes. 'Where?'

'They picked it up with the lights on the skirt of the pool.

A small amount on the coping. It may have been washed off, or may have washed away with the water when the body was pulled out – but since they also found what appears to be the charred remains of some sort of cloth in the fireplace up there, I'm voting for washed off.'

'Two votes.'

'The morgue team confirmed both contusion and laceration on the back of the vic's head, and that it would have bled some. It's her prints on the bottle we found on the bar up there – contents of which will be confirmed by the lab – and on the corkscrew. They'll also run DNA on the cigarette butts, but the brand matches what she had in the case in her bag. It held twelve. She had two left. Marlo's and Matthew's prints on the glasses outside the dome.'

'Okay. Let's take Julian. Give me a minute to feed some of this to Nadine and get her out of here.'

She turned to Roarke. 'Do you want to hang in here for the last interview?'

'Darling, I wouldn't miss you interrogating my counterpart for worlds.'

'Hah. Peabody, go ahead and get him in here. Read him his rights, get him settled. I won't be long.'

She separated Nadine from Roundtree and Connie while Peabody took a reasonably sober Julian into the dining room.

'The way it looks she hit her head on the pool skirting, either fell or had help. Could have fallen in. Or tried to get up, drunk and dizzy from the fall, gone in. I'll know more of that after the ME's had a look at her.'

'That's it?'

'That *is* it, at this point. If she had help, I've got statements, interviews, impressions, and a basic time line. If it was an accident, I have the same and we can close it down. But for now it remains undetermined – and either way, I need you to wait thirty minutes before you call it in and start the machine. I want Julian's statement on record, and him tucked into his place before the frenzy.'

'What difference does—'

'Nadine, if I didn't trust you'd wait the thirty because I tell you I need it, you'd be held here, without your e-toys until. But I do trust you'll wait.'

'Understood.' Nadine sighed it out. 'Appreciated. If I didn't believe you wouldn't screw with me just because, I'd have found a way to get to a 'link before this and had the story out by now.'

'Also understood and appreciated.'

'There's one more reason I opted against sleeping with Julian.'

'Okay.'

'He's not like Roarke, but he gives the illusion of being a lot like him when he's in the mode. So the idea of sleeping with him felt disloyal – and just, well, icky.'

Eve started to laugh it off, then realized Nadine was perfectly serious. 'Really?'

'Yes, really.'

'All right, not completely understood, but appreciated anyway.'

'I hear he bangs like a turbohammer.'

'I thought you said he wasn't like Roarke.'

'Oh, that was cruel. Maybe I'll give him a spin after all.' Nadine fluffed back her hair. 'I'm going to say good night to Roundtree and Connie. I've got my car service, so if you're done with the Miras I can give them a lift home.'

'And pump her for impressions.'

'Naturally.' Nadine gave one of her strands of pearls a quick twirl. 'But I'd give them a lift anyway.'

'Yeah, you would. They can leave anytime.'

When she returned to the dining room, Julian was slumped, pale and obviously miserable, over a cup of coffee.

'You've been read your rights?' Eve began.

'Yes. She said it was for my protection.'

'That's exactly right.' Eve took a seat across from him. 'Do you know what happened?'

'What?'

'You know Marlo and Matthew found K.T.'s body on the roof.'

'Yes.' He shook his head as if coming out of a dream. 'God. *God!* It's horrible. I don't know what to do.'

'You're doing it right now by talking to us. Were you up on the roof tonight, Julian?'

'No – I mean, yes.' He sent Eve a pitiful look. 'I'm confused. I had too much to drink. I shouldn't have, but I was upset after that scene at dinner. I want you to know I wasn't – I'd never try to, ah, start something with you, and right in front of you,' he said, appealing to Roarke.

'But you would in back of me?'

Julian actually went a shade paler. 'I didn't mean—'

'Just winding you up, mate,' Roarke said, smile very, very cool.

'Oh. Okay, I wouldn't want you to think I'd hit on your wife. She's fascinating – I mean to say I'm kind of fascinated, and playing you, it gets intense with Marlo. But I – and Marlo and I aren't – not really. Just for work, for show. It's just part of the deal. I mean, I would – they're both beautiful women, but—'

'Is that a requirement?' Eve asked. 'Being beautiful.'

'All women are beautiful,' he said and smiled for the first time.

'Including K.T.?'

'Sure. Well, she could be.'

'And did the two of you start something?'

'Not recently.'

'What would be "not recently"?'

'Oh, well, a couple of years ago, I guess. We had a little fun. And a couple months ago. She was feeling down, so I cheered her up.'

'Did she want more cheering up?'

He shifted, stared hard at his coffee. 'The thing is, she didn't really want that. She really wanted to complain about Marlo, or to get me to complain about her – Marlo, I mean – to Roundtree.'

He looked up then, met Eve's eyes with his own dull, bloodshot blue. 'I wasn't going to do that. She got bent over it, really hammered at me. I finally went to Joel and asked him to get her off my back. I didn't like to do it, but she was really putting me off, and screwing with my focus. I guess it just bent her more. I don't know why she has to be that way.'

He looked away again, shook his head. 'I don't understand why people can't just be nice, have a good time.'

'Why did you go up to the roof tonight?'

His gaze dropped again. 'The view's mag.'

'Were you alone with the mag view?'

He said nothing for a long moment. Peabody reached over, touched his arm, spoke gently. 'Julian?'

He looked at her. 'She didn't really look like you when she wasn't made up. You have a prettier mouth, and your eyes are nicer. I like your eyes better.'

'Thanks.'

Though Eve saw Peabody's color come up, her partner maintained.

'Who was on the roof with you tonight?' Peabody asked him.

'When I went up, she – K.T. was there. I didn't want to talk to her, not when she was in that mood. We'd both been drinking. I didn't want to talk to her.'

'But you did?'

'A little. I asked her why she'd acted that way at dinner. Connie went to all this trouble. It was our job to be friendly, to make sure all of you had a good time. But she just started up about Marlo, you, Matthew, everybody. I didn't want to be around her, so I came back downstairs.'

'You argued,' Eve prompted.

'I don't like to argue.'

'But she did.'

'It's like she just can't be happy. I don't get that when there's so much to be happy about. Look what we get to do for a living. Yeah, sometimes it's hard, but mostly it's just fun. And they pay us a lot of money. Everything's easier, it's better when you let yourself be happy. It's like she can't.

'Do you have a blocker?' He rubbed at the back of his neck. 'Sober-Up always gives me a headache, a hangover, and makes me feel kind of dull. I don't get like that if I just sleep it off. That's what I was trying to do, just sleep it off.'

Roarke took a small case out of his pocket, offered one of the tiny blue pills.

'Thanks.' Julian smiled at Roarke. 'I feel like crap.'

'When were you on the roof with K.T.?' Eve asked him.

'Tonight.'

Eve thought Nadine's assessment of Julian being a little dim hit bull's-eye. 'What time?'

'Oh. I don't know. I'd been drinking, and . . . after dinner. I know it was after dinner.'

'Did you watch the gag reel?'

He stared off into space, brow furrowed. 'Sort of. I want to see it again, when I can focus. I just couldn't. I guess I went up for some air before I watched, then I couldn't focus anyway. I was falling asleep, so I went out and lay down on the couch.'

'When you came down, K.T. was still on the roof?'

'Yeah. She was still there.'

'Did you see anyone else go up?'

'I didn't see anyone go up. I wanted to lie down, but Roundtree wanted us in the theater.' His gaze tracked back to Eve. 'Are you sure she's dead?'

'Yes, very sure.'

'It doesn't seem real. It doesn't feel real. Did you tell me how she died? I can't remember. Everything's mixed up.'

'It appears as if she drowned.'

'She drowned?' Julian dropped his head in his hands. 'She drowned.' He shuddered. 'K.T. drowned. Because she was drunk, and she fell in the lap pool?'

'I can't tell you.'

'Because she was drunk,' he repeated, 'and she fell in the lap pool, and she drowned. God. It's horrible.'

He lifted his head when Peabody came back with a glass of water.

'Thanks.' He laid a hand over Peabody's. 'I wish this hadn't happened. I wish she'd never gone up on the roof. She wouldn't let herself be happy. Now she never will be.'

She had Peabody take him out, and sat where she was a moment, sorting through her thoughts. Roarke shifted chairs to sit across from her.

Odd, she thought, really odd to have him in the same chair that Julian just vacated. Odd how clearly she could see the differences between them. The body language, the clarity of eye, the stillness – and the ease of being still.

'He's a bit of a gobdaw, isn't he?'

'I couldn't say. What the hell is a gobdaw?'

'Slow-witted. I don't think it's just the drink or the abrupt sobering.'

'Not entirely. Gobdaw.' She shook her head at the term. 'Even gobdaws kill.'

'He strikes me as more the harmless sort.'

'Even them. But he's the only one, so far, who's admitted to being up there, with her. Could be the gobdaw in him, or the harmless. Or just honest innocence. He goes up, thinks, "Hell, I'm not dealing with her again," staggers back down. Someone else goes up and does the deal with her. Or she stumbled on her stilts and deals with herself.'

'Roundtree finally talked Connie into taking a soother and going to bed,' Peabody announced as she came back in.

'Probably a good thing,' Eve decided. 'I don't need her – or him – anymore tonight.'

'What do you need?' Roarke asked her.

'To go home, I guess, and let this work through in my head. It's rare to interview so many witnesses/suspects in one lump. We're witnesses, too, and right now I feel like a lousy one.'

'Because you can't zero in on the killer – if indeed there is a killer – almost before the body reaches the morgue?'

'We were right here.'

'I keep going over and over it.' Peabody blew out a breath. 'Asking myself did I see, even sense, somebody sneaking out, sneaking in. But I was so into the show. It was funny and so iced. I remember different people calling out some remark, but can't pinpoint the timing. Mostly it was just a lot of laughing or good-natured groaning. I've got nothing.'

'We'll sort it out.' Eve got to her feet, wobbled a little. 'I forgot I had these damn things on.' She scowled down at her shoes. 'I'm going to make sure the sweepers blocked off the roof access.'

'They did,' Peabody assured her. 'I already checked.'

'Then let's get out of here.'

'Ride with us,' Roarke invited. 'The car can take you downtown once it drops us home.'

'Oh, boy, thanks. Limo ride! You know, if you take out the chunk where there's a dead body and a couple hours of interviews, this was a mag evening.'

Eve stripped off the shoes the minute she stepped in the house. And winced. 'Why do they hurt more when I take them off than when I have them on? Harris probably did a header into the pool on purpose because her feet were already killing her.'

Roarke scooped her off her aching feet. 'You earned a ride.'

'I'll take it,' she decided as he was already carrying her up the stairs. 'You know it's about fifty-fifty, murder or accidental death.'

'That sounds about right.'

'But it wasn't an accident.'

'Because?'

'She was asking for an ass-whooping, and too many people

who were there had reason to give her one. Blood on the pool skirt, which, yeah, could mean, she fell, got up, fell again – didn't get up. Dinged-up shoe heels – the one in the pool had dings, too, and a broken strap. Could've maybe happened in a fall. And traces of a burned rag in the fireplace.

'The vic pisses everybody off, causes a potentially ugly scene at dinner in front of what I'd call civilians – us.'

'It's nice to have company in my civilian status for a change,' Roarke commented and carried her straight up onto the platform, dumped her on the lake-sized bed.

'*Then* she goes up to the roof and conveniently drowns.'

'Convenient would be relative.' He picked up her feet, set them in his lap. 'Drowning with the cleverest of murder cops on the premises wouldn't be convenient for the killer.'

'Sure it would. It . . . ' She trailed off to a low, happy groan as he began massaging her foot. 'Oh, that's good, really good.' She nearly purred when his knuckles pressed on her arches. 'And you're getting so much sex.'

'Always my plan. Consider this foreplay.'

'Who wouldn't? Anyway, it has that clever murder cop looking at everyone in the same place, at the same time – while everybody who didn't kill her is trying to think straight enough to remember where they were, what they were doing when. And what everybody but the vic and killer was doing was sitting in a dark theater for a good forty minutes.'

'Focused on themselves.'

'Exactly. Nadine gets tagged, but she takes herself and her 'link off to a private area, and is too distracted to notice if anybody left or came in. Nobody mentioned seeing her go out, not even Andrea, and Nadine had been sitting beside her. We're in the front, so we wouldn't see any traffic behind us.'

'And it's very likely none of them believe any of the others are capable. Everyone who didn't kill her believes, or wants to believe, it was an accident.'

'Add in they're united in their dislike of her, and their commitment to the project. It's always smart to kill in a crowd if you can blend in.'

As he started the same treatment on her other foot, she sighed. 'You know that almost – almost – makes it worth wearing those ankle breakers.'

'I figure I owe you as I had the pleasure of enjoying your legs and ass while you did.'

'Business question.'

'All right.'

'When this breaks, which with Nadine leading the charge it already has, how will it affect the project?'

Interesting, he thought, to be discussing murder with his cop while she lay on the bed in her finery. Their life was nothing if not interesting.

'Spun right – and it will be – it'll power up interest and anticipation. They've just been handed a lorry-load of free publicity. An actual murder while producing a major vid about murder? The real-life cop the vid centers on investigating same. It's a bloody bonanza.'

'That's what I thought.'

'I see your motive angle, Lieutenant, but it seems a bit extreme to do murder for some media buzz, especially when they've already been buzzing.'

'But it's a nice side benefit. I'm going to think about it. But now I think you should get me out of this dress.'

'I've been considering my method on that.'

'I'm pretty sure you just yank the zipper down.'

He smiled, gave her calves a series of squeezes that made their muscles sing. 'Over you go then.'

She flopped onto her belly. 'Roundtree knew the timing, just how long he could be out of the room. But I feel like I would've noticed him leaving. He was up front. Connie knew the timing, and did leave the room by her own admission. I bet Preston had not only seen the reel before, but probably helped edit it together. If this was planned—' She lost her train of thought for a moment when his lips replaced his hands on her calves, and felt even better.

'They're top candidates. Steinburger and Valerie – they may very well have had that time down, too – and any one of them would know the value of murder and spin.'

He worked his way up to her thighs, warm lips, a tease of tongue.

'And any of the actors could have slipped out,' she murmured as part of her mind began a lovely, lazy drift.

'How would they know she'd be on the roof?'

'The killer could have arranged to meet her there. Or ...' The zipper eased down fraction by fraction as his mouth continued to play her. 'Or she arranged to meet the killer, which would lean toward impulse killing or crime of passion. Or . . . I can't think when you're doing that.'

'You'll have to give thinking a pass then, as I've no intention of stopping.' He slid the narrow triangle of panties down her hips.

With his mouth at the small of her back, he slid his fingers into her.

Her hands curled into the sheets. 'I'm still in the dress.'

'Only parts of you. You're hot and wet. Soft and smooth.'

The orgasm rolled through her, one extended, luxurious swell that left her steeped in pleasure. He gave himself the delight of her back, long and lean under the sparkle of diamonds, to the curve of muscle in her shoulders, her arms. And back to the heat again so she cried out when the fire took her.

He turned her over, peeled away the dress.

'You're still wearing a suit.'

He leaned down, circled her nipple with his tongue. 'Give me a hand with the tie, would you?'

'You're making me crazy,' she managed as she struggled to loosen the tie, tug it off.

'Still no intention of stopping.' But he shrugged out of his jacket as he feasted lazily on her breasts. 'You look like a pagan. A pagan warrior queen.' He scraped his teeth along her throat. 'Naked, glowing, wearing nothing but ropes of diamonds.'

'I want you inside me.' Breath tearing, she bit at his ear. 'Hot, hard inside me.'

'My hands are busy at the moment.' He filled them with her breasts. 'I'll need help getting out of this shirt.'

She reached up, tore it open, sending buttons flying.

'Well, that's one way.'

'It's how it works when you're a pagan warrior queen. Take me.' She gripped his hair, yanked his mouth to hers. 'I want you to take me like there's nothing you need more.'

'There isn't. It's you. It's always you.'

But he eased back to deal with the rest of his clothes and used his eyes on her as effectively as he had his hands.

'Everything in me skips and scrambles when you look at me like that.'

'You're mine.' And that brought him something beyond excitement, something deeper than passion. 'You're mine,' he said again.

And when she lifted her arms to him, brought him to her, chained him to her, he took her as if there was nothing he needed more.

6

Peabody yawned until her jaw cracked as she contemplated her breakfast choices. In order to start the day right, in a healthy, body-conscious state, she shouldn't have the bagel and schmear. She should choose the fruity yogurt. She certainly shouldn't have the bagel and schmear *and* the fruity yogurt.

And she shouldn't even think of the possibility of the cherry Danish she could pick up on the way to Central.

Why did she always think of the damn cherry Danish in the morning? She wasn't entirely sure the thought of it didn't put an extra pound on her ass.

'I'm having the fruity yogurt, and that's it.'

At his seat at their tiny kitchen table, McNab poked at his bowl of Crispy Crunchie Charms and said nothing.

Peabody doctored her coffee first and wished the stupid low-cal sweetener tasted as good as the wonderful zillion-cal sweetener. But she felt righteous if deprived, sitting down with the healthy yogurt and the low-cal coffee.

She wished she could eat bowls of Crispy Crunchie Charms with an ocean of soy milk like McNab and his skinny ass that never seemed to gain an ounce.

Life was definitely unfair when your metabolism had all the zip of a lame turtle.

She drank some coffee, and felt her brain start to clear. She liked the way the sun came in their kitchen window in the morning, and played through the bright yellow curtains she'd made herself – still hadn't lost her Free-Ager skills, she thought.

She'd enjoyed making the curtains, selecting the fabric, designing a pattern, sitting down at her little machine to whip it all together into something pretty and functional.

Plus McNab had been mega-impressed.

One day she'd actually finish hooking the rug she'd started for the living area, and that would knock him right out of his gel-boots.

He got such a kick out of the fact she could make stuff, so that added more pleasure and satisfaction to the making. It was good to have their things mixed and matched together in their own apartment. Her dishes with his pub glasses, her chair, his table. Just theirs now.

And it was good, really good, to sit with him in the mornings when their shifts meshed, eating together, talking.

As she drank more coffee, she realized he wasn't eating, or talking.

'Your triple C's are going to get soggy,' she warned.

'Huh? Oh.' He shrugged, pushed the bowl aside. 'I'm not really hungry.'

'I don't get you people who aren't really hungry in the morning.' The entire concept put her in a sulk. 'I wake up starving, then have to talk myself into not eating everything in sight so my butt doesn't become an ad blimp.'

When he didn't respond – and he always had something cute to say about her butt – she frowned. He looked a little pale, she thought now. Heavy under the eyes, and very broody.

'You okay?' She reached across to touch his hand. 'You don't look so good.'

'I didn't sleep much.'

'Are you sick?' Instant concern had her leaning over to lay a hand on his brow. 'I don't think you have a fever. Why don't I make you some tea? I've got that blend from my gran.'

'No, that's okay.' His pretty green eyes lifted, met hers. 'Peabody . . . Delia.'

Oh-oh, she thought. He only called her Delia when he was upset, pissed, or feeling very, very horny. And he didn't look horny.

'What is it? What's the matter?'

'I just wondered . . . I love you.'

'Oh, I love you, too. I was just thinking how much I like sitting here with you in the mornings in our kitchen. Just starting the day together. And—'

'Do you want to get married?'

If she'd been drinking coffee, she'd have sprayed it all over his face. Instead, she swallowed hard. 'Oh. Um. Huh.' How did her tongue get so fat all of a sudden? 'Sure, yeah. Eventually.'

'To me, I mean.'

'Well, yeah, to you, dummy. Who else?' She gave him a light punch on the shoulder, but he didn't smile, and her stomach went queasy. 'Didn't I just say I love you? Did I do something to make you think I don't? Ian . . .' Like her first name, his was reserved for bigger moments. 'I can be stupid about—'

'No. Dee, no. You don't want to get married now?'

'Well . . .' Her stomach fluttered, clenched, fluttered again. 'Do you?'

'I asked you first.'

'Maybe you should tell me what brought this on.'

'I couldn't sleep. I kept seeing K.T. Harris lying beside the pool up on that roof. And the way the light made her look so much like you. And how for a minute, it *was* you, in my head. I couldn't breathe.'

Concerned, relieved, in love, she got up, sat on his lap, cuddled him in when he pressed his face to her shoulder. 'It's okay. I'm okay, we're okay.' She kissed his hair, bright as her curtains. 'It's all okay.'

'It just made me think how much you mean to me, and I started to wonder if I was – if we were – wasting time. That maybe we should get married. I wanted to ask if you wanted me to ask. You have to know you're it. You're it for me, Peabody. The one.'

She eased back, cupped his face. 'You're it for me. Ian McNab. The one and only. I've never felt about anybody the way I do about you. It makes me happy. All of this makes me so happy – my dishes, your pub glasses. *Our* place.'

'Me, too.'

'We don't want to get married now. That's for grown-ups.'

She said it with a smile that brought one to his pretty green eyes.

'But one day, down the line?'

'Oh yeah. We'll have a big, crazy wedding. A mag wedding. Get married, have kids.'

Now he grinned, patted her belly. 'A little She- or He-Body.'

'When we're grown-ups.' She kissed him with the sun playing through the curtains, made it count. 'The best part, right now, is you'd ask if I wanted you to ask. I love that you'd do that.' She wrapped him up again. 'I really love you for doing that. Ask me again, one day down the line.'

'You could ask me.'

'Uh-uh.' She drilled her finger playfully into his belly. 'You.'

He dug his fingers into her ribs. 'Why not you?'

'Because you started it.' She giggled her way into the kiss. 'Crap,' she muttered when her com signaled.

She angled back, reached over to slide it across the table. 'Text from Dallas. She says to meet her at the morgue.' She calculated the time, grinned. 'We've got fifteen minutes.'

She popped up to race him to the bedroom. Fifteen minutes with the guy who loved her enough to ask if she wanted him to ask?

Even better than a cherry Danish.

*

Eve walked down the white tunnel of the morgue. She'd long ago gotten used to the smell of death coated with lemon-scented industrial cleaner. She'd stopped thinking that the men and women at Vending or heading to an office had recently lifted the internal organs out of a corpse, or were going to after the next hit of coffee.

She no longer wondered how many occupants resided in the cold drawers, or how many gallons of blood washed down the gullies of the tables on a daily basis.

But when she passed through the doors of the autopsy room and saw Harris on the slab, the resemblance to Peabody gave her a hard jolt.

Chief Medical Examiner Morris turned away from a comp screen. He wore a navy blue suit with razor-thin lines of silver. He'd twisted his ebony hair into a ladder of sleek tails at the back of his head.

Some sort of gritty, back-beating rock played at low volume, and a vending cup of coffee steamed away where he'd set it down on a steel tray.

His exotic eyes skimmed past Eve, then back. 'I'd hoped Peabody would be with you.'

'She's on her way.'

'It's a . . . I'm not sure what to call it.' He walked to the body, naked on the slab, the Y incision tidily closed. 'Really, the resemblance is only surface. And yet.'

'I know.'

'I'll admit I'm grateful Carter was on last night, and did the work here.' He tapped a finger to the screen to bring it on.

'I would have found working on her very disturbing. You didn't request me.'

With a shrug, Eve slid her hands into her pockets. 'It was late.'

'No.' Now those dark eyes softened a bit as he looked at Eve. 'You thought because I'd lost Amaryllis, that we'd had to bring her here to my house, even this surface resemblance to a friend would cause me pain.'

'There wasn't any point in it.'

'There's a point in thanking you for your consideration. I miss her.' He brushed his fingers over his heart. 'I think I'll always miss the potential of what we could have been together. But I'm better than I was.'

'That's good.'

'When I came in here this morning, looked at her, it made me unspeakably sad. People who do what we do, who work with death day after day, we can still find it unspeakably sad. I think it's important we do, from time to time.'

'I barely met her, and I didn't like her. I've made a point in picking out all the physical differences between her and Peabody. And still, it hits a spot.'

'I think, after all this time, all this death, it's good we still have a spot that can be hit. Coffee?'

'That?' She glanced at the steaming cup, could smell the raw bitterness from where she stood. 'Pass.'

'It's foul,' he agreed with a bit of cheer. 'I don't know if it's a good thing or bad that I've gotten used to it.'

'I could hook you up with some real.'

'If I had real coffee in here, there'd be a stampede. Even the dead might rise like zombies. I'll stick with foul, avoid the horror.'

'I don't think real coffee's going to make Harris rise up and bite your throat.'

'Brains,' Morris corrected. 'Zombies eat brains.'

'Okay, that's just sick.'

'Well, they are zombies, after all. In any case,' he said as the foolish moment took the edge off. He glanced at the screen, at the hard data. 'After the initial sadness came the gratitude. This loss isn't mine, or yours. I think, from time to time, we have to be grateful, too.'

'I wanted to kiss Peabody on the mouth last night. I resisted, but I wanted to.'

It made him smile. 'Aren't we the softies, the murder cop and the dead doctor. Well. Someone else will just be sad this morning.'

'Not so much,' Eve told him. 'She was a bitch. I haven't talked to one person who knew her who liked her, with the exception of her mother. And I don't know if that was "like" or just shock and grief over the loss of a child.'

'Even less like our girl then. A pity for the victim, though I doubt she suffered much as, according to the results of the tox screen Carter ordered, and I've just reviewed, she was very drunk. Blood alcohol level point-three-two – along with some considerable traces of zoner.'

'She drank her way through the evening. She had herbals

in her bag, and I found six butts on the roof. They're at the lab. Could be she had some zoner mixed in.'

'She sounds like someone who didn't care for her own reality very much.'

'COD?'

'Drowning. Water in the lungs. She was alive when she went in. The head wound . . . ' He brought it up on-screen, split it with a magnified section of the pool skirt. 'It was severe enough to render her unconscious, but not fatal. Without the dunk, she'd have suffered a mild concussion, required a couple of stitches, and a blocker for the headache. Carter's reconstruction, and I concur, indicates a fall.'

He switched data, brought up the computerized reconstruction.

'She fell or was pushed backward, struck her head on this pebbled surface. The blow would have rendered her unconscious, as I said, for several minutes. Longer, I expect, with her BAL and the zoner.'

'The way she hit, and where she hit. She couldn't have fallen, bounced, rolled, fallen into the water. Not on her own.'

'No.'

'Could she have regained consciousness, tried to stand, and fallen in? Off her balance?'

'If she had, I'd expect to see another injury as the water was shallow. This mildly lacerated contusion on her temple is consistent, as you see on-screen, with a roll over the coping. Also, as you noted in your on-scene, her shoes had scraping at the heels. Here—'

He turned to the body again, moved down to the right hip. 'Another slight contusion. That's consistent with her initial fall, and with the sweeper's report on where they found the blood.'

'Blood that had been washed off. It wouldn't have been, even if she'd fallen in, splashed up water. It's not enough, and the distance doesn't work for that.'

'Not on Carter's reconstruction.'

Eve saw it clearly. 'So she went down, on her own or with help. She's out cold. And when she's out cold somebody drags her a couple of feet to the edge, then rolled her into the pool, where she drowned.'

'That's our conclusion. This wasn't an accidental death. It's homicide.'

'That's all I need.' She turned as Peabody rushed in, stopped.

'Wow. Still really weird,' she said as she stared at the body. 'I think her legs are longer than mine. Why can't my legs be longer?'

Morris stepped around the slab, walked up to her. He took her shoulders, kissed her on the mouth.

'Wow.' Peabody blinked several times. 'Um, thanks. That was nice.'

'It's very good to see you,' he said, and his eyes laughed into Eve's when he stepped away.

'So far this is the best morning I've had in ever.'

'Well, hold on to that,' Eve advised. 'We've got homicide, a media circus, and a long list of suspects. Let's get to work. Thanks, Morris.'

'Anytime. And Peabody? I like your legs just as they are.'

'The day gets better and better.' Dazzled, Peabody walked back into the tunnel with Eve.

'Try this. You're late. And I can see damn well from the bounce in your step you're late due to sex, which means I have to catch you up on the ME's findings, and this does not make my day better and better.'

'I couldn't help it. McNab asked me to marry him.'

The second hard jolt of the morning stopped Eve in mid-stride. 'What? Jesus. What?'

'I'm eating fruity yogurt instead of the bagel and schmear I wanted, and he's sitting there with his bowl of Crispy Crunchie Charms, and he asked if I wanted to get married.' The residual thrill bounced her on her pink boots. 'Really, he asked if I wanted him to ask, which is even sweeter and better, and wow oh wow, I had to have sex.'

'Okay.' How many shocks, Eve wondered, was she supposed to rebound from? 'So . . .'

'So we're going to get married. One day. Not now. We don't want to get married now.'

'I'm confused.'

'I think he needed me to know it's what he wants one day, with me. And needed to know it's what I want one day, with him. And it is.' Peabody hiked up her shoulders in a kind of self-hug. 'It really is. It shook him, you know, seeing somebody who looks like me, who's *being* me, you know. Dead.'

'Yeah, that I get.'

'And he needed me to know, and he needed to know, so he asked if he should ask, and we ... I'm crazy about him, Dallas. But it's more than crazy. I really absolutely love every bony inch of him.'

'I guess you do.' Eve took a minute as they walked outside. 'I may never say these words again, but you're good together. And you're both being smart, to wait awhile before you jump to the next level.'

'You didn't,' Peabody reminded her.

'Nothing about me and Roarke was smart. Nothing about us should've worked, when you look at it close.'

'You're wrong about that. The closer you look, the more it's clear why it worked. Why it works.'

'Maybe so. But if you're late due to sex again, I'll kick your ass.'

'Understood.'

'We're going to swing by to talk to Mavis and Leonardo before we head in. They left before the body was discovered, but they were there through the evening, and during the gag reel, so we need their statements. Added to it, Mavis played herself so she did some work with the cast and crew. She may have something to add to the mix.'

It was still a little odd to return to the building, and the apartment that had once been hers. Now Mavis, Leonardo, and their baby had the space – and more, as they'd taken the neighboring apartment and torn down walls, redesigned to accommodate the family and their work.

Odder still in some ways that Peabody and McNab had taken an apartment in the same building.

A lot of changes, Eve thought, in a short time.

'It's early,' she began as they started up the stairs she'd once climbed daily. 'But I want to get this done even if we have to wake them up.'

'Dallas, they've got a baby less than a year old. Believe me, they're up.'

'If you say so.' She knocked, noting the security – solid – and the fact somebody had recently painted the door hot candy pink.

Leonardo, his big, gilded, tawny eyes a bit sleepy, his coppery hair in long dreads, opened the door with a huge smile. 'Good morning! What a nice surprise.'

He wore what Eve supposed was his home wear – a long cream-colored tunic with elaborate embroidery on the cuffs over loose chocolate brown pants.

Though he'd seen them only hours before, he greeted them both with enthusiastic bear hugs. 'Mavis is just finishing getting Bella dressed for the day. We're going to a family yoga class later this morning before Mavis goes to the studio for a recording and I start a round of meetings on spring designs.'

'Yoga? The kid does yoga?'

'It's a good activity for the family.'

'Okay. And spring? It's barely fall.'

'Fashion is forward. Coffee? I have some of Roarke's blend. I've been spoiled.'

'I'll get it.' At home, Peabody moved through the open space to a newly designed kitchen.

Eve took a moment to glance around. Everything was color – the walls, the art, the fabrics hanging here and there as if at random. They'd separated the kitchen from the living space with half walls of some sort of textured glass.

Every time she came by, it looked less and less like what she'd left behind.

'It looks like you,' she decided. 'Like all of you.'

'We're happy here.'

'Yeah, it feels happy here. Look, Leonardo, I'm sorry to crash into your morning, but—'

Before she could finish, Mavis bounced out, hair bundled up in a curly topknot, a sunburst of color in her snug top with her knee-length pants picking up the pattern with wide cuffs. On her hip, Bella wore similar pants in the same pink as the front door and a white top with *Namaste* spelled out in sparkling rhinestones.

Bella squealed. 'Das!' After that, her current name for Eve, she babbled out a stream of the incomprehensible.

'I thought I heard somebody. And Peabody!' Mavis did a quick dance on sparkly red skids. 'You're just in time. Wait till you see this. Okay, Bellissima, go see Dallas!'

'Das!' Bella called as Mavis set her carefully on her feet with the baby gripping Mavis's fingers.

'You can do it, baby. You can do it.'

Blue eyes huge, Bella took a shaky step on her pink skids. Then another, with her hands waving like bird's wings when she let go of Mavis's fingers.

'What's she doing? How can she do that?' Eve had to will herself not to retreat as the little legs and hands worked, and the blue eyes shone with the thrill of it.

'She's walking!' Leaving the coffee behind, Peabody eased out of the kitchen. 'She's taken her first steps.'

And finished them by ramming into Eve's legs, clutching her trousers like a rope off a cliff.

'Just this morning,' Mavis sniffled, 'Leonardo put her down to play on the floor while we got her breakfast. And she pulled herself up on the chair, and walked to him. She walked to her daddy. It still waters me up,' she managed, and swiped at her eyes.

Behind Eve, Leonardo sniffled in stereo.

And Bella, head tilted back, fingers clutching, eyes imploring, said, 'Das.'

'What does she want?'

'She wants you to pick her up,' Mavis said.

'Why? She can walk.'

'Das,' Bella said again, and managed to infuse the single syllable with absolute love.

'Okay, okay.' With trepidation, Eve reached down, hauled her up.

Bella kicked her feet in delight, shouted, 'Slooch!' and pressed her mouth – always damp – to Eve's cheek. 'Hi! Hi!'

115

'Hi.'

Bella patted Eve's cheeks, babbled, then threw out her arms. 'Peebo!'

'That's me,' Peabody said, stepping over to take Bella. 'I'm Peebo. You're so pretty. You're so smart.' Peabody gave Bella a toss in the air that all but stopped Eve's heart.

'Are you crazy?'

'She loves it.' Peabody tossed the kid again, and made Bella laugh like a lunatic.

'We're actually here officially,' Eve began, and noted Mavis didn't seem to mind a bit that Peabody threw her kid around like an arena ball. 'K.T. Harris was murdered last night.'

'Murdered?' Mavis's mouth dropped open. 'Come on, we were all there. She was fine, for a total mega b-word.'

'She drowned in the lap pool on the roof. She had help.'

'This is horrible. This is . . . ' Leonardo passed a hand over his wide face. 'I don't know what to say.'

'You'd left before the body was discovered, but we need to talk to you both.'

'Listen, why don't I take Belle in to play?' Peabody suggested. 'It'll go faster and easier that way.'

'Yeah, would you? I don't want her around the murder vibes anyway,' Mavis decided. 'It can't be good.'

Bella leaned over Peabody's shoulder as they started out, waved her hand, blew kisses. 'Bye-bye. Bye-bye.'

'I'll get the coffee.' Leonardo brushed a hand over Mavis's shoulder as he went to the kitchen.

'This is total shock time. I mean, we were there, we talked

to her. Sort of. And that crap she pulled at dinner . . . Do you know who did it?' Mavis demanded. 'Do you have a target suspect? They're all actors and stuff. How could one of them kill her? They've got a major vid going.'

'Sit down, sweetheart.' Leonardo brought out steaming cups on a tray. 'I made you some nice jasmine tea.'

'The coffee smells a lot better. Still nursing,' Mavis added, 'so I'm mostly off coffee. I had scenes with her, you know? And once we were in the mode, she was good – she was Peabody. I liked her when we were in the mode.'

'Did she have trouble with anyone?'

'Try everyone. Out of the mode, she was the big b-word, and nothing like Peabody. She was always looking to screw with Marlo, and she gave Matthew grief every chance she got.'

Mavis brought up her legs, crossed them under her, sipped at the tea. 'I heard her yelling at Julian inside his trailer one day when I was going to mine. And she treated Preston – who's a total doll baby – like s-h-i-t. She didn't mess much with Andi. I think she knew Andi would have decked her, plus Andi's got a mouth and a way of using it that's better than a punch in the face. She got on Roundtree's back a few times, but he rolls with that, as far as I could see.'

'What about last night?'

'I wish I'd paid more attention. Honeybee?' she said to Leonardo.

'It was tense. I don't like when things are tense, especially that way. She broke into my conversation with Andi about a dress for the premiere, insisted I design hers, too. She was drunk and rude, and Andi told her . . . ' His color came up. 'It was a suggestion that was physically impossible, if you follow. They got into it a little. K.T. said she had the bigger, more important role, she should come first. Andi made another suggestion. It was very uncomfortable. K.T. backed off, and Andi went right back to discussing the dress as if it had never happened.'

'That's good to know. Andrea Smythe didn't mention any of this last night.'

'Oh, I saw K.T. corner Matthew, really in his face,' Mavis added. 'I didn't hear anything, but it looked intense, and she gave him one of these' – Mavis jabbed her middle finger in the air – 'before she stomped off. He looked peeved.'

'When was this?'

'Um.' She shut her eyes. 'Right before dinner. Yeah, a few minutes before we went in to dinner. And she was talking to Julian right before the show. He didn't look peeved; he looked bored and annoyed. She did, though – look peeved. They were both pretty lit by then. I'm pretty sure she went off, sat in the back by herself. I didn't pay much attention to her because I wanted to see the show. It was fun.'

'Did you notice anybody else? Anyone who left the theater during it?'

'No.' Mavis looked at Leonardo who shook his head. 'We were sort of cuddled up together, me and my moon pie. We left pretty much right after. Trina's aces at sitting, but we didn't want to be away from Belle too long. We said good-bye to

Roundtree and Connie, and sort of eased out. Oh! We saw Julian. He was passed out in the living room.'

'All right. If either of you think of anything else – any detail, let me or Peabody know.'

'K.T.'s dead.' Mavis shook her head as if still trying to take it in. 'What happens now?'

'Now we find out who made her that way.'

Eve filled Peabody in on the way to Central.

'Nobody that Mavis or Leonardo saw having a moment with Harris mentioned it in Interview,' Peabody pointed out.

'Let's find out why.'

'Do we bring them in?'

Eve considered it. 'Yeah. Let's play this as a routine follow-up, but make them come to us. Contact each one, make the arrangements. I want to get this new info down, start the board and book. Then we'll see them one at a time. Jog their memories.'

Keep it friendly, Eve thought.

For now.

7

'Start a deeper run on the vic,' Eve ordered as she and Peabody rode the elevator in Cop Central. 'Let's see if we can find any other connection between her and the other people at Roundtree's last night, including staff and catering.'

'On that.'

When they stepped off, Eve spotted two of her detectives huddled at Vending outside the bullpen.

Carmichael, her hair twisted up and secured to the back of her head by some sort of clamp, turned. 'LT.'

'Detectives.'

'Sanchez here is running down our choices of liquid refreshment.'

'I merely pointed out that the lemon fizzy sold here contains no actual lemons. If you want actual lemons in a fizzy, you go to the deli around the corner. They make theirs on site.'

'And my contention is, the body's full of chemicals anyway. Why not add more?'

'Fascinating.'

'Well, we're after some liquid refreshment before we haul in a bunch of lowlifes,' Carmichael told her. 'We caught one last night. A couple of bangers went out in that illegals stall disguised as a basketball court on Avenue B. One guy's dead on scene with a lot of holes in him. The other was still breathing, got holes, and also had his head bashed in with an old iron post – which had his blood, skin on it, but no prints.'

'More interesting than lemons,' Eve decided.

'Since the bashed-in guy croaked this morning, we've got a double, that maybe looks at first glance like the two DBs just DB'd each other.'

'But since the DB with just holes didn't have gloves, wasn't sealed, and was really completely DOS,' Sanchez added, 'it's hard to buy he wiped his prints off the iron post before he became dead. Plus the ME didn't find any cloth, rag, or handy shirt inside the DB on the off chance he wiped and ate, and we didn't find anything that could have done said wiping on scene. We conclude a third party did the bashing and wiping.'

Sanchez was fairly new to her division, but Eve liked his style. 'At this point, I would be inclined to agree with that conclusion.'

'So we're going to haul a bunch of bangers known to associate with both vics, which means a long day of bullshit.'

'Hence the desire for liquid refreshment prior to,' Sanchez finished.

'Hence. Was the iron pipe from the scene?'

'A few of them lying around,' Carmichael confirmed. 'Used to be a fence.'

'Look for an initiate, younger banger wannabe or a girl-friend who's not a full combat member. Another banger would more likely use a sticker. Pipe's a weapon of opportunity, and any self-respecting banger wants to cut, not bash.'

'Good point.' Carmichael nodded. 'And potentially less bullshit.'

'I'm still not drinking fake lemons.'

'There's a deli on Avenue B that still does genuine egg creams,' Eve told them. 'Cost you ten, but worth it.'

'I know that place.' Carmichael pointed at Sanchez. 'I know where that is.'

'Good. You're buying.'

They started toward the glide, arguing over who should pick up the tab. It was, in Eve's mind, a good, solid partnership forming in a short amount of time.

'Now I want an egg cream,' Peabody muttered. 'I missed breakfast due to asking if I wanted to be asked and sex.'

'Settle for fake lemons, because you're not going to Avenue B. Do the run, set up the follow-ups. I'll put the board and book together.'

She walked through the bullpen, through the familiar sounds and smells – fake sugar, fake fat, fake coffee, real sweat, voices, beeping 'links, humming comps – and into her office.

The message light on her desk 'link flashed like neon on Vegas II. She scowled at it, hit the AutoChef for coffee, then ordered a list of callers without the messages.

Reporters, she thought with mild annoyance as the list ran down. And more reporters. Nadine, of course – twice. She'd have to deal with them, and before much longer. But they'd just have to wait until she set up her board, wrote up her notes.

As she began, she had a low-level urge for that egg cream, which made her think of chocolate, and the candy she'd successfully hidden – again – from the greedy hands of the nefarious Candy Thief.

She glanced toward her rickety visitor's chair where the candy sat snugly inside – she hoped – the bottom of the seat she'd carefully removed and replaced.

The candy would have to wait, too, she decided.

She finished the board, pinning up both ID and crime scene shots of the victim, ID shots of everyone who'd been at the dinner party, more crime scene photos – the purse, the herbal/zoner butts, broken glass – the sweeper's initial reports, ME Carter's reports and results.

She sat at her desk, drank the rest of the coffee while she studied the board.

She'd started on her notes, writing up a time line, when she heard footsteps approaching.

Not Peabody, she thought idly. Peabody had a distinctive clump. This was a purposeful stride.

Whitney, she thought, straightening at her desk seconds before her commander stepped in.

'Dallas.'

'Sir.' She got to her feet, uneasy. Commander Whitney rarely came to her. More rarely came to her office and shut the door as he did now.

'K.T. Harris,' he said.

'Sir. The ME has determined her death a homicide. As I was on scene at the TOD, I was able to interview, with Detectives Peabody and McNab, all individuals also present.'

'Including yourself?'

'I'll be writing that up, yes, sir. I should have a full report for you shortly.'

'Sit down, Lieutenant.'

He lowered to her visitor's chair, frowned. 'Why in God's name don't you requisition a replacement for this? It's like sitting on bricks.'

She felt weird knowing her commander's ass was one crappy cushion away from squatting on her candy. 'Because nobody sits on bricks for long. Take the desk chair, Commander.'

He waved that away, sat for a moment, studying her board. He had a wide, dark face, lined from years and the weight of command. His hair, cropped short and close to the skull, showed thickening threads of silver.

'We have some areas of complication with this matter.' He nodded toward her flashing 'link. 'Media?'

'Yes, sir. I'll deal with it.'

'Yes, you will. That's one complication. Another is your connection to the victim.'

'I had no connection to the victim.'

'Dallas, you had dinner with the victim shortly before her murder.'

'I had dinner with several people. I met the victim, spoke to her, only once. We had no connection, sir.'

'You had words with her.'

Eve's face registered nothing, but inside there was a quick flick of surprised annoyance. 'She had words, would be more accurate, Commander. The victim had been drinking, was, by all statements taken, a difficult individual. She spoke inappropriately and offensively during dinner, but not to me directly. My response was, I believe, brief and appropriate. And that was the end of it.'

'She was also portraying your partner in a major vid.' He gestured to her board. 'Suspects at this time include individuals who are portraying yourself, your husband, other members of this department, other people who are associated with you personally.'

'Yes, sir.'

'The media will take that hay and mix it with manure.' He laid his wide hands on his thighs. 'We need to get in front of that. Having you pass the case to another investigator won't help at this point, and' – he said before she could speak – 'could bog down the investigation. But that can't be ignored,' he added, pointing to her 'link. 'We'll need a clear statement from you, and from Peabody. We'll hold a media conference this afternoon. And you'll work with the media liaison on that statement, and on approach to the conference.'

'Sir,' she said, thinking she'd rather be stabbed in the eye with a needle pulled out of that manure-ripened hay.

'Both of us might prefer you and your partner give the case your complete energy and attention, but this is necessary. There are already media reports about bad blood between you and the victim, others playing up the angle of you heading the investigation into the death of the woman playing your partner. All of them grinding up the fact you were at dinner, that you were present when K.T. Harris died. We'll deal with it, and will continue to deal with it until – as I trust you will – you close the case.'

He rose. 'Conference Room One. Now. With Peabody.'

'Yes, sir.'

Goddamn it, she thought as she walked with him to the bullpen, as he peeled off and she called to Peabody. 'With me.'

This crap was already slowing down the work.

'What's up?' Peabody asked.

'Fucking media,' Eve said under her breath. 'Fucking media liaison, fucking media conference, fucking statements to same.'

'Oh.' Peabody blew out a breath. 'I guess we knew this was coming.'

'Yeah, but I figured I'd have time to finish my prelim report first, get the labs back. Somebody already put it out there I had "words" with the vic.'

'You didn't, not really. She was just an asshole.'

'Remember that.'

They walked into the conference room. There another board stood, immediately pissing Eve off as she saw her own ID shot beside Marlo's, Roarke's beside Julian's, and right down the line.

The man who completed the board stood tall in a snappy

smoke-gray suit. His glossy black hair curled to the nape of his neck. Cuff links glinted silver at his cuffs.

He turned, a stranger to her, a striking face highlighting his mixed-race heritage with mocha cream skin, long, dark eyes tipped at the corners and heavily lashed. When he smiled, his mouth bowed and showed a hint of dimple at the left corner.

'Lieutenant Dallas.' His voice was the same as his skin, rich and creamy. 'Detective Peabody.'

'This is Kyung Beaverton,' Whitney told them. 'He works with Chief Tibble, who has assigned him to us for the duration of this matter.'

'Kyung, please.' He held out a hand to Eve, then Peabody. 'I'm pleased to help you navigate the media maze we expect, and are, in fact, already in. Will you sit?'

Eve ignored the question. 'Start by telling me why you've got us up there with the suspects.'

'Because the media will, and again, have already done so. It's annoying, but reality often is. You aren't she; she is not you, but this connection will be made over and over. So we address it.'

He spread his long-fingered hands. 'While you respect the actor portraying you, she is only portraying a reflection, and indeed on a case already investigated and closed. You expect Marlo Durn will continue to portray other characters, fictional and nonfictional, while you will continue to investigate homicides. Your priority, at this time, is the investigation of the unfortunate death of—'

'The ME's determined homicide,' Whitney told him.

'Ah. The murder of K.T. Harris. You will be pursuing all possible leads in this matter, and can and will not discuss the details of an active investigation.'

'Okay.' Eve relaxed a little. He didn't seem to be as much of a dick as liaisons she'd dealt with before.

'It's been reported you argued with the victim prior to her death.'

'That's inaccurate.'

'Good.' He lifted a finger, wagged it like a teacher at an exceptional pupil. 'Excellent, in fact. Please sit. I was able to ... requisition the brand of coffee you prefer. We'll have coffee, and you'll tell me – *exactly* – what passed between you and the victim. Detective Peabody, please feel free to add your own thoughts, or anything you overheard said at the table during this byplay.'

'Byplay.' Eve studied Kyung as he programmed coffee for all. 'That's a good one. Quick spin.'

'Good, quick – and plausible – spins are my job. I'm good at my job, Lieutenant, as I know you and your partner are at yours.' He smiled, winningly. 'You don't like, even resent all of this. I don't blame you. You're not required to like the media maze, which is why you'll do well to let me guide the direction.'

He smiled again as he set the pot of coffee on the table. 'I do like it. We do better at our work if we enjoy it, don't we?'

No, not a dick, but a manipulator. A smooth one. That she could respect. 'Okay, Kyung, here's how it went.'

She gave him the 'byplay' essentially word for word.

'An appropriate response to an inappropriate statement,' Kyung commented. 'Was anything else said?'

'Not between us. I figured she had a problem with members of the cast, and that problem was enhanced by her drinking. As I didn't know she'd end up dead, I didn't pay much attention to her.'

'She called you a bitch.' Peabody hunched her shoulders when eyes shifted to her. 'After everybody started talking again, she muttered "bitch" under her breath. McNab told me later. He was sitting next to her. It pissed him off, but he said he ignored her because he figured you didn't want any more, um, byplay.'

'He was right. Plus, if somebody doesn't call me a bitch once a day, I figure I'm not doing my job.'

Kyung smiled at that. 'I think you'll do very well with the media, with just that tone and attitude.'

Eve eyed him. 'The liaison usually pushes me to play nice, be diplomatic. And wear lip dye.'

'Different circumstances, different styles.' He merely shrugged. 'I believe you should be just as you are, just have responses ready for questions we expect will be asked. And when you're asked about this incident at dinner – and you will be – you should respond as you did to me. Argument is inaccurate. Ms Harris made an inappropriate comment to which you casually responded. This byplay was the only time you and Ms Harris spoke during the evening. If you would say this in a matter-of-fact, unhurried way, then take another question, it should do well enough.'

He lifted his hands, palms up, cuff links glinting. 'If the point is pressed, repeat, expand only that you and Ms Harris had only met twice, briefly, and simply didn't know each other. At this point you are focused on finding the person responsible for her death. I've heard you say in other statements involving murder that the victim belongs to you now. If this feels right and suitable, say that.'

'She does belong to me now.'

'Yes, keep the dialogue on that point, on the investigation insofar as you can discuss it publicly. They will ask, and often, how it feels to investigate the murder of the woman who portrays your partner, who resembles your partner.'

'K.T. Harris was not my partner. She was an actor doing her job. My job is to find out who took her life.'

He smiled again. 'I feel a bit superfluous. Is Marlo Durn a suspect?'

'Ms. Durn, as everyone who was present at the time of the murder, was interviewed. She's been cooperative. It's too early in the investigation to term anyone specifically as a suspect.'

'How do you feel about questioning, investigating the woman who plays you in *The Icove Agenda*?'

'Again, she's not me, but okay, yeah, there's a thread of strange. Most homicide investigations have a few threads of strange woven in.'

'Don't you feel this unusual connection may bias you or affect your work?'

'Why would it?'

'Here, I can help.' He pressed his palms together, gestured them forward like in prayer. 'If you follow up that natural question with the statement that if you believed the investigation would in any way be affected by the fact the actors in *The Icove Agenda* are portraying you, your associates, you would not head the investigation.'

'Because I'm standing for K.T. Harris now,' Eve finished. 'And identifying the individual who caused her death, bringing that individual to justice is what I'm sworn to do as an officer of the NYPSD. Period. Now fuck off so I can do my job.'

'Perfect. If you'd just think that last part rather than verbalizing it, perfect.' He gave her his big, white-toothed smile. 'I'm having a hard time understanding why you're considered such a difficult assignment by my colleagues.'

'Because most of them are assholes. So far, you're not.'

'Hopefully that will continue. Now, Detective Peabody, let's go over potential questions and responses.'

'I have to talk to the media?'

She didn't squeak it, but came dangerously close.

'Harris played you, you were present at the dinner party, there when Harris was killed. You are second lead on the investigation. It's best to handle this through this media conference rather than piecemeal.'

Eve watched him coach Peabody. He seemed satisfied with her responses as well, tweaking them here and there, helping her stay brief and on point.

'You'll be fine,' he decreed. 'Let me say the media will continue to squeeze every ounce of juice out of this story, then find a way to make more. Lieutenant, I understand your husband will have his own media team, and that someone in his position knows how to handle the media. But, in this case, I'd like to coordinate with his people.'

'That's up to him.'

'Yes, but if I tell you my intentions up front, I won't be an asshole.'

She let out a half laugh. 'I'll get word to him that you're not one.'

'Appreciated. I'll be with you both prior to the conference, and through it. If you need anything from me beforehand, I'll make myself available.' Kyung got to his feet. 'Commander Whitney, I'll get to work.'

'Thank you for your time.' He sat another moment after Kyung went out. 'Who are you bringing in for follow-ups?'

'Andrea Smythe, Julian Cross, Matthew Zank. To start, sir,' Eve told him.

He nodded. 'Let's keep it as quiet as possible. Arrange for them to come in through the secured garage. I'll clear it. Have someone who won't be starstruck escort them to Interview.'

'Yes, sir.'

'Are you leaning toward one of them?'

'Not at this time.' Knowing he expected at least a general oral report, she itched to stand. But it seemed awkward. 'We're going to look for any connection between the vic and any of the household staff, the catering crew. But none of the cast members or crew who attended had any liking for the vic, and in general the opposite. That's often enough motive for murder, particularly when the death appears, as this one, to have been the result of an argument or confrontation. A shove, a fall, a drag and roll into the pool. Alcohol may have been a factor. There was a lot of it. The vic made herself disagreeable, difficult. She caused delays and friction on set, made demands.'

Eve nodded toward the board. 'She was, at various times, intimate with both Zank and Cross. Both men volunteered this information. Zank also stated that the victim continued to pursue him after he'd ended the relationship, was violent and obsessively jealous.'

'And Zank's the one who claims to have found her, pulled her out.'

'Yes, sir, along with Marlo Durn. I believe Zank and Durn are currently engaged in a personal, sexual relationship. If the vic was aware of this, it would have added yet more friction. At TOD, the guests were gathered in Roundtree's home theater watching what they call a gag reel. We know Harris left the theater during the show as TOD confirms she died during its run. We can't, as yet, pinpoint who else left the area, joined her on the roof. We do know there was time to leave, get to the roof, kill Harris, and return before the end of the reel.'

She paused a moment. 'We'll dig into backgrounds, prior conflicts, any violent behavior. The initial shove, or fall, that feels impulsive, a moment of temper. But dumping an unconscious woman in the water, that's a deliberate act, as is walking away while that woman drowns. It may or may not have been calculated, Commander, but it's cold.'

'And the probability one of the staff had a relationship with her that turned murderous?'

'Very low. It's going to be one of the cast or crew, one of the people who worked with her, one of the people she pushed, insulted, threatened.'

'Who pushed back.' He got to his feet. 'Celebrity murders,' he muttered. 'They'll probably make another goddamn vid.' At Eve's stunned, slightly horrified expression, he smiled. 'You could make book on it,' he said. 'Keep me updated. And don't be late for the media conference.'

'Shit,' Eve said when he'd gone out. 'Shit. He could be right.'

'Who'd play me in this one? I mean, it's really wild, isn't it? Somebody playing me investigating the murder of somebody who was playing me. And then there's—'

'Don't. You're giving me a headache. Get those runs done.' Eve rubbed the back of her neck as they headed back to the bullpen. Inside, she stopped, scanned the room, considered. 'Uniform Carmichael.'

When his head popped around his cube, she gestured. 'My office.'

She strode off, texting Roarke to expect a contact by Kyung, and that Kyung wasn't an asshole.

'Sir?' Uniform Carmichael said, standing in her doorway.

'Are you a vid fan, Carmichael? Do you like watching,

keeping up with the Hollywood gossip, reading up on the celebrities?'

'When I have time to watch any screen, I like sports. That's real action.'

'Right. You'll do.' She assigned him as escort, ordered him to keep a lid on it, dismissed him.

Happily she transferred all messages from reporters to Kyung, and got back to work.

She'd completed her initial report, including her own statement, had just started a deeper run on Harris when her 'link signaled an incoming text from Roarke.

Not an asshole. From you, glowing praise. Will deal with it.

Satisfied, she leaned back, studied the data on Harris.

Parents divorced, Eve noted, when she'd been thirteen. One sibling, a brother two years her senior. She'd grown up in Nebraska until the divorce. The mother, who'd sued for and had been granted sole custody due to domestic violence, relocated with her children in Iowa.

Eve couldn't see much difference between Nebraska and Iowa. As far as she was concerned they were both big states with lots of fields, barns, and cows.

She dug a little deeper, scanned some of the police reports, court documents on the domestic violence, frowned over the photographs in evidence of Piper Van Horn – the mother – after her husband Wendall Harris had tuned her up. Also documented was a broken wrist, black eye, minor concussion on then fifteen-year-old Brice Harris – now Van Horn as he'd taken his mother's name as she had after the divorce.

Wendall had done a stint in an Omaha pen, completed anger management and substance abuse courses. Then, Eve saw as she poked a bit more, had died of injuries incurred in a bar fight when Brice had been twenty.

Interesting, Eve thought, that K.T.'d kept her father's last name. Interesting she appeared to have inherited or chosen – who the hell knew – his bent for pissed-off violence enhanced by too much alcohol.

She scrolled through school records. Average student with some disciplinary issues. No extracurricular activities until the age of fourteen when she'd hooked up with the theater program at her school.

'And look here,' Eve murmured. Harris had racked up a string of DUIs by the time she'd been twenty-two, and had her license revoked. Like father, daughter had completed a substance abuse program.

By eighteen, Harris had left Iowa for New LA. Had a couple brushes in addition to the DUIs for assault – charges dropped in both cases. Another for D&D – fine paid, rehab program completed.

Didn't take, Eve thought, and remembered the face, the voice, the grief of Piper Van Horn when she'd contacted the woman to tell her K.T. was dead.

The mother grieved, she thought. Most of them did. Not all, but most. Her own hadn't given the child she'd birthed, abused, and abandoned to a monster a second thought. Hadn't even recognized her when they'd stood face-to-face.

Doesn't apply, she reminded herself. Think of the victim. The more she understood the victim, the better chance she had of understanding the killer.

What she saw here was a woman who'd grown up with violence and anger, one who looked to have found escape or pleasure in acting, but who'd continued that anger/violence cycle to her own death.

Why? Eve wondered. And did why matter, really?

She swiveled around to her board. Had the victim known something about one or more of the cast and crew? Something she'd threatened the killer with, some sort of exposure – a career-damaging embarrassment?

Or had she just pushed somebody too hard for too long?

She swiveled back to read an incoming from the lab.

'Dallas?' Peabody stood in the doorway.

'Zoner mixed with the herbals – almost fifty-fifty.'

'Jeez, between that and the wine, she didn't need the knock on the head to pass out.'

'Pretty sure bet once she went down, she didn't get back up. Blood trace on the recovered pieces of burned rag. Vic's blood. Only vic's DNA on the butts recovered on scene. Drag marks on the heels consistent with skirting material and pattern.'

'That's pretty quick work.'

'For a change. Let's keep the zoner on the QT for now, see if anybody mentions that area of her habit.'

'Yes, sir. Carmichael's bringing Andrea up.'

'Good.' Eve kept her eyes on the data. 'Let's give her a few minutes to settle in.'

One at a time, she told herself. They'd scrape away at some of that Hollywood polish and find out what was under it.

The more she learned about Harris, the less she liked her. But that didn't make the dead less hers.

8

Dressed in traffic-stopping red, her hair in glinting gold waves rather than Mira's subtle sable, Andrea Smythe sat at the scarred table in Interview. She wore bold black hoops at her ears and a sparkle of black stones forming an elongated heart at the hollow of her throat.

She tipped her head with a smile when Eve and Peabody entered.

'It's satisfying to know our set designer was so accurate. This looks very much like what we're using.'

'Not much to design,' Eve commented. 'Record on. Dallas, Lieutenant Eve, and Peabody, Detective Delia, entering Interview with Smythe, Andrea, on the matter of Harris, K.T. Case number H-58091.'

'So formal.'

'It's not black-tie, but we take murder pretty seriously around here. We appreciate you coming in.'

'It seemed the wise choice, given the circumstances.'

'You've already been informed of your rights and obligations. Do you need me to read them to you again?'

'No. I have an excellent memory.'

'That should help.' Both Eve and Peabody took their seats.

'Do you have anything to add to your statements from last night? Any corrections or changes to same?'

'No.'

'Would you like anything before we get started?' Peabody asked her. 'Coffee? A soft drink?'

Andrea smiled again. 'You're to put me at ease while your lieutenant keeps me on edge. It's a good rhythm. I think Marlo and K.T. captured it well for the camera. Not perfectly, but very well. I'm fine, but thanks for asking.'

'This isn't a scene,' Eve reminded her. 'There's no script. And the body is very real.'

'I'm aware. Should I have played the part?' Andrea lifted her shoulders. 'Worn mourning black, put on my solemn face? I could call up a tear or two. But black's not my best color, and it's no secret K.T. and I weren't close. I'm sorry she's dead. I'm sorry, philosophically, that death is part of life, and I think – outside fiction – murder is a fucking coward's game. A selfish, self-serving fucking coward's game. Other than that, her death means little to me.'

'Inconvenient though, isn't it? Given the shooting hasn't wrapped?'

Andrea lifted her shoulders again, crossed her legs. 'Her scenes were nearly done, and Roundtree will find a way to work around her. He's a brilliant and innovative director.'

'And there's the boost from the media buzz.'

'True enough. It's the nature of the beast. The machine will make a great deal more out of K.T. dead than they did – or would have – out of her alive. Ironic, isn't it? She'll finally have all the fame and attention she craved. She only had to be murdered to get it. And that's unnecessarily cold,' Andrea added with a sigh. 'Even for her. I'm sorry I said that.'

'You've made it clear you didn't like Harris, found her personally and professionally ... difficult's the word that keeps coming up. Is that accurate?'

'Bloody bull's-eye.'

'You and she had the occasional confrontation?'

'Occasional. I doubt there was anyone working on the Icove project who escaped a confrontation with K.T. Again, the nature of the beast.'

'You've been forthcoming about the tone of your relationship with the victim, your feelings about and toward her. That's why I have trouble understanding why you haven't been forthcoming about the argument you had with her last night, shortly before she was murdered.'

'Did we argue last night?' Andrea spread her hands and smiled. 'I couldn't say. We exchanged unpleasant words so often, they blur.'

'I don't think so. Not with that excellent memory of yours. I think an argument with her, on the night she was murdered, would stick with you.'

'She'd been deliberately rude at dinner, upset Connie. I told her she was a flaming git, deserved to be tossed out on her considerable ass. She'd been drinking enough to tell me to fuck off. That was about it, and hardly made any impact with me.'

'Again, I don't think so. If it had been that simple you

wouldn't lie and evade. That tells me it was more – more personal, more intense. Word is she usually avoided you, but last night the two of you were seen having a heated discussion – one you failed to mention in your statement. One you're lying about now. What did she have on you, Andi? What was she shoving in your face?'

Andrea looked Eve dead in the eye. 'I have no idea what you're talking about.'

'See, that just makes me wonder more. What happens when I start wondering, Peabody?'

'When you start wondering, you start digging. When you dig, you tend to find things people want to stay buried. A lot of things,' Peabody added. 'Sometimes they don't have anything to do with the case, but once they're uncovered, they have to be picked over.'

'Yeah, and when you start uncovering things, you have to ask more questions, talk to more people. And the media's got its collective ear to the ground. In fact, I have a media conference this afternoon. Who knows what questions might come up?'

'Now who's threatening whom?' Andrea demanded.

'It's not a threat. It's an outline. The more you try to cover up, the more I'll dig. I'll find out, and it'll be messy.'

Leaning back, Eve rocked a little on the back legs of her chair. Andrea's foot – shod in red with a slender black heel – had begun to jiggle.

'And then I'll wonder if you didn't take that argument up on the roof for more privacy. Maybe it got more heated, maybe it got physical. You shove her. She hits her head. There's blood. She's unconscious. You're so *pissed*. The bitch just wouldn't quit. She got in your face. You've had enough. What's one more shove, this time into the pool. She deserved it. She fucking *asked* for it.'

'No one deserves to be killed, and you're a bleeding loon if you think I'm going to tumble for the hard sell. I didn't kill her. I never went up to the roof last night. And I have nothing more to say to you.'

'That's your right. We'll dig, and we'll find, because now I know whatever you and the vic got into last night mattered. It scares you.'

'She didn't scare me.'

'Maybe, maybe not. But I do.' Eve leaned forward. 'You think because you're in the public eye, the media's already broadcast everything there is to know or find out. Not even close. If you stole an ice pop when you were six, I'll find out. If one of your husbands skimmed on his taxes, I'll find out. If one of your kids cheated on a spelling test in grade school, I'll find out.'

Andrea leaned forward in turn, and once again met Eve's eyes dead on. But this time they held fury. 'Leave my children out of this.'

There, Eve thought. Weak spot.

'You've got a son about the age of the victim.' She glanced at Peabody.

'Cyrus Drew Pilling, age twenty-six. Only child with second husband, Marshall Pilling. Married October of '34, divorced January of '36. No children with first husband, Beau Sampson, married June '30, divorced April '32. Twin girls with third and current husband, age eighteen. Married Jonah P. Kettlebrew, September '40.'

'My family has nothing to do with this. I don't appreciate these goddamn insinuations.'

'I bet your family's visited the set. Maybe Harris made a play for your son – or your husband. Hell, maybe she wanted to try out a couple of girls. Maybe one or all of them caught the ball and ran with it. That'd be a pisser.'

'That's a filthy thing to say, and about decent people. People you don't even know.'

Eve stood, planted her palms on the table, crowded in. 'I will know them. That's your choice. It was personal between you and Harris, wasn't it? It wasn't the work, her bitchiness. It was personal. It's all over you.'

'I've taken care, and worked hard to protect my children, to keep them out of the public eye. I'm not going to let you expose them to this ugliness because you're shooting fucking craps.'

'A lot of police work is a crapshoot. Was Harris messing with your family, Andi?'

'It had nothing to do with my family. My family of record.' She passed a hand over her brow, back into her hair as she studied Eve, then Peabody in turn. 'Are we wrong about you? Am I now in the position of trusting the words on the page as to who you are? If you're a woman – if you're women – of integrity?'

'This one's got a medal for it,' Eve said, gesturing to Peabody. 'But, I guess, it's a crapshoot.'

Andrea managed a strained laugh. 'It was about my godson. He's like one of my own. He's a couple years older than Cy, and they've been friends since birth. Dorian's mother and I go back to grammar school. We're family.'

Eve sat again. 'Okay.'

'He's a good boy, young man. But a few years ago he got in some trouble. He came to California looking for a break, as so many do. He stayed with us awhile, and I was able to get him some work. But he ... he was young.'

'Okay,' Eve said again. 'What kind of trouble did he get into?'

'Too many parties, too many people able and willing to provide him with illegals. There was nothing we could do, nothing his mother could do. Over a year, nearly a year and a half, he spiraled down. We bailed him out of jail. He'd go to some meetings, then back to the clubs, to the parties, to the street corners. He stopped getting work.'

'It's hard,' Peabody said gently, 'when someone you love hurts themselves, and you can't stop it.'

'Yes.' Andrea steadied herself. 'It's bloody brutal. He stole or prostituted himself to get the next fix. He lied and schemed and ... I felt responsible. He'd come to me, so bright, so shiny and young. Then I barely recognized him in what the drugs made him. A liar, a thief, a cheat. A violent young man. One day, it caught up with him, and the dealer he'd stolen from beat him nearly to death. He was almost ...'

145

She trailed off, shook her head. 'In any case, the police contacted my son. Dorian had Cy's 'link number on him. Hitting bottom they call it, for good reason. When he could walk again, Dorian went into rehab. I knew a place with an exceptional reputation. A discreet place in Northern California. It brought him back, helped him find Dorian again.'

'How did she find out?'

'She was there. Fate is a cold, hard bitch.' Bitterness crackled in the words. 'K.T. was in the same place, at the same time. They attended group together a few times, and Dorian held nothing back in group. As I said, it brought him back. He lives in London, where he's a solicitor. He's engaged to be married, a lovely girl. They came to New York for a visit a week or so ago – and to the set, of course. She recognized him. And seeing our connection, thought it would be amusing to suggest how it might be if the media got wind of the story, of the trouble he'd been in.'

'Was she blackmailing you?'

'No. Taunting me. She understood it upset me, unsettled me, as little else she could say or do would. Dorian made restitution for that period of his life. Why should she want to expose him, his family, his fiancée to public shame? To hit back at me, of course.'

'Did you go up with her to the roof? Did she push and push, Andi, until you finally pushed back?'

'No. No,' she repeated. 'During the argument you're talking about, I told her to do her bloody worst, that I'd make sure the media knew how they'd come by the information, and she'd be the one digging out from the shit storm. I'd talked to Dorian that morning, and I'd told him what was happening.'

Her eyes filled, but she blinked back the tears. 'He told me to stop worrying. To stop letting her bully me, and use him as a cudgel. He'd told his girl everything long before he'd asked her to marry him. He'd given the partners at his firm full disclosure during the hiring interview. And he'd only be sorry, should she follow through with the threat, if it embarrassed me.'

This time she didn't manage to blink back the tears. 'It wasn't about being embarrassed.'

'You wanted to protect him,' Peabody murmured.

'I'd done such a poor job of it before. But he didn't need me to protect him. So when she started on me about it at the party last night, I said everything I wanted to say. The upshot of which is, fuck off, you ugly cunt. Those were the last words I spoke to her, and I'm not sorry for them. Not in the least.'

When they'd ended the interview, had Andrea escorted out, Eve sat another moment. 'Do you buy it?'

'Yeah. The facts can easily be verified. The rehab center, the timing, if they were both there and so on. It would be stupid to lie about it.'

Eve nodded in agreement. 'Let's verify anyway.'

'You don't buy it?'

'I'd say the odds are good she had a godson who was in the

same rehab as K.T., that they went to group together. That K.T. recognized him when he came to visit the set.'

'So we bump her down the list.'

'No, we don't. I believe "fuck off, you ugly cunt" were likely the last words Andi said to K.T. Harris. But she may very well have said them to her on the roof, right after she rolled an unconscious Harris into the pool.'

'Aw, man.'

'Family's the weak spot, and Harris zeroed in, stuck a shiv in it. So, yeah, maybe Smythe pushed back – *Go on, spill it, bitch, and it'll be worse for you.* Harris is drunk and aggressive, and they take it up to the roof. Smythe doesn't want this confrontation public. It escalates. Hell, maybe Harris got physical first, but when Harris goes down, Smythe's enraged, had her fill. Drags Harris into the pool, mops up the blood, and goes down for another drink. And the world, as she sees it, is minus one cunt.'

'Do you really think she could do it?'

'I think she's got the balls for it, yeah. I don't know whether she's got the cold. But she stays on the high side of the list.'

They took Matthew next. He struck a casual note with a dark green shirt over a lighter tee with jeans and high-top skids. He jumped on Peabody's offer of a drink, opted for a citrus cooler. He studied the two-way-mirror wall, shifted his butt on the chair.

'I always wondered what it felt like in one of these rooms. It feels nervous. Like the air's just a little too thin.'

148

'Do you have something to be nervous about?' Eve asked him.

'When a cop wants to talk to you in a room like this, you're going to be nervous. That's part of it, right? The interviewee is already a strike down at the plate.'

He took a swallow of his cooler. 'Do you think I can get a look at EDD while I'm here? I was setting that up with McNab before . . . before.'

'I'll check with Captain Feeney.' Casual dress and attitude, Eve thought. She'd play on that. 'How are you doing, Matthew?'

'Okay. No, not really. She was dead when I pulled her out of the water. I know it's probably stupid, but it hit me later. She was dead when I pulled her out, when I gave her CPR, mouth-to-mouth. She was dead the whole time. My head keeps going back to that. Not that I tried, but that she was dead the whole time.'

'And the two of you had once been intimate.'

'Yeah. I knew the shape of her body, the feel of her skin, her mouth. And last night, I touched her, put my mouth on her. And she was dead. But she . . . felt the same. I can't get past it.'

'You said last night you hadn't been involved sexually for several months.'

'That's right.'

'But she wanted to be.'

'I think she just wanted what she couldn't have. Some people are wired that way. Maybe.'

'It had to put you on the spot, especially since you were playing lovers.'

'I wouldn't say she made it easy, but she had a lot of ambition. She wouldn't screw up the work to screw with me.'

'You said she wrecked your trailer.'

'Yeah.' He took another swallow. 'Had to be. She didn't even want me or care about me that way – not really. She just ...' He shrugged. 'I should've let her break it off. Looking back, I wish I'd held out until she dumped me. Then she wouldn't have stayed so pissed.'

'The way you talked last night made it sound as if she was obsessed. In fact, I believe you used that term.'

'I don't know.' His gaze, green as his shirt, flicked to the two-way glass again. 'I guess, sort of. I think she just didn't like not being the one calling it off. When I think about it,' he continued, 'she had more grease than I do, career-wise. She could've pushed to have someone else cast as McNab. Maybe she figured we'd hook up during the shooting, then she could dump me. I don't know. I don't even know why I'm thinking about it. She's dead.'

'It couldn't have gone over well with her when you and Marlo started sleeping together.'

His face went blank, utterly, as he set down his drink. 'I don't know what you're talking about.'

'You don't know you're sleeping with Marlo Durn, or you don't understand the term?'

'Listen, I don't know where you got that information, but—'

'Are you denying it?' Eve flattened her voice. 'Because lying to a police officer in Interview doesn't go over well. It just makes us all suspicious and pushy.'

He hesitated, shifted. 'My relationship with Marlo doesn't have anything to do with K.T. – or anybody. It's personal.'

'You and Marlo romping on the sheets doesn't have anything to do with a woman who, by your own statement, was obsessed with you? Stalked you? Vandalized your trailer? Does that fly for you, Peabody?'

'It doesn't even get off the ground.' Peabody's tone, her expression radiated soft sympathy. 'I'm sorry, Matthew. It's awkward and uncomfortable when you have to talk about private business, but if you try to avoid and evade, it just looks bad. The way I see it, you and Marlo are both adults, both free to, you know, enjoy each other.'

'You'd think,' he muttered. 'It doesn't have anything to do with K.T.,' he insisted. 'We were done, over – finished before Marlo and I even met.'

'But K.T. didn't want it to be done, over, finished,' Eve prompted.

His tone, his face hardened. 'That was her problem.'

'She made it yours.'

'She was a pain in the ass, okay? A serious pain in the ass even before she found out Marlo and I were together. It just got uglier once she found out we were.'

'When was that?'

'A couple of weeks ago, I guess. She went to Marlo's trailer, got in her face about it, told Marlo a bunch of crap about me, how I was just using her, and how she – I mean K.T. and me – how we were still making it. We weren't. We did some publicity, some photo shoots where we were in character. That's just part of the job, but we weren't seeing each other. In fact, it got to the point were I could barely stand to do a scene with her.'

'Did that confrontation cause friction between you and Marlo?'

'No. Marlo didn't buy in to K.T.'s bullshit.'

'But it upset you,' Eve pressed.

'Yeah. Okay. When Marlo told me, I got pissed. And okay, I got into K.T.'s face about it. I shouldn't have. I should've listened to Marlo and just let it go, but I didn't. I told K.T. to kiss it, and stay the hell out of my personal business. To stay away from Marlo off the set. She tried to play me, telling me how Julian and Marlo were screwing around. How I could ask him; he'd tell me.'

The temper showed now, in his face, his body, his voice. 'I told her she was pathetic. And hell, it was like a flashback, with her screaming and crying and threatening to ruin my life, my career. All I did was make it worse.'

'Define worse.'

'Marlo and I got this loft. It belongs to a buddy of mine, outside the business. He's away for a couple months, and we're using it. We've been careful, using disguises to come and go, keeping it quiet.'

'Because of Harris?'

'No. Well, that, too. But the suits and the publicity

machine really want to play up the Eve/Roarke/Marlo/Julian angle.' He managed a wan smile. 'Just not as sexy if Eve and McNab are hooked up.'

'You're putting me off, Matthew.'

Now his grin came quick, easy. 'See? Marlo and I are team players. And the fact is, this project's a big break for me. We decided to keep it private – for that, and because we wanted it to be. It's easy to get caught up in that machine, then you're hearing or reading about how you're this or that, or she's doing whatever. We just want a chance to see where this goes without the hype and the circus. I know a lot of people figure it's just Hollywood, and actors hit up for shagfests instead of the real. But it feels real with Marlo. The first time I met her . . . I've never felt about anybody like this. We just want a chance. So we've been keeping it quiet for us, for the project.'

'K.T. found out about the loft.'

'I guess we got a little careless. I know it seems stupid, putting on a wig or dressing up just to go home – and it is. But at first it was fun, too. But I guess we slipped up somewhere. Coming to the end of the project, thinking we were nearly there. She must've followed me. It's the only thing we could figure because she knew all about the loft. And she said . . . '

His color came up, and he lifted his drink, gulped some down. 'She said she had pictures. That she'd made a vid of the two of us. In bed.'

'From inside the loft?'

'She said she found my swipe and code when she broke

153

into my trailer. How she'd cloned it. And she hired this private investigator to set up a camera in the bedroom, over the closet. Maybe she was blowing smoke, maybe not. But she knew stuff about the loft, the colors, the setup. And when we checked out the security discs, there were a couple of blank areas on two separate days.'

'That must've been upsetting.'

'Yeah. Yeah, you could call it upsetting.' His hand fisted on the table, then relaxed, reached for his drink again. 'I wanted to kick her ass, okay? I've never hit a woman in my life, but I wanted to hurt her. But I didn't. You know what she said?'

'I'm all ears,' Eve told him.

'She said I had to dump Marlo – and make it a hard dump. And I had to pick up with her where we left off, only she'd be calling the shots. She wanted a big media announcement on how we'd fallen in love on the set. Who does that?' he demanded. 'Who wants somebody who doesn't want them?'

'And if you refused?'

'She was going to put the video on the 'Net. And she had guys lined up who'd talk about how Marlo had sex with them – all kinds of weird sex.'

The anger seemed to drain out of him, and he said, quietly, 'I think she'd lost her mind. I swear to God, I think she'd just lost her fucking mind.'

'When did she give you the ultimatum?'

'God.' He scrubbed at his face. 'The day she was killed. That morning. I said I didn't believe her. She said I was making a fool of her, making her a joke, and nobody got

154

away with that. She said she'd give me a preview that night, so I could see she had the goods.'

'Did she ask you to meet her on the roof, Matthew?'

'She *told* me I'd better meet her. I told Marlo. I wasn't going to. I was going to handle it on my own, but one of the things we promised each other was to be up-front. No pretenses, no game playing. So I told her. We decided, screw it. It's our life, right? And like you said, we're free to be with each other. Being team players doesn't mean letting some crazy bitch call the shots. Plus, if she had a vid, and made it public, we'd press charges.'

He heaved out a sigh, shoved his drink aside. 'Marlo was all over that, maybe it's being inside a cop's skin for the last few months. But she said if K.T. paid somebody to break into our place, set this up, and she used it this way, we'd damn, well see her ass in jail – and if the producers, Roundtree, the public, the media didn't like it, well, screw them, too.'

'But the two of you went up to the roof,' Eve reminded him.

'Yeah. We had this plan. We went up earlier, before dinner – just to take a look around, sit down, and talk it through. We decided we'd go up together, confront her, make her threaten us again, talk about the PI and the camera, all that. Marlo had a recorder in her purse. Then we'd tell K.T. if she followed through, we'd take the recording to the cops. Maybe people would get off watching the two of us in bed, but they'd get off big-time when K.T. Harris went to jail for blackmail and accessory to . . . I don't know. Marlo had a whole freaking list.'

'And how did that go over with Harris?'

'It didn't, because she was dead when we got up there. Look, I argued with her earlier in the evening. I asked her to forget all this, just grab some sanity and back off before it went too far to handle. And she grabbed my crotch.'

He tipped his head back, stared at the ceiling. 'Jesus. She grabbed my balls, and said, "I've got you by these, baby, and you'd better remember it."'

He took a breath, looked back at Eve. 'We should've told you. We should've told you everything straight out, but it all seemed so . . . huge. And we didn't have any proof. After we realized she was dead, after the CPR didn't work, Marlo looked through K.T.'s purse.' He winced. 'I know that sounds cold, but she was dead, and we wanted to . . . How would you feel?' he demanded. 'How would you feel if a bunch of strangers sat around watching you and Roarke in bed, or you and McNab?'

'I'd probably want to cause harm to the person responsible.'

'We were going to. Marlo's way – your way. But there wasn't any vid or any part of one in her bag. She must've been lying all along. I don't get it. I swear to God, I don't know why she'd lie. Maybe she thought I'd just cave, then when I didn't she had to save face. I don't know.'

'Or maybe you'd had enough. You got mad, and you pushed. Who'd blame you? After that, it just happened so fast. Impulse and rage. Maybe you didn't mean to kill her, didn't mean for her to drown. You just wanted the video, wanted to protect yourselves, your privacy, the project. But then you didn't get her out in time.'

'No. No. No. She was in the pool, facedown, when we got up there. We didn't even think of the video until ... I tried. We both tried. Everything happened exactly the way we told you. We left out the blackmail, the threats. But it happened exactly the way we said. I swear to you.'

'Including Marlo going up with you, with a recorder on her?'

'Yeah. Like I said, we were going to—' The light seemed to dawn, like a switch flicked. 'Jesus Christ, we're idiots. We've been so ... We've got a recording. Marlo turned it on when we started up. We tested it first. We have a recording.'

9

Eve decided to reserve judgment on whether Marlo and Matthew qualified as idiots, innocents, or calculators. In the meantime, she kept Matthew cooling his heels in one interview room while Peabody contacted Marlo, requested she come into Central.

'We'll take Julian while we're waiting for her to come in,' Eve told her partner. 'When she does, we'll see what we see — or don't. And we'll see if pretend Roarke has any little secrets pretend Peabody sussed out.'

'I don't like to think of her as pretend Peabody anymore. The more we find out, the meaner and crazier she gets. It's like it's bad enough fake Peabody got murdered, but now fake Peabody is a dead, blackmailing asshole on top of it. It's depressing.'

'Yeah, it's all really too bad for you.'

'Well, it kind of is. How am I supposed to enjoy the vid now, when I'll be thinking how behind the scenes I was trying to blackmail McNab into bed, and the whole time he's in love with you? And that maybe there's a vid of the two of you all naked and sexy and—'

'Stop right there before I boot.'

'Hey! Maybe there's a vid of fake Peabody and fake Roarke all naked and sexy. That would definitely make up for it. Maybe I can get a copy.'

'There's going to be a vid of me tearing strips off your ass then using them to wallpaper my office. I'll make copies for everybody. Get Marlo down here. I'll start on Julian.'

Eve headed to Interview. Inside Julian sat, head in hands. When he lifted his face, he was pale, hollow-eyed, unshaven.

'I don't feel well,' he began.

'Don't look well either. Record on. Dallas, Lieutenant Eve, in Interview with Cross, Julian.' She added the pertinent data, sat.

'I'm fasting,' he told her.

'Is that so? Is that a mourning for Harris deal?'

'A – no. I drank too much. Then the Sober-Up, the blocker, and I took a sleeping pill when I got back to the hotel. It's all too much for my system. I'm taking nothing but clear liquids today, to flush out the toxins.'

'That's one way.'

'Do I need a lawyer this time?'

'Do you want one?'

'I want to go home, go to bed. I want to wake up yesterday before all of this happened. It's like a dream, a really bad dream.'

'You argued with K.T.'

'At dinner.'

'After dinner. Before the gag reel.'

'I did?' His eyes, bloodshot and dull, stared into hers.

'About what she said at dinner? I was upset, embarrassed. Did I tell you already?'

'Some of it. How about when she came banging on your trailer door yesterday? What did she want then?'

'I . . . don't remember.'

'Bullshit, Julian. You weren't drunk then. I have a witness who saw her banging on your door. And she was angry, insistent.' The timing worked, Eve thought, and she was banking Peabody had heard Harris yelling outside Julian's trailer.

'She was always angry about something,' he said with a shrug.

'She wanted you to claim you and Marlo were having an affair.'

'That's just studio hype. It's—'

'No, Julian. She wanted you to tell Matthew you and Marlo were screwing around behind his back. Matthew and Marlo are involved. Harris didn't like it. She wanted you to help her break them up.'

'I didn't know Matthew and Marlo were a thing.'

'Until?'

'Yesterday. When K.T. started raging about it. They're really good at keeping it low. I could see it last night, when I looked for it. Up until then, I just thought they were friends. Maybe they had sex – it happens – but I didn't know they were a thing.'

'Why would she expect you to do what she wanted, to tell Matthew Marlo cheated on him with you?'

'Hell if I know. And I wouldn't. I like Marlo. I like

160

Matthew.' Sincerity shimmered in his voice. 'I'm not going to do anything to hurt them like that.'

'It didn't bother you that Marlo preferred Matthew to you?'

'Actually, it was good to find out there was a reason she turned me down.'

'Not used to getting turned down, are you?'

'Not much,' he said, without a whiff of pride or shame. 'I get a lot of sex. I like it. It's fun, and after, I'm really relaxed. I'm okay that Marlo wants to be with Matthew. Somebody else will want to be with me, right?'

Hard to argue, she thought, with someone who seemed to think sex was as simple and available as a fizzy at the corner 24/7. And for him, maybe it was.

When Peabody walked in, Julian visibly winced, then looked down at the table.

'Peabody, Detective Delia, entering Interview. Thanks for coming in, Julian,' Peabody continued. 'Do you want anything? Something to drink?'

He shook his head, then glanced at her. 'Actually, could I have some water? I'm pushing fluids.'

'No problem.' Peabody recorded her exit.

'You didn't want to let Harris in to your trailer yesterday,' Eve continued. 'Why is that?'

'She was yelling. I didn't want a confrontation.'

'What did she have to confront you about?'

'I don't know, I don't know.' He dropped his head in his hands again. 'It was always something with her.'

Peabody came back, set a bottle of water on the table by Julian.

'What was she holding over your head, Julian? That was another "always something" with her. What did she say she'd do if you refused to lie about Marlo?'

'I don't want to talk about it.'

Eve glanced at Peabody, nodded slightly.

'Julian.' Peabody reached out, and when she touched Julian's hand, he pulled back.

'Sorry.' He glanced up, looked down again. 'It – you – remind me.'

'But I'm not K.T. I'm not going to yell at you, or threaten you, or say things to make you feel bad. She did that. To you. To a lot of people.'

'I don't know why some people can't just be nice. Be happy.'

'She wasn't happy, and she wasn't nice. And she always looked for the bad side. Everybody's got a bad side, or something they don't want other people to know. She liked to find out, and then use that to make someone hurt, or to pressure them to do something they didn't want. What did she find out about you?'

'It was a long time ago.'

'Okay.'

'And it wasn't my fault.'

'I believe you.'

'We were clubbing. I'd just landed the lead in *Forgiven*. It was mega, a career-maker, so a bunch of us were celebrating.

We'd partied pretty hard all night. Drinking, illegals. I don't do them anymore, but I did. Maybe a little zoner or Hype, something was always right there, like party favors. Women, too. Just there.'

'*Forgiven*. That came out about ten years ago. You were really young,' Peabody said in that same understanding tone. 'Hardly twenty.'

'Twenty-three. It was a major break, a lot of money. We were all high from celebrating, and at this sex club. In and out of the privacy rooms, you know how you do.' He shrugged, drank some water.

'Sure,' Peabody agreed, though she didn't.

'Then we went back to my place, and some of the women came so we could party some more. And two of them went back to my room with me. In the morning, they're still there. We just passed out together after. And this guy's at the door, and he's screaming. How he's going to kill me. One of the girls is his daughter. She's sixteen. Both of them are fucking sixteen.'

He covered his face with his hands, rubbed hard before he dropped them. 'How was I supposed to know? They shouldn't have been in the club. They had bogus IDs, and they said they were twenty-one. I didn't make them have sex with me. I didn't force them. But I bought them drinks, I gave them illegals, I had sex with them. If I'd known they were only sixteen I wouldn't have. I swear. They didn't look sixteen or act sixteen, and they were in a sex club and all over me.

'He said he was calling the cops, having me arrested for

statutory rape. Everybody's screaming, and he slapped his kid. He really hit her hard, and he jumped me when I tried to stop him from hitting her again. My buddies dragged him off. The girls are hysterical. One of my friends is a lawyer, and he started talking all this legal shit about how the girls were going to end up in juvie, and this guy was going up for assault. It just got worse and worse.'

'What happened?' Peabody asked when he fell silent.

'I gave them money. A lot of money to make it stop. To make it go away. It was a long time ago, and I didn't know I was doing anything wrong when I was doing it. But it would've ruined me. If I'd gotten charged with rape, I'd have been finished. It could still ruin me.'

'And K.T. found out.'

'That's what she does,' he said, bitterly now. 'She finds out. Then she puts the screws to you when it suits her. I never did anything to her, but she said she was going to leak what happened to the media. She even had the names of the guy and his daughter. She said I'd go to jail, and no studio would hire me again. It was almost ten years ago, and she said I'd go to jail.'

'Unless you played along with her and lied about Marlo?'

'Yeah. She said I had to tell Matthew we were screwing on the side, and give him details.'

'What did you tell her?'

'I said no. I wasn't going to do that to friends. And she said they weren't my friends. Did I think either of them would go to jail for me? She scared me.'

He took another drink, a long one.

'What did you do?'

'I got ahold of my lawyer friend and told him what K.T. said. He said I should stall her, and he'd find out where the girl was now, what she was doing. He said I wouldn't go to jail because there's a statute of limitations thing, and I was okay there. But still, I didn't want all this hashed around in the media. My friend said it was a good bet the girl and her father wouldn't want all that coming out either, so it would be K.T.'s word against mine. But I should stall her, tell her I had to think about it until he looked into it a little.'

'Did you talk to her about it last night?' Eve asked him.

'I tried to stay out of her way. Then she pulled that bull-shit at dinner. It was worse because I knew what she wanted me to say, to do. So I just kept drinking so I wouldn't think about it. She cornered me, started on me again. I told her to just leave me the hell alone. I wasn't going to talk to her about it with all those people around. I think I said some-thing stupid about my lawyer looking into it.' He rubbed his head. 'Or I thought it, and didn't say it. I don't know. It's blurry. I drank too much.'

He dropped his head into his hands again. 'Connie's right.'

'About what?' Eve asked.

'Drinking doesn't make problems go away. Just because you can't remember them doesn't mean they're not there.'

To keep it rolling, Eve shifted straight to Marlo, and won-dered if she should tell her fictional counterpart she was currently showing too many nerves for a cop. Instead, she read the data into record, dropped down at the table.

'You got here fast.'

'I was . . . already downtown.'

'Waiting for Matthew to finish up. Let's save more time. We're aware you and Matthew are involved, and hoped to keep the relationship private. We're aware K.T. clued in, found the loft you and Matthew are using, and of her attempt to blackmail you with a recording of the two of you in an intimate situation.'

'You're aware of quite a bit. I hope you're aware that Matthew didn't hurt her. We weren't going to take her blackmail, bullying, and bullshit anymore, but we didn't kill her.'

'She told you she'd hired a PI to break into your place, to plant a camera, to subsequently break in again to retrieve same. But you didn't bring this information to the police.'

'No. It was *private*. Do you know how precious private is when you have so little of it? Besides, we didn't know who she'd hired. If we'd gone to the police with the story, she'd have just denied it. How could we prove it? We decided that was how to handle the whole ugly mess. Prove it.'

'How?'

'Matthew agreed to meet her on the roof, but we were both going – with a recorder I had in my bag. We'd get her to talk about the break-in, the blackmail. Then we'd tell her to shove it. We'd have something to bargain with, you see? If she went public with what she had, we'd not only go public with her admission, we'd file charges.'

She nodded briskly, righteously. 'Criminal trespass, extortion, sexual harassment. But when we got up there, she was in the water. She was already dead. Matthew – listen to me – he didn't even hesitate. He went in after her. Despite what she'd done, what she threatened to do, he tried to save her. He tried so hard.'

Tears shimmered now along with the urgency in her voice. 'He'd have saved her life if he could have. But we were too late. And now, we didn't tell you all of this because we didn't want the suspicion, the media nightmare, the fallout. We didn't deserve it. We haven't done anything but fall in love.'

'That's nice for you, but you've also obstructed justice by withholding relevant information.'

'Fine.' She sat back, shrugged in a jerk. 'Arrest me. We didn't do anything wrong.'

'Where's the recording K.T. had on you?'

'I don't know.' Marlo all but spat it out. 'Maybe it was all a lie, all of it. A bluff. She said she'd show Matthew a preview, so if she had it, she should have had it with her. But . . .'

'You looked for it.'

'All right, yes. Maybe that was cold and self-serving, but she was dead. We couldn't do anything about that. And if you found the recording, who would you look at for her murder? And the recording would find its way to the damn media, you can count on it. So I looked in her bag, but it wasn't there. It wasn't on her, or in the bag, or anywhere I could find up there. So I guess you can add attempted theft and compromising a crime scene to my list of sins.'

'It's a bad time to cop an attitude, Marlo,' Eve said mildly. 'Where's your recording?'

'I just told you, she didn't have any recording.'

'Not hers. Yours.'

'My . . .' Her face froze. The hand she lifted to shove at her hair dropped to the table. 'My recorder. It was on. God, it was on the whole time. I got so focused on hers, I forgot. It's in my bag. It's still in my evening bag. Everything was so crazy and complicated and awful. It's still in my bag, at the loft. I'll go get it.' She shoved to her feet. 'I'll go get it, and you'll see what happened. You'll see we didn't kill her.'

'I'm going to have two officers escort you back to the loft. They'll bring the recording in. Just an aside, Marlo. We have an excellent EDD here. If it's been tampered with, edited, screwed around with, we'll know.'

'Good.' She squared her jaw, her shoulders. 'Because it hasn't been, so you'll know that, too. I hated her. She was a sick, bitter bully. A manipulator who would have been happy to ruin my life. But I didn't want her dead. I wanted her to know, and to live with the fact that I was smarter, stronger, and just better than she was. I wanted her to live with the fact that when the project was complete, I was going to show the recording I'd made to Roundtree, to the producers, and her life would be ruined. She'd have been lucky to get a part playing a housewife on an ad blimp. That's what I wanted.'

'I believe her,' Peabody said when Eve assigned the officers to escort Marlo back to the loft. 'It plays. It makes sense.'

'She's an actor. Actors make fiction play and make sense. But yeah, I'm leaning in the same direction. So where's K.T.'s blackmail preview?'

'Maybe it was a bluff.'

'I don't think so. What interests me is why the killer took it. For another dose of blackmail, or for protection? After we get this damn media conference behind us, we need to head over to the vic's hotel room. If she had part of the recording with her, the whole shot's somewhere else.'

'I could take the search now while you do the media deal.'

'Nice try, Peabody.' She checked her wrist unit. 'Let's go get it over with so we can get back to doing what we actually get paid to do. I want this PI *if* he exists,' she added as they walked to Central's main media room. 'If he exists, he got paid. If he got paid, we can track it through the vic's financials.'

'Maybe a cash deal. PIs who break–and–enter don't like leaving a trail.'

'Maybe cash, but it would've been recent, and substantial for the trespassing. She had to find one who'd do it. We'll find him.'

'He'd have checked the recording, to make sure he had something worth taking to the client.'

'Oh yeah. And odds are he made himself a copy for insurance. A PI who'd do this kind of sleazy domestic work probably specializes in same. It's what she'd be after. With his client dead, he's got two choices. He destroys the evidence, cleans up anything that he feels connects him to a DB – or he tries to cash in on the recording. I think with what we've got, we can finesse a tap on Marlo's and Matthew's 'links.'

'You don't think they'd come to us if they got squeezed again?'

'They didn't the first time, which is weight on getting the warrant. Meanwhile we want a thorough search of K.T.'s hotel room, her trailer, do a search for any safe boxes rented in her name – or yours.'

'Mine? Why – oh.' Peabody puffed out her cheeks. 'In case she used that to cover herself.'

'I bet they have IDs – the cop characters. Prop badges to flash for the vid. Easy to use that to rent a safe box. It's what I'd do. We'll check the banks and rental facilities near the hotel. She'd want quick access if she stashed it away.'

They went into the prep area of the media room where Kyung waited.

'Timely,' he congratulated. 'Is there anything you need or want before we begin?'

'To make it fast,' Eve said. 'We've got a couple of new leads we need to get on asap.'

'Anything you want to share with the media?'

'No.'

'All right then, we'll stick with what we've already discussed. There's water on the table. You'll be—'

'I'm not sitting at a table,' Eve told him.

'All right,' he said without missing a beat. 'We'll set up a large podium. I'll give the media the rules of the road, introduce you both. You'll take questions for about fifteen minutes. When it's time, I'll cut it off, and you're done, free to pursue your new leads.'

He had a way, Eve decided. The podium appeared without delay. Kyung took his place behind it to make the announcement. He managed to do so with smoothness, friendliness, and sobriety all at once.

When he stepped back, Eve moved forward with Peabody just behind. Questions careened out instantly, shouted, overlapping, clashing. Eve simply stood, silent, scanning the crowd.

Full house, she thought, with most of them jumping out of their seats, hands raised. Cameras aimed like laser rifles.

She recognized Nadine's usual camera operator, but Channel 75's ace was noticeably absent.

Smart, Eve decided. You couldn't get the story if you were the story. She imagined Nadine had arranged with Kyung to observe from one of the rooms honeycombed through the media center.

'K. T. Harris was murdered last night at approximately twenty-three hundred hours.'

Eve didn't bother to pitch her voice above the fracas, ignored several shouted commands to speak up. 'Her death occurred during a dinner party,' she continued in the same tone, 'in the home of Mason Roundtree and Connie Burkette, and attended by several individuals connected to the in-progress vid adaptation of Nadine Furst's book based on the Icove investigation.'

She gave it half a beat.

'Detective Peabody and I will take questions pertaining to

this matter as long as said questions aren't shouted at us by a roomful of reporters behaving like bratty children on a school field trip. You've got one,' she said to one of the reporters who dropped back in his chair, shot up a hand.

'Gralin Peters, UNN. As you were on the scene at the time of the murder, have you interviewed all attendees, and do you have any suspects at this time?'

'All individuals in the household at the time of Ms Harris's death were interviewed and gave statements immediately after the body was discovered. At this time we are reviewing those interviews and statements, doing follow-ups, and actively conducting the investigation. We can name no suspects at this time.'

'How does it feel knowing K.T. Harris, who was playing your partner in this vid, was murdered while you were right downstairs? BiBi Minacour, Foxhall Media Group.'

'It feels the same way it does when someone's murdered anywhere in New York. It feels as though I need to find out the identity of said killer, gather evidence against him or her, and make an arrest.'

'Detective Peabody! Detective Peabody! Jasper Penn, New York Eye. Is it difficult for you to investigate the murder of the woman who played you in this vid and who resembled you so closely?'

'It's an unusual situation, but no, it's no more difficult than any other investigation.'

'Why aren't both of you considered suspects? Loo Strickland, Need to Know.'

'We have alibis,' Eve said and earned a quick roll of laughter.

'But you and the victim argued publicly shortly before her murder.'

'That's inaccurate. The victim made an unfortunate comment during dinner. I commented on her comment. I met the victim once, earlier that day on the set, very briefly. As the victim was late for the dinner party, then seated at the opposite end of the table from me during the meal, we did not have an opportunity to converse, and, in fact, this brief byplay was the only time the victim and I interacted, though indirectly.'

She started to take the next question when Strickland called out again. 'What was her comment, and your response?'

She considered ignoring him, then figured someone else would ask. 'You don't "Need to Know" as neither have any bearing on the investigation. Again, we didn't speak directly, and there were many comments, responses, conversations before, during, and after the meal. It was, after all, a social occasion.'

'Lieutenant! Doesn't having a social connection with not only the victim but other members of the cast and crew – including Marlo Durn, who's playing you in this project – pose a conflict for you?'

'First, I only met Ms Harris, Ms Durn, and other members of the cast and crew yesterday morning, and this dinner party was the first social contact. So "social connection" is a stretch.

If either my partner or I believed the contact, the unusual connection would in any way influence or impede the investigation we would not be heading said investigation. K.T. Harris is our priority now. We stand for her.'

'Someone took her life,' Peabody said. 'It doesn't matter who she was, what she did for a living, whether she was a stranger or a friend. Someone took her life, and Lieutenant Dallas and I will use every resource of the NYPSD to identify her killer and see that Ms Harris has justice. Those of you only looking for gossip are wasting our time. Time we need to spend doing our job.'

'But the circumstances are unusual, as Lieutenant Dallas stated herself,' someone called out. 'You're investigating the murder of an actress who would speak and act as Detective Peabody. During the course of the investigation you would interview and investigate the actors who speak and act as Lieutenant Dallas, as Roarke, as Detective McNab, Commander Whitney, and so on.'

'Murder's hardly ever usual,' Eve said. 'And I'm betting it never feels usual for the victim or the friends and family of the victim. Actors,' she continued. 'Playing roles. The victim is not Detective Peabody. Marlo Durn is not me. I expect Ms Durn will continue to portray other characters, both real and fictional, as I intend to continue to investigate murders and murderers. Right now, my focus, and my partner's focus is on K.T. Harris. She's ours now. My partner explained that very well. The Hollywood hype?' Eve added. 'Play it up if that rocks you, if it bumps your numbers. I figure it's your job. So, do your job. I'm going to do mine. Peabody.'

She stepped back from the podium, turned to walk out while more questions hammered at her back.

'Not quite as discussed,' Kyung said quietly. 'But very good. Celebrity drives this train,' he added. 'Hers, yours, the others at the dinner.'

'I'm not a celebrity.'

'You are, and you'll just have to deal with that. On your own, as the wife of a wealthy, powerful man, as the central character in a best-selling book – and screen adaptation. Actually, while the celebrity is the juice, it may give you more room and freedom on the priority. On the investigation. Many of these stories will chase the star angle. If the victim had been just anyone drowned at a party, there'd be no particular interest. For a time, the interest will be on her, you, the others who are stars, not on the workings, the nit and grit of what you're doing about her death.'

'That's a point. We're going to get to the nit and grit now.'

'Good luck with it. And Detective Peabody? Very well done. Very well done indeed.'

'Thanks.' She cleared her throat as she walked with Eve. 'I didn't even know I was going to say anything until I was already saying it. It just seemed like nobody really cared she was dead – murdered. Just that she was murdered during the shoot, while we were there, while she was playing me. It just wasn't really about her at all.'

'No, it wasn't. Kyung's right. Let them play that up, roll around in it. We'll do the caring.'

'Even though she was a bitch.'

'Even though. Contact McNab, get him to start looking through her financials, see if he can find anything that connects to the PI. We'll take it to the vic's hotel after we get Marlo's recording.'

'You know what would happen if it leaked? The recordings – either or both?'

'Yeah, so let's make sure we keep it plugged.'

10

Eve unsealed the recording her escort officers had bagged, labeled, and logged. 'Close the door, Peabody.'

Wanting a bigger screen than the mini, Eve plugged it into her comp, ordered a read-and-play. Then crossed her fingers her machine would cooperate.

It hiccupped a couple times, flickered, then steadied with Marlo's face filling the screen.

'Marlo Durn and Matthew Zank.'

'Hey, how come you get top billing?'

She laughed, then angled the recorder so both of them came into view. Eve recognized the earrings Marlo had worn the night before. 'Durn and Zank – alpha order. Let's make sure it worked.'

After a short blank space, the recording picked up. 'Okay.' Marlo's voice, quieter now, and the view a semi-obstructed one of an elevator. 'We both know how we're going to deal with it. She's going to be pissed, right off, that I'm with you.'

'Fuck her. She may be crazy, but she can't be as pissed as I am. I want to punch her face in.'

'Matthew.'

'Okay, you punch her. Girl on girl – better, and sexy.'

'Jesus,' Eve muttered, 'what *is* it with men and girl fights?'

'Plus,' Matthew continued, 'you're ripped – seriously ripped – since you've trained for Dallas.'

'I'd love to try it.' The recorder caught a partial view of flexed female biceps. 'But this is better. It's good she'll be pissed, like we talked about. She'll go off about what she did, she'll go off on her threats about making that sex recording public.'

'Bitch. Still . . . I'd kind of like to see it. Private showing? You and me?'

Marlo laughed again, and the angle changed so Eve saw Matthew's torso, then up to his grinning face. 'I'll bring the popcorn. But we need to get it first. And if this works, she'll trade it. She won't risk her career over this. Will she?'

'It's going to be okay, babe. It'll all work out. She's going to find out she can't mess around with Zank and Durn. Inverted alpha order.'

'I really love you.' The screen shifted as they walked into the lounge. 'When this is finished, when we're all done, let's go somewhere for a while. Find an island, a mountaintop. Somewhere we can keep us between us, just a little while longer.'

'Anything you want. Anywhere you want.' The screen blurred.

Obviously, Eve thought, however Marlo had rigged up the opening in her bag, it was now pressed to some part of Matthew as they embraced.

'Doesn't sound like murder being planned,' Peabody commented.

'Not yet.'

'Okay.' Marlo moved back, let out a deep breath. 'Action.'

'Exterior scene, night,' Matthew murmured as they walked out on the roof terrace. 'God, it's gorgeous out. I liked it better when we came up before, just sat out.'

'We'll do it again. When this thing's settled.'

'It's a date. Okay. K.T.!' he called out. 'You wanted to have this out. Let's do it.'

'I don't see her. Maybe she didn't come up yet.'

'She wasn't in the theater. Damn it, K.T., stop screwing around.'

They continued to walk. Lights played off the surface of the corner of the pool as they entered the dome.

'Maybe she's—'

'Oh God!'

'Marlo, what – oh Jesus!'

The image tilted, tipped, showed Matthew racing toward the pool, jumping in fully dressed, turning over the floating body to reveal K.T.'s face.

Marlo let out a choked scream, and the view slid and blurred as the purse fell to the pool skirt. Eve saw her legs and feet, running, watched her drop to her knees, reach out to help Matthew pull the body to the side. Their voices, their words, mixed and jumbled.

What happened?

Help me get her out.

179

Is she dead? Oh God, is she dead?

Give me room, give me room. She's not breathing.

She watched Matthew perform CPR, try mouth-to-mouth while Marlo rubbed K.T.'s hand between hers as if to try to warm it.

Come back, come back! Come on!

She's cold. She's so cold. Should I find a blanket?

She's gone, Marlo. She's gone.

He sat back on his heels, pale, dripping. His breathing sounded raw, labored, while Marlo knelt, shuddering.

'We should call for an ambulance. My 'link.'

But Matthew took her hand. 'She's dead. She's dead, Marlo.'

'But, she can't – how? There must be something.'

'I can't get her back. She's dead. She's . . . she's cold.'

'Oh, Matthew.' With the body between them, they leaned toward each other, all but fell on each other. 'What do we do? What should we do? Dallas and Peabody. We have to go down, tell them.'

'Yeah. Jesus, I'm shaking. Some hero. I need a minute. I just need a minute.'

'It's okay. It's okay.' She held him, then jerked back. 'The recording. We have to get it.' She scrambled to her feet.

'Marlo, don't touch anything.'

'I'm just going to take the recording. It must be in her purse. It's right here. If the police find it, they could think – Matthew, they could think we killed her, or fought with her, or . . . It's not here. There's nothing here. Does she have a pocket? Is it on her somewhere?'

'Marlo, stop. Stop. She doesn't have anything. She must've lied. Just lied, and now she's dead.' His words came out as if they'd been scraped against a rasp. 'She's dead, and we're not doing anything.'

'You did everything you could.' Marlo dropped down beside him, stroked his dripping hair. 'She must've hit her head and fallen in. She was drunk, and she fell and drowned. Look, there's her glass, some wine spilled and a broken glass. It was an awful accident. God, Connie's going to be sick about it. We should go down now. Come on, baby, let's go down, get help.'

'Yeah. Yeah. What do we tell them, Marlo?'

'The truth. We came up, and we found her. You pulled her out, and you couldn't save her. We don't have to tell anybody the rest. It doesn't matter to anybody but us.'

'You're right. I wanted to hurt her, Marlo. I wanted to see her squirm. I don't know how to feel about that now.' He took a breath, took another, got to his feet. 'How did you feel when I told you she was dead?'

'What? Horrible. Horrified. Scared. Sick.'

'Okay, that's what you feel when we go down. We haven't had time to calm down any, or think about it. We found her, pulled her out, tried CPR, then went down for help. None of the rest changes what happened, right?'

'No. No, it doesn't.' She picked up her purse. 'Ready?'

'Ready. We should run.'

They said nothing as they ran downstairs. The record continued as they played it out for Eve. At some point Marlo laid her bag aside. For a time there was a snatch of conversation, the partial image of someone going by. Then the record announced end of time.

'It's the way they said it happened,' Peabody said.

'Yeah. They're both pretty good at their work, so . . . We make sure it's legit. I want Feeney to run the original through all the tests. We'll make a copy for the files.'

She ordered the copy, drummed her fingers. 'It's a disrupted view, but it angled well enough. No blood. The blood had already been washed off when this recorded. I couldn't see the vic's purse, whether it was open or closed when Marlo went at it. We'll see what she says about that detail.'

'If this was real, the killer cleaned up the blood, took the recording – so he or she knew about the recording.'

'Assuming there was a recording. And assuming there was, let's go find it.'

By Eve's order K.T. Harris's hotel suite and trailer had both been locked and sealed. The hotel manager wasn't happy about it.

'The police seal is upsetting to our guests,' she told Eve as she escorted them – at her insistence – to the suite.

'I bet the need for the police seal probably bums out your former, now dead, guest.'

The manager flattened her lips as she strode briskly out of the elevator on high, thin heels. 'All of us at the Winslow are very sorry about Ms Harris's death. But we do have a responsibility to our guests. It's not as if Ms Harris was killed here. The suite isn't a crime scene.'

'Are you a cop?'

'No, I'm the manager of this hotel.'

'Okay, here's the deal. I won't tell you how to manage your hotel. Don't tell me how to manage a homicide investigation.'

At the door, Eve broke the police seal. 'I want the data from the key card or cards for this suite for the day before yesterday, yesterday, and today.'

'No one has entered this room since it was sealed last night by two police officers.'

'Then the data will so confirm, won't it?'

'If you're doubting my word, or the security of this hotel—'

'I'm not doing either – yet,' Eve said as her patience went as thin as the manager's lips. 'I'm doing my job. Now you can unlock the door as you brought your master, or I can use mine. Either way you can go back to doing your job.'

The manager swiped the card with an angry jerk of the wrist. 'When will the room be unsealed, and Ms Harris's belongings removed?'

'Her belongings will be taken into evidence later today. The room will be unsealed when I'm satisfied there's nothing in said room that pertains to my investigation. You'll be notified. Until then—' Eve opened the door, waiting until Peabody went in, then turned and shut the door in the manager's face.

'I don't think she likes you.'

'Oh, come on. I was really warming up to her.'

Eve set her hands on her hips, looked around. They'd come into a parlor, one with plenty of space, color, and fancy touches.

A plush sofa in rich, textured gold curved against a wall covered with mirrors of varying sizes and shapes. Flanking it were tables topped with tall lamps shaped like peacocks. Chairs of peacock blue faced the sofa over the expanse of a boldly patterned rug. Another set of chairs, smaller in scale, circled a table by the window with its view of downtown. A small bowl of fruit centered on the table.

An enameled cabinet – peacocks again – spread over another wall.

Curious, Eve opened it to find an entertainment screen, a bar, fully stocked, and an impressive library of vid and book discs.

'Nice,' Peabody said. 'And there's a little kitchen through here. AutoChef, full-size fridge, dishwasher, glassware, dishes. 'Everything's clean, shiny, and tidy.'

'They'd have done their evening service before we sealed the room. Little powder room here, and the end of the tp roll's folded in a point – a sure sign nobody used the john since housekeeping was in.'

'I like when they do that. My aunt used to do it when I'd stay at her place. And she'd leave a piece of her homemade candy on the pillow.'

Eve walked into the bedroom. 'Maybe your aunt's been here.' She glanced at the gold-foiled chocolate, the neatly folded coverlet. The basket on it held slippers, a folded robe with the hotel's logo, and a printed card wishing Ms Harris sweet dreams.

Eve sometimes wondered if the dead dreamed, wherever they went, wherever they waited. But she doubted the murdered dead's dreams were sweet.

'What do you see, Peabody?'

'Lots of pillows, good linens, good service. It's a mag layout for reading or watching some screen in bed. And it's quiet. Good soundproofing. You can hardly hear New York.'

'What don't you see?'

'Clutter. No clothes or shoes, no personal debris. No personal anything,' Peabody realized. 'No pictures or mementos. She'd have stayed here for weeks. Months really. And there's nothing of her out here. Or in the parlor.'

'Exactly. Nothing to make it feel like home. She must have liked being in a hotel. The service, again, the lack of the personal. Comfortable, spacious, well-appointed, and anonymous.'

Eve opened a closet. 'Plenty of clothes. Stylish, designer – even the casual stuff. Laundry hamper – it's empty. She must have used their valet service. Let's find out when they picked up her laundry, get a list. Get it back.'

'You got it.'

Eve stepped into the master bathroom. Oversized jet tub, separate multihead shower, drying tube – pounds of thick white towels for those who preferred them.

The long gold counter boasted wide double sinks, a tray of full-sized hotel amenities.

'Kept her face and hair gunk in drawers,' Eve said after opening a few. 'Your basic stuff, too. Tooth stuff, deodorant, blockers, mild tranq – prescription. Most people tend to leave something out on the counter, right? Hairbrush, toothbrush, something. But she keeps it all closed up in drawers. Don't look at my stuff. Mine, mine, mine.'

'Maybe she was just really tidy and organized.'

'It's not put away tidy and organized. It's jumbled some. Put it away, shut the drawer. It's all anonymous again. Start on the drawers,' Eve decided. 'I'll take the closet. Full-out search.'

Valet service, definitely, Eve thought. Everything was hung perfectly, and in order by type, by color within type. Shoes, and plenty of them, stood on the shelves running along the side wall. Handbags nestled in cubbies, with one hanging on a hook.

Current day bag, Eve concluded, and from the weight, the vic liked to carry half her life with her. Eve hauled it out, dumped it on the bed.

'Jesus, who needs all this stuff? And this is what she carried in addition to what she had in her evening bag last night.'

'Some people like to be prepared for anything.'

'Like famine, pestilence, alien invasion?'

'Any of that could happen.'

'So a loaded handbag is a sign of paranoia. Good to know.'

Eve sorted through the electronics, the snack food, the

breath mints, the enhancers, the case of pills – blockers, she noted – and a couple of those tranqs.

She sniffed at the contents of a go-cup. 'Vodka,' she announced. 'Pretty sure. We'll have it checked. Looks like she also wanted to be prepared for drought and a return of Prohibition.'

'Either of which could happen.'

Amused, Eve shook her head. 'No recorder. Also no money, no plastic, and she wasn't carrying enough of either on her at TOD for it to be all. She must be using the safe.'

'I've got nothing so far but really beautifully folded underwear. The valet must be top-notch here. It's sexy heading toward slutty underwear, by the way.'

Interesting, Eve thought, and contacted management for the hotel bypass code for the safe.

Perhaps in retaliation for the door in the face, the manager refused to relay the code. Instead she insisted on sending up someone from Security.

While she waited, Eve continued the search.

'She's got a tell on the safe,' she called out. 'A single hair loosely taped to the lower corner.'

'That is paranoid,' Peabody decided. 'She had a framed picture of Matthew buried under all that underwear. That's kind of sad.'

'Take it out of the frame.'

Loose credits and coins, Eve noted, checking pockets. More breath fresheners. A mini-flask. Had to be vodka, Eve decided after a sniff.

'How did you know!' Peabody hustled to the closet waving a key.

'Because she's paranoid, so she hides things. And she's obsessed. Matthew's the current obsession. Safe box key.'

'That's what it looks like.'

'Bag it and keep going,' Eve ordered at the sharp ding of the doorbell. 'That's Security for the safe.'

Security was big and burly with a hard handshake and little to say. He had the safe open quickly, gave her a nod, then strode out again.

'Safe's loaded,' she told Peabody. 'Cash, plastic, jewelry, notebook. Oops, tsk-tsk. This looks to be most of a dime bag of zoner. Envelope here of photos – probably the PI shots – of Matthew, Matthew and Marlo. Some in disguise, some not. Matthew and Julian, Matthew and Roundtree, and so on. And a small lockbox. Safe in a safe. Paranoia.'

'I've got script pages, notes on the script, what are they – call sheets – in this desk.'

Eve carried the lockbox out, studied it, considered. Roarke could have it opened in two seconds – maybe less – and probably just with the power of his mind.

'Hell with it.' Eve dug out her pocketknife. 'What local bank did she use for business in New York?'

'Liberty Mutual, down by Chelsea Piers. McNab's on those financials.'

'She wouldn't have used that bank, that branch for whatever's in the safe box. She's the "spread the chickens in many coops" type.'

'I think that's eggs and baskets.'

'Chickens, eggs. Same thing.' Once she'd removed the code plate, Eve tried prying, poking, jimmying.

No one was more surprised than Eve when the lockbox popped open. 'It's not so hard,' she murmured.

'Another notebook, a business card for A. A. Asner, Private Investigations and Security. Stone Street address. And a sealed recording. I'm betting it's a copy. If she got the original, it's in that safe box.'

Eve picked up the notebook, tried to open it. 'Pass coded.' She thought a moment, then keyed in MATTHEW. The screen flickered on.

'Paranoid, but obvious.' She began flipping through, working from the latest entry back. 'She's got the dinner party in here – time and date, a few pithy comments.

Expect elaborate by Overboard Connie to impress Skinny Bitch and Pleasebody.

'Pleasebody! What the hell.'

'I'm Skinny Bitch, and I barely met her.'

Had enough from Asshole Andi. She'll shut the fuck up after tonight. And it's time for Foolian to fall in line. Harlo's over, and Matthew's going to come back where he belongs and like it.

Tonight's the night.

'I guess it was,' Eve said. 'Just not the way she figured.'

She flipped back. 'I've got a note of a cash payment of a hundred grand to Triple A. That would be the PI. Two half payments. First a week from the last entry, second and last three days ago. And there's a code. 45128. #1337.'

'Lock code and box number?'

'I'd say so,' Eve agreed. 'Let's check banks, Lower West to start, see if she rented a box under her name. Or yours.'

'Mine again?'

'Paranoid,' Eve said again. 'And she's playing you. It's a natural fit. We finish here, find the bank and box, and pay Triple A a visit.'

Another hour of searching proved they'd already hit the mother lode. While Peabody worked on pinning down the bank, Eve called for sweepers and EDD. She wanted the room processed, the 'links and security checked – and all personal belongings of the vic bagged, sealed, and logged into evidence.

'Still working on it,' Peabody told her.

'We'll head toward Asner's office. Keep at it.'

A paranoid, obsessive personality with a substance abuse problem. Why bother to kill her, Eve thought, when she'd probably self-destruct before long anyway?

She could hide her flasks and illegals, but nobody ever hid them well enough. Her colleagues had to have known she had a drinking and an illegals problem. Come at one of them – any one of them could counterweight it with Harris's secrets.

She considered Matthew and Marlo. They could have killed her, then gone back, made the recording of the discovery. Elaborate, dramatic – but that was their business, wasn't it? Their nature, to some extent.

The motive seemed weak to her. Sure, having the public

consume a vid of them having sex would be embarrassing, but they'd done nothing wrong. The public would goggle, snicker – and sympathize.

Then again, the push/shove/fall, that played like an accident or impulse. It could even be touted as self-defense. She came at me, I pushed her back. She slipped.

The rest might have been panic.

No, it didn't play like panic. It played like calculation. It said to Eve: *I've gone this far, let's just finish it once and for all.*

Why take the recording? Why clean off the blood?

Because the recording had value. Because whoever did it was new to the game, assumed her death would be termed accidental drowning as a result of a fall *into* the pool.

Back to square one. It could have been any of them.

'Got it! New York Financial, and she *did* use my name.' Peabody hunched her shoulders. 'That's a little creepy.'

'But not unpredictable. What address?'

Eve programmed it into the navigation when Peabody read it off. 'Only a block from the PI. We'll go see him first, get a warrant for the box in the meantime.'

Peabody put in the request, then sat back. 'All this, over a guy? And one who dumped her, and was hooked with someone else.'

'No, he's the – what do they call it – McGuffin. All this is about her. If not Matthew, somebody else or something else. It's about ego and greed. Power plays and a generally pissy nature.'

'I can't believe I was juiced when they cast her to play me.

Pleasebody,' Peabody muttered. 'She didn't have any respect for me at all. I wish I'd known what a crappy human being she was before she got dead. I'd have shown her a Pleasebody.'

'How long do you figure you're going to stew over this?'

'Awhile. I've never worked on a vic I wished I'd punched in the face before somebody killed her. I've been working on my hand-to-hand.'

'Is that so?'

'That is very so. I think I'm improving. Plus I lost two pounds. Well, one-point-seven pounds.'

'One-point-seven.' Eve slanted a look over. 'Seriously? You weigh in decimals?'

'Easy for you, Skinny Bitch.'

'Hey, that's Lieutenant Skinny Bitch to you, Detective Pleasebody.'

That got a lip twitch that spread to a reluctant smile. 'But the point is, I've been working on that hand-to-hand, on not telegraphing my moves and all that. I could've taken her down, one-on-one.'

'Damn right. You'd have mopped the floor with her if she hadn't gone and got herself killed first. Selfish fucker. The least she could've done is lived long enough for you to bloody her.'

'I don't care how that sounds.' After folding her arms, Peabody jerked up her chin. 'It's true.'

'Maybe when we collar the killer, there'll be an opportunity for you to engage in a bit of hand-to-hand. If you punch the killer, it should have some level of satisfaction.'

'It would. I think it would. Yeah, I feel better. Thanks.'

'Anytime.' Eve decided the fates had rewarded her for placating Peabody when she snagged a street-level slot half a block away. 'Maybe you can lose that point-three pound walking to Asner's office and back.'

11

Since Asner's office was situated over a pierogi place in a pockmarked brick building that squatted between a dingy tattoo parlor and a particularly seedy-looking bar, they added a flight of stairs to the walk.

'Pierogies. Even smelling pierogies can offset weight loss. It's a medical phenomenon.'

'Hold your breath,' Eve advised as they started the climb.

As the building squatted between bar and parlor, Asner's office squatted between a law office Eve figured specialized in repping sleazeballs and a bail bondsman who no doubt shared clients.

Eve opened the door into a claustrophobic reception area with barely enough room to hold the desk manned by a bored, busty blonde who sat painting her nails murderous red.

Clichés became clichés, Eve deduced, because they were rooted in fact.

'Good afternoon.' The blonde spoke in squeaky Brooklynese as she straightened at the desk. 'How can we assist you today?'

Eve took out her badge. 'We need to speak to Mr Asner.'

'I'm sorry. Mr Asner is not in the office presently.'

'Where is he?'

'I'm sorry. I'm unable to give you that information.'

'Did you see this?' Eve tapped her badge.

'Uh-huh.' Cooperatively the blonde nodded, widened her eyes. 'If you tell me the nature of your business I can tell Mr Asner on his return.'

'When is he expected back?'

'I'm sorry. I'm unable to give you that information.'

'Listen, sister. We're the police, get that? And we're here on police business. We need your boss's whereabouts.'

'I'm sorry—'

'Don't keep reading that same line.'

'But it's *true*.' The blonde waved her red-tipped fingers in the air. 'I can't tell you, 'cause I don't know. He said how he had some outside business, and I should hold the fort.'

'Can you contact him?'

'I *tried*, 'cause Bobbie came by and said why don't we go out for a drink, but I can't go out for a drink if I'm holding the fort. So I tried to tag him to ask when I could stop holding it, but I went right to v-mail.'

'Is this usual?'

'Well ... it depends. Sometimes A's outside business involves, um, wagering. When it does he maybe doesn't answer his 'link for a while.'

'Do you know where he wagers?'

'Different places. They move around.'

'I bet. Do you have a name?'

'Uh-huh.'

195

Eve waited a beat. Then two. 'What would your name be?'

'It's Barberella Maxine Dubrowsky. But everybody calls me Barbie.'

'Really? Okay, Barbie, let's try this. Do you have a client who resembles my partner here?'

Barbie caught her bottom lip between her teeth – a method, Eve assumed, of concentration. 'Um, no, I don't think.'

'One named K.T. Harris?'

Now the lashes fluttered, a reflex of anxiety. 'Am I supposed to tell you?'

'Yeah, you are.'

'Okay. No, at least I don't remember that name. There's an actress who has that name. She used to go with Matthew Zank. He's totally cute. I saw her in this vid about corporations and crime or something. I didn't get it. But she looked good, plus it had Declan O'Malley in it, and he's—'

'Totally cute,' Eve finished.

'Uh-huh.'

'How about a client named Delia Peabody?'

'Oh sure. She came in to see A about a week ago. Something like that. She was in with A for a long time, like maybe an hour, and he was really excited when she left. But . . .' She glanced over her shoulder, dropped her baby-doll voice to a whisper. 'I thought she was kind of a beyotch – you know?'

'Is that so?'

'She, like, ordered me around. Like—' Barbie snapped her

fingers, then frowned down at her nails. 'Shoot. I smudged them. I'm really polite with clients, but I wanted to tell her, Listen, you, just 'cause you're rich doesn't mean you can snap your fingers at me and look at me like I'm dirt.'

'Why did you think she was rich?'

'She had on these mag-o-mag shoes. I've seen them in *Styling*, and they cost *huge*. And she wore this swank dress. Some redhead comes in here in a swank dress and mag-o-mag shoes, I know she's rich. But that doesn't mean she can boss me around and tell me to go out and get her a decent cup of coffee – cream no sugar – for which she didn't even pay me. It's not like I get an expense account working here, and that coffee cost me ten. A made it good a couple days ago, but she shouldn't have done like that. Right?'

'Right. Do you know why she hired A?'

'I wrote up the file. It's okay to tell you? We're confidential.'

'I'm the police,' Eve reminded her.

'Yeah, I guess. Well, I wrote up a domestic surveillance file, and the contract for it. We do lots of those 'cause people really cheat, and that's just not right. A said to leave the amount blank.'

'Is that usual?'

'No way, but I just work here. He said to leave it blank, then he didn't give me a copy for my files. He said not to worry about it, but I do the billing and the books. I'm good with numbers. Numbers and people.' She smiled, poked out her impressive breasts. 'They're my strengths.'

'Did she come back?'

'No, she only came in the one time. Fine with me. I don't like people talking down to me. But A's been in a really good mood since. Except, I guess this morning. He came in and barely said hello, and he locked himself back in his office. He was okay when he left, though. He gave me a wink. Not that we're like that, if you know what I mean. I wouldn't get like that with the boss. You've got to keep that out of the office, right? Or you don't get respected.'

'That's smart, Barbie.'

'Anyway, I haven't seen Ms I'm-Too-Good-to-Pee-Body since the one time. Is she in trouble? I wouldn't care, except because of A.'

'You could say she had some trouble. When A comes back, or you're able to contact him, I'd appreciate it if you'd tell him I need to talk to him.' Eve dug out a card.

'I sure will. I don't think I'm going to hold the fort much longer, though. We don't have any appointments in the book anyway. So I'll leave him a message if I go before he gets back.'

'Thanks. You've been very helpful.'

She beamed. 'That's good. I like to help.'

After they left the office, Peabody shoved her hands in her pockets. 'These nicknames are pissing me off.'

'But you're not I'm-Too-Good-to-Pee-Body. Harris is.'

'It's *my* damn name. And now I have to pee. It's like my bladder has to prove something.'

'Pee at the bank. Consider it a deposit.'

*

They found another recording in the safe box, more cash, and two dated, handwritten receipts from A. A. Asner for fifty thousand each.

They bagged and labeled, and transported everything back to Central.

'Get the cash logged in and secured,' Eve told Peabody. 'I'm going to take the recorders up to Feeney for a quick analysis. Write it up. When I've finished with the recordings, I'll swing by the studio, check out the vic's trailer before I head home.'

'You don't want me with?'

'Figuring her, she's too paranoid to have much of anything in her trailer. But we've got to look, so I'll take care of it. Get it written up, copy Whitney. And you can send the file to Mira, get me some time with her tomorrow.'

'Okay. Dallas? I've been thinking. There's no murder weapon. We have motive all over the place, and the same for opportunity. Because this is a tight-knit group, when you think about it. They've been spending hours together every day for months – and they're all in the same business – the same world.'

'No argument.'

'Well, I don't know if any one of them would tell us if they actually saw someone slip out of the theater. I don't know if any one of them would tell us if they actually knew which one of them killed Harris.'

'Probably not. Or not yet.'

'I don't see how we're going to pin this one, or prove it, unless the killer decides to come in and confess.'

'Maybe we'll arrange just that. For now we take the steps, work the case. And don't put that you think we're screwed in the report.'

But she had a point, Eve thought as she headed up to EDD. They had a victim no one liked, one who'd threatened or manipulated or pissed off everyone who'd been on scene at the murder.

Three cops, she thought in annoyance, a shrink, and a former criminal now expert consultant, civilian, right there at the time and the place, and they couldn't appreciably narrow the list of suspects.

It was as embarrassing as it was infuriating.

She walked into the color and sound of EDD. And movement, she thought when she spotted McNab doing a kind of prancing pace around the room. He weaved or sidestepped when one of his fellow e-geeks strutted or boogied in his path.

Like a strange, disjointed dance, Eve thought, where even the chair-sitters bopped, swiveled, or tapped to some constant internal beat.

She stepped in front of McNab, poked him to get his attention.

'Hey.' He flicked off his earpiece. 'Got those financials for you.'

'Two withdrawals of fifty large, each within the last ten days.'

'Well, hell. You spoil the fun.'

'We tracked her PI. Anything else interesting?'

'As a matter of fact. Come, have a seat in the parlor.'

He led the way to his cube, recently decorated, Eve noted, with a poster of a monkey in a tutu riding an airboard with a PPC in one hand, a sandwich in the other while its earpiece flashed green. A smaller monkey rode in a pack on her back.

It was titled MULTITASKING MAMA.

'So, I figured I hit the gold with the 50K withdrawals, but I ran through the rest anyway. She's got auto-payments on her place in New LA, standard autos for standard home expenses, the usual blah stuff. Fees to her agent, her manager. She doesn't spend a lot considering what she pulls in. Mostly it goes to face and body treatments, wardrobe.'

He swiped through what Eve supposed he considered the usual blah stuff.

'Then I find this nice chunk charged up to I Spy, so I dig down, and it's the shop here, in Times Square. Follow that up. She bought two spy cams a couple weeks ago. Microminis, with audio, motion, and sound activation, remotes, timers – the works. I got the clerk who sold them to her, and he remembered her. Except he described her as a redhead – a "pushy, hard-ass redhead," to use his words.'

'Fits. She was a redhead when she hired the PI, and when she rented a safe box at a downtown bank. That must've been her go-to disguise. Two cams. Interesting. And interesting timing. That's good work, McNab.'

'All kudos accepted. One more deal. She also put a hefty deposit down on a high-end, high-class villa – for a two-week stay starting December twenty-third. Olympus Resorts, and she booked a private shuttle – two passengers. She had to give the names. Hers, and Matthew Zank.'

'And again interesting. Send the data to my home unit. I'll take a look when I get there. Is Feeney in his office?'

'Last I saw him.'

She headed over. The captain of the ship of noise and eye-blasting colors sat hunched at his desk in rumpled shirtsleeves. Silver threaded through his minor explosion of ginger hair. His face sagged like an old, comfortable hammock and looked as lived-in as the rumpled shirt.

As he worked his screen, he reached for one of the candied nuts in the lopsided bowl on his desk.

She gave his open door a one-knuckle rap. 'Got a minute?'

'I'm working on a goddamn budget. You can have an hour.'

'I finished mine.'

'Shut the fuck up.'

She smiled, shut the door. And Feeney's droopy eyes sharpened like arrows.

'You got doughnuts? I don't smell doughnuts.'

'Because I don't have any doughnuts.'

'Then why'd you shut the door?'

'I need you to analyze something.'

'I did your anal. The purse recording. It's clean. Straight through, no edits, no splices.'

'Good. But this is another one. And it's sensitive.' She helped herself to a couple nuts, studied the crooked orange, green, and blue bowl. 'Mrs Feeney make this?'

'Nah. She can do better than that now. Mostly. My grand-daughter made it for me. Now the kid wants a frigging pottery wheel and a kiln for Christmas. Who can think about Christmas this early?'

Apparently Harris had.

'Do you ever take off,' Eve wondered, 'go away, like a vaca-tion, for Christmas?'

'Why the hell would we do that? It's Christmas.'

'Yeah. Okay, so my vic hired a PI to plant a cam in her former bedmate's and his current bedmate's loft. I've got two recordings, one she kept in a lockbox in a safe in her hotel suite, one she kept in a safe box at a bank.'

'What did she catch them at? Screwing Dobermans? Plotting a terrorist attack?'

'I can't say as I haven't viewed them yet, but I expect she caught them doing what people do in bedrooms.'

'Has to be more than that to lock two copies in separate locations.'

'Well, I have to watch it and see. And I want to know if either of the recordings is the original. Can you tell?'

'Yeah.' He turned to his comp, called up a program, fiddled a moment. 'Let's have 'em.'

Eve took them out, unsealed each, noted down the time, the location, her name, Feeney's. He cued them into his machine. 'Run them simultaneous, split screen. The program will pop out any anomalies, determine generation of the recording.'

He ordered the run.

The screen flickered on with identical scenes as Marlo walked into the bedroom of the loft.

'That's the actress, right? I heard she looked just like you. I don't see it.'

'It's closer when she's made up for it.'

Offscreen, Matthew called out, asking if she wanted some wine.

'I wouldn't say no.' She walked to a long dresser with a soft silver gleam, opened a drawer. She tossed what looked like a T-shirt and drawstring pants on the bed, then pulled the sweater she wore over her head.

Eyes closed, she stood a moment in her bra and cargo pants, rolling her shoulders.

Matthew walked in with two glasses of wine – and smiled. 'I like your outfit.'

She smiled back. 'I got banged around some in the fight scene today.'

'You rocked it.'

'And I'm feeling every bit of it.' She took the wine, sipped, let out a pleased sigh. 'But that's a start. I'm going to get comfortable, then try to stretch some of the aches out.'

'I can help you with that.' He set his wine aside, put his hands on her shoulders, made her groan when he rubbed.

'You've got some bruises, babe.'

'Tell me about it. I can't imagine how many Dallas had after doing it for real. We should finish it tomorrow, if I can walk. Did you hear K.T. got all over Nadine and Roundtree? She wanted Peabody written into the scene.'

'I heard something about it. Don't think about her. You're tensing up just thinking about her. She's not worth it.'

'I know, I know. She doesn't care about the production. She just wants more screen time. She screamed at Preston today. I could hear her all the way in Wardrobe. She threatened to have him fired because she didn't like the angles he used in the bullpen B roll he directed.'

'Oh, for Christ's sake.'

'And she made Lindy from Craft Services cry, something about the pasta. I swear, she gets meaner and crazier every day.'

'A few more weeks, we'll be wrapped, and she'll be out of our lives.'

'Until the rounds of publicity and promotion, the media tours, the premieres. Even the thought of . . . No. I'm stopping. Why am I thinking about that lunatic when my guy's giving me a shoulder rub?'

He bent his head, kissed her between the shoulder blades. 'Just relax.'

'I will. I am. In fact.' She turned around, reaching behind to set her glass beside his. 'I have so many aches, so many places that need a good rub.'

'Poor baby.'

She laughed as she caught his hands to draw him to the bed. Then gave him a little nudge to send him down on his back. 'I really think skin-to-skin's the only answer,' she continued as she reached around, unhooked her bra.

'Anything I can do.'

'I've got some ideas on that.' She tossed the bra, unbuttoned her pants.

As she slid naked onto him, Eve felt the heat spread over the back of her neck. She had to fight an urge to shift her feet.

What had she been thinking, bringing this to Feeney? Viewing it with him. Maybe it was stupid, but she knew damn well he was as mortified and miserable as she was.

If they'd been watching bloody murder – axes hacking, blood spurting, blasters burning into flesh, neither of them would have blinked. But a naked woman, a half-naked man – okay, shit, altogether naked now – enjoying some playful sex?

Torture.

'Okay.' The sound of Feeney's throat clearing was explosive. 'End run,' he ordered. 'That's enough for the analysis. No edits or compromises on either.' He didn't look at her as he spoke, which made her profoundly grateful. 'And both are second-generation copies.'

'Neither is the original?'

'That's what I'm telling you.' Very carefully he resealed them for her.

'Asner.' Embarrassment faded away as she considered the probabilities. 'The PI. Keeping the original, maybe to try a little squeeze of his own. Or maybe he just likes to watch.'

'You can watch a copy.'

'Yeah. He kept the original, and if he sold it, he could bill it that way.' She'd still have to search K.T.'s trailer, but she leaned heavy toward the PI. 'Sell it to some gossip channel, or do a little double-dipping with the players. I need to have a conversation with A. A. Asner.' She gathered up the recordings. 'Thanks, Feeney.'

'Yeah, yeah.' Cheeks still mortification pink, he hunched back over his work.

As she headed down to her office to gather what she wanted to take home, she pulled out her 'link to try Asner's office.

Barbie's squeaky voice informed her the offices were closed, gave her the hours of operation, and invited her to leave a detailed message.

'This is Lieutenant Dallas, NYPSD. I need to speak with Mr Asner as soon as possible. I have some routine questions regarding an active investigation.'

She left it at that. Asner had at least a hundred thousand, and might be tempted to rabbit if she pushed too hard.

Considering the time, how long the trip to the studio, the search might take – especially now that she intended to search Matthew's trailer as well – she tried Roarke next.

'Lieutenant.' His face came on-screen. 'What nice timing. I've just finished a meeting.'

'You had a meeting. What a shock.' She frowned at the background noise, the blurred view behind his pretty face. 'Are you at transpo? Do you have to go somewhere?'

'No. I had to come back from somewhere. Cleveland, actually.'

'Okay. Listen, I've got to go back to the studio, do a search of the vic's trailer and some other stuff. I'm going to be late.'

'You're going to be late? What a shock.'

'I should've seen that coming.'

'I'll meet you. There's an errand I could take care of downtown. I'll meet you at the studio – Harris's trailer, you said. When we're done, we'll have some dinner with a river view.'

'Sounds like a plan. Nothing fancy, okay?'

'Pizza and beer.'

'Are you trying to seduce me?'

He laughed. 'Always. I'll see you shortly.'

She loaded up what she wanted, swung back into the bullpen. 'Neither recording's the original,' she told Peabody. 'Asner is still AWOL as far as I know. We'll try him at home first thing in the morning. Unless you hear otherwise, just meet me there.'

'LT,' Sanchez called out when she turned to leave. 'It was the girlfriend – the two dead bangers.'

'Right.'

'Former boyfriend who doesn't want to be former pulls a knife on the current boyfriend, and sticks him pretty good before current can get his own sticker out. Current's losing a lot of blood while ex is putting holes in him, and doesn't have much left to put holes in the ex. The girlfriend picked up the pipe and whaled on the ex. She says she was trying to stop him from killing current – too late for that, but it holds up pretty well. Maybe she whaled harder and longer than might be strictly on the line, but current's lying there dead or dying.'

'Are you charging her?'

'The thing is, we talked to some people, and they confirm the ex was hassling them, threatening them, started other fights. And he knocked her around pretty good, too, which is what makes him her ex. Maybe we get Man One, maybe Man Two. The PA made some noises, but isn't enthusiastic about it. Carmichael and me don't see the point in it.'

'See if Carmichael can talk her into going into one of the victim programs, then spring her if the PA's good with it.'

'Thanks, LT, that's the way we wanted it to work.'

Sometimes, Eve thought, as she sprinted to catch the elevator to the garage, things worked the way you wanted them to work.

She badged her way through security at the studio, and informed them to clear through her expert consultant, civilian, on his arrival.

She went straight back to the small city of trailers.

Lined up close, she noted. Not much privacy here. They looked the same from outside, she thought, except for the names on the doors.

She followed the guard's directions until she came to Harris's and the sealed door. Between the woman playing Nadine and the guy playing Feeney. Not, she noted, beside Matthew's or Marlo's or Julian's. She bet that gave Harris something else to bitch about.

She unsealed the door, stepped in.

Sitting or living area, she mused, with brightly colored

sofas, an oversized swivel-style leather chair. A table held a bowl of fruit, not as fresh as it had been. In the small kitchen area, the Friggie was fully stocked – water, wine, soft drinks, a selection of cheeses, berries in a clear, unopened container. A bottle of vodka in the freezer.

To get the feel of the place, she started back toward the sleeping area, glanced in the bathroom. Flowers, again not as fresh as they had been, on the counter, and a low-sided box holding soaps, shampoo, lotions.

While the bedroom wasn't spacious, it held a bed, neatly made, a fancy side chair, a wall screen. The closet was outfitted with rods and drawers.

She started there. She found another bottle of vodka – opened and half empty – in a drawer, and a small bag of zoner tucked into the toe of a boot.

She'd nearly finished the bedroom when she heard the trailer door open. Laying a hand lightly on her weapon, she stepped out – and Roarke came in.

Jesus, would she ever get over how gorgeous he was?

He smiled at her – only more gorgeous – and closed the distance to kiss her.

'Hi,' she said. 'How was Cleveland?'

'Windy. And what are we looking for in the late, largely unlamented K.T. Harris's trailer?'

'Nothing I think we'll find, but I've got to look. I'm about finished in the back. I'll fill you in.'

He skimmed a fingertip down the dent in her chin. 'One of my favorite times of day.'

'You're in a good mood,' she observed as they walked back.

'I am. It was a productive day.'

'You didn't buy Cleveland, did you?'

'Just a small piece.' He lifted his eyebrows at the vodka bottle, the bag of zoner, and the box of herbals Eve suspected was laced with the illegal. 'Are we having a party?'

'It's looking like the late and largely unlamented spent a lot of time at least partially drunk or stoned. And she'd been busy the last couple weeks.'

While she finished the room, she caught him up to date, moved to the bathroom, found the tranqs – another prescription, a different doctor.

'She sounds like a sad woman, one who found it more natural to make enemies than friends.'

'And because of that I have a houseful of suspects she'd alienated, upset, pissed off, or threatened.'

'I hate to ask, as he seemed a likable sort, but with her booking the transportation and vacation for both of them, could Matthew have been working with her to scam Marlo somehow? Get close to her, arrange for this blackmail, and then add the actual payoff in later.'

'It's a thought, and I've had it.' But she shook her head. 'It's not gelling well. Why the actual PI and payment? All they had to do was convince Marlo there'd been a PI, a break-in, a plant. Matthew could have planted the camera and saved them a bundle.'

'True enough.'

'I'm going to take a dip in his financials anyway, see if

there's anything hinky. I tagged him, asked for permission to look through his trailer. He gave me the go.' She shrugged. 'There's nothing here.' Eve shoved at her hair. 'She wouldn't risk it. The drugs, the drink, the illegals, they're only here because she needed them.'

He walked out with her, waiting while she sealed the door. 'My money says she planted the cameras she bought in Times Square in Matthew's trailer, then trashed it when she heard or saw something between him and Marlo.'

'I figure, yeah. It's the old "hell's got nothing on a woman dumped."'

'Or words to that effect,' Roarke decided.

'So, I've got his go-ahead, and can look through. If I'm right and we find them, I'm free to see what's on them.'

She led the way down the alley between trailers, turned, and walked to Matthew's.

While the layout in his was the same as K.T.'s, the feel was entirely different.

Here was casual, lived-in, a little messy. Instead of a bowl of fruit, the table held a music pod and a basket of PowerBars, candy bars, gum. There was a bottle of wine in his Friggie, but it stacked heavily toward fizzies and soft drinks. His freezer held a trio of frozen dessert bars.

Roarke found the first camera fixed to the top of the window trim in under two minutes.

'The other will be in the bedroom,' Eve told him. 'You might as well go get it while I finish in here. No point in not looking through his stuff since he gave permission.'

They walked out again in less than a half hour. 'No illegals, no drugs except standard blockers, one bottle of wine, no sex toys, and enough snack food for a grade-school class.'

She looked around again. 'He and Marlo wouldn't have snuck in here for a quickie. Too many people wandering around, too much too close. Maybe she thought they would, or maybe she just wanted to spy on him, ended up seeing them do a little kissy-face, or do the kissy-face talk.'

'You have such a way with words,' Roarke observed, and slid an arm around her shoulders. 'Let's hear some kissy-face talk.'

'I'd have to be drunk first.'

'Too true.'

'Either way you work K.T. and the cameras, it's sick. She was sick and sad.'

'She makes you angry, and she makes you sad.' He hooked an arm around her waist now, pressed his lips to her temple. 'Let's go get that beer and pizza, take a little time away from this.'

'Yeah.' She hooked her arm around him in turn. 'Let's do that.'

12

Recharging and refueling were fairly new concepts for Eve. Before Roarke, unwinding time might have been downing a beer at a cop bar, surrounded by other cops talking shop. Occasionally, if Mavis could talk her into it, a night out at a club. But for the most part she'd done the solo, in the apartment now full of color and Mavis's family.

She'd never looked, particularly, for anyone to share the end of the day with, but doing just that with Roarke – whether it was work or like this, a short interlude without it – had become a habit.

And it was better.

She liked the busy pizzeria with its clatter and conversations, its pretty view of the marina and the boats swaying in their slips. She had cold beer, hot pizza, and a man who loved her to share them with.

Yeah, it was a whole bunch better.

'Why don't you have a boat?' she asked him.

'I believe I do have one or two.'

'I don't mean big-ass cargo boats or whatever for shipping your loot from point to point.'

'Loot? That's a shadowy word. I try to stick to the light

now that I'm married to a cop.' He cocked a brow, lifted his beer. 'Think of how embarrassing it would be for both parties if she had to arrest me.'

'I'd front your bail. Probably.'

'Good to know.'

'I mean, why don't you have one of those zippy boats or the sailing jobs?' She bit into her slice, gesturing toward the window and the view with her free hand. 'The kind of boats people have who think skimming all over the place on top of the water is such a good time.'

'You don't want one.'

'Me? No. Looking at the water – it's nice. Being in the water – a pool, the beach – all good. Riding on it where you might end up in it way out there with things that live under it and want to eat you? Why go there?'

'I've been out there, and in addition to the things that live under it and want to eat you, the ocean herself can be very unforgiving.' He looked out, as she did, at the water and beyond. 'I've lived on an island, one way or the other, my entire life,' he reminded her. 'I must like them.'

'But not boats.'

'I've nothing against them.' He slid another slice of pizza onto her plate. 'I've enjoyed some of my time on them – for business, for pleasure. There was a time, when loot was more applicable to my business, I spent considerable time on boats.'

'Smuggling.'

He smiled, so easy, so wicked. 'That's one way to look at it. Another would be engaging in free enterprise. But there's more than cops and crooks in the mix when engaging in free enterprise on the high seas.'

'Such as?'

'Well.' He glanced at the boats again, then back at Eve. 'Once, in the North Atlantic, somewhere between Ireland and Greenland, we hit a storm. Or it hit us, more accurately. That would be my description of hell. The utter dark, then the blinding flashes of lightning that brought waves, taller than a building, wider than the world into terrifying relief. The sounds of the wind and water and screams of men, and the cold that numbed your face and fingers, froze your bones inside your skin.'

He took a sip of beer, shook his head. 'That's a memory.'

And the sort he rarely shared and she rarely asked about. 'What happened?'

'Well, we fought all night, and into the day, to keep afloat. It was like being rattled about like dice in a cup. The water heaving over the deck. You're never so alone as that, I think, than in a storm at sea. We didn't all make it, and there was no help for those who went into the water. The instant they did, they were lost.'

She could see he'd gone back, felt it through and through, so said nothing while he took a moment for the rest.

'I remember being slammed, tumbling toward the rail and the sea that waited to swallow a man down. And ramming into something, I can't say what even now, that stopped me before I pitched into the maw of it. And as I managed to brace myself, I caught someone's hand as those bloody waves heeled us up, caught it as he was sliding by me. I saw his face in a sheet of lightning. Little Jim, they called him as he was small and slight. Tough one though, Little Jim. I'd taken fifty from him the night before the storm in a poker game. I'd had a heart flush over his full house. I had him, I thought, I had him, but the water slammed us again, and he slipped out of my hold, and went over the side.'

He paused, lifted his beer, sipped it, like a toast. 'And that was all of Little Jim from Liverpool.'

'How old were you?'

'Hmm? Ah, eighteen. Maybe younger, maybe a bit younger than that. We lost five men that night. You wouldn't have called them good men, I suppose, but it was a hard death for them just the same. And still, we got the cargo in. So . . .'

He shrugged, bit into his pizza. 'I've no yearning to travel about on a boat. But I can pilot one well enough if you get a sudden yen.'

'I think we're both safe from that.' She laid a hand over his. 'Was it worth it?' she wondered. 'All the risks you took?'

'I am where I am, and you're with me. So it was, yes, worth it all just for this.' He turned his hand over under hers, linked fingers. 'For this.'

She thought about it on the drive home. She rarely asked specifics about the life he'd led before they'd met. She knew about the misery of his childhood, the poverty, the hunger, the violent abuse at the hands of his father.

Neither of them had cheerful, happy Christmas memories from what people called the formative years.

She knew he'd been a Dublin street rat, a thief, pickpocket, an operator, and one who'd used those street skills and more to build the foundation for what was, essentially, a business empire.

She understood that while he'd been moving toward full legitimacy when they'd met, he'd still had his fingers in a few messy pies – more for amusement than need. He'd pulled his fingers out, plugged up those holes for her. For them.

She knew bits and pieces of the time between, but there were large chunks, like a storm at sea, she didn't know.

When she wondered – and cops always wondered – she usually just let it be. Because he was right. Whatever he'd done, wherever he'd gone, it had all brought him to her.

But there were times she wondered why, and how.

'What do you think hooks people together? Besides the physical. I mean, sex hooks all sorts of people together that don't work.'

'Other than chemistry? I suppose recognition plays a part.'

She rolled her eyes toward him. 'That wifty Irish woo-woo.'

'Wifty?'

'You know.' She shook her hands in the air. 'I see how Matthew hooked up initially with K.T. Harris. Same business, same place, both attractive. I even see, to a point, why when he shook her off she dug in. That can be pride, stubbornness, or just obstinacy. But this is – was – more.

218

Obsession's more than pride and obstinacy. She followed him, spied on him, hired a PI at considerable expense to perform illegal acts, and hoped to blackmail him with the results. She was so dug in on it she planned their holiday vacation together. It didn't matter to her he didn't want her, or that if he caved and went along with her it would be under duress. It's a kind of rape.

'So I just answered my own question.'

'Power, control, and careless violence. Everything you've told me about her speaks to her wanting power, over people, her image, her career.'

'You know more about power – getting it, keeping it – than anyone I know. When you want something, you find a way to get it. You wanted me.'

Reaching over, he danced his fingers over the back of her hand. 'And I've got you, don't I?'

'Because I wanted you back. I mean, think of the coffee alone. I'd've been a fool to say no.'

'And you're no fool.'

'But if I'd been one, if I'd said no—'

'You did, initially.'

'Yeah, and you walked away. That was pride, but it was also strategy. You cut me off, and because I was stupid in love with you, I came to you.'

'Came to your senses.'

'I needed the coffee. But if I hadn't. If I'd found another means to feed my need for coffee, what would you have done?'

'I'd have done anything I could to persuade you you'd never be happy without my coffee.' Including groveling, he thought. But why bring that up?

'Not everything,' she corrected. 'A man in your position *could* do anything, that's the point. You could have pressured me, threatened me, blackmailed me. You could've used violence. But you wouldn't have.'

'I love you.' His eyes met hers briefly, and it was there. The simplicity of it. The enormity of it. 'Hurting you wasn't the goal – or an option.'

'Exactly. For K.T. hurting was just a means, because possession was the goal. And in fact, hurting was a bonus, I think. She wouldn't have stopped.'

'What does that tell you?'

'Killing her was the means to stop her. Not personal in the intimate sense, but like closing and locking a door when what's inside the room is dangerous or just really unpleasant. The lack of real violence in the killing's part of that. She falls – or gets pushed. The killer doesn't keep at her, doesn't strike, hit, choke. What he does is drag her into the water, tidy up a little. There now. All better.'

'You've eliminated Matthew.'

'The recording covers him, and Marlo, though we could argue they staged it. It's what they do. But you add the lack of physical payback. Her intentions were to force him into a sexual relationship he didn't want. That's personal, it's intimate – but the murder wasn't. So yeah, Matthew's low on the list. Marlo now ...'

'Really?'

'Not as low. I'd expect more physical from her – punch, slap, scratch – something. But I can see them intending to confront her as they stated. I can also see Marlo facing off with her first, giving her a shove, then either panicked or just really pissed off, finishing it off with the pool. Matthew would cover for her. He loves her. It doesn't play real pretty for me, but it makes a tune.'

She let it simmer while he turned in the long, winding driveway toward home. The setting sun washed the stones in gold, flashed spears of red against the many windows. Leaves, still green from summer, took on that light and hinted of the creeping autumn.

When she got out of the car, the air held that same hint – fresh, she thought, rather than chilly.

'Summer's toast,' she said.

'Well, it had a long, hot stretch of it. It's cool enough we could have a fire in the bedroom tonight.'

The idea appealed so much she continued to smile even when she walked in and saw Summerset looming in the foyer.

'Halloween's weeks off yet, but I see you've got your costume. It's good to be prepared.'

He merely cocked an eyebrow. 'I have a box of your clothes that came with you into the household and haven't been used as rags, as yet. In the event you want to trick-or-treat as a sidewalk sleeper.'

'A predictable home,' Roarke put in as he took Eve's arm to pull her upstairs, 'is a comfort to a man.'

'Did he mean that?' she demanded as the cat streaked up after them. 'Or was he yanking my chain?'

'I have no idea.'

She shot a dark look behind her. 'My clothes weren't that bad.'

'No comment,' Roarke said when she turned the look on him. 'Whatsoever.'

'All he wears is mortician black anyway. What does he know? Hey,' she objected when he continued to pilot her toward the bedroom. 'I've got work.'

'Yes, and I'd be interested in helping with that. But I want to show you something first.'

'In the bedroom?' Now she narrowed her eyes, gave him an up and down. 'I've seen it before. It's nice. I can probably make time to play with it later.'

'You're too good to me.'

He steered her straight in, and toward the box tied with a gold bow on the bed.

'Oh man. You got me something in Cleveland.' In reflex, her hands dove into her pockets. 'You should put it away until Christmas.'

'It's barely October, and you'll want this before Christmas. It's not from Cleveland.'

'I already have everything. You just keep buying stuff.'

'You don't have this, which you'd see for yourself if you'd open the bloody thing.' He gave her a finger flick on the head.

'Okay, okay. It's too big for jewelry, so I probably won't

lose it. It's clothes because everything I used to have is rag fodder. It's something nice.' She gave the ribbon a tug. 'So I'll probably destroy it at work, then Summerset'll give me the hairy eyeball. Which is just one of the reasons I wish you wouldn't—

'Oh . . .' There was a flavor to the sound she made, as a woman might make eating soft, creamy chocolate. 'Nice.'

She had a weakness for leather and rich colors, which he knew very well. When she pulled the jacket out of the box, he saw the deep, burnished bronze suited her just as well as he'd hoped. It would hit her mid-thigh, and fall very straight. The deep, slash pockets – reinforced – would hold everything she needed to carry. The buttons on the front, and on the decorative belt in the back, were in the shape of her badge.

'It's great.' She pushed her face against it, inhaling the scent. 'Really great. I love the coat you got me last year.' Even as she spoke she rubbed her cheek against the leather. 'I really don't need—'

'Consider this one a transition. The other's long and for colder weather. You can wear this now. Try it on.'

She saw the label. 'Leonardo did it, so it's going to fit – ha ha – like it was made for me. Look at the buttons!'

'We thought you'd like that.'

Yes, he thought, it fit her perfectly, suited her perfectly – the color, the cut, the subtle embellishments. When she turned toward him, the hem swirled around her thighs.

'It feels great, too. No pull in the shoulders because of my weapon harness.' She slid a hand inside, drew her weapon

223

smoothly, and smoothly replaced it. 'It doesn't get in the way.'

'There's a knife sheath worked into the lining – right side as you prefer the cross-draw, and use your right hand for your main weapon.'

'No shit.' She opened the jacket, checked. Mimed by crossing her arms, and drawing both gun and imaginary knife simultaneously. 'Handy. Pretty damn handy. What's with this lining? It feels sort of dense. It's not heavy, but it doesn't feel like coat lining.'

'Something we've been working on in R and D for a while.' He crossed to her, ran his fingers over the lining himself. 'It's body armor.'

'Get out.' Her forehead creased as she examined it more closely. 'It's too thin and light. Plus it moves.'

'Trust me, it's been thoroughly tested. Leonardo was able to take the material and fashion it into the coat. It will block a stun on full, though you'll feel the impact. It'll protect from a blaster, though the leather would suffer. And it will block a blade – though again, pity about the leather.'

'Seriously?' She pulled her weapon again, offered it. 'Try it.'

He had to laugh even as he thought: *Typical. Just typical.* 'I will not.'

'Not very confident in your research and development.'

'I'm not firing a stunner at my wife in our bedroom.'

'We can go downstairs to the range.'

'Eve.' With a shake of his head, he guided her hand back

until she holstered the weapon. 'Trust me. It's been tested. You have the prototype in a very flattering and fashionable form. We'll be moving into production shortly, and negotiating with the NYPSD to be the first police force so equipped – not as fashionably, of course.'

'It's like nothing else. And it really moves.' She tested by going into a crouch, a spin, trying a side kick. 'Doesn't hamper range of motion or—' It struck her then.

'You said you've been working on it awhile.'

'It takes time to develop something new, and one that fits specific requirements.'

'How long a while?'

He smiled a little. 'Oh, I'd say about two and a half years. Since I fell for a cop.'

'For me.'

'For me as well. I want to keep you.' When she reached up, laid a hand on his cheek, he took her wrist, turned her palm to his lips. 'We were close, but I pushed a bit in the last few weeks.'

'Since Dallas.'

'He hurt you. I realize you wouldn't have been wearing body armor when McQueen attacked you in our hotel room, but all the same. He hurt you and I wasn't there.'

'You were there when I needed you. I beat him, again, but I nearly lost myself.'

'You wouldn't have.'

'All I know is you were there when I needed you. I don't know if I could've gotten through any of it without you. I don't ever want to go back there.' She closed her eyes briefly. 'But if I have to, I know you'll go with me.'

'You'll never go back alone, Eve.'

'You've been careful with me since we got back. Nothing too obvious, but you've been careful. You don't need to be.'

'I could say the same.'

'I guess we both went through the wringer, so we've been trying not to push the wrong buttons. One of us will forget, or get pissed, and push one. And that's all right. We're all right.'

'You haven't had nightmares since. I thought you would, worried that . . . Eve,' he said, flatly, when she stepped back.

'Not nightmares. Not like that. Just . . .' She shrugged, then took off the coat, carefully laid it on the bed. 'Dreams. Just dreams. Sometimes it's just her – Stella – sometimes with McQueen or with my father. Sometimes all of them. But I can pull out of them before they get bad. Really bad.'

'Why haven't you told me?'

'Maybe because we're being careful with each other. I don't know, Roarke. They're dreams. I *know* they're dreams, even when I'm having them. They're nothing like on the level of what I had in Dallas. And I can stop them, before they get really bad, I can stop them. I need to.'

'You don't need to do this alone.'

'I'm not.' She touched his face again. 'You're right there. If I need you, you're right there.'

'Have you talked to Mira?'

'Not yet, not really. I will,' she promised. 'I know I have to.

I'm not ready, just not ready. I feel ... good. Strong, normal. I know I need to talk to her, go through the process, and that during the process I won't feel good, strong, I won't feel normal. I'm not ready for that yet.'

'All right.'

She smiled again. 'Still being careful.'

'Maybe, but I believe you'll know when you're ready. And that I'll know. You're not.' He laid his lips on her brow. 'But you will be.'

She leaned into him, laid her head on his shoulder. 'Thanks for the magic coat.'

'You're welcome.'

She shifted, wrapped her arms around him for the kiss. Then sighed. 'Okay, we'll have to do this now.'

'What would that be?'

She stepped back. 'As usual, you're wearing too many clothes. Start fixing that.'

She stepped past him to take the coat and box off the bed.

'Is this a seduction?' he asked. 'I'm all aquiver.'

'Here's how it is.' She set the box and coat on the sofa, unhooked her weapon harness. 'One of the things I have to do is watch Matthew and Marlo have sex – all the way through this time since Feeney and I aren't reviewing it together and suffering the mortification from hell. After doing that having sex with you is just going to be weird. So we'll do it now, before it gets weird.'

'Maybe I'm not in the mood.'

She let out a snort. 'Yeah. As if.' She sat to pull off her

boots, eyed him. 'I'd buy you dinner first, but we already ate.'

'We didn't have dessert.'

She sent him a wicked grin. 'That's what I'm saying.'

He laughed, then sat on the side of the bed and took off his shoes. 'Well, since you're so determined.'

'Oh.' She stood, took off her shirt, her pants. 'I can take no for an answer.'

'Who said no?'

She crossed to him, long and lithe, and sat on his lap, facing him. Grabbing his hair, she crushed her mouth to his, drawing the kiss down, down, coloring it dark and dangerous. She slid her hand down between them, gave him one hard stroke. 'Yeah, you seem to be in the mood now.'

She angled away, slithered onto the bed, then rolled, lifted her eyebrows at him. 'About those clothes.'

It took him roughly ten seconds to get rid of them. 'What clothes?' he asked, and tumbled down to her.

She was laughing when they rolled. The cat, who'd assumed it was nap time, leaped off the bed to stalk away in disgust.

She needed to play, Roarke thought, to offset the brief journey into bad dreams and hard memories. He played his fingertips down her ribs, made her squirm and gasp out what was close to a giggle.

'Foul!' She grabbed his ass in a hard squeeze.

'What, this?' He tickled her ribs again until she bucked, choking on a laugh.

'Keep that up, you won't get laid.'

'Oh, I think I will as you'll be too weak to fight me off.' He drilled his finger into her side, and when she squealed – a sound so rare and foreign for her – he dissolved into laughter of his own.

'Got you now,' he murmured, nipping lightly at her shoulder. 'A bit of a tickle and you turn into a girl.'

'You're looking for trouble.'

'Oh, that I am, and as you're all naked with girlish squeals under me, I think I can find it.'

'We'll see who squeals, pal.' She caught his earlobe, not so lightly, between her teeth.

'That was a yelp,' he claimed. 'And a manly one.'

She levered up, so he used the momentum to roll again, once, twice, until they ended up in the same position but across the bed.

'You're outweighed, Lieutenant. And outmuscled.' He gripped her hands, drew them over her head. 'Might as well give it over.'

He lowered his mouth to take her, and the sound she made now was pure pleasure. Her body went soft beneath his while the sole of her foot slid up to stroke his leg.

The next he knew he was on his back, her knee at his balls, her elbow at his throat. Her eyes glinted down into his.

'Weight and muscle fall beneath agility.'

'You're a slippery one, you are.'

'Damn right, so you might as well give it over.' Now she lowered her mouth, then stopped a teasing breath away, drew back, teased in for a sampling nip, then another before she covered his mouth with hers.

'Who's a girl?'

'You're mine.' His hands glided down her back, around and up to her breasts. 'You're my girl.'

'Sap,' she said, but in a little sigh as she gave him her lips again.

She'd never been anybody's girl, had never wanted to be. It had always seemed a weak term to her, one of submission and vulnerability. But with him, it was sweet and foolish, and just exactly right.

With more affection than passion – passion would come – she dropped kisses on his face. Oh, how she loved his face, the angles of it, the planes of his cheekbones, the line of his jaw.

She felt that affection, the simplicity of it, the scope of it from him as he wrapped his arms around her.

For a moment they stayed quiet, body to body, her lips resting on his cheek.

When she pressed her face into the side of his throat, he thought it the most magnificent thing.

His girl, he thought as hands and lips began to stoke the first embers of passion. His strong, complicated, and resilient girl. He loved every corner of her mind, her heart, even when she maddened him. There was nothing he wanted or treasured more truly, nothing he had craved or dreamed of in those dark, often desperate years of youth that was as rich or as powerful as what she'd given him.

He'd believed in love despite the lack of it in those early years, or perhaps because of the lack. But it had taken her to show him what love meant, what it gifted, what it cost, what it risked.

Breath quickened as the fire built to a blaze. She moved over him, supple as silk, then under him when he turned her. When he filled her.

Once again he took her hands, once again their eyes met, then their lips. Joined, they let the fire take them.

Later in her office, her board set up, her computer on the hum, she studied the faces, the facts, the evidence, the time line.

And felt as if she studied a blank brick wall.

'I don't understand them. Maybe that's why I can't get a good hold on this. Acting, producing, directing – and all that goes into it. It's a business, an industry, but it's based on pretending.'

'You're equating pretending with pretense,' Roarke responded. 'They're not the same. Imagination's essential to the healthy human condition, for progress, for art, even for police work.'

She started to disagree about the police work, then reconsidered. She had to imagine, to some extent, the victim, the killer, the events in order to find the reality.

Still.

'These people – the actors. They have to become someone else. They have to want to become someone else. Playacting, isn't that a term for it? Play. But they have to make a living at it. So you get agents and managers, directors, producers.'

She circled the board. 'The director. He has to see the big picture, right? The whole of it even while he separates it into sections, into scenes. He calls the shots, but he's dependent on the actors taking his direction, and being able to . . .'

'Become,' Roarke finished. 'As you said.'

'Yeah. The producer, he's got the financial investment and the power. He's the one who says yeah, he can have that, or no, you can't. He has to see the big picture, too, but with dollars and cents attached. So he needs more than what the actors and director put on-screen. He needs them to cultivate image and generate media so the public can imagine the real lives – the glamour, the sex, the scandals – of the actors who make their living being someone else.'

She circled again. 'So specifically, you've got Steinburger as producer – and I imagine the suits that line up with him, because suits always line up – seeing to it the public are fed Julian and Marlo as an item. Because they consider the public largely made up of morons – and I don't disagree – who'll buy into the fantasy. More, who *want* that fantasy and will fork over the ready for more tickets, more home discs. Because, back to business, everybody wants a return on their investment.'

'What does that tell you?'

'For one thing, Julian, Marlo, and everyone involved went along with that angle. Most of their interviews are playful,

232

flirtatious, without actual confirmation or denial. If one or both of them is asked if they're involved romantically, they give clever varieties of the old "we're just good friends" – with little teases about chemistry and heat. The same goes for Matthew and Harris.'

Eve stopped her pacing in front of the board. 'That's more low-key, as the investment in their fantasy isn't as important. K.T. did more playing that up – chemistry again, how much she enjoys her scenes with Matthew. He talks more about the project as a whole, or the cast as a group. He's careful, even in the interviews, not to connect himself too solidly with Harris. He doesn't want that fantasy in his head, or the public's. That's strictly the work on the set. He's careful,' she said again.

'And that tells you?'

'She wasn't important to him, not really. People kill what – or who – isn't important, but that's not what we've got here. He and Marlo were upset, pissed off, but not murderous. If they'd argued, and it got physical, that would have been that. She was alive when she went in the water. She wasn't important enough to either of them to kill, because over and above the invasion of privacy, some embarrassment, they'd both have gotten through that – and reaped public support – everybody loves a lover.'

'They're happy,' Roarke added. 'Happiness is exceptional revenge. If she'd played it through, she'd have looked the fool, not them. I agree, it doesn't work.'

'There's Andrea. K.T. threatened her godson, his hard-won

233

peace, his reputation. Mothers kill to protect their young. She didn't give me a buzz in Interview, but she's a seasoned and talented pro. So she's on. Then there's Julian. If the relationship between Marlo and Matthew came out – now, before the end of the project, before he'd had any opportunity to walk back all that flirting and chemistry, some might see it as Marlo preferring the lesser star, the sidekick you could say, to the big guns. That could make him look like a fool, or less – chip that women-can't-resist-me image he's got going. Added, she embarrassed him at dinner. Added, he was drunk. A confrontation, a scuffle, temper, ego, pride, and alcohol. That's got a solid ring.'

'I think you enjoy considering me – my counterpart in any case – as your prime suspect.'

'It has a certain entertaining irony. But more, he's just not too bright, and the drunken stupor on the sofa afterward could read as burying his head in the sand. Let's make this go away.'

She nodded as it played out in her head. 'In the imagination portion of police work, I can see him killing her – mostly through accident followed by cover-this-up, followed by avoidance of reality.'

Eve eased a hip on the corner of her desk. 'Steinburger, who I need to talk to again. She's threatening his profits, the shiny gleam to the project. She's a major pain in his ass. And, as she had something on several other players here, she may very well have had something up her sleeve on him. Same scenario. Confrontation, fall, cover up.

234

'She's threatening Preston — same deal. This project's a major break for him, working with Roundtree, major stars, major budget, and she wants to screw him because he can't give in to all her demands. He doesn't have the power, but she doesn't care about that.'

'So far you've only eliminated Marlo and Matthew,' Roarke pointed out.

'And Roundtree. He just couldn't have gotten out of the room, up on the roof, killed her, and gotten back in the time frame. He was too much front and center. But Connie wasn't, and by her own admission left the theater. She was furious with Harris, and since my impression is Roundtree talks to her about the work, the ups and down, likely already had a nice store of pissed-off going. Again, no buzz, but again, she's a pro. And again, K.T. may have had something on her, or on Roundtree.

'Then there's Valerie. Keeps quiet, does the work, follows orders. She's the one spinning the promotion wheel, and K.T.'s threatening to throw pliers in it.'

'That's wrench, but just the same.'

'She could've confronted K.T., warned her to cooperate, and the scenario plays out.'

'All right, Lieutenant, you've laid it out. Who do you like for it?'

'Just hunch and supposition, or imagination, I guess. In descending order: Julian, Steinburger, Valerie, Andrea, Connie, Preston. Which means I talk to all of them again, go back to the beginning, and try to shake them up. After I talk to the PI. I may get something out of him that changes that order.'

She pushed up to go around the desk and sit. 'But it's one of them, and whichever one is nervous, worried, and sweating it out. First kills will do that to you.'

13

Eve yanked herself out of the dream and into the hazy light of dawn. Breathing, just breathing, to give herself a moment to be sure she was awake, and not making that jerky transition from one segment of a dream to another.

Her throat begged for water, but she lay still another moment, eyes closed, waiting for her pulse to slow.

Roarke's arm came around her, drew her close against him. Anchored her. 'I'm here.'

'It's nothing. I have to get up, get started.'

'Ssh.'

She closed her eyes again. She hated this waking fragility, this thin, shaky sensation as if she'd crack if she moved too quickly. She knew it would pass, it would smooth away again, but she hated it nonetheless. Hated, too, knowing he'd broken his habit of being up, dressed, and having accomplished God knew what in the business world before she stirred.

'Tell me.'

'It's nothing,' she repeated, but he brushed his lips over her hair. Undid her.

'Stella, in the bedroom of the place she had in Dallas. The one we searched. But it's like the bedroom from before, too, when I was a kid. I don't know where we were then. It doesn't matter. She's sitting at this little table, with all her lip dyes and creams and paints – all that stuff. I can smell her, that perfume – too sweet. It makes my stomach hurt. Her back's to me, but she's looking at me in the mirror with all that hate, that contempt. I can smell that, too. It's hot and bitter.

'I need some water.'

'I'll get it.'

She didn't argue, no point. In any case, she felt a little better, a little stronger. Just a dream, she reminded herself. And she'd known it for what it was while she'd been in it.

That had to matter.

She took the water Roarke brought her, ordered herself to drink it slowly.

'Thanks.'

He said nothing, only set the empty glass aside, took her hand.

'Her throat,' Eve continued, bringing her fingers to her own. 'Blood pouring out of her throat, down the front of the pink dress she was wearing when I busted her, when I wrecked the van. She's so angry. It's my fault, she says. Look at her dress. I ruined it. I ruined everything. Then I see him in the mirror, I see him behind me. McQueen. Or my father. It's so hard to tell. I reach for my weapon, but it's not there. I don't have my weapon. And she smiles. In the mirror, she smiles, and it's horrible.

'I have to get out, I have to wake up. So I wake up.'

'Is it always the same?'

'No, not exactly. I'm not afraid of her. I want to ask why she hated me so much, but I know there's no answer. I'm not afraid until, at whatever angle the dream takes, I go for my weapon and it's not there. Then I'm afraid. So I have to wake up.'

'None of them can touch you, not ever again.'

'I know. And when I wake up I'm here. It's okay; I'm okay, because I'm here. I don't want you to worry about me. I'll just feel guilty.'

'I'll try to worry only a little so you'll only feel a little guilty.'

'I guess that'll have to do.' She shifted so they were nose-to-nose and heart-to-heart. 'Don't change your routine because of this. That'll get me wired and worried. Besides, if you don't keep up with your predawn quest for world financial domination, how are you going to keep me in coffee? If you slack off, I'll have to find another Irish gazillionaire with coffee bean connections.'

'That would never do. I'll continue my quest if you promise to tell me when they come.' Gently, he trailed his hand over her hair. 'Don't keep them from me anymore, Eve.'

'Okay.'

'And since it appears the very core of my happiness rests on your addiction to coffee, I'll get you some.'

'I won't say no, but I've got to get moving. I'm meeting Peabody at Asner's place. I want to hit his apartment early before he gets out.'

'Asner?' Roarke said as he rose and walked to the AutoChef.

'The PI.'

'Ah, yes. A light breakfast then.' The cat bumped against his legs, wound through them. 'For some of us.'

She got up, knowing he'd try to pamper her into taking her coffee – and possibly the light breakfast – in bed. She took the mug from him, knocked some back.

'I'm going to grab a shower,' she told him. 'You'd better catch up on the world domination.'

'I'll get right on that, after I feed the cat.'

He did so while she went for the shower. Then, drinking his own coffee, stood by the window.

Careful with each other, she'd said. Yes, they were just now. And it looked as if they'd need to be for a little longer yet.

She felt like herself – maybe even just a little better due to the magic coat – when she drove downtown. She left the windows down so the brisk air could slap her cheeks, pleased that the ad blimps had yet to start their hyping lumber in the sky, and the snarl and piss of New York traffic could rage on without the blast from above.

Too early for blimps, too early for most tourists. It felt like New York nearly belonged to New Yorkers. Glide-carts did their morning business, heavy on the soy coffee and egg pockets. Maxibuses burped and farted their commuters to the early shift or breakfast meetings while those on foot clipped along or swarmed the crosswalks like purposeful ants.

She had a plan, and it started with cornering A. A. Asner.

Charges of breaking-and-entering, criminal trespass, electronic trespass, accessory to blackmail – to start – and the threat of losing his license and livelihood should make him talk like a toddler on a sugar high.

She'd bargain some of that against him turning over the original recording – and all copies, as well as spilling any and all data he had on K.T. Harris, her movements, her intentions, her meets.

If he hadn't done some research on Harris, some shadowing, she'd eat her new magic coat.

And to cover bases, she'd requested a warrant for both his home and offices, citing his business with the victim.

She expected to get it.

She settled for a second-level spot a block and a half from Asner's apartment building. Decent neighborhood, she noted. Better than what he'd chosen for his office. Packs of kids shuffled down the sidewalk, heading for school, she imagined, some of them herded by parents or nannies. Their chatter piped through the air as most headed along the sidewalks in what she assumed was the latest kid fashion of mid-calf boots with soles thick as a slab of wood.

Those who didn't shuffle, clumped.

A woman in overalls hefted up the safety grill on a small market. She shot Eve a smile.

Fresher weather, Eve thought, fresher people.

She enjoyed the walk, promised herself she'd get in the solid workout the preshift visit to Asner had postponed until the evening.

She spotted Peabody coming from the opposite direction in kind of a quick march. The cowboy boots Roarke decided Peabody had to have from Dallas flashed sizzling pink with every stride.

The stride hitched, and Peabody's mouth formed a stunned O. Instinctively, Eve laid a hand on her weapon, checked behind her, but Peabody was already dancing – the only word that fit – down the sidewalk.

She said, 'Ohhhh,' and reached out.

'Hey. Hands off.'

'Please. Please, please, soooo pretty. Lemme just have one little touch.'

'Peabody, isn't it embarrassing enough you're wearing pink cowboy boots, again, without standing here drooling on my coat?'

'I love them. Love, love my pink cowboy boots. I think they're going to be my signature footwear.' She snuck in a stroke along the sleeve of Eve's coat. She said, again, 'Ohhhh, ultra-squared. It's like butter.'

'If it was like butter it'd be melting all over me.'

'It sort of does. It's all gushy and soft and so completely uptown. When you were walking it just swished. It's just as mag as your long one.'

'Now that we've discussed our wardrobe choices for the day, maybe we can go roust Asner. Since we're here anyway.'

Peabody's hand came up again, and Eve pointed a warning finger. 'You already touched.' When she turned to the building's entrance, Peabody let out her third *ohhhh* of the morning.

'The belt detail in the back. It highlights your butt.'

'What?' Stunned, Eve tried to crane her neck and look. 'Christ.'

'No, no, in a *good* way, not in a skanky way.' She snuck in another stroke. 'Was it a just-because? I love just-because presents the best. Last month McNab gave me the cutest pair of earrings – like chains of hearts – just because. You know a guy's stuck on you if he springs for just-because jewelry of any kind.'

'Okay.' Which, by Peabody's measure, would mean Roarke was stuck on her like a man in quicksand. She stopped at the door, pulled out her master. 'It's lined with body armor.'

'Say what?'

Eve opened the jacket. 'The lining, it's a new material his R and D people developed. Blast-, stunner-, and blade-proof.'

'Seriously?' This time Eve made no objection when Peabody fingered the lining material. It was, in Eve's opinion, a cop thing and allowed.

'It's so thin, and light – and it moves. It shields a blast?'

'So he says, and he'd know. I figured you could stun me later to test it out.'

'Hot damn. You know what, the jacket's like the car.'

'Is this a riddle?'

'No,' Peabody said as Eve swiped the master. 'It's an ordinary thing – well, special, but a jacket, right? And the car, it's ordinary, it even looks it. But both of them have the special inside. Cop special especially, you know? He so gets you. That's even better than a just-because present.'

'You're right. He does. And it is.' Inside, Eve paused another moment. 'He's worried about me.'

'Going to – being in – Dallas had to be hard on both of you,' Peabody said carefully.

'You don't push.'

'I read your reports, and I figure there's a lot of stuff, personal stuff, not in them. I get you, too. Partners better get each other, right?'

'Yeah.'

'One day maybe we'll have a drink, and you'll tell me what wasn't in the reports.'

'We will.' And could, Eve realized, because Peabody got her. Because she didn't push. 'I will. Asner's place is on the second floor.'

As they started up Eve heard the usual morning sounds from an older, unsoundproofed, working-class building. The mutter and pulse of morning shows on-screen, music, doors closing, the whine of the elevator, and of kids not yet shuffling or clomping toward school.

No palm plates on the doors, she noted, but plenty of sturdy locks, security peeps. She studied the Secure-One plate on Asner's door, and figured it for show, a deterrent rather than the real deal.

She used the side of her fist, gave the door a good trio of bangs. Almost immediately the door across the hall opened. The man who came out wore sweats, a warm-up jacket, running shoes. He carried a gym bag over his shoulder. He gave them an easy smile as he fit a ball cap over scraggly brown hair.

'I don't think A's home.'

'Oh?' Eve responded.

'I gave him a tag a few minutes ago. We're gym buddies, and usually head out together most mornings. He didn't answer, so . . . ' He shrugged.

'Did you see him yesterday?'

The smile faded into suspicion. 'Yeah. Why?'

Eve took out her badge. 'We need to talk to Mr Asner. When did you see him yesterday?'

'About this time. We hit the gym. What's this about?'

'We need to talk to him about an ongoing investigation.'

'Then you should probably try his office.' He gave them the address they already had. 'It's a little early, but if he's working on something that kept him out all night, he might've just bunked there.'

'Out all night?'

The man shifted, obviously uncomfortable. 'I'm assuming. We made plans – loose ones – to watch the game together, with a couple other guys last night. My place. He didn't show, and he's not one to miss game night, especially when we had a bet on it. So I figured he got caught up on work. Look, you should just go to his office. I don't like talking about a buddy to the cops. It feels off.'

'Understood. We appreciate the time.' Eve took out a card. 'Listen, if you do happen to see him at the gym, just tell him to contact me.'

'Sure. I can do that.' He slipped the card into his bag. Relaxed again, he smiled. 'If you see A first, tell him he owes me twenty.'

'Will do.'

Eve waited until the neighbor jogged down the steps. 'We might as well try the office. It's not far, and he might've bunked there, especially if he spent the day gambling and got stung.'

Once they were in the car, Eve ran through her suppositions, conclusions, and theories reached the night before.

'I agree about Matthew and Marlo,' Peabody said. 'They're happy lovebirds. Not that lovebirds don't kill – the inconvenient spouse or "rich, just won't give up and die" Great-aunt Edna. But not only doesn't Harris apply, but neither has a spouse, and they're both more than sound financially. Was there anything on the recording I should know about?'

'They had sex, some post-coital mushy pillow talk. They did some yoga together, then ordered Chinese food, ate it while they – what do you call it – ran lines on upcoming scenes. He helped her with the choreography of a fight scene. Talk that wasn't work-oriented stuck mostly to choices of a getaway. It's between Fiji and Corfu – or was. They watched some screen in bed, had another – shorter – round of sex, went to sleep.'

'Sounds kind of normal,' Peabody observed, 'settled. Happy lovebirds.'

'The morning routine was no surprises. A workout, shower sex – which I assume, as they left the bathroom door open and the audio picked up some sex sounds – fruit and yogurt for breakfast, more work and getaway talk. They laugh a lot. Dressed and out the door.'

'No sign of Harris, or the PI picking up the cameras?'

'He'd have edited himself out, if he had a brain. Since the recording ends with them leaving, he has a brain. No sign of Harris, and very little said about her from either spied-on party. Which probably burned her ass.'

Eve parked, checking Asner's office window as she got out. The overcast sky made the day a little gloomy, but no lights shone in his office.

'He's either not in yet, or still asleep.'

As they went in, started up, she asked herself why, if he had a brain, he dodged the cops. He had to know they'd pin him down, and the longer it took, the less friendly the pinning. Maybe working out a story, a cover, maybe consulting his lawyer.

Or maybe he'd taken his big paycheck and smoked.

She didn't much like that idea, and liked the other possibility that circled her mind even less.

She approached Asner's office door, started to rap on the glass. 'It's not secured.'

The other possibility stopped circling to hover. She drew her weapon, as did Peabody.

'He could have forgotten to lock it,' Peabody said quietly.

'A waste of good locks.' She nodded, counted off, and they went in the door together.

The quick initial sweep showed her the disorder of the reception area. All that was left of the computer on the desk was the screen. The drawers had been pulled out, upended.

Again at Eve's signal Peabody moved toward the inner office. She pulled open the door, swept right while Eve swept left.

Disorder reigned here, too, as well as death. A. A. Asner lay facedown on the floor. The back of his skull had been smashed in, presumably with the statue of a bird that lay nearby covered in blood and matter.

He wouldn't be paying his gym buddy the twenty, Eve thought, and was beyond being pressured to talk about his equally dead client.

Eve holstered her weapon. 'Go get the field kit, and I'll call it in.'

'Hit him from behind,' Peabody said. 'Hard, and more than once. No calling this one an accident.'

She hurried out while Eve contacted Dispatch, reported the DB, requested uniforms for securing the scene and canvassing, a sweeper unit, and a morgue team.

She took out her recorder, fixed it on, engaged it. 'Dallas, Lieutenant Eve, and Peabody, Detective Delia, entered the offices of Asner, A. A., Private Investigations. The door was not secured. Detective Peabody has returned to our vehicle for a field kit. Dispatch has been contacted, and support teams have been requested.

'The victim, identity yet to be confirmed, has suffered multiple blows to the back of the head. The weapon appears to be a statue of a black bird, wings folded in, beak – Maltese falcon,' she murmured. 'He got bashed with a replica – souvenir – whatever from the vid. Book, too,' she remembered.

Both were among Roarke's favorites.

'Hero in the story's a hard-bitten PI, early twentieth century. More irony, I guess.'

She walked out, studied the entrance door. 'No visible sign of forced entry. He let the killer in, or came in with him. He either knew him or wasn't worried about him as the killing blow came from behind.'

Careful to touch nothing, she walked toward the office again. 'Moving toward the desk, back to the killer. Small table to the left of the office door. Easy reach. Grab it, smash it. Asner goes down.'

Avoiding the congealed blood pooled on the floor, she moved closer to the body. 'Another blow as he's going down. Maybe a third and fourth for good measure when he's on the ground. Messy. The office has been ransacked, as has the reception area. Computers are missing, drawers searched. The vic is not wearing a wrist unit, possible robbery. But that's bogus. Bogus. Coincidence, my ass. Whoever did Asner did Harris. And wanted the recording, wanted information, wanted . . . silence.'

She glanced over as Peabody came back, panting slightly, with the field kit. 'What are the chances of it being a coincidence that the PI Harris hired got bashed to death in the neighborhood of twenty-four hours after she drowned?'

'Slim to none,' Peabody responded and offered Eve the Seal-It from the kit.

'I say even extra-slim to none. Let's verify his ID for the record, get TOD.'

'Take off the coat.'

'What?'

'It's brand-new, Dallas, and extreme. Why risk getting blood or dead yuck on it? I put three coats of protective shield on my boots, so they won't get yucked up.'

She had a point, Eve thought as she took off the coat. Which was why, in her view, cops shouldn't wear anything they had to worry about getting yucked up.

With the coat set safely aside, she crouched by the body.

'Victim is confirmed as Abner Andrew Asner,' Peabody said when she checked prints. 'Age forty-six, licensed private investigator, and owner/operator of the business at this location.'

Working with the gauges, Eve nodded. 'TOD, twenty-three-twenty. So, a late appointment or meet.' She checked pockets. 'No wallet in his back pockets, none front pants pocket my side, no loose change, no nothing. Your side?'

'Nothing,' Peabody confirmed. 'No wrist unit either. No pocket 'link on him, or memo book, no weapon.'

'There's a jacket on the floor over there, under that peg. Check it, then the desk. Tried to make it look like a robbery,' Eve continued, 'the way they tried to make Harris look like accidental drowning. Make-believe, but not convincing if you know *squat* about police work.'

'Because we're not idiots,' Peabody confirmed. 'Nothing in the jacket. A couple of wrapped mints on the floor, like

250

maybe they were in the pocket.' She moved onto the desk as Eve sat back on her heels.

'The vic got a hundred K, but he kept the original record-ing. Just couldn't resist. Maybe a little more to make here, he thinks. From who? He has to figure Harris is going to hit Marlo and Matthew. Would he try a double dip there? Or would he try for another interested party?'

'I guess we find out what all interested parties were doing right around eleven-thirty last night.'

'That would be good information.'

'They're all probably at the studio. Preston contacted me last night to tell me they're scheduled to shoot my scene on Saturday, and if I had any time free, I could swing in, take a look at some wardrobe today.'

'You're still doing that?'

'Well . . . ' Peabody stopped sifting through the debris on and around the desk. 'Do you think I shouldn't?'

'No reason not to. If we don't have this nailed down by then, cops playact with killers all the time.'

'I hadn't thought of that. McNab's going with me. They may sneak him into a scene, too. And I can handle some wussy smash-from-behind Hollywood killer. Buffing up on hand-to-hand, remember?' She flexed her right biceps.

'When you're picking out wardrobe, pick out something that can handle your weapon, or an ankle piece.'

'Good idea. No memo or appointment book, no pocket 'link, no recording.'

'Keep looking. I'll take reception.'

She'd barely started when the uniforms arrived. She sent them both out to canvass the building and a two-block radius. The killer had hauled out electronics, which meant he'd had transportation or a partner with same. So he'd had to park, and make at least two trips up and back. They'd see how late the restaurant on the street level operated, and the tattoo parlor. She had no doubt the sketchy-looking bar would have been open and doing business at the killing hour.

She looked up again at the click, click, click of heels in the corridor – the giggle, and the lower male laugh.

Eve moved to the door, stepped out to see Barbie in a red skirt barely bigger than a dinner napkin, doing the hair-toss, eyelash-bat routine for the benefit of a lanky, lantern-jawed guy in a wrinkled suit.

Bobbie, Eve presumed. It appeared they'd done more than have a drink.

Still giggling, Barbie turned her head, and this time batted her lashes in surprise. 'Oh. You're back.'

'Yeah.'

'A let you in? I didn't expect him so early. I came early 'cause I felt a little guilty about leaving before closing yesterday.'

'Did you speak to Mr Asner after my partner and I left?'

'No. He never tagged back, so I just v-mailed I was closing up.' She bit her lip. 'Is he mad? I didn't think he'd care since—'

'No, he's not mad. I'm sorry to tell you Mr Asner was murdered last night.'

'What? *What?*' She screeched the second what. 'A doesn't get murdered. He's a professional.'

'It appears he came in with, or let someone into his office last night. He was struck on the back of the head with the statue of a black bird.'

'Birdie! No. Are you sure, are you sure? Because A can take care of himself. He shouldn't be dead.'

'I'm very sorry for your loss.'

'But – but.' Tears erupted like spurts of lava, rolled down her face as she turned it in to her companion's chest. 'Bobbie.'

'Robert Willoughby. I'm an attorney. My office,' he added, gestured to the neighboring door. 'I know you need to ask, so I'll save you time. Barbie and I left the building around four-thirty, went over to the Blue Squirrel for a drink, stayed for a couple of sets. I think it was about seven when we left, and caught dinner at Padua, a little Italian place on Mott. We decided to make a night of it, and went for music and drinks at Adalaide's. I guess we stayed till about midnight, then we ...'

'We went back to my place.' She sniffled. 'We can do that. We're not married or anything – to other people, I mean. Bobbie, somebody killed A.'

'I know. Why don't you go in my office, honey, and sit down?'

'Can I?' she asked Eve. 'I feel really bad.'

'Sure.'

Bobbie unlocked the door, settled her in, then stepped out again. 'She wouldn't hurt a fly. Literally.'

'I've no reason to believe she had anything to do with Mr Asner's death.'

'You said he let somebody in, or came in with someone. So it wasn't a break-in.'

'There's no evidence of a break-in, but we can't rule it out at this stage.'

'It wasn't a break-in.'

Eve eyed him. 'Maybe you and I should have a talk, Bobbie.'

'Yeah, we should. Listen, I want to call my assistant. She and Barbie pal around some. Barbie would do better if she had somebody with her right now. Just let me get somebody to stay with her, and I'll talk to you. It won't take long. Sunny only lives a couple blocks away.'

'All right.'

He glanced toward his office. 'It's the first night we ...' He blew out a breath. 'This is a hell of a morning after.'

14

Since Peabody was better with weepers – had a way of easing and eking information out between sobs – Eve had her talk to Barbie while she took Bobbie.

The layout of the law office was identical to Asner's with a no-frills decor. She left Peabody with Sunny the assistant and the teary Barbie in the reception area, and sat with Bobbie in his office.

'What do you know, Bobbie?'

'It may not be anything. I know A was riding high the last couple days. Big payoff from a client. I don't know the details, and I'm not sure I'd tell you if I did.'

'It's okay. I've got most of them already.'

'Well.' He shrugged. 'He liked to gamble, and he was flush. I know he was going to hit a game yesterday because he stopped by, said I should go with him, he'd front me. I don't do that kind of thing – gamble. I can't afford to. And I don't play with money I don't have in the first place. So I said I'd pass. I had work anyway.'

'Okay.'

'It could be he played too deep, lost what he didn't have, or needed to get more from his office.'

'Did he keep money there?'

'I don't know. Maybe.' His eyes tracked to the door as Barbie let loose another spate of sobs.

'My partner's good with the grieving,' Eve told him.

'Yeah, okay.' Bobbie pressed his fingers to his eyes, took a couple long breaths. 'Okay.' Dropped his hands back to the desk. 'Anyway. It could be he got into it over the bet, and whoever he owed or was there to collect killed him. But—'

'Kill him, you don't get paid,' Eve finished. 'But we have to check these things out. Do you know where he played yesterday?'

'They move around. I think he said he was picking it up in Chinatown. The thing is – Lieutenant, right?'

'That's right.'

'The thing is, yeah, A liked to play, but he wasn't stupid about it. I went with him a couple times, and I never saw him play past his limit, never used a marker, never swung toward the high-stakes, break-your-legs-if-you-welsh kind of game. He just liked to play, have some fun at it. So I don't see it going here.'

'You see something else.'

'Maybe. Listen, do you want some coffee?'

'I'm good, thanks.'

'I'm just going to get some coffee.' He rose, went to a shoe box–sized AutoChef on a short counter. It made ominous grinding noises, then clunking ones. 'I've got to replace this piece of crap.'

He pulled out a mug, and the steam sent out a scent worse than Morris's morgue coffee.

'I don't know if it's anything. But . . .'

'But.'

Bobbie sat, sipped, winced. 'God, this is truly horrible. A asked me some legal questions, hypothetically. Bought me a beer the other day, made it like conversation. But I'm not stupid either.'

'Did he hire you?'

'No, or I wouldn't be talking to you. It still doesn't feel right, but he's dead. Not just dead. Murdered. I liked him, a lot. Everybody liked A.'

'What was the hypothetical?'

'He wondered if somebody had something come into their possession, and they requested compensation of a monetary nature for that something from an interested party, how much legal hassle would there be? I asked straight out if he was talking about stolen property, and he said no. Just a kind of memento. Nothing exactly illegal.'

'Exactly illegal,' Eve repeated, and Bobbie managed a faint smile as he choked down another swallow of coffee.

'Yeah, I caught that, too. I said I couldn't tell him specifically since I didn't have specifics, but if he had something that had come to him, without crossing the law, requesting compensation shouldn't be a problem. But if that something was legally the property of the interested party, or obtained by illegal means, he was in a very shadowy area.

'He said something about finder's fees, possession being

nine-tenths of the law. I hear bullshit all day, and I know when somebody's trying to rationalize. I also know sometimes A skirted the line in his work. I also know he wanted to retire.'

'And adding things up,' Eve prompted.

'Yeah, adding them up I told him maybe he should give this idea more thought, which isn't what he wanted to hear. He had this thing about moving to the islands – and opening a little club or casino/bar deal. I got the feeling he saw this as a big score, something that would polish off his retirement plan. I actually thought that's why he was flush yesterday, and asked him if he'd exchanged the memento for compensation. He said he was working on that. Then . . .'

He rubbed his eyes. 'Sorry, still taking it in. Yesterday when he dropped in about the game, I poked at him a little about it. It just bothered me. He said how current events had changed – how did he put it – changed the complexion. How he was rethinking his position, and maybe he'd just pass the memento over to the interested party, take his bird in the hand and be done. He said how we'd grab some coffee tomorrow – today – and he'd tell me how it went.'

Bobbie stared down at his hands. 'I'm afraid it didn't go well, at all. I'm afraid I wasn't clear or strong enough in how I answered when he asked me.'

'Hypothetically?' Eve waited until Bobbie looked up, into her eyes. 'I'd say this event was in motion, and that there was very likely nothing you could have said to stop that motion. I'm sorry you lost a friend.'

'Will you notify me about his body, its disposition? He's got a couple of ex-wives, no kids. I don't think either of his exes would be interested in seeing to that. He had a lot of friends. I think we could pool together, take care of him.'

'I'll let you know.' She started to the door, stopped. 'What are you doing in this place, Bobbie?'

'Kind of a dump, huh?' he said as he looked around. 'But it's my dump. I did a couple years as a PD. It's necessary work, but you don't get a choice. This may not be much, but I get to choose my clients, when I get one.'

'Good luck. I'll be in touch.'

Outside Peabody took a gulp of air. 'She was really broken up. I got the impression she thought of him as sort of an honorary uncle. She didn't have anything, Dallas. Nothing she didn't give us yesterday.'

'Bobbie might have.' On the drive to the studio, she gave Peabody the rundown.

'It pretty much confirms, hypothetically, that he was trying to sell the recording. Or maybe after he heard his client got dead, just give it over.'

'And his interested party found killing easier the second time. Stupid, and greedy. It looks like he saw another big windfall, all for one job of work. Wanted to pad his retirement fund. Now he's retired, permanently.'

'The killer must have the recording. If Asner took him or her to the office, the recording must have been in the office.'

'We search his apartment. He might've been in negotiation mode in the office, still feeling it out. I had the uniforms go over and seal it. We need to check with the night shift at the restaurant, the bar.' Fat chance, Eve thought, but shrugged. 'We could get lucky.'

'This isn't over a sex recording of a couple of single actors breaking no laws or moral codes.'

'You're right about that. It's a power struggle turned very nasty. It's about greed, obsession, and a need to control. About eliminating obstacles or problems.'

'Back to it being almost any one of them. If the killer wanted the recording – whatever the reason – and it was in Asner's possession at the time of the murder, he'd had enough time to destroy it, lock it up, make a million copies. Whatever, again, the reason.'

'Yeah,' Eve said, and began to think about it.

An assistant to somebody's assistant met them at Security and escorted them through the labyrinth to a soundstage where a set had been dressed as the conference room in Eve's home. There, in reality a year before, they had interviewed the three clones known as Avril Icove.

In the observation area, Marlo and Andi enacted a tense, emotional scene between Eve and Mira. Roundtree cut, retook, and cut again, pushing them both. At the end of a take Marlo walked to the observation glass, stared through, face set.

At nothing Eve could see. She supposed that would be added with vid magic. Julian walked in, and to her so they both looked through the glass.

'And cut! Perfect. Let's reset for reaction shots.'

Now Eve stepped forward. 'I need you to hold on that.'

Roundtree turned, scowled at her with the expression of a man deep in his work and unwilling to surface. 'Five minutes while we reset. Preston—'

'I'm going to need more than that.'

'If you need to ask questions, again, ask one of us who isn't trying to *work*. We've lost one of our cast members, we have the media and the paparazzi *and* the goddamn cops crawling up our asses. I'm going to finish this scene before—'

'You're going to have the media, the paparazzi, the goddamn cops – especially me – crawling up your asses for a little while longer. There's been another murder.'

The fury on Roundtree's face died off into sick dread, while others on the set reacted with gasps, mutters, and oaths.

'Who?' he demanded, looking around swiftly, like a father doing a head count of his brood. 'Who's been killed?'

'A. A. Asner, a private investigator.'

Something like relief chased with annoyance took over, face, voice, the sweeping gesture of his hand. 'What the hell does that have to do with any of us?'

'Considerable. Now we can arrange for me and my partner to interview the individuals we feel pertain in a manner that causes the least amount of time and inconvenience to your production, or we can shut this production down until we're satisfied.'

She wasn't entirely sure she could pull that threat off, but it sounded ominous. Roundtree went the color of over-cooked beets.

'Preston! Get legal on the line, that asshole Farnsworth the studio stuck us with. I've had enough of this shit. Enough.'

'Mason!' Before Eve could respond, Connie rushed onto the set. 'What's going on here? You take a breath.' She pointed a finger at him. 'I mean it. You take a breath.'

He looked as though he might explode first, but he took the breath, then another when Connie wagged that extended finger at him. His color cooled a few degrees.

'She wants to shut us down because some private dick got killed. I'm not taking any more of this harassment.'

'A private investigator? Murdered?' Something in Connie's tone had Eve focused on her.

'A. A. Asner. I don't think that name's unfamiliar to you. I'm not looking to shut anything down, if I get reasonable cooperation. I've got a job to do,' she said to Roundtree, who'd gone back to tugging on his red goatee. 'We can both do our jobs, but mine comes first. That's not negotiable.'

'An hour,' he told her.

'We'll start with that. I need to speak, individually, to everyone who attended the dinner party.'

'Steinburger and Valerie aren't here. They're off dealing with this fucking mess. Nadine's probably off somewhere writing another book about this fucking mess. Matthew's not on the call list today.'

'Let's get them here. The sooner we can get this done, the sooner we can get out of your ass.'

His lips twitched in what might have been a reluctant smile quickly controlled. 'Preston.'

'I'll take care of it.'

'Take an hour!' Roundtree boomed it out. 'I want everybody back here and ready to work in one hour.'

'Nobody leaves the premises,' Eve added. 'We'll speak to the cast members in their respective trailers. Go there,' she ordered. 'Wait. I need a place to talk to non-cast members,' she told Roundtree.

'I've got an office here. You can use it.'

'That'll work. I'll take you first.' She turned to Connie.

'All right. I'll take you to the office.'

'I'll follow up with you,' she said to Roundtree. 'Then Preston. I want to know when the others arrive on the premises.'

'I'll take care of it,' Preston said again, then scurried off.

'Peabody, why don't you go after Preston, make sure everybody goes where they're supposed to go. And to save some time, contact Nadine yourself. Get her whereabouts and so on.'

'Yes, sir.'

'This way.' Connie, in sensible flats and casual trousers, led the way.

'Why are you here today?' Eve asked her as they exited the soundstage.

'Everyone's on edge, upset, as is to be expected. I'm useful. The cast and crew can talk to me. I make a good wailing wall.'

'And you can keep your husband from imploding.'

Connie sighed, negotiated a turn. 'Yesterday was grueling. In our business we're used to the microscope of the media. But yesterday, even with buffers in place, was grueling. I don't know how many contacts I fielded, or avoided, or passed on to Valerie. Not just reporters, bloggers, entertainment site hosts, but from vid people – actors, directors, producers, crew – who either knew K.T. or just wanted to know what was going on.'

She unlocked a door, stepped into a roomy office with a huge, deep sofa, a trio of generous club chairs, a shiny galley kitchen, a private bath.

'I want coffee. Would you like coffee? I've had too much already, but, well, it's too early to start drinking, isn't it?'

'I wouldn't mind coffee. Black.'

'Mason feels responsible,' Connie began as she pro-grammed coffee. 'He won't admit it, but I know him. We hosted the party, she died there. We've been annoyed and impatient with her, and he regretted casting her in this proj-ect. We both knew she was difficult, but she handled herself so well initially.'

Connie shook her head, passed a hand over the hair she'd pulled back in a casual tail. 'She was so enthusiastic, so coop-erative – at first. But in the last two or three months, it's been a series of arguments, demands, frustrations, delays.'

'Makes it tough to work. Tough for Roundtree to keep it all going.'

'It does – did. He's not one to suppress his feelings or

thoughts – as I'm sure you've observed. So he made it very clear how he viewed her behavior. He swore he'd never work with her again. And now, of course, he won't. And he feels responsible.'

'He's not, unless he's the one who drowned her.'

'He couldn't.' Graceful, contained, Connie moved to the sofa, set both cups on the table that fronted it. She sat, folded her hands. 'I want you to listen to me. He rants, yells, stomps, and snarls. He'd have blackballed her if he could – and that's not out of the realm of possibility. But he'd never do physical harm.'

Eve took a seat. 'How about you?'

'Yes, I'm capable. I've thought about this. I think most of us are capable of killing under the right – or wrong – circumstances. I would be. I think I would be. I know I could happily have slugged her, then done a victory dance. I was that angry with her on the night of the party. I can only tell you I didn't. I want you to find out who did, but I don't want it to be anyone I care about. It's hard to reconcile that.'

'Tell me about Asner. The PI.'

'You know about Marlo and Matthew.'

'And apparently so do you.'

'She confided in me yesterday. She told me everything – that they'd fallen in love, were sharing a place in SoHo, that K.T. found out, hired a detective. She told me about the recording. As I said, I'm a good wailing wall. It has to be the same detective who's been killed. You wouldn't be here asking questions otherwise. But I don't understand it.'

'He had the original recording, and from what we've gathered, intended to sell it to an interested party.'

'The media.'

'I don't think so.'

'Who else? Marlo or Matthew?' Obviously exasperated, Connie threw up her hands. 'I hope to God they have more sense than that, or that I talked some of that sense into them yesterday. Who cares?' She flicked the wrist of one lifted hand. 'Yes, yes, the media would salivate, the blogs will bloat. The video would garner millions of hits. Is it unfair – certainly. Is it a terrible invasion of their private lives – absolutely. If you want fair and privacy, find another line of work.'

'That's pragmatic?'

'It's survival,' Connie said flatly. 'I was furious for them, disgusted with K.T. – even though she's dead. It was a horrible, unstable, selfish thing to do. But they're two young, gorgeous, happy, talented people. And this is nothing to get so worked up over. If the recording leaks, it leaks, then you deal with it. Someone like Valerie will take that ball and spin it.'

'Even if it leaks before the project's finished, while Julian and Marlo are supposed to be the hot ticket?'

'That's just nonsense anyway, isn't it? Maybe it does boost the numbers, at least initially, but it's nonsense. The numbers people latched onto this angle, partially because Marlo and Julian do have wonderful chemistry, and partially because the characters they're playing are real people – a couple, a hot ticket, that the media and public are fascinated with.'

She smiled at Eve's expression. 'If you wanted to stay out

of the public eye and consciousness, you should have found a different husband, and shouldn't be so good at your work.'

A little hard to argue, Eve decided, with pithy common sense.

'Does your husband share your opinion over the nonsense?'

'He liked the idea of Marlo and Julian perpetuating a relationship offscreen. He felt it kept them in character for longer stretches. But he didn't know about Matthew. I don't think anyone did.'

'Where were you between ten and midnight?'

'Home. Yesterday was exhausting, and it wasn't the time to go out and socialize.'

'Was Roundtree with you?'

'Of course. They shut down production for the day yesterday, for obvious reasons. And also to add to security. Added to it all was the problem of logistically shooting a handful of scenes that involved K.T. Mason, Nadine, and the scriptwriter holo-conferenced off and on during the day, working that out. After dinner, Mason went down to view and edit, to make some of the changes work more smoothly. I don't think he came to bed until after two, then he wanted to be at the studio by six, for a breakfast meeting with Joel and two of the studio execs who'd come in from California.'

'What were you doing while he worked?'

'I put a droid on the 'links, programmed to get me only in case of emergency. I'd had enough. I read scripts in bed, or intended to. I think I must've gone under by nine.'

'So you and your husband weren't actually together in the same area of the house during the time in question?'

Connie sat silent for a moment. 'No. If you're asking if either of us has an alibi, I'd have to say I don't. I didn't take any communications, didn't speak to or see anyone from about eight-thirty until Mason took the script I'd been reading out of my hands and climbed into bed at about two this morning.'

'Okay. Thanks for the time.'

'That's it?'

'For now. If you could send Roundtree in, we'll keep this moving so he can get back to work.'

While she waited, Eve made notes, took a moment to poke around the office. The walls held numerous framed photos. Roundtree with various actors – some she recognized, some she didn't. Of Roundtree on some outdoor location, high in a crane, baseball cap backward on his head as he scowled at a monitor. One of his Best Director Oscars sat on a shelf along with some other awards, and she noted a football trophy for MVP, from his Sacramento high school, in what she calculated would have been his final year.

Family photos sat on the desk, facing the chair.

He walked in, kind of lumbering, like a bad-tempered bear. 'I'm supposed to apologize, but fuck that. I don't like anybody coming on my set and telling me what to do.'

'Yeah, I got that.'

'And if you try shutting us down, you're going to have a fight on your hands.'

'Then why don't you take the stick out of your ass, sit down, get this done so we don't have to face that issue?'

He bared his teeth at her, then grinned. 'Fuck it. I like you. You piss me off, but I've been living with you for better than six months now. You're a hard-nosed, hard-ass, hard-working bitch. I like that.'

'Yay. Where were you between ten and midnight?'

'Working. I'm a hard-nosed, hard-ass, hardworking son of a bitch.'

'At home. Alone.'

'I don't like somebody breathing over my shoulder. We've got a goddamn problem. I have to fix it. I've got a cast and crew tied up in knots. Connie . . . ' He dropped into a chair, and for the first time let the fatigue show. 'She loved that fucking lap pool.'

He sat, tugging his goatee, brooding. 'I surprised her with it a couple years back. Had it done when we were back on the Coast. She loved to swim, and she uses it every day we're in New York. Every morning, even if she's working and has a six A.M. call, she uses the pool first.'

He trained those sharp blue eyes on Eve, and the anger and bitterness came clearly. 'Do you think she's going to be able to do that now? Go up there, enjoy her morning swim? She feels responsible for what happened to K.T.'

Eve angled her head, thinking how Connie had said the same of him. 'Because?'

'She laid into K.T. after dinner. She planned the party, right down to the goddamn mints. It was her idea to have the

269

whole stinking thing, and now she's sick about it, and trying to hold up for everybody else. That's who she is.'

He rolled his shoulders back. 'Now what the fuck is this about some PI, and what's it to do with any of us?'

'Harris hired Asner to plant cameras in the loft Marlo and Matthew are living in, in SoHo.'

His brow beetled. 'What? What the hell are you talking about?'

Eve laid it out for him, or as much as she wanted to lay out. And watched him absorb, chew on, spit out until he shoved to his feet and prowled the office.

'Idiots. Bunch of idiots. What the hell do I care if Marlo and Matthew want to screw like college kids on spring break? Christ's sake. And I swear to fucking *God* on a mountaintop, if that stupid, selfish, crazy-ass bitch wasn't dead I'd strangle her.'

He kicked his desk, a sentiment and gesture she understood as she was prone to the same.

'Why the hell didn't you arrest this Asner asshole?'

'I would have, but it's hard to book a dead guy.'

'Shit.' He dropped into the chair again. 'What a fucking mess.'

'How much damage would the recording do, if it leaked?'

'How the hell do I know? You can't figure the public. You just do good work, try to pick good people, good scripts, then throw the dice. It'll be embarrassing, for Marlo and Matthew, and for Julian, but that won't last. It'll make the studio look stupid, at least to those who know how they fabricate some of the hype. Other than that, it's still rolling the dice.'

Peabody poked her head in when Eve sent Roundtree out.

'Want an update?'

Eve crooked her finger.

'Nadine's still a little pissed she didn't latch onto the Marlo/Matthew connection before you did. She wants exclusives right, left, and sideways. She contacted everybody we're talking to via 'link yesterday, and actually managed to get into Julian's hotel room – with his permission – for a one-on-one in the afternoon. She didn't have much to add, which I figured was what you wanted me to find out, but she's digging like a terrier.'

'Good.'

'Preston's alibied. I verified. He and Carmandy were in her room until after midnight. We can check hotel security on that, but it feels solid.'

'All right.'

'Matthew's in the studio, was actually in his trailer. He and Marlo came in together this morning. Steinburger and Valerie are also here. They've been in his office working on spin and media angles.'

'Why don't you take the lovebirds – separately. Then Andrea. I'll take Valerie first, then Steinburger, round it out with Julian.'

'Works for me. I'll get Valerie on her way.'

Eve busied herself with more notes, linking names with lines until Valerie clipped in on her important shoes. She wore an earlink, had a pocket 'link, and a PPC clipped to what Eve supposed was a fashionable belt. She carried two go-cups.

'Mango smoothies,' she said, setting one on the table. 'I thought you might like one. Now.' She sat, crossed her legs. 'How can I help you?'

'You can start by giving me your whereabouts last night, between ten P.M. and midnight.'

Valerie held up one finger in a one-moment gesture, and unclipped her PPC. 'Let me check my calendar. It's cross-checked, of course, in my memo book. I have that in my briefcase in Joel's office. I holoed with reporters on the West Coast until ten. I believe my memo book will have that conference ending at approximately ten after the hour, as it ran over a bit. I had a meeting scheduled with Joel at ten-thirty. I believe we brainstormed and handled a variety of issues until about one this morning.'

'And where did you conference and meet and brainstorm?'

'At Joel's pied-à-terre. I stayed in the guest quarters last night to simplify the situation.'

'Situation?'

Valerie maintained her pleasant, slightly smug expression. 'K.T. Harris's murder is a situation.'

'At least. Are you and Joel Steinburger sexually involved?'

'No. That's insulting.'

'Insulting because you're no longer sexually involved? Because I have two different statements verifying you had been previously.'

'It's no one's business, and not at all pertinent. Mr Steinburger and I are not involved in the way you imply.'

'But you were?'

'Briefly. Several months ago. We ended that phase of our relationship amicably, and work together. Nothing more.'

'Uh-huh. And last night, you and Mr Steinburger worked together in his pied-à-terre, from ten-thirty until one.'

'That's correct. I conferred with my assistant, as I recall. All of us are putting in considerable overtime.'

'On the situation.'

'Yes.'

'How are you handling the Matthew-and-Marlo-as-lovers portion of the situation?'

'I'm sorry, what?'

'Tell me this. How much overtime did you put in on K.T. Harris while she was alive?'

'I don't know what you mean.'

'I mean, how did you spin, cover up, keep quiet, her addiction problems, her threats, the blanket dislike for her on this project?'

'K.T. was a talented actor whose work was celebrated and respected. As is often the case with artists, her temperament was often misunderstood by those outside.'

'Does anybody actually buy that bullshit? Amazing.'

In response, Valerie just folded her hands in her lap.

'Send me the list of your holo-conference attendees, and a copy of your brainstorming notes. I'll take Steinburger now.'

'It would help considerably if you could speak with Joel in his office. We're enormously busy this morning.'

'Sure. Lead the way.'

The offices were in the same section, hardly more than a thirty-second walk.

Power play, Eve decided when she went in – after Valerie's knock and Steinburger's answer. He sat behind his desk, a busy man. His office boasted a wall of screens, several of them tuned to media channels with the sound muted. His comp, 'link bank, disc files, memo cubes, crowded his expansive desk.

He, too, had a sofa, chairs, awards, photos – and a small conference table now holding the debris of meetings.

'Yes, yes, sit. I'll be right with you. Valerie, I don't know where the hell Shelby went off to. Get Lieutenant Dallas some coffee.'

'I'm good. You can leave,' she said to Valerie.

'I need Valerie to—'

'It'll have to wait,' Eve interrupted. 'This isn't a business meeting, but a police investigation. You're entitled to have your lawyer present, or you can designate Valerie as your legal representative. However, she would be under no legal constriction to hold what's said in this room confidential.'

'This won't take long, Valerie. We'll deal with the next round in …' He checked his wrist unit. 'Twenty. Take a break.'

'I'll be close by.' Valerie stepped out, shut the door.

'I'm sorry to be abrupt,' Steinburger began. 'We're dealing

with a great deal of difficulties, on every level. I'm told you're here about some private investigator's death, and you think it's connected to K.T.'s murder.'

'That's right. I need your whereabouts for last night, from ten until midnight.'

'Well, let's see.' He scrolled through his book, searching with shadowed eyes. 'I watched Valerie's media conference, she did one via holo with the West Coast last night. It was booked from nine to ten. We reviewed that, then spent considerable time working on how to handle the situation.'

'There's that word again.'

'Sorry?'

'Go on.'

'We discussed a memorial, here at the studio, and holding another on the Coast.' He sat back, swiveling in the chair. 'We covered a lot of ground, how to respond, which specific interviews to accept or assign. It was a very full day as I'd worked with Roundtree and some associates earlier on what editing and amendments needed to be done on the script and the vid already shot. I think Valerie and I stayed at it until about one in the morning. Right now, I'm living on coffee and boosters.'

'Valerie stayed in the guest quarters in your New York residence.'

'We worked late, and wanted to get back at it early this morning.'

'While you were working late did you decide how to handle the media regarding Marlo and Matthew's relationship?'

'You mean Marlo and Julian.'

'No, I don't.' She stood up. 'Thanks for your time.' She paused on her way to the door. 'I meant to ask. Do you keep a car, a vehicle of some kind in the city?'

'I have a car, yes, but most often use our car service and driver so I can work more easily coming and going. Why?'

'Just curious.'

She stepped out.

Roundtree and Connie both had a vehicle, as did Steinburger. Easy enough to check rentals on the others.

She reconnected with Peabody. 'We'll take Asner's apartment next. What did you get?'

'No alibi for Andi or Julian. Both of them claimed they stayed in, keeping a low profile due to the media hunt. Andi spoke with her husband, but that was about nine in the evening. He's heading in to New York today so she won't be alone. Julian admitted – or claimed – he had a bottle of wine, took a tranq with it. He remembered he contacted several friends back home during the evening, but doesn't remember who or when, due to wine and tranq. And that he dropped his 'link, broke it, and threw it in the recycler.'

'Convenient.'

'Yeah. And you?'

'A lot of calm and compassion from Connie, which seems genuine, but again. A lot of pissed off from Roundtree, and surprise that again seemed genuine re the two Ms Connie knew. Marlo confessed all to her yesterday. The Roundtrees have two vehicles in New York, and were in separate areas of the house during the time in question.'

'No alibi.'

'No. Valerie and Steinburger state they worked together until one. Their stories match. And real neatly, too.'

'Oh-oh.'

'She bunked in his guest quarters, for efficiency.'

'And another oh-oh.'

'He also keeps a vehicle in New York. But most interesting to me was learning they both should stick with their jobs and not try acting. They suck at it. Valerie's plugged in like a valve in a heart, and yet she pretended she didn't know anything about the two lovebirds and kissy-face. I might've bought that if she hadn't been so crappy at lying to me. And if she knew, Steinburger knew — and vice versa. But he also opted to lie, then didn't even bother to demand what the fuck. He just let it slide away.'

'The third oh-oh might be the charm.'

'Just might. Let's see if Asner's apartment has anything to tell us.'

15

Unlike the early-morning pulse and mumble, Asner's building held quiet midday. Everyone off to school, Eve thought, or to work, or to the shops, running errands.

The minute she unsealed and unlocked the door, she thought someone else had run errands.

'Well, either Asner was a really messy guy, or somebody beat us to it.' Peabody stood, lips pursed, as they surveyed the jumble of the small living area.

The contents of upended drawers scattered over the floor mixed with debris from closets, cabinets. In limp gray puffs, the stuffing spilled out, like disgorged intestines, from the cushions of the faded sofa and armchair.

'It's empty, but let's clear it anyway.' Eve drew her weapon, peeled off toward the tiny bedroom.

It wouldn't have mattered if they'd come in sooner, she thought, replacing her weapon. But damn, it was annoying.

'The killer wanted to make sure he got all copies of the recording. Or Asner didn't have the original in the office. Either way, this is a thorough job. Careful, too,' Eve observed as she picked her way through, 'even with the mess. He didn't heave things around – too much noise, somebody might complain that time of night.'

'He kills Asner, tosses the office. He took Asner's wallet, and the vic didn't have any key code on him. So—'

'Yeah. And I missed something. The vehicle. The killer didn't have to have transportation. No PI can function without his own ride. He could have taken Asner's vehicle.'

She took the steps in her mind. 'Loading it up, driving it here, tossing the apartment, then ditching the car somewhere, ditching or destroying the electronics. It's thorough. He had more time to think this one through.'

'But it's still stupid, Dallas.' Peabody toed a pile of drawer junk. 'It's a recording of a couple of Hollywood stars getting some. It's just . . . it's just not big enough for all this.'

'Yeah, it seems stupid. Seems like overkill – all around. So, there's more somewhere. Could be Harris had Asner do another job, and he dug up something on the killer. We could be chasing our tails on the recording. Red herring, or only part of the story.'

'His fee was pretty steep.'

'So, maybe fifty for each job. Fuck.' Eve slapped her hands on her hips. 'We're running in circles. Let's get a search team in here, save ourselves the time. And we need to verify Asner has a ride, and if so get a BOLO out for it. I want the search team to bring sensors. Asner might've had a hidey-hole the killer didn't look for or find. No computer or 'links here, so he took them. It's a lot of hauling. Let's check around, see if anyone saw somebody loading up last night.'

After spending considerable time learning nobody saw anything, heard anything, knew anything, there or at the office building – and being offered tattoos at ten percent discount, Eve and Peabody walked back to the car.

'Sometimes I think about it.'

'What?'

'Getting a tattoo,' Peabody told her. 'Just a little one. Something fun, or meaningful, or—'

'Why would you pay somebody to cut a picture into your flesh?'

'Well, when you put it that way.'

'Stick with temps.' Eve pulled out her communicator at its signal. 'Dallas. Yeah,' she said after a moment. 'Have it hauled in. It'll need to be processed.' She turned to Peabody. 'They found Asner's ride parked at the Battery Park Marina.'

'Marina, water, dumping ground.'

'Yeah. I think we should do a run, see which of our friends has a boat. What's better than dumping a bunch of electronics off a pier?'

'Dumping them out in the river.'

'It could be our killer's using a brain this time around. Let's head in.' She wanted to put her feet up, and start using hers.

She found the ME's report when she got to her office, and wished she'd felt able to carve out the time to talk to Morris in person. Still, the report verified her own on-scene. Multiple blows from behind, with the falcon statue. Reconstruction indicated two blows of considerable force came after the victim was prone, and the first two of four had been enough to kill.

The tox showed the vic had several ounces of bourbon in his system at TOD. No other signs of violence or struggle.

Eve added the report, Asner's picture, the crime scene and apartment photos to her board.

Then she got a large coffee, sat down, put her boots on her desk.

She studied the board while she drank her coffee.

All sorts of connections, she thought. All sorts of egos. Throw in sex, money, fame.

Start with sex, she decided.

Connect Harris to Julian and Matthew. Indirect to Preston, due to her threat to shout sexual harassment. She was tossing his alibi for now. In a tight-knit group, people lied for each other.

Possibility Harris connected by sex to others on the list, she mused. Sex was always a possibility.

Connect Matthew with Marlo, and again indirectly due to publicity hype, to Julian. That connects Harris and Marlo through sex, one degree removed – times two.

Connect Roundtree and Connie. Possibility one or both unfaithful at some time, either with the vic or one of the others. Harris claimed to have had an affair with Roundtree, cannot verify. Claimed Marlo engaged in sexual acts with Roundtree, cannot verify.

Connect Steinburger and Valerie, whether that sexual

connection was past or present. Harris had had a talent for digging up dirt. Very possible she'd known, threatened to use the information somehow.

No discernible connection through sex with Andrea.

Money.

It just didn't feel like money. These people had money, though more was always good. Then again, numbers, which equaled money in this case, were the reason for the publicity hype re Julian and Marlo, and the spin and cover on the continual problems with Harris.

So, money. She needed to find out more about how that end of it worked for all involved.

Fame. That was like sex, wasn't it? A rush, a need, and particularly applicable to this set of individuals. Celebrity. The need to have it, the need to maintain it, or grow it. And like sex and money, celebrity held power. Could be used to wield power, and to control.

Circling, circling, she thought. And yet . . .

Sex, money, fame, power. It was all a mix, all a stew these people worked in, lived in. And all of those things could be weapons, vulnerabilities. Could be threatened, lost, diminished.

Motive. To maintain power at all costs.

First murder. A snap of temper, or even the victim's own clumsiness. Followed by impulse/calculation. Quick, opportunistic, no real plan or deep thought.

But the second, blow after blow? That's anger, she thought, with a little desperation thrown in. From behind, not personal. Opportunistic again, grabbing the heavy statue. But not face-to-face. And a careful, thorough follow-through on murder two.

Laborious even, transporting the electronics, loading them into the victim's car, doing the same at his apartment. Risky, too, though on the low side. Pumped with adrenaline, a definite task to accomplish, a plan of action.

And there had to be more to it than recovering a recording of two people having sex who were perfectly free to have sex.

Add blackmail to sex, money, fame, power.

'Dallas?'

Distracted, she frowned over her shoulder at Peabody. 'Working.'

'I know, but K.T. Harris's brother came in. He asked if he could talk to you. He's been to the morgue. They're going to release the body tomorrow. I thought you might want to talk to him, and didn't think you'd want to do it in here.'

Eve looked back at the board, the crime scene and dead photos of Harris.

'Have somebody escort him to the lounge. I'll be right there.'

She sat for a moment, checking Harris's family data to be certain she had it straight. She stood up, surprised to see rain splatting against her window. She'd been in too deep to notice.

When she walked into the lounge with its vending machines, spindly tables and chairs, she picked out Brice Van

Horn right away. He didn't look anything like a cop. A big man, broad in the shoulders, with short, dark hair that looked freshly cut, he sat brooding down at a tube of ginger ale.

He had a rawboned, sunburned look about him – a corn-fed, farmer's look to her eye. He wore jeans and a plaid shirt with boots that had seen a lot of miles.

He lifted his head when Eve approached the table, and she saw eyes as faded a blue as his jeans, and the lines fanned out from them from squinting into the sun.

'Mr Van Horn, I'm Lieutenant Dallas.'

'Ma'am.' He got to his feet, shifted the other chair. It took Eve a moment to realize he'd pulled it out for her. She sat so he would.

'I'm very sorry for your loss,' she began.

'We lost Katie a long time ago, but thank you.' He cleared his throat, folded his big, calloused hands. 'I felt like I should come here. I didn't want my ma ... I guess it doesn't matter what a child does or doesn't. A mother's always going to love her anyway. I didn't want her to make this trip, so I asked her to stay back home with my wife and kids, told her she had to help look after the farm while I came to bring Katie home.'

He stared down at his ginger ale again, but didn't drink. 'I went to the place where she is. The doctor there ...'

'Doctor Morris.'

'Yeah, Doctor Morris. He was very kind. Everybody's been kind. I've never been to New York before, and I didn't think people would be kind. You shouldn't feel that way about places you haven't been, people you don't even know, but . . . '

'It's a long way from Iowa.'

'Lord, yes.' A smile ghosted around his mouth, then vanished. 'I know you're the one who's been looking after her.'

Eve felt the phrase keenly. 'That's right.'

'I wanted to thank you for that. Katie, she was a hard woman, but she was my sister. You know, it's been more than five years before today since I laid eyes on her. I can't do anything about that. Can't do anything to change being mad at her all this time, having all the bad feelings I had for her. But she didn't deserve to die like that. Do you know who killed her?'

'We're actively investigating . . . ' He looked so sad, she thought, so big and out of place. So lost. 'I think I do, but I can't prove it yet. I'm working on it. We'll do everything we can to identify her killer, to get justice for your sister.'

'Can't do more than that. Even after all Katie did, my ma's kept up with what she's doing. All the Hollywood shows and that – Ma watches. She told me Katie was working on a movie about you.'

The old-fashioned word suited him, Eve thought. 'Not about me. About a case I worked.'

'They said how you were there when she died.'

'I was, yes.'

He nodded, looked off. 'Ma wants to bury her back home. Katie hated everything about home, but Ma wants it, so . . . did you know her?'

'No, not really.'

'I guess we didn't either – now, I mean. We only knew her before.' He took a drink, set the tube aside again. 'My father was a hard man. He lived hard, died hard. Katie loved him. Or I don't know if love's what it was. She was like him, and I guess that's why she was the way she was.'

Eve said nothing. If he needed to talk it out, she might learn something.

'He used to hurt my ma, used to hit her. He was big, like me. Like I am now, I mean. She's not. She used to tell me to look after Katie, because Katie was younger. When he came home drunk and mean, she'd tell me to take Katie off, keep her away. I was just a kid. I couldn't do anything to help my mother, not then. And Katie? She didn't want to be away from him.'

He pressed his lips together, shook his head. 'Nothing he did was wrong in Katie's eyes, even when our ma was bleeding, she didn't see he did wrong. When she got a little older, she'd tell him things – like if Ma talked to one of her friends too long or didn't get some chore done. Sometimes she'd just make it up, make up something to get him going on Ma, especially if Ma said no to her about something, or wouldn't let her have what she wanted.'

Learned early, Eve thought. Go with the power/take the power.

'He called Katie his princess, told her how she was better than anybody, how she had to go out and get whatever she wanted, take it if need be. She took that to heart. She was only a child, so maybe it wasn't all her fault. And he'd buy her things, like a reward when she told him something about Ma. It got so Ma would give Katie most everything she wanted. You can't blame her. But it was always more, and never enough.'

'It was hard on you,' Eve observed, 'caught in the middle, without the power to stop it.'

'One day I thought I was big enough to stop him. I wasn't, and he beat me so bad I pissed blood for – I beg your pardon.'

Eve only shook her head. 'Is that when your mother left him?'

'I guess you know some about it. It seemed she'd take him beating on her, but when he did it to me, she wouldn't take that. She waited till he passed out drunk, then she took me to the hospital, and she called the law. And there's Katie screaming how she's a liar, and her daddy never touched me. People around there knew my father well enough, and his hands were raw from beating on me. Then she—' He paused, took a careful drink. 'Then she said how he'd been protecting her because I'd tried to get at her. That way.'

He lowered his head, shook it. 'My own sister. They didn't believe her, and she kept changing the story. But they had to ask questions, do tests and that. Anyway, at the end of it they locked him up.'

'And your mother took you to Iowa.'

'Yeah, packed up and left. This woman talked to my ma, about things she could do, and gave her the name of a place we could go, live awhile till we got settled in. I had to stay in

287

the hospital near a week, but when I could travel, we left. Katie hated her for that, hated the both of us, I guess, as she surely made our lives a misery whenever she could. But she had to stay, go to school and counseling because the judge said so. Besides, the old man, he didn't want anything to do with us, Katie either, when he got out of jail. She blamed Ma for that, too.'

He looked up again. 'I'll tell you something, ma'am, when we got out, it's the first time I could ever remember my ma going a full week without being hit. How can you blame somebody for wanting to go a week without being hit?'

'I don't know. I think for some, violence becomes a way of life. It becomes the normal.'

'I guess that's true. Anyway, he got in more trouble when he got out, and I guess he took on somebody meaner than he was, and that was the end of it. Katie blamed us both – blame, I guess that was her normal, too. She got into trouble at school, stole things, got drunk whenever she could, started smoking zoner, and whatever else she could get. And when she could, she lit out for California. Ma had changed our names legal, but Katie took his back. That shows you something.

'I don't know why I'm telling you all this.'

'It helps me to know her. Whatever she was, whatever she did. It helps me know her. And knowing her will help me find who killed her.'

His eyes watered up, and he struggled in silence a moment for composure. 'I don't know how I'm supposed to feel. My ma's grieving, but I can't. I can't grieve for my sister.'

'You came here, all this way, to take your sister home. That shows me something.'

'For my ma.' A single tear spilled out. 'Not for Katie.'

'It doesn't matter. You came, and you'll take her home.'

He closed his eyes, sighed. 'When my wife was carrying our first, I was so afraid. I was afraid I'd be what he was, that I'd do what he did. That it was in me – in the blood – like in Katie's. Then I had my boy.' He turned his palms up, as if cradling an infant. 'And I couldn't understand how, how a father could – I'd cut my arm off first. I swear to God. But Katie, it was like she couldn't be any other way. Now someone killed her, like someone killed him. Was it supposed to be like that, right from the start?'

'No. I don't believe that. No one had the right to take her life. She made bad choices, and it's hard for you to reconcile that. Murder's a choice, too. I'm going to do everything I can to make sure the person who made that choice pays for it.'

'I guess that's what I needed to hear. I guess that's why I came to see you. I can tell my ma that, and I think it'll comfort her some.'

'I hope it does.'

He sighed again. 'I guess I better figure out what to do with myself until I leave tomorrow.'

'You've got two kids, right?'

'One of each, and we're having another.'

She pulled out a card – her last – made a note to dig out

more. 'There's this kid. Tiko,' she said, scribbling on the back of the card. 'He sells scarves and whatever else, on this corner in Midtown I'm writing down. He's a good kid. Go buy your wife and mother a scarf. Tell Tiko I sent you, and he'll make you a deal. And ask him where to get your kids some souvenirs from New York at a good price. He'll know.'

'Thank you. I'll do that.'

'You can contact me if you need to. The information's on the card.'

'People oughtn't say New Yorkers are cold and rude. You've been kind and friendly.'

'Don't spread that around. We New Yorkers have a rep to uphold.'

When Eve walked back into the bullpen, Peabody got up from her desk to meet her. 'How'd it go?'

'He's having a rough time. Guilty because he thinks he's not grieving, but he is. He couldn't be more different than Harris – like a big sturdy tree, and she's that itchy vine that climbs up it. He gave me some insights into her.'

'Speaking of insights, Mira's in your office.'

'Shit. I forgot about the consult.'

'She's only been here a few minutes. She said she had an appointment in this sector, and just came by.'

'All right. Stay on top of the forensic guys. Maybe the killer got sloppy with Asner's car. And I want the search team on the apartment to let me know if they find a drop of dried spit that wasn't Asner's.'

'Will do. Meanwhile, I dug on the boat angle. None of them has a boat in New York.'

'Crap.'

'But. Roundtree and Steinburger both had one back in New LA – and Julian and Matthew are both experienced sailors, as is Andrea Smythe. She and her husband have a sporting yacht in the Hamptons. So I was thinking, maybe one of them has a friend with a boat docked at the marina, and borrowed it. Or just stole one to do the dump.'

'That's good thinking. A good angle. Work it.'

'Can I use McNab?'

'I've told you I don't want to hear about your sex life.'

'Ha ha. This is going to take a lot of search and cross-referencing. He's got skills. Oops, I forgot not to mention my sex life.'

'And again, ha ha. Ask Feeney if you want him before end of shift. Once you're both off, it's your party. And that's the end of allusions to your sex life.'

She walked to her office, saw Mira standing at her skinny window.

'A dreary kind of rain,' Mira commented. 'It's going to make traffic a little slice of hell going home.'

'That balances out the easy, stress-free drive I had in this morning. I'm sorry about the delay. I'd have come to you.'

'I was nearby anyway, and Peabody told me you were talking with K.T. Harris's brother.' She turned, pretty in her rosy suit and favored pearls. 'That sort of thing is rarely easy or stress-free.'

'He's a very decent sort of man beating himself up some because his sister wasn't a very decent sort of woman. His father tuned the mother up regularly. Harris not only sided with him but passed on info – often false – so he had an excuse to smack the mother around, and reward the daughter for her loyalty. When the son finally got old enough to try to stop him, he ended up in the hospital. The mother finally called the cops and had the fucker put in a cage. Harris wasn't pleased, claimed it didn't happen even though her brother's pissing blood in the hospital. Then claimed the brother tried to molest her, and the father protected her.'

'Lie, blame, lie to shift blame and protect your status quo.'

'Whatever it takes. She also wasn't pleased when the mother relocated herself and the kids. It seems she made it her mission to follow in Daddy's footsteps.'

'Taking his name professionally and legally makes a statement,' Mira agreed. 'She saw her mother as weak, her father as the one with the power. She sided with power and enjoyed being rewarded. When her mother ended that cycle, it wasn't just seen as punishment, but again, as taking *her* power away.'

'And she spent the rest of her life finding ways to have it and keep it. Lies, blackmail, threats. Everyone says she had talent, and she must have enjoyed the work. But that was secondary to taking control of the people around her. And I think making them fear her. Fear and respect? The same thing to her.'

'I agree. She compensated with drugs and alcohol, which probably made her feel more powerful. Did the brother indicate there was any sexual component between father and daughter?'

'No. But I'd say her father was her first obsession.'

'Young girls often fantasize about marrying their father. A benign fantasy, nonsexual, normally outgrown. Harris's may have been more complicated. She took her power from him, from the bond of violence and betrayal. The men she became involved with later – like Matthew – became obsessions, yes, but not substitutes. She wanted to take more power from the men she involved herself with, wanted to take her father's and have the control. Her mother severed her father's power by leaving him. This couldn't happen to her. It couldn't be accepted.'

Eve turned to the board, to the face that, oddly enough, brought nothing of Peabody to mind any longer. 'The more we lay her out, the more she sounds like killer rather than victim.'

'Had she lived, she might have escalated to that. Your killer's escalated with the second victim. More violence, more complicated planning. The first murder was passive. This, with multiple blows, shows a rage he hadn't felt, or perhaps admitted with Harris. There's a pattern – taking her 'link, taking Asner's electronics. The attempt to make Harris's death look like an accident or misadventure, and the attempt to make Asner's look like burglary.'

'Crappy attempts both times.'

'Also a pattern. Your killer believes himself – or herself – clever, careful, believes he can create this deception – and with Asner went to considerable time and trouble. He's intelligent, organized, focused. There was a purpose to the killings, making the motive of this recording feel weak.'

'Oh boy, do I agree with that.'

'It could hold up with Harris's murder if we theorize an impulsive, angry act, then a hurried cover-up. Asner's takes this to another level.'

'think Harris hired Asner for at least one other job, and th he ound something more damaging than a couple of H wood types in an offscreen sex scene. It may be Marlo a latthew used that recording as a blind — gave me that so 't look under it. Or, if they're not involved in the mur, something damaging to the killer. Something the rich l famous would risk killing for.'

'You may be right. We know it fits Harris's pathology. You've already discovered she held threats over several heads.'

'And again, like Marlo and Matthew, nothing worth killing Asner over, since the individuals had related those threats on record. Asner gave her something else, or the killer feared he would. Something that didn't come out in the interviews.'

She glanced at the board. 'I need to look at it all again. I told her brother she didn't deserve to be killed.'

'Do you believe that?'

'I believe she needed to be stopped. You'd say she needed help — therapy, counseling. I lean toward she needed to be punished. No, it's not a lean,' Eve realized, 'it's a solid stand. Bullies need to pay, but murder's not the price. So I take that solid stand on punishment, and still stand for her.'

'I think she needed help, and punishment. She had an abusive childhood. I know you don't see it that way,' Mira continued at Eve's instinctive shrug, 'but she did.'

'Maybe, but she found a way to make it work for her. I wonder . . .'

'What?'

'Sometimes I wonder what kind of family or environment Stella came from. Was she born bent – selfish, violent, heartless? Or did she get caught up in the cycle? I don't excuse what she did or was either way. Cycles have to be broken.'

'I'm sure you know Roarke could find out.'

'What I'm not sure of is if I really want to know. Maybe. Eventually. He's worried about me. I know he wants me to talk to you.'

'Should he be worried?'

'I don't want him to worry.'

'That didn't answer the question.'

Eve sighed. She found, for once, she didn't want coffee, and got them both a bottle of water. 'I dream about her. Not nightmares, not really. But strange, lucid dreams. She blames me, which would fit with the way she thought, was.'

'Do you blame you?'

Eve took a moment before answering. 'Harris's brother? Part of him feels guilty because he couldn't love his sister, and part of him grieves for her. I don't know if it's guilt or just acknowledgment that part of me feels. There's no grief. I told you that before, and it hasn't changed. I know I'm not responsible for what happened to her. She is. McQueen is.

Even my father holds more of the blame than me. But I started the chain when I took her down in Dallas, before I ever knew who she was.'

Eve studied her water bottle even as that moment flashed through her mind. That defining moment when she'd yanked a suspect around, and looked into her mother's face.

'I started the chain when I pushed her to flip on McQueen. The chain McQueen broke when he slit her throat. I can't and won't pretend otherwise. I was doing my job. And other lives, innocent lives were on the line. But doing my job was a factor in her death.'

'Doing your job saved those innocent lives. The choices she made ended hers.'

'I know that. I believe that. But, I'm involved in the death of both my parents. Directly with my father as my hand held the knife. A child, self-defense, yes, all true, all logical. But . . . ' She fisted her hand, as if around a hilt. 'My hand held the knife. With her, I started the chain. It's hard knowing that, no matter what they did to me, no matter what he'd have continued to do to me. It's hard knowing I ended, or had a part in ending, the two people who made me.'

'They didn't make you. They performed an act that resulted in conception, and did so with the purpose of investment and profit. They weren't your parents, and were your mother and father only in the strictest biological terms.'

'I know that.'

'Do you? You've begun to call her Stella, that's an

296

emotional distance. But you continue to call him your father. Why is that?'

Eve stared, fumbled. 'I . . . I don't know.'

'It's something to think about, something we might talk about again.' Mira rose from the visitor's chair, laid a hand briefly on Eve's shoulder. 'Tell Roarke we talked. He may worry less.'

'Okay.'

Alone, Eve frowned at her board. Only her mother and father in the strictest biological terms. By that same benchmark, K.T. Harris was only a daughter, a sister in those same terms.

By choice, Eve decided, Harris had died no man's child.

16

Return to the scene of the crime, Eve decided, and revisited all three locations on her way home. Where, she'd determined, she'd attack the case fresh.

At Asner's apartment building, she talked to the gym buddy neighbor again. Shaken, but cooperative, the man couldn't add anything relevant to his earlier statements.

She knocked on some doors. Everybody liked A, and nobody had seen anyone entering or exiting his apartment or skulking around the building the night before.

She toured his apartment, the search team's report fresh in her mind. They hadn't found so much as a stray data disc. Prints, yes. The victim's, the gym buddy's, another neighbor's who checked out, and a licensed companion named Della McGrue. Eve intended to make another stop and have a chat with Della.

She imagined the apartment before it had been tossed.

Spare, she thought. Inexpensive furnishings, except for the monster wall screen. A guy thing, she noted. A couple of prints on the walls to spruce it up, average-looking land-scapes.

Two sets of sheets, one that had been on the bed, she assumed before the killer yanked them off to check the mattress. Spare and simple wardrobe in the closet and drawers. A couple of suits – one black, one brown, a half-dozen shirts, some socks, some boxers. Three pair of shoes, four with what he'd worn when he'd had his head bashed in: one black dress, one casual scuff, and gym shoes.

Sweats, shorts, T-shirts, a couple of ties.

The same style in toiletries, nothing fancy. Nothing fancy in the goody section either, she decided. A sexual performance aid in pill form, one box of condoms – three missing.

She sat on the side of the bed. A simple guy who liked to gamble, who went to the gym in the morning, had a brew and watched his majorly big-ass screen in the evenings. Had an LC over occasionally.

A PI who didn't mind blurring the line for work. She imagined he enjoyed it, the slightly shadowy areas. Dreamed of owning his own little casino bar somewhere warm and tropical.

A friendly sort. One who inspired grief in his neighbors at his death, genuine tears from an employee.

A. A. Asner. Had Harris picked him because his name came first in the listings? She imagined he'd gotten a lot of clients just that way.

'Should've taken a pass on this one,' she murmured.

As Della McGrue lived only three blocks away, Eve tried her next.

The buildings mirrored the same style, but when a puffy-eyed Della let her in, Eve saw her apartment couldn't be more different than Asner's.

Color and clutter, the yippy bark of a little fluff-ball dog Della clutched to her ample breasts. A harem's worth of pillows piled on the red sofa, fat candles, decorative bowls, sparkly glass animals covered tables.

Della stood, her blond hair a luxurious wave framing a face of tipped-up nose, baby-doll lips, and red-rimmed blue eyes. She cooed to the dog to soothe it.

'We're both so upset,' she told Eve. 'Frisky just loved A. Can we sit down? I haven't felt good since I heard about A. I'm having a soother. Do you want one?'

'No, I'm good. Was your relationship with Mr Asner professional?'

'Sort of, but not really.' Della cuddled the now quiet but trembling dog in one arm as she drank a pink soother from a tall glass. 'If we had sex, I had to charge him. I've got to make a living, and A knew that. I always gave him a discount, though. But sometimes we'd just go out to dinner or a vid. Just to spend some time with a friend, without the sex. I liked him a lot.'

'I'm sorry you lost your friend.'

'He was in a risky business, I guess. I mean mostly it was insurance stuff, or divorce stuff. But detective work's risky. But I never thought anyone would ...'

'When did you last see or talk to him?'

'Just yesterday. He got a big payoff from a client, and he

was going to buy into a game. He wanted a good-luck bang first. I don't work that early in the day unless it's a friend or a regular.'

'Did he tell you about the client?'

'Not really. Except he didn't like her. He said she had a nasty streak, but her money was good. Oh, and she wasn't who she said she was. Did she kill him?'

'No, but any information on or about her might help me find who did.'

'He didn't say much. He was in such a good mood. He brought Frisky her favorite doggie treats, and he brought me chocolates. He was sweet that way.'

'Did he tell you why he was in a good mood?'

'Not really. He just said how he'd made some decisions, and something about how sometimes bad things happen to wake you up, to tell you to play it straight, even if straight put you in a squeeze.'

'Did he talk to you about it, give you any details?'

'No, just that he felt good about it. And, oh, he said he was going to retire. He said that a lot, but it sounded like he meant it this time. He was going to go down to the islands next week, check out some property. He said maybe I could come. Maybe I would've. He was fun to be around. Then we went to bed for a while. After I made him a sandwich, then he – oh, I forgot. Somebody tagged him. He got all professional, so I figured it was a client.'

'Did you hear any of the conversation?'

'Not really. He walked back in the bedroom with the 'link.

I did hear him say something about meeting at ten. I think it was ten. When he came out, he was . . . thoughtful. That's how I'd say it. He gave me a big kiss, gave Frisky a rub, and left. I'll never see him again.'

Eve tried a few more angles, but realized she'd wrung that source dry. Asner hadn't given names of clients or specific business with them to friends.

But she had a fresh bone to chew. It appeared as though the killer had contacted Asner, not the other way around.

When she arrived at Roundtree's the house droid informed her Mr Roundtree was still on the set, and Ms Burkette was not at home. Better yet, Eve decided.

'I need to review the theater area and the roof.'

'Do you want me to contact Ms Burkette?'

'What for?'

'I . . . It's not the usual practice to allow someone to wander the house without Ms Burkette or Mr Roundtree in residence.'

'I'm not someone. I'm the cop serving as primary investigator on a homicide, one that occurred in this house.'

'We're all very upset.'

'I'm sure you are. You'll probably be less upset when the individual who murdered Ms Harris is identified, apprehended, and charged. So, I'm going to work toward that by reviewing the areas I mentioned.'

'Of course. I'll show you to the theater.'

'I know the way.' Eve took out her PPC, pulled up Asner's ID shot. 'Does he look familiar?'

'No.' The droid went into that momentary dead pause as it scanned. 'No. I don't know him.'

'You never saw him around the neighborhood?'

'I have nothing in memory. Is there something I can get for you while you . . . review?'

'No, but thanks. I'll let myself out when I'm done.'

Eve went directly to the theater. She stood for a few minutes, bringing the scene back into her mind as it had been that night. Everyone milling around, getting drinks or desserts, talking in little groups or lounging in the chairs.

Big, happy group, she thought. Except for Harris. She'd been sulky and withdrawn, off to herself.

Drinking and watching, Eve thought now, annoyed she'd paid so little attention to the woman.

Of course, neither of them had known Harris would end up dead in under an hour.

She dimmed the lights, took the chair she'd had that evening, and tried, again, to bring it back.

She'd been focused on the screen, but Roundtree had never been far away. Seated near during the show.

People laughing, or calling out remarks. She closed her eyes, heard Mavis's wacky giggle, Andrea's voice making some comment. But when? When?

She couldn't be sure.

Lots of laughter – gurgles of it, shouts of it, groans of it. Roarke murmuring in her ear when Marlo fumbled her prop weapon during a take.

All right, not what she heard then, there was too much of it. What hadn't she heard.

No comments from Harris, at least none that had reached the front of the theater. None from Valerie, Preston, Steinburger. Again, not that she'd heard. Nothing from Connie after the first few minutes.

Julian? He'd said something, his voice slurred from the wine. Early on, she thought. Maybe.

She brought up the lights again, studied the layout. A good-sized room, the sloped floor allowing every chair or sofa a good, unobstructed view of the screen. One exit on the side, and the main in the rear.

Easy in and out, and they hadn't been seated in a tight group. People had spread out, and as Roundtree had drawn both her and Roarke to the front, seated them, she hadn't seen exactly where everyone settled.

She pulled out her notes, did a rough outline from the statements of seating arrangements. Dimming the lights again, she tested by sitting in each area, getting the angles, the views.

Interesting, she decided, but a long way from conclusive.

She left the theater for the roof.

She took the elevator. The killer would have, she thought. The quickest way, a way least likely to be seen by other guests or staff. Direct to the rooftop lounge.

Two minutes or less, then out to the pool.

Harris, pacing? Smoking her laced herbals, drinking. Argumentative, threatening, bitchy.

Had the killer argued with her? Impossible to say, or, if so, if the argument had been brief or protracted. The fall, the decision. Drag her in, search the evening bag. Get the bar rag, use the pool water to wipe up the blood, toss the rag in the fire. Take the elevator back down.

Minutes really. It could have taken only minutes. Hardly more than a quick run to the john. Why would anyone notice?

Eve looked up. The dome had been partially opened. A nice October night, but . . .

Curious she went downstairs again, hunted up the house droid.

'Question. This time of year is the pool dome generally opened or closed?'

'Oh, closed. Ms Burkette uses the pool every day – or did. It's been a warm autumn, but she likes to keep the dome heated, the water very warm. And the mechanism needs to be seen to.'

'For what?'

'It sticks off and on. It doesn't close completely unless you turn it off then on again when it sticks. She was going to have someone come out and fix it, but since the night of the party, she hasn't used the roof. No one was allowed up there.'

'Did anyone else know about the trick to close it?'

'Mr Roundtree, of course, most of the staff, the pool maintenance crew.'

'No one else?'

'Not to my knowledge, no.'

'Okay, thanks.'

So the killer opened the dome, Eve thought as she drove home. If Harris had opened it, why close it? Or try to. The information bumped Connie down the list. If she'd wanted it closed, she knew how to make it close.

The killer hadn't. Maybe hadn't noticed it hadn't closed completely. Just flick the mechanism and go.

Why open it in the first place?

Smoke, from the zoner-laced herbals. Good possibility, she decided. Maybe the killer disliked the smell, was allergic, or just wanted the fresh air.

With her mind rolling that angle over and what it might mean, she zipped through the gates of home.

Rain smacked at her as she made the dash to the door, and inside she found the foyer empty.

Too quick for you this time, Scarecrow, she thought, and deliberately shed her jacket and tossed it over the newel post. She missed doing that during warmer weather just because she knew it got under Summerset's skin.

Pleased with herself, she bounded up the steps and into the bedroom to change to workout gear.

An hour in the gym, some hard laps in the pool, would loosen her body and her mind. To avoid running into Summerset, she took the elevator down, then stopped short when she saw Roarke, already sweaty, doing bench presses.

'Fancy meeting you here.'

'I didn't know you were home.' She walked over, looked down at him. 'Did you buy everything already?'

'Everything worth having – today. Did you catch all the bad guys?'

'Made my quota. I thought I'd sweat out some theories, suppositions, and probabilities, then shower before scooping up another load of bad guys.'

'Good plan. Nice to see you.' He clicked the weights on their safety, sat up, and reached for his water bottle. 'After a run?'

'Initially.'

'I wouldn't mind one. Where are you going?'

'Hadn't decided.'

'I've got a new VR program, and two can play.'

She narrowed her eyes. 'I'm not after sex sweat.'

He tipped back the water, eyes amused. He'd tied his hair back, and his skin gleamed.

He could probably change her mind on the sweaty activity, she decided.

'Strange, isn't it, how often your mind leaps straight to sex?'

'Maybe because you're always nailing me.'

'Maybe. But for now.' He pushed off the bench, walked to a built-in cabinet for the VR gear. 'It's more than a run. There are various obstacles, choices in directions, all of which have their own consequences or rewards. Different scenarios. We have urban, rural, suburban, seemingly deserted landscapes of myriad types. Night, day, a combination. Whatever you like, basically.'

'Is it a game or a workout?'

'It's both. Why not have fun at it? Where would you like to go?'

307

She started to pick an urban background – it's what she knew. But if it was a game, too, that meant competition.

'Let's go rural.'

'You surprise me.'

'We'll both be off our turf. Mix up day and night.'

He passed her a set of goggles, began to program. 'The goal is to reach the destination that will be shown on the map in the insert at the bottom of your play screen. If you fail to navigate an obstacle or you're injured, you lose points and distance. Clear one, gain them. Clear so many, you're rewarded with something useful.'

'How many times have you played this?'

'A few, but not the scenario I'm putting on. We'll start even on this. Thirty minutes do you?'

'Yeah, that should do it.' Eve fit on the goggles, studied the landscape that surrounded her, checked the insert, and saw the snaking, winding paths, intersections, blocks, and the pulsing light that indicated the goal.

Thick woods, dim light, a rough track and a lot of under-growth. The sort of place strange animals wandered. Animals with teeth.

She'd be more comfortable running through a dark ware-house full of homicidal chemi-heads.

Which was exactly why she'd gone against type. She'd work harder.

'Watch for pulses on the map, they'll indicate obstacles or some element of trouble. Ready?'

'Okay.'

The roar of wind came up, whipped the trees as the scene came to life around her. She heard crashing – branches falling, and a kind of whoosh and pound that might have been a waterfall.

But what did she know?

Eve started off at a warm-up jog, chose the left fork on the track. Another, bigger crash, and a tree fell across the path only a few feet ahead of her. She vaulted over it, racked up a few points. Increased her pace.

She veered right, heard a rumbling, echoing growl, and decided to backtrack. She'd just take the longer route.

She ran flat out now, finding her rhythm, muscles warming.

She saw the narrow, swaying bridge ahead – rope and open planks – with some gaps – over a wide chasm. A river, the color of mud, roared and churned below. She rushed the bridge, leaping over gaps, nearly crashed through when wood cracked under her feet.

Then the whole business began to vibrate. She thought, *Oh shit,* as frayed rope snapped, and the planks behind her tumbled down to splash into the swirling river.

She sprang up, snagged dangling rope and propelled herself forward. The surge of wind, speed, struck her, as exhilarating as it was terrifying. She landed hard – a jolt from ankles to knees – on a narrow ledge.

To the right, the ledge widened and stacked into rough stone steps. On which stood a howling pack of wolves. Even as she considered her options they began to slink forward.

She stopped, considering, and started climbing, dragging herself up the cliff face.

Sweaty, straining, she reached the top.

Reward, the screen flashed. *You now have a knife.*

She patted her hip, felt the sheath.

Frosty.

Panting a bit, she ran left, away from the wolves. Just as she found her rhythm again, something snaked around her ankle. The next thing she knew she hung upside down, dangling from a rope from a tree branch.

Somewhere, drums began to beat.

Probably cannibals, she thought. It would figure.

By the time she levered herself up – oh, her aching abs – and cut the rope, landed hard on the forest floor, the drums sounded a whole lot closer.

She caught her breath, glanced at the map to choose directions.

An arrow dug with a thwack into the tree an inch away from her braced hand.

She ran hard. Climbed a mountain of stones, fell into a bog, jumped off a cliff into a river to avoid a really big bear.

Her next reward – a flashlight – came in handy when dark fell like an avalanche.

Wet, winded, momentarily lost, she found herself surprised when the screen flashed END TIME.

She pulled off her goggles, turned to Roarke, and was pleased to find him as winded as she.

Plus, she'd edged his score by three points.

'Apparently I have a broken arm,' he told her. 'It cost me.'

'I was nearly snack food for a bear, and lost my knife when I fell into a bog. That was fun.'

He grinned. 'It was. Want another thirty?'

She'd planned on an hour, she reminded herself. So why not?

'You're on. I want a quick swim after, then I've got work. Questions. Lots of them. Maybe if I bounce some off you, you'll have an answer.'

'All right then. Loser deals with dinner. I've a mind for red meat after this.'

'Again, you're on.'

'From the beginning, or where we left it?'

'Where we left it.'

At the end of thirty, she slid down to the floor – limp.

'I was attacked by a pig.'

'A boar,' Roarke corrected.

'A mutant pig. I always knew there were mutant pigs with really sharp teeth in the woods. Why do people like to go there? And there was a meadow. Pretty. It looked safe. Snakes. I should've known there'd be snakes.'

'I had a machete. It came in handy.' Seated beside her, he studied the tallies. 'Make my steak rare, would you, darling?'

'Crap. I was kicking ass here until the pig. Fucker cost me the game. And neither of us got to the goal.'

'Next time.' He pushed to his feet, offered her his hand. 'Still want that swim?' he asked as he pulled her up.

'I had one. In a river. With jagged rocks. There may have been alligators.' She rolled her shoulders. 'Hell of a workout, though.'

She grabbed a shower instead of a swim. And fair being fair, put the meal together. With fair being fair, she put it together in her office. But didn't object when Roarke opened a bottle of wine.

They'd earned it.

'So.' She took a long, slow drink. 'Could you say who you heard, maybe who you didn't hear, while we were in the theater watching the gag reel?'

'Not for certain, no. I wasn't paying attention.'

'Me either. That part of my to-do list was mostly a bust. I talked to an LC Asner used for palship and sex.'

'Always nice to have sex with a pal.'

'She has sex with her pal the afternoon Asner was murdered, then made him a sandwich.'

'Now that is a pal.'

'Says the man eating steak.'

'Where's my sex?'

'You ought to be able to find it.' She sent him an easy smile. 'So, Asner told the sandwich-making LC he'd decided to play something straight, even though it might put him in a squeeze.'

'Interesting. Do you think he'd decided to turn over the recording?'

'Maybe. Piecing together his state of mind – from his secretary, conversations he had with his lawyer friend, and now this – I'm leaning toward him learning his client, who I'm betting he made as Harris, had been murdered, which caused him to rethink any possible bonus round with the recording. Play it straight, turn it in, retire, and move to the islands.'

'But end up dead instead.'

'Yeah. His sex pal said he got tagged on his 'link right before he left. She didn't hear the conversation, except that he agreed to meet the caller in his office that night at ten.'

'Indicating his killer contacted him.'

'Exactly. Indicating the killer knew about him, and how to contact him.'

'From Harris's 'link?'

It was good to have someone who connected the dots. 'That's my bet. He arranges the meet, kills Asner, hauls out the files and electronics – covering all the bases. People kill for all sorts of strange reasons, but I'm not buying this is over that recording.'

'You think Asner – through Harris, or vice versa – had something on the killer.'

'Something he intended to turn over along with the M and M recording, yeah. Or the killer was afraid he would. Digging into dirt, that was Harris's MO, and that's what fits. Her brother came to see me today.'

They ate as she told Roarke about the conversation.

'It's a sad commentary on a life, isn't it?' he commented. 'She not only turned against those who loved her, but used them for her own gain. She'd rather have had that gain, wield that power, than have real affection, real friendship.'

'Did she choose to be like her father, or was she just like him?'

Roarke laid a hand over hers. 'You're living proof of the power of choice.'

'Mostly I believe that's how it works. You decide. Like the workout game. Go right, go left, up or down, and deal with the results. So, yeah, I think she made the choices. I think she believed she liked it that way. But she wasn't happy. You could see she wasn't happy with the choices.'

'Yet she continued to make them.'

'Until someone chose to kill her. It wasn't Roundtree or Connie. I'm saying – at least with what I have now – it wasn't Marlo or Matthew. It wasn't Preston.'

'You've narrowed your list considerably.'

'The killer opened the pool dome.'

'How do you know?'

'Because he or she tried to close it. If Harris had opened it, there'd be no reason for the killer to close it. None I can see. The dome was partially open when we discovered the body.'

'I remember that, yes.'

'It's acting up, doesn't close properly unless you turn it off and on again. The killer didn't know. Connie would have, as she used the pool daily.'

'Are you thinking someone came in from the outside?'

She paused with a fry halfway to her mouth. 'Outside what?'

'The dome, darling.'

'Shit. Shit. I hadn't thought of that. How would they get up there?'

'All manner of ways,' he said, smiling. 'Sometimes the best way to get in is to go down. A remote to open the dome, a weak spot security-wise, I'd imagine.'

'You're thinking like a B-and-E man.'

'Not anymore. Or only in the service of my wife.'

'Ha. I'll have to run probabilities now that you put it in my head, but I don't think anybody came from out or up. I think the killer opened the dome from the inside. Harris had or was smoking those doctored herbals, and six of them would put up a hell of a cloud in a smallish, enclosed area. She couldn't have been up there long, but there were six butts.'

'Enclosed dome, smoke. Yes, I can see that. He wanted the fresh air. Or she. You seem to be down to two of each. Julian and Steinburger, Andrea and Valerie.'

'Or a combination thereof. Somebody could be covering for somebody. And I'm looking at Steinburger and Valerie, as – as far as I know – they're the only ones lying to me. She'd be more likely to cover for him than him for her.'

'Unless she knows too much about him, things he'd prefer didn't get out. He might be willing to cover for her then.'

'Yeah. They used to bang, and people tend to blab after a bang.'

'I'll be sure to guard my tongue.'

'It's usually tired from all the work during the bang,' she pointed out, and made him laugh.

'True enough.'

'What I can't get is – saying it is Steinburger. Why kill her? I mean, lots of reasons, sure, but why now? Why not string her along, pay her off, do what she wants until the project's complete? He'd have given himself a major headache by offing one of his own stars.'

'The boar or the river,' Roarke said. 'Neither choice is particularly pleasant, but you have to make one. Sometimes under pressure.'

'That's good.' Eve pointed at him. 'That's pretty good. On one hand you've got the mutant pig with the big, sharp teeth who wants to chew your leg off. On the other, the river with jagged rocks where you may or may not bash yourself into bloody pieces.'

'Most people jump.'

'Because the threat from the mutant pig is more immediate. Better to take your chances with the water and rocks. But better altogether to kill the mutant pig, then stroll away on dry land.'

'I'm beginning to wish I'd suggested pork instead of steak.'

When she laughed, he topped off her wine.

'Easy on that,' she said. 'I'm going to switch to coffee. I have to dig into Steinburger and Valerie. If I'm right and they're in this, there's something to be found. If a PI can find it, I sure as hell can.'

'I have every faith, and so have faith you can handle a glass and a half of very nice Cabernet. Tell me why you've zeroed in on Steinburger. It's not just because he wasn't truthful.'

'If you lie to a cop, you've got a reason. Often the reason's stupid, but it's there. More, he went on the offensive in the first interview.'

'And offense is defense.'

'There you go. Add one more. This has been about power and control. Hers against the freaking world from what I can tell. Who has the most power and control on this project – in the industry – among the players we've got?'

'The one with the money. It's nearly always the case.'

'Yeah, being a rich bastard, you'd know.'

'Naturally.'

'Steinburger's the one with the money. He owns the production company, and has the longest, shiniest rep. He's labeled one of the most powerful men in Hollywood.'

'You've been reading the trades.'

'Know your turf,' Eve said. 'He likes the spotlight, does a lot of publicity, pumps on the hype. And he's a liar, he's defensive, he's the hand on the money wheel. He's also got a young, attractive liar at his disposal in Valerie. It's enough for me to choose that direction.' She smiled again. 'Even if I fall into a bog.'

17

Roarke lingered over his wine while Eve updated her board.

She seemed relaxed in the work, and despite the manner of her waking that morning more rested than she'd been since their return from Dallas.

Her wounds had healed. He thought – hoped – the wounds that didn't show had begun their healing as well.

'I can hear you worrying from over here,' she told him.

'Actually I was just enjoying the view of my wife, and thinking she looks well.'

'It's the first solid workout I've put in since ... awhile. I needed it.' She continued her update. 'I talked with Mira a little.'

'Did you?'

'She gave me some things to think about, and I will. I'm dealing, Roarke.'

He got up, walked behind her, wrapped his arms around her. 'So am I.' He kissed the top of her head, then stepped back. 'If I didn't think you were dealing, I would've let you beat me in the game.'

'Like hell.'

He laughed, hugged her again, harder. 'You're right. But that just shows I'd never pander. I have too much respect for you.'

'And the shit keeps rising. You have too much ego to take a dive.'

'My ego and my respect both cast long shadows.'

'What shape is the respect shadow?'

'I'm sorry?'

'Because the ego shadow's shaped like a penis. So I wondered.'

He turned her around, flicked a finger down the dent in her chin as she sent him a big, sunny smile. 'I believe I'll take the shadow of my penis to my office. Is there anything in particular you want me to look for?'

'Sex and money.'

'I thought we'd done talking about my ego.'

'That's a good one. Sex and money as applies to Steinburger and/or Valerie. Because there's something there. She looked too damn smug this morning. Like she'd just got laid, or got a big bonus in her paycheck. There's something.'

'I'll see if I can find the something.'

'One thing I'm chewing over. If the killer arranged the meet with Asner with murder in mind, he'd have taken a weapon. But he used a statue – Maltese falcon.'

'Really? Killing the erstwhile Sam Spade with the black bird. It's very nice irony.'

'I don't imagine Asner thought so, but yeah. Point is, either the killer opted for the irony and the convenience, or didn't bring a weapon. If no weapon, the meet wasn't about murder. It just ended up that way.'

'Another fork in the road, another choice.' Roarke nodded. 'Maybe the meeting was to be a negotiation, and the killer didn't care for the terms.'

'So, the hell with it. I'll just bash your brains in. Killing comes easier the second time for a lot of people. Once it's seen as a solution, why not use that solution again?'

She studied the crime scene stills of both victims.

'I don't think either of these murders was planned as much as decided on the spot. Back to the game again. Once you make one turn, you have to make another, or backtrack. You can't unkill, so he made the next turn.'

'And there's usually another to come. If it's Steinburger, and he's used Valerie for cover, she's another threat. Another turn may be to eliminate that threat.'

'Yeah, it might. Taking it now, that's very risky, but down the road, at another fork. He might see it as another viable choice. I need the why. I can pressure him with the why. Otherwise all I've got are impressions.'

Hands in her pockets, she rocked back on her heels thinking about turns in the road, choice, consequence.

'For an amateur he's done a good job of cleaning up after himself. So far.'

'Maybe he's done it before,' Roarke suggested. 'Taken this fork, made this choice.'

She stopped, turned. 'Done it before? Wouldn't that be interesting? Could that be the why? Sex and money,' she said to Roarke as she strode to her desk. 'I'm going to take a deeper look at his background, see who else might be dead.'

'That's perfect, isn't it? I'm sex and money; you're dead bodies. What a team we are.'

'Best to stick with our strengths.'

What if he had done it before? she wondered. Accidental, deliberate, momentary impulse.

And got away with it.

And what if, she continued, Harris either knew or suspected – had Asner working on digging deeper.

Eve sat back a moment. And who was running down a fork in the road now? A waste of time, a rush to nowhere if she was wrong. But with no evidence, what choice was there but a walk in the dark?

'Computer, search for Steinburger, Joel – as identified in these files. Match with any deaths associated with him.'

Acknowledged. Working . . .

'Secondary task. Search for any unsolved murders in which subject was detained, questioned, or connected. Further task, search for any self-terminations or accidental deaths connected to subject or Big Bang Productions.'

She pushed up as the computer acknowledged the tasks. She went into the kitchen, programmed coffee, and took it with her back to her board.

Facts, she thought. Harris threatened Marlo, Matthew, Julian, Preston, Andrea, Connie.

Harris had words or confrontations with Matthew, Julian, Andrea, and Connie on the night of her death.

Harris spent time in the dome on the roof, smoking zoner and herbal tobacco.

Harris incurred an injury due to a fall on the back of the head.

Death by drowning.

It was only supposition that she'd had a 'link in her bag, and the preview of the recording as well. Solid supposition, high probability, but not fact.

Dome partially opened.

Blood washed away with bar rag and pool water.

As she went through it again, Eve fiddled with the arrangement on the board.

Harris hired Asner to plant recorders in the loft shared by Marlo and Matthew.

Asner did so, retrieved same, provided Harris with a copy.

Again, it was only supposition he'd retained the original.

Witness statement rather than hard fact had Asner tagged on his personal 'link, then making arrangements for a meet.

Asner met the killer in his office. That was fact.

Asner died as a result of multiple, violent blows with a bronze statue.

Killer, because who the hell else, removed all records and electronics, using Asner's car to transport.

Asner's vehicle found at marina.

Task one complete . . .

'Okay, let's see what we've got. Data on-screen.'

The list was long, but she'd expected it. She'd deliberately aimed the first search wide.

Three out of four grandparents, his father, a stepmother, one sibling – various cousins, aunts, uncles, and one ex-wife. She ordered family members as a subset.

Nonfamily made for a longer list. A college roommate, several actors, other industry professionals, his gardener, his longtime family doctor, a business partner, his current wife's former voice coach (retired at the time of her death).

Eve ordered subsets of professional associates, another of nonbusiness or nonindustry connections.

She then ordered the computer to cross-reference any connections on or between subsets, and to generate another subset with those results.

As she studied the list, the computer informed her there were no unsolved murders, other than those currently under investigation, connected with the subject.

'That's too damn bad,' Eve muttered.

Accidental or self-termination proved a different matter. There were plenty.

Eve got more coffee and began to sift through.

At some point Roarke sent her the record of a transfer, the evening before, of fifty thousand from Steinburger's to Valerie's account.

She copied it to her file before starting a second board.

She believed coincidence was as rare as an honest thief, and that if she scraped away long enough, thoroughly enough, coincidence revealed pattern.

It was pattern she saw now as she took a step back from the new board.

'Son of a bitch.' She walked over to Roarke's open office door. 'Come have a look at this, will you? I need a fresh eye.'

'I have two you can borrow. I've just been playing around a bit with the financials,' he said as he rose.

'There may be more of that to come.'

'I do love the legitimate opportunity to poke into other people's private affairs. It keeps me honest.'

'More or less.'

'You've expanded, I see,' he commented about her second board. She'd centered Steinburger's ID shot, fanned out others from it. Below each circling photo was a date.

'What do these people have to do with Steinburger, and your current case?'

'Oddly? They're all dead. Chronologically. Bryson Kane, college roommate. They, along with two others, shared an off-campus rental. Kane died as the result of injuries sustained in a fall down a flight of stairs. His death was ruled accidental, the high level of alcohol in his system a contributing factor. Due to a similar intake of alcohol, the other roommates, including Steinburger, slept through the sound of the fall. The body was discovered by one of the other roommates in the morning. Kane was twenty.'

'Young.'

'The next wasn't so young. Marlin Dressler, eighty-seven, great-grandfather of Steinburger's fiancée at the time – and first ex-wife. Also a bigwig in Horizon Studios, where Steinburger had his first job in the industry – basically an assistant to Dressler's assistant. Dressler had a getaway place in Northern California. He fell off a cliff.'

'Is that so?'

'He was an avid hiker, an amateur botanist. He had, allegedly, hiked up the canyon from his getaway place, collecting samples. He lost his footing, broke his leg, a couple of ribs, incurred internal bleeding. The ME estimated it took him twelve hours to die. After Dressler's death, Steinburger moved a couple rungs up the ladder.'

'Handy for him.'

'Yeah, isn't it? Dressler died six years after Kane. Three years later – I'll add Steinburger had married the fiancée, and had moved up again at Horizon – Angelica Caulfield, an actress—'

'Yes, I've seen her work.'

'She was known for her excesses as much as her work. Nobody was particularly surprised when she died of an overdose. There was some surprise that she was pregnant at the time of her death, about five weeks into it. Father unknown. While it was rumored Steinburger might have been romantically involved with her – which he vehemently denied – the rumor was never substantiated, and in fact there were plenty of rumors about Caulfield's other lovers. Steinburger, however, was one of the producers of her last project, and had, in fact, campaigned hard with the studio to cast her. His wife was also expecting their first child at the time of Caulfield's death. While her death was officially ruled accidental, there was – and still is – speculation of self-termination.'

'But not foul play.'

'Not yet. Forward four years. Jacoby Miles, a paparazzo who'd hounded Steinburger, among hordes of others, was beaten to death with a ten-pound dumbbell inside his home. All of his cameras and electronics had been taken. Police believed Miles had walked in on a robbery in progress, and in fact, subsequently arrested a B-and-E man apprehended in the same neighborhood a few weeks later. While the B-and-E man denied the burglary and murder, he served twenty-five years for same. Within a month of the murder, Steinburger and his wife separated and filed for divorce. Two days after the divorce was final, Steinburger married his second ex-wife.

'Sherri Wendall,' Eve added, tapping the next ID. 'An actress known for her comedic timing and fierce temper. Their marriage lasted four years, was described as tumultuous. Three years after their divorce, Wendall died in what was determined to be an accidental drowning due to a fall and alcohol consumption. It was the tragedy and scandal of the Cannes Film Festival that year. Steinburger attended, as one of the partners in the fledgling Big Bang Productions.'

'She was brilliant, really. You've seen some of her vids.'

'Yeah. Funny lady. Five years after the funny lady drowned in the south of France, Buster Pearlman, one of Steinburger's partners, ingested a terminal cocktail of barbiturates and single malt scotch. The ruling of self-termination was additionally fueled by speculation of embezzlement on his part, and what Steinburger regretfully testified was the threat of internal audit.'

'Yes,' Roarke murmured, 'I'll be looking more at finances.'

'We go seven years. A long stretch, so I'll be going over the interim again. Allys Beaker, twenty-two. An intern at the studio, found dead in her apartment. She'd slipped in the shower, the report claims, and fractured her skull. Her ex-boyfriend was detained and questioned, but there was no evidence to charge him with anything. He did, in his statement, claim he believed Allys was seeing someone else, an older man, a married man. This supposition was reinforced by a female friend of the deceased, who stated Beaker believed the man she was involved with intended to leave his wife and marry her. Steinburger was two years married to his last ex-wife.

'Which brings us to current events. So, with this data, what do you see here on the board?'

'A pattern. You believe he's been killing for — Christ — forty years? Without slipping, without suspicion?'

'I stopped thinking it halfway through the forty. I know it. It's a way to solve a problem, it's a choice. It's going to take more to find out what the problem might have been in each case. Some are obvious,' she continued, gesturing at the board as she paced in front of it. 'An affair resulting in a pregnancy, and the other party wouldn't let go. Money difficulties pawned off on a partner, one who might have either been in on the skimming or learned of it. A nosy photographer who saw or photographed something damaging. A stupid young girl who pushed for marriage, likely threatened to tell his wife.'

'Sex and money, as you said all along.'

'Most are violent, somewhat impulsive. A shove, a blow. A cover-up. He might even see them as accidents. Or self-defense in a twisted way.'

Roarke laid a hand on her shoulder when she stopped beside him. 'Nine people.'

'Very likely more, but it's a hell of a start. He's a serial killer who doesn't fit the standard profile. He doesn't escalate, or stick to type, stick to method. His connections or involvements with each pop out when you lay it out, but otherwise, it's just a four-decade span of accidents, suicide, misadventure. Just bad luck. Who's going to connect an almost ninety-year-old hiker slipping off a canyon path with a drunk twenty-year-old college kid falling down the stairs six years earlier?'

'You.'

She shook her head. 'I don't know if I would have. I looked at this – at Harris – as a first kill. I looked at the list of suspects and thought argument, impulse. Period. Panic, cover-up. Mira thought the same, though she did talk about there being two different styles – the impulse, the calculation. I saw it, but I didn't. Not clearly. Then you said maybe he'd done it before. I never considered that. Never considered this.'

'What do you see now, when you look at the pattern?'

'Ambition, greed, self-indulgence, an obsessive need to preserve status and reputation. Sociopathic tendencies and a need to control, absolutely. He killed Asner rather than pay him off, risking that second kill. But there's calculation there. He's alibied, and while Asner was connected to Harris, he was also connected to any number of unsavory types given his line of work. He paid Valerie off for the alibi. He can't afford a third kill, not now. But eventually she'll have an accident. He'll make sure she's paid and rewarded until he can get rid of her.'

'He killed Harris because she'd seen the pattern.'

Eve nodded. 'Or some of it – even one element – and she hired Asner to dig into it. He may have seen more of the pattern. We'll probably never know the full extent of what he and Harris knew.'

She sat on the edge of her desk, picked up her empty coffee cup, scowled at it. 'I can't prove any of it.'

'Yet.'

'It's nice having somebody believe I can work small miracles.'

'Every day. It's likely he's made other payoffs. I can look for that, near the dates of each of these deaths. I can look into the embezzlement for accounts opened during that period. And starting with the college roommate, into his academic records.'

'I've got a couple of ex-wives I can approach, police reports I need to go through again – investigators to nudge. There's no such fucking thing as a perfect murder. There will be mistakes, more connections. He may have gotten away with this for longer than I've been alive, but his time's up.

'It's up,' she murmured. 'And he's going to pay for every

face on these boards. I need coffee. Then let's start working some small miracles.'

Cold cases had their own tone, approach, dynamics. Memories faded or altered. Evidence was misplaced. People died.

For once she had an advantage in the time zone area. It was early enough in California for her to start making contacts, asking questions, requesting additional data.

She got lucky with Detective McHone – now Detective-Sergeant – who'd been secondary lead on the Buster Pearlman suicide.

'Sure I remember. Pearlman downed enough barbs to kill himself twice. Waste of good scotch, or so my partner said at the time. He had the lead on that. He's retired now, lives out in Helena, Montana. Spends all his time fishing.'

'The data I've been able to access indicated Pearlman was – allegedly – embezzling funds from the studio.'

'He'd skimmed fifty large just that morning, into an offshore account under his wife's maiden name. She swore he wouldn't steal a gumball. They weren't living over their means. Their means were pretty damn good as it was. The funds skimmed came up to ten times what we found. Never could zero in on the rest.'

'What tipped you to the embezzlement?'

'The wife. She and the kids had been visiting her parents for a few days. When they got back, they found him. She said it couldn't have been suicide. He'd never kill himself, never leave her and the kids. Pushed and pushed. It didn't take long for us to find the money, or to smell out the problem at the studio. They had an audit scheduled for the next week.'

'Tell me about Steinburger.'

'Is he on your list for K.T. Harris?'

'He was there, so he's on the list.'

'I remember he was adamant about Pearlman being innocent. About it being some kind of accident. Pretty damn pissed we'd smear a good man's name, upset his family. Went public on it, too. Got a lot of play for standing up for his friend and partner, trying to support the widow and kiddies.'

'Did it ever angle as a setup to you?'

'It looked straightforward. The rest of the money was a puzzler, but from what the forensic accountants could pull out, he'd been dipping here and there for a couple years. Could've washed it a dozen different ways.'

'No records,' Eve prodded. 'No second set of books?'

'He'd wiped his electronics. Given every last one of them a virus. We couldn't do as much back then as we can now.'

'Do you still have them?'

'Jesus, that's a while – what, fifteen years, give or take. I can't tell you.'

'I'd appreciate it if you'd check, D-S McHone. And given what we can do now, if those electronics are still in evidence, you may find something relevant on them.'

'I haven't thought about this case in God knows. I can check. You're liking Steinburger for Harris.'

'I am. And if he killed my vic, I'm betting he killed yours, too.'

'Son of a bitch.'

'That's what I said.'

She talked to more cops, made more notes, drank more coffee.

Roarke came in, eyed the coffeepot on her desk. He went into the kitchen, came back with a bottle of water. 'Change it up a bit.'

'What, are you the coffee police?'

'If so, you'd be doing life without parole. I've a couple of potentially interesting transactions. One a transfer from an account Steinburger has quietly buried under the name B.B. Joel.'

'Big Bang Joel? Really?'

'Not particularly inventive, but B.B. pays his taxes like a good boy. The day of Angelica Caulfield's death, he transferred twenty thousand into a new account, one opened by Violet Holmes.'

'The day of?'

'Yes. The body wasn't discovered until the next day.'

'Possible premeditation. Setting up the alibi in advance. Wait a minute.' Eve swiveled back to her machine, calling up files as Roarke continued.

'Holmes was, at that time, an emerging star – young, fresh, primed for her first major starring roll. Steinburger and Big Bang made her a full-fledged star. He and Holmes have been linked together a few times between marriages.'

'She has a boat, moored at the marina where we located Asner's car. Peabody and McNab found four possible connections between individuals who have boats here and Steinburger and others on the list.'

'Holmes and Steinburger lived together, for a few months, at one time,' Roarke told her. 'Apparently remain friends.'

'Friendly enough I bet he knows where she keeps her boat, how to operate it.'

'I wouldn't be surprised. There was also a withdrawal of ten thousand from the B.B. Joel account the day after the ex-wife drowned. No transfer, but then some people will insist on cash in the hand.'

'Fussy. Where does the money in this account come from?'

'Working on that. Going back, small – under five thousand – deposits were made during the first months after the account was opened. Which was some twenty months prior to the partner's supposed suicide. They graduated to larger amounts, but still under ten. He taps the account regularly. He may see it as a kind of petty cash drawer. Want a bit of something you'd prefer your accountant didn't see? Tap.'

'To the public, he lives a high life – power, glamour, shiny friends, juicy travel. But it's a straight one. Maybe B.B. Joel likes the more sinuous.'

She looked over at her boards. 'Time to tie it together so it holds enough weight to convince Whitney and the PA.'

'Eve,' he said when she turned to the 'link. 'It's past midnight. Who are you waking up?'

'Peabody. We need a conference room in the morning, with Whitney, Reo if we can get her, Mira—' She paused, gave Roarke a thoughtful look.

'I have several steps toward world financial domination scheduled in the morning, but—'

'No, who wants to get in the way of that? Can you just copy everything to Feeney? I'll bring him in, with his favorite boy.'

'I'll see to it.'

There was a breathy pause on the 'link, then a husky 'Peabody,' with blocked video.

'Locate Violet Holmes,' Eve ordered.

'Huh? Who? Oh. Sir?'

Eve ignored the sound of rustling, a slurry male murmur, a quiet, groaning sigh. 'Holmes – the boat. I want her location. Arrange a conference room, zero-eight-hundred. Be there. Bring McNab.'

'Okay. What . . . Sorry, we were just—'

'I don't want to know what you were just. In fact, I'll issue a thirty-day rip if you so much as hint what you were just. Holmes, conference room. Report to my office thirty minutes prior for an update.'

'Yes, sir.'

'Good work on the boat.'

'Thanks.'

'Go back to just,' Eve said and cut her off.

She sent priority requests to the others she wanted at the briefing, but through message only.

'In case they're just?' Roarke wondered.

'I'm ignoring that, because I'm not picturing that. I need to put this in solid order. I'm close, but I want to fine-tune.'

'I'll do the same so Feeney can easily intercept the pass.'

'Appreciate it. I guess I just owe you.'

He laughed, leaned down and kissed her head. 'I'll just have to collect another time. In the meanwhile, lay off the coffee.'

She waited until he'd gone into his office to roll her eyes. But she reached for the water instead.

18

When he felt her stir beside him, Roarke drew her closer, rubbed her back.

'Ssh,' he said. 'Ssh now. Hold on to me and sleep.'

She shivered a little, burrowed closer still.

He'd lit the fire before they'd slipped into bed. Now, only a few hours later, it simmered in the hearth and tossed its gold-washed red light into the room.

Quiet, warm, soothing. It's what he'd wanted for her in sleep.

Yet she clung, anchored to him against the dreams.

He brushed his lips over her hair, wanting to will the tension in her body away, to erase those images and emotions that gave her so little peace.

With his eyes closed, he continued to stroke her back in light, rhythmic movements designed to lull.

In the dark, curled against him, her body seemed so fragile. It wasn't, he knew. His Eve was strong, tough and athletic. He'd seen her take a punch – more than once – and execute one. He'd been on the receiving end of her fist, so could attest she packed some power.

He'd tended her wounds, as she had his, and knew she healed well, healed fast. His resilient, hardheaded cop.

But there were parts inside that tough, disciplined body that remained fragile – perhaps always would. And those vulnerable places pulled at him to protect, to comfort, to do anything he could to spare her a bruise or blow.

The vulnerability undid him even as the strength brought him pride. And the whole of her brought him love beyond the measuring of it.

Of all he'd craved in his life, all he'd dreamed of having, all he'd fought to gain by fair means or foul, he'd never imagined having such as she as his own. Never imagined himself the man he'd come to be because she was.

Now he felt her begin to relax again, degree by degree, and hoped she drifted toward that quiet and that warmth where there were no bruises or blows. And he let himself drift with her, wrapped around her like a shield.

So when she lifted her face to his, when he lowered his lips to hers, it was another kind of dreaming, as soft and lovely as the firelight playing on the walls.

His heart poured to hers, a murmured stream of Irish while she melted against him.

She knew some of the words; he'd said them before. But there was more now. He always seemed to have more to give her. Now he gave her tenderness when she hadn't known she'd needed the tender. He gave her unity when alone hurt.

A touch, a taste, all slow, all easy, as if patience and love were one steady heartbeat.

Worries that had dogged her in sleep broke apart, dissolved so there was only the welcome weight of his body, the lazy stroke of his hands, the stirring taste of him on her tongue.

She flowed along that gentle current of sensation, its lazy rise, its graceful fall. Breathing him, touching as she was touched. As if nothing in the world mattered more than the moment. And nothing existed in the moment but them.

When she opened, he filled. When he filled, she surrounded.

As they moved together in the dance of firelight, the tenderness brought tears to her eyes, a catch of them in her breath.

'I love you.' Overwhelmed, undone, he pressed his face to her shoulder. '*A ghra. A ghra mo chroi.*'

'Love,' she sighed as she rose to peak, light as a feather on a cloud.

'Love,' she repeated when she lay warm against him. She rested her hand on his cheek. He curled his over her wrist.

She slept, in the quiet and warm.

Roarke slept with her.

When she woke to sunlight, it pleased her to see him in the bedroom sitting area, drinking coffee – the cat sprawled over his lap – while he watched the financial reports whiz by on-screen. And fully dressed in one of his god of the business world suits.

Which meant he'd been up an hour, probably more, and tended to some of his realm.

So not as worried about her.

She glanced at the time, grunted, then rolled out of bed to shower. In the drying tube, she closed her eyes as the warm air swirled around her. Time to get your head in the game, she ordered herself.

Who the hell had a head to get in any game before coffee?

She grabbed the robe on the back of the door, shrugged into it as she strode back into the bedroom and straight to the AutoChef.

She drank half the first cup as though her life depended on it, then turned, studied Roarke again.

'Morning.'

'She speaks.'

'And she's going to have to do a lot more of it.'

She crossed over to the closet, started to reach for clothes at random.

'Not today,' Roarke said from behind her.

'What? I'm not wearing clothes today?'

'Oh, if only. Today, you take a rare moment to think about clothes.'

'I think about them. They keep me from being arrested for indecent exposure. And if I have to tackle some asshole during the course of the day, it prevents him from thinking I'm a sex fiend.'

'Both excellent purposes for wardrobe. Another is presentation. You're going to be presenting your case – and yourself – to your commander and others.'

'Which is cop work.' She may have been barefoot, but she

prepared to dig in her heels. 'I'm not fancying up for cop work.'

'There is, Lieutenant, considerable area between indecent exposure/sex fiend and fancying up. Such as . . . '

He selected fitted trousers in chocolate brown with a kind of nubby finish, matched them with a three-button jacket in deep, strong blue, then managed to add an Oxford-style shirt with stripes that picked up both tones.

'A clean, confident presentation of someone who's in charge and prepared to get down to the business at hand.'

'All that?'

'Wear your new boots.' He passed her the clothes. 'They'll work well with that, and with the coat as well.'

'What new boots?' Her eyebrows drew together as he took them off a shelf. 'And where did they come from?'

'The boot elves, I assume.'

'The boot elves are going to be pissed when they're dinged and scuffed inside a week.'

'Oh, I think they're more tolerant than that.'

'Those elves keep this up I'm going to need a bigger closet.'

But she dressed as advised, then sat to pull on the boots while Roarke programmed breakfast for two.

They slid on like – as Peabody might say – butter. 'Okay.' She stood, took some strides. 'They're great. Sturdy – I could definitely kick some teeth in with these.'

'The elves had that as top priority.'

'Huh.' She did a quick squat and rise then paddled her

340

heels. 'But they're not stiff or heavy, so they could handle a serious foot-chase.'

'Second priority. I'll pass your satisfaction on to the elves.' He set two plates of waffles on the table, gave Galahad a cool, warning stare, then looked Eve up and down. 'You look confident, streamlined, and absolutely capable of kicking in those teeth.'

'I like the last part the best.'

'Only one of the myriad reasons I love you.'

She sat, and when he joined her, she laid a hand over his. 'I feel confident and streamlined. I woke up that way because you were with me last night, because you loved me. And because you were sitting here this morning, doing what you always do instead of worrying about me.'

'Does that mean you're going to stop worrying about me worrying?'

'It's moving that way. We probably just need to have a good fight over something, finish it off. A good fight can work like a good orgasm, and clear things out.'

'Well now, I'm longing for a good fight. We'll have to schedule one in.'

'Better, I think, when they're more . . . organic.'

'Organic orgasm through temper.' He laughed as he passed her the syrup he knew she'd pour on in a flood. 'I'm filled with anticipation.'

'Remember that when I piss you off next time.'

She drowned her waffles in syrup.

*

Within thirty, primed by waffles, Eve checked her 'link. 'Everybody's a go for the briefing. I'm going in early, make sure everything's set up the way I want it.'

'Good luck. I should have some time this afternoon, either to deal with that fight we need to have or give Feeney some help.'

'Maybe we can work in both.' She gave him a quick kiss before heading for the door.

'Look after my cop,' he called after her. 'Just you try licking off that plate, boy-o,' she heard him say to the cat, 'and see what happens.'

It made her grin all the way downstairs.

She didn't have as much luck with traffic as she had the day before, but used the time in snags and snarls to work out her approach.

She wanted a warrant to search Steinburger's residence, his office, his vehicle – and one to dump all his electronics on Feeney and EDD.

Odds of getting them were slim, she knew. She could – she damn well would – convince everyone in the briefing that Steinburger had been killing people who annoyed him, got in his way, or just posed a serious inconvenience, for forty years.

And yet the pesky issue of probable cause would remain.

Still, she'd push for it, and if – most likely when – she got shut down, she'd push for one to monitor his 'links and comps.

And she wanted that in place before she talked to his ex-wives – the surviving ones – his boat pal, former college roommates, Buster Pearlman's widow. Before she had another round with the Hollywood set.

A lot of people were going to feel the heel of her new boots on their necks before she was done.

She pulled into her slot in Central's garage. She rode up in an elevator that stopped to let cops on, let cops off. And wished she'd opted for the glides when an undercover detective she recognized stepped in hauling a midget.

The midget boasted a shaved head covered with tats and showed gaps in his teeth in a feral snarl. That bald head might have only reached McGreedy's waist, but its owner looked mean as a rattler.

Both of them smelled, strongly and distinctly, of shit.

'Jesus, McGreedy.' One of the cops stepped as far to the side as the car would allow. 'You sleep in the sewer?'

'Chased this fucker into one. Caught you, too, didn't I, you fucking little fucker. Fucker bit my ankle. I got midget teeth marks in my ankle.'

Even as he said it, his prisoner issued a sharp kick to the wounded ankle, another to the shin, and let out a kind of war cry as he leaped, fast and nimble as a spider, on the back of the uniformed cop ahead of him in the car.

Amid the chaos, and the unbelievable stench, Eve considered. Two cops were currently trying to haul the crazy little bastard off while he yanked hair, kicked feet, sank teeth.

She decided on a different approach. She drew her weapon, and keeping a careful distance, leaned forward, pressed it to the crazy little bastard's head.

'Want a taste of this?'

He swung around, bared his gapped teeth, and she calculated he intended to use the uniform as a springboard into her face.

'I'll drop you like a stone,' she warned. 'No, like a pebble. An ugly, smelly pebble. Then I'll personally drop-kick your ass into a cage.'

'I got him, Lieutenant.' Panting, snarling, sweating, McGreedy ripped his prisoner off the uniform, shoved him facedown on the floor of the car. 'Fucker.'

'Officer?'

'Shit. Shit. Bingly, Lieutenant.'

'Officer Bingly, as you're already due for a shower and a change of uniform, why don't you assist Detective McGreedy in securing his little fucker and hauling same into detox?'

'Yes, sir. Shit.'

'It ain't roses,' McGreedy agreed.

'Hold him back, would you?' Eve requested, and hopped off the elevator.

Never a dull moment, she thought as she took a cautious sniff of herself just in case.

She bypassed her office for the conference room where she re-created her case boards, loaded data into a computer.

By the time she was finished, she expected Peabody to clock in. Deciding she wanted another hit of decent coffee before things got rolling, she secured the conference room and started to her office.

She spotted Marlo – despite the long, sun-streaked

brunette wig and oversized sunshades – coming off the glides.

'Dallas.'

'Not working today?'

'I'm not due in hair and makeup until nine, so I thought I'd take a chance you'd be in, and have a few minutes.'

'I'm in, and a few minutes is all I've got.' Eve nodded as Peabody and McNab came up the next glide. 'Hang on a minute,' she told Marlo.

'Is that Marlo?' Peabody asked.

'Yeah, I'm going to talk to her. The two of you can head right into the conference room. I've got boards set up. Study, ponder, prepare to discuss. What's in the box?'

'Doughnuts.' McNab grinned at her. 'We figured, hey, cops, breakfast time, briefing. It's the necessary ingredient.'

'It couldn't hurt. I won't be long.'

Eve considered the fact her murder board stood in her office, and deciding it might be an advantage, led Marlo in.

'Thanks for . . . ' Marlo trailed off, her gaze on the board. 'God, that's stark. And really, really disconcerting to see my own face up there, those of people I know and care about. Can I sit down?'

'Sure.' As she did, Eve rested a hip on the corner of her desk. Her mind went, unfortunately, to the idea of how many asses had sat on her candy in the last couple of days.

'You know, I thought I'd gotten so tough, prepping for this part. I've always kept in shape, but Christ, I trained for this. Physically, I mean. And, I thought, mentally. But I learned, fast, I'm not half as tough as I thought. I can work. I can put myself there, but as soon as I step out of you and into me? I'm just Marlo Durn, and I'm scared.'

'Of what?'

'There's no way around the fact one of us . . . ' Her gaze went to the board again. 'One of us killed K.T. There's no way around it. And I know you believe whoever did that killed the man she hired to spy on Matthew and me. So I'm scared because I'm working with someone who could do that.'

'Did Asner approach you, Marlo, or Matthew about compensation in exchange for the recording?'

'No.' She stared at his photo on the board. 'I've never seen him before. He was in the loft, in our bedroom. And now he's dead.'

'Has anyone approached you?'

'No. I'd tell you. It's way beyond the invasion of privacy, the embarrassment. Even the anger over it. I wanted to come here, see you, ask you if you're any closer to finding out who. And I know you probably can't tell me, but I hate being this way. Hate being scared, hate wondering about these people I care about. Hate locking my trailer door, even when I'm inside.'

'Are you afraid of anyone in particular?'

Marlo shook her head. 'Matthew's handling it better, and so's Andi. Julian's worse than I am. He's a wreck. Connie was supposed to fly to Paris to shoot some ads. Their daughter was going to meet her so they'd have a few days over there together. She rescheduled because she doesn't want to leave Roundtree. I know that's not really important in the bigger sense, but—'

'It's hard to reorder your life, even in the short-term. It's hard to wonder if someone you know isn't someone you know at all.'

'Yes.' Marlo closed her eyes. 'God, yes. Can you tell me anything? Anything at all.'

'We're having a major briefing on the investigation and some new angles this morning.'

'That's good then.' Marlo let out a breath. 'That's good.'

And that would get around, Eve thought. She wondered what Steinburger would think when he heard.

'There's a minor detail I meant to check out,' Eve continued. 'You'd probably know, save me some steps.'

'Anything.'

'Does anyone besides Harris smoke? Herbals, or otherwise?'

'Oh.' Marlo slumped a little. 'I do. A little. Occasionally. Not herbals. Tobacco, and I know, I know, I know. Bad for me, painfully expensive. And you have to hide like a thief. I've cut them out almost completely because of that, and more – might as well be honest – because Matthew dislikes it so much. He insists I can get the same effect with yoga breathing, which only proves he's never smoked anything.'

'So he objects?'

'Disapproves. Worries. I tried to switch to herbals as he's not as rabid about those, but hell. It's not the same.'

347

'Anyone else? Smoke or object to it?'

'Andi will bum a drag now and then, either from me or off an herbal. A lot of the crew sneak off for an herbal during breaks. Roundtree designated an area for them, though the studio wouldn't approve. And Joel pitched a fit.'

Inside, Eve smiled. 'Did he?'

'He's the smoking gestapo.' She straightened again, rolled her eyes dramatically. 'I swear, he can tell if you've had a single puff an hour before from a half mile away.' She made sniffing sounds, lowered her brows, roughened her voice, and did a dead-on mimic of Steinburger. 'Who's been smoking! I won't be exposed to it. Preston! Valerie! Get this place aired out, right now!' She made hacking noises, covered her mouth with her forearm. 'Somebody get me a lozenge and some spring water!'

Then she laughed, sat back. 'I swear, his eyes start watering if somebody so much as thinks about smoking. He and K.T. were at it on that all the time. They'd . . . Oh, I didn't mean. It's not like he'd kill somebody over it. He just can't stand it, and his eyes do get red.'

'Understood.' Eve smiled. 'We know Harris smoked herbals on the roof, inside the dome. DNA. From what you've said it doesn't seem likely she got them from someone else at the party.'

'She wouldn't ask, believe me. Or share.'

'Then that covers that. Just a minor detail, as I said. I've got to get to the briefing, Marlo.'

'Okay. Thanks. Really.' She rose, took Eve's hand. 'It's probably stupid, but I feel better just talking to you.'

348

'Glad I could help. I'll walk you out.'

'You probably think it's silly,' Marlo said and tugged on her wig. 'Wigs and shades and oversized coats.'

'I think I'd hate it if I couldn't walk down the street, buy a soy dog, take a stroll, grab a slice without having people staring at me, pushing at me, taking pictures of me.'

'It's part of the package.'

'Everybody's got a package. You don't have to like all of it.'

'Matthew and I are talking about going public. What the studio wants, it just doesn't seem important now. Two people are dead. That's what's important, so ... And you know what else?' She pulled off the wig, shaking out her short hair as she stuffed it in her bag. 'God! That feels better. Screw it. I'm Marlo Durn.'

She shot Eve the megastar smile and strolled toward the glide.

Armed with the additional data, Eve strode to the conference room. Inside, McNab stuffed the last of a doughnut into his mouth.

Peabody turned from the board, goggled. 'Holy shit, Dallas.'

'Convinced?'

'Are you kidding? The pattern's there. Right there. He kills people.'

'Not quite a habit,' McNab put in, 'more than a hobby. Or maybe there are others, people who didn't have a connection to him. In between he kills complete strangers.'

'Possible. But it strikes me as more likely his killing is, to him, just part of doing business. Sometimes you fire, some-times you dissolve a partnership. Sometimes you kill.'

'It's almost sicker that way.' Peabody looked back to the board. 'If he profiled like a true serial, we could at least say he's compelled. But it's not compulsive when you go years between. It's—'

'Convenience.'

'Sicker. And to think I was so juiced because he talked to me about the cameo, and how they'd play me up.'

'We'll get him, She-Body.'

'Now I want a damn doughnut.'

'Got your cream-filled with sugar glaze right here.' McNab pulled it out of the box for her.

She took the first enormous bite as Whitney came in.

'Commander,' Eve began. 'Thank you for making the time.'

'You made it sound urgent. Are those doughnuts?'

Peabody, unable to speak with a mouth full of cream, nodded.

'Detectives Peabody and McNab thought they were called for,' Eve told him.

'When aren't they?' Whitney selected a jelly, topped with sprinkles. But the board caught his eye before he could sample. In silence he studied the data, the pattern.

'Nine?'

'Yes, sir. It's possible there are more, but these dates, times, circumstances I can verify. I'm expecting Doctor Mira, Captain Feeney, APA Reo, and would like to brief everyone on the data and my conclusions at once.'

'Yes. Kyung will join us here at oh-nine-hundred. I can bump that time if you need more.'

'Hopefully not.'

Whitney shook his head. 'This is a shit storm.'

A lot of that going around, Eve thought.

She stayed out of the way as Feeney came in, reacted enthusiastically to the doughnuts, then stood munching one as he studied the board. Mira and Reo came in together, and Eve heard a snippet of their continued conversation about a shoe sale.

Eve waited as each caught the board, as Mira accepted the cup of tea Peabody brought her. As she sat, sipped, studied.

Eve judged the timing, then walked up to the board, faced the room.

'The data, my gut, and a probability of seventy-three-point-eight say that Joel Steinburger killed the nine individuals on these boards. Motives may be murky as yet, but beginning with Bryson Kane, when the victim and the suspect were twenty and twenty-one respectively, the suspect had received a warning of imminent academic suspension due to spotty attendance and failing grades. While records show the suspect's attendance did not significantly improve, he went from near suspension to honors list in a four-week period.'

'You figure he cheated,' Feeney commented.

'I do. I figure he paid the victim, who was a straight honors student, to write his papers, crib any tests or exams. I believe the victim either wanted to stop or asked for more money. They argued, and the suspect pushed him down the stairs. The suspect's grades dipped sharply for the three weeks after his roommate's death. This was put down to natural emotional upheaval at the time. I call bullshit. His grades dipped because he killed his source. He had to find another.'

'How do you prove it?' Reo asked her.

'By analyzing financial data from that period. By interviewing the other roommates, instructors, students.

'Second victim,' she continued. 'His fiancée's wealthy, influential great-grandfather, and the suspect's boss. At his death, the great-granddaughter – who married the suspect – came into a considerable inheritance. And from the pattern that emerges here, the suspect has a fondness for women.'

'A cheat's a cheat,' Feeney commented. 'He cheats on the girlfriend, Granddaddy finds out, tells him to blow.'

'That's the one I like,' Eve agreed. 'The suspect ends up with a wealthy wife, a solid position at the studio, and the potential to become heir apparent.

'Victim three,' Eve said and worked her way down.

She juggled data and theories, answered questions, reasserted time lines.

'Considering the length of time we're dealing with,' Reo began, 'it would take a miracle to access all the data. The financial records, travel, wit statements. Much less locate and interview all parties involved. Then we have to jog, and trust those memories and impressions.'

'So he keeps getting away with it, because he scatters his kills, changes his method. Nine people – maybe more – are dead because Joel Steinburger wanted them that way. Because he wanted money or sex or fame or a reputation he'd never earned. They're dead because he wanted the easy way to the red carpet, the media spotlight, the power chamber of a glamorous industry. And he wanted all the benefits that go with it. The money again, the sex, the envy of others.'

'I don't disagree with you, Dallas. But you've got pattern – a logical pattern, a convincing one. You don't have evidence.'

'We'll get it.'

'How close are you to getting him for K.T. Harris and/or Asner?'

'Closer than I was. Closer still when you put them together with the others – when you *see* the pattern. Get me a warrant to search his residence, his office, his vehicle. Get me one to confiscate and search his electronics.'

'And would you like me to get you a pony while I'm at it?' The Southern in Reo's voice went to steel. 'Where's the cause? The judge and any decent lawyer, which believe me Steinburger will have a fleet of, will point out that many men in their sixties can be connected to nine deaths over the course of their lives. That only one of these cases was designated homicide, for which the individual charged was convicted. I can get a judge to look at this, to see what you see, what I'm damn well seeing, too. And we still won't get a search warrant.'

'So that's it?' Eve shot back. 'You don't even try.'

'Of course I'm going to try. Damn it. I want to put this creepy bastard away for the rest of his life. I'm telling you we're going to get a big, fat, solid no on a search warrant.'

Eve paced away.

'I'll talk to your boss,' Whitney told Reo, 'and as many judges as it takes. If Doctor Mira will reprofile. If you have some thoughts on this, Doctor Mira.'

'Yes.' It was the first word she'd spoken since entering the room. 'I have some thoughts.'

'Before that, as a backup.' Eve turned back. 'What about a warrant to monitor his transmissions? An EDD trace on his 'links, his comps. Everything. He's my primary suspect in two current murders. I can eliminate several of the others present at Harris's death. I have a partially open dome, evidence the vic was smoking herbals laced with zoner. And a statement that can and will be verified that the suspect has a strong, even passionate aversion to smoke. The dome was closed, and the mechanism faulty. The suspect was unaware of this. When he opened it to clear the smoke, he was unable to close it completely after he killed Harris.'

'I can work with that,' Reo calculated. 'I could work a trace. And we'll work with the prosecutor on the Pearlman suicide. If your contact on that can locate the evidence, the files, we may be able to toggle back now that we have this secondary account. But if you don't get something off the trace in short order, we're going to have a tough time keeping it in place when he leaves New York. And the rest.'

Reo turned to the boards again. 'I want to believe we can prove it, but realistically, it could take years to put it all together.'

'He'll kill again.' Mira spoke up now. 'He won't wait years

between this time. He's killed twice in two days. It's a new kind of power. He murdered Asner with extreme violence, the kind he's only exhibited, that we see here, one other time. There's a pattern there as well. His privacy was infringed. He reacted with violence, then took and we assume destroyed all that pertained to him. In this case, Asner isn't the end of it. If Valerie was paid or compensated to give him an alibi, she's now a new threat. He'll need to eliminate her, and I don't believe he'll wait. Not years, not months. Weeks perhaps. He'll need to finish it to feel fully in control again.'

She looked at Eve. 'He's more dangerous now, without that feeling of control. He is organized, so he'll plan. He's self-serving and can justify all his actions as necessary. And he is ruthless. Whatever gets in the way of his comfort, his success, his ambition must be eliminated. He's killed for his own needs for forty years, and has become a powerful, respected, famous, wealthy man. On the one hand, killing is the same for him as it is for a paid assassin.'

'Business,' Eve said.

'Yes. And on the other, it's intensely, intimately personal. Friends, lovers, former wives. You may find he had a sexual relationship at one time with K.T. Harris. Only twice were his kills not part of his intimate circle.'

'And those he killed with extreme violence.'

'He could let that violent nature out with them. I believe when you interview his ex-wives and any former or current lovers they'll tell you – if they're honest – he preferred rough sex, likely with rape role-playing. The violence is there, always. Ending lives gives him a sense of control, and at the same time, the need to end them when threatened controls him.'

'He's going to be real unhappy when we take away his control and put him in a concrete cage. Get me a warrant,' Eve told Reo. 'Whatever you can get.'

After a quick knock, Kyung stepped in. 'Do you need me to wait?'

'No.' Eve angled her head. 'It's good timing. If everyone could stay a few minutes more. I've got a way I think we can get something on that EDD trace sooner rather than later.'

She jerked a thumb at the box on the conference table. 'Have a doughnut,' she invited Kyung.

19

'You need to set up another media conference,' Eve said to Kyung.

'I'm afraid so.' After a brief perusal, he selected a conservative glazed, broke it tidily in half. 'It's necessary.'

'Okay, but it has to wait until APA Reo finesses a warrant, and EDD is set on a tap and trace.'

'Well.' Kyung spread his hands in surprise. 'You're very agreeable.'

'I hope to say the same about you. We're going to announce there's been a break in the case, and I feel an arrest is imminent.'

'Excellent news.' Kyung continued to study her face. 'If it's true.'

'The break part's true. In my opinion. The arrest depends on how the killer reacts to the true part.' Eve turned toward Whitney. 'With your permission, of course, Commander.'

'I follow you,' Whitney told her. 'You expect the suspect to make some sort of contact after this announcement. That he'll be compelled, through panic or curiosity.'

'He'll want to know what we've got, and if any of it casts a shadow on him. His alibi for Asner is another person, a person and an alibi I believe he bought. Price could go up. His alibi may contact him to renegotiate terms.'

'They could deal with that face-to-face.' Feeney lifted his shoulders. 'May not use a 'link or comp to work it out.'

'True. But I've got someone else who'll engage the suspect face-to-face. Nadine's good at getting people to say things they don't expect or intend to say. Every and any little slip he makes adds weight. I want to bring her in, Commander. Not only does she have a vested interest, but I know she won't go public with any information I give her until I give her the go. Especially when I agree – reluctantly and with some annoyance – to giving her an exclusive on *Now* in exchange for her assistance and discretion.'

'He manipulates,' Mira commented. 'No one can live as he's lived, do what he's done for four decades and not have a mastery of manipulation. Nadine also manipulates expertly. And so,' she said to Eve, 'do you. You know he'll lie to her.'

'Yeah. But about who? Because at a point where he believes we're nearly ready to make an arrest, he has to throw some dirt on someone else. There's a limited number of suspects. He's going to have to toss one of his own into the fire to feel safe. He'll have to lie, or shave the truth into another shape. The more he does that, the better chance he'll slip up.'

'He may kill one of his own,' Mira pointed out. 'And, as he did with his partner, stage it as a self-termination, one executed out of guilt.'

'Yeah, so we'll have to take steps there. I'm working it out.'

'Excuse me.' Kyung held up a hand. 'I'm not a detective, but am I seeing what I think I'm seeing?'

Eve glanced at the board when he gestured. 'That information stays in this room.'

'Understood. Of course. But … have you actually connected nine murders to Joel Steinburger? One of the most respected, revered, successful, and celebrated producers in the industry?'

'Just because he makes a good vid doesn't mean he's not a stone killer. And I'm about to end his streak and his celebrated status.'

'This is going to be huge. The media will explode over this, and the NYPSD – and you, Lieutenant, will be at ground zero.'

'You sound happy about that.'

He only smiled, took a neat bite of his doughnut. 'We all do what we do.'

'You got that right.'

Eve went straight to her office from the conference room to contact Nadine. 'Boat lady,' she said to Peabody.

'Lives in Tribeca with her cohab.'

'Contact her. I want her to meet us at the boat.'

'At the boat?'

'Asap, Peabody. Nadine,' she said the minute the reporter came on. 'We have to talk.'

'I have a window this afternoon, about—'

'Now.'

'Dallas, I'm right in the middle of—'

'Believe me, whatever you're in the middle of isn't as juicy.'

'Really? What's juicier than finalizing arrangements for an exclusive with Isaac McQueen as he awaits transport to his new facilities – an off-planet, maximum-security penitentiary? To tie in with interviews with the Jones twins, with the young girl McQueen and his accomplice snatched from the Dallas mall, *and* interviews with every survivor a certain rookie cop freed when she took McQueen down in New York over twelve years ago? We're getting a six-hour special, in three parts, on this. It's going to be mega.'

'Good for you. Want something else mega? The kind of mega that could mean another book, and sure as it's sweaty in hell, would have Hollywood beating down your door.'

'When and where?'

'The Land Edge Marina, Battery Park. Hold on.' She glanced over as Peabody came back, held up a finger, mouthed: *In an hour.* 'In two hours. Don't be late.'

She clicked off.

'It is mega,' Peabody said. 'I don't mean books and vids. I mean cop mega. When I became a cop it wasn't for cases like this. I mean, it's hard to even imagine anybody could do what he's done, for forty years. It makes me feel . . . '

'Depressed,' Eve finished. 'Like he should've been stopped long before this. If one cop had looked right instead of left, up instead of down, had asked one more question, maybe he would have been stopped.'

'Yeah. I know some people never get caught, or they slip

through because you just can't nail the case shut. But this is . . . It's been decades, Dallas. And I look at the board, and I see that college guy, a guy younger than me. He'll never get older, never graduate or fall in love. He'd be old enough to have grandkids now, but he's always going to be twenty.'

'He's a good one for you to keep in your head. A good one for you to stand for in this. You remember his face and his name, Peabody, and remember he never had a chance to be older than twenty because Joel Steinburger cut off that chance. He cut it off, and he got away with it. So he cut off other chances.

'We're going to make sure he never does it again.'

She answered her beeping 'link. 'Dallas.'

'McHone. I got lucky. Found the evidence box, case book, the tagged electronics. The works. Couldn't get it off my head after I talked to you, so I went in, started digging.'

'I owe you. Look, we're hot here. If I could have what you found, I can get our top dog in EDD and a civilian consultant with mad skills to dig into the e-stuff. I'd appreciate getting my hands on that case book, and the rest.'

'If you find something that lets me tell Pearlman's widow he wasn't a coward and a thief, we'll be square. I've got to push through some paperwork to clear sending this out to you, then make arrangements for secure transport.'

'I can expedite some of that. I'll have my commander deal with the red tape, and I'll get the transport. If you ever need anything from me, D-S McHone, just reach out.'

'I'll do that.'

'Get Whitney to get this rolling,' she told Peabody. 'I'll get the transport moving.'

She started to contact Roarke, winced, hissed, paced to the window and back. It was wrong, she knew it, to interrupt him every time she needed something he could supply.

Maybe it was like swallowing sand, but she contacted Summerset instead.

'Lieutenant?'

'I need a fast, secure shuttle to transport two NYPSD officers to California, and bring them and sensitive evidence back to New York.'

'I see. I'll need the exact destination, and your preferred departure center.'

'That's it?'

'I assume you wish this transportation expedited, so yes, destination and departure centers will suffice.'

'Okay.' Still suspicious, she told him.

'Very well. Have your men at departure, with valid identification and signed authorization, of course, in thirty minutes.'

'Signed authorization from who?'

'From you, Lieutenant. As the shuttles are, always, at your disposal, the officers only require your authorization. Unless you intend to accompany them, then it won't be necessary.'

'No, I'm not going. They'll be there in thirty.' She swallowed more sand. 'Thank you.'

'Of course.'

She frowned at the blank screen on the 'link. How was she

supposed to know it was that easy? If she'd known it was that easy, she could've contacted the transpo station herself. Still, Summerset could likely cut through it all faster anyway.

'Dallas.'

'What?' Distracted, she glanced over, saw Reo at the door. 'Yeah.'

'You got your warrant. I let Feeney know.'

'Good. We'll start rolling the ball.'

'You don't want to hear it, I know, but you're going to have to be really lucky for him to say anything you can take to court on these murders.'

'He may say something that leads to something else, that can be. It's a process, Reo.'

'And one that may take years – if ever – to build a case against him for the old murders. Shouldn't you focus on the two already in your hands?'

'I can focus on more than one goal at a time. A college kid, a pregnant woman, a husband and father, an old man, a woman smart enough to divorce him, some guy just doing his job. Who do you want me to forget?'

'None of them. But if you can close it down on Harris and Asner, he's never going to see daylight again. He's only got one life, Dallas, and if we do this right he'll spend what's left of his in a cage.'

'That'd be fine, if it was only about him. It's also about seven people and the lives they'll never get to live. Did you look at them?' Eve demanded.

'Yes. I know. I *know*, Dallas. I want him for all of them.

I want to prosecute him for every one, and win. Which is a fantasy because if we ever got enough to take him down for all of them, my boss would be all over it, and I'll settle for first chair. But I'd settle, now, for a solid case on one count – put him away, and hope we can gather the others over time.'

'I'm not ready to settle. When we get enough to box him on Harris and Asner – or either – I'm going to break him to pieces on the rest. On the whole. Then I'm going to hand you those pieces on a platter.'

'And I'd take them. Mira's worried. You got that, too? She's worried he'll find a way to block the light on him and beam it on someone else. Or worse. We don't want to add another to his scoreboard.'

'I know how he thinks now. I'm going to stay ahead of him.'

'Keep me in the loop. And if you get me a couple more slivers, I'll do a hard push for the search warrants.'

'You could try it now.'

Reo only shook her head. 'I try it now, I'm going to get a no. I get a no, it's harder to get a yes later.'

Eve saw the logic, even if she didn't like it. 'You know when we – me and Peabody – went to the set before Harris got dead and things got sticky, they were shooting this scene where a feisty young APA accompanies two homicide cops into the Icove residence, and when they find a DB, the APA passes out cold.'

'Crap. Crap. They put that in there?' Her face a study in

mortification and annoyance, Reo did a quick circle. 'Crap. It was my first body. It could've happened to anyone.'

'It happened to you. The actress went down really graceful.'

'You enjoyed it.' Eyes slitted, Reo pointed a finger. 'You enjoy my video humiliation.'

'It doesn't suck for me. And if memory serves, you made up for it. You stuck your neck out, you got things done.'

Reo sighed. 'Get me a sliver. One sliver, and I'll stick it out again.'

'Get ready to do just that.' Eve grabbed her coat.

'Oh my God.' Reo made a hum of almost sexual pleasure.

'Really?' Keeping some distance, Eve shrugged into the coat. 'Seriously, sex noises over a coat?'

'It's . . . delicious.'

'Don't lick it. Once,' Eve said, knowing damn well she wouldn't get past Reo without it. 'You can touch it, but just once.'

'Mmmm. It's gushy.'

'What is that word?' Eve muttered, striding out into the bullpen. 'Peabody, with me. We'll get you the sliver,' she said to Reo.

The wind whipped over the water and blew the scent of it inland. It was a pretty enough day, and the tourists took advantage, wandering the park, piling on ferries for a trip to Liberty Island. Gardens continued to bloom, the colors edged toward the rusts and umbers of fall.

Vendors had their stalls – the ever-enterprising locals – to hose those tourists on the price of a soy dog, souvenirs, guides, toss-away 'links and cameras for those who'd lost or forgotten their own.

Eve stood studying the marina, where sleek boats rocked on the busy water.

The private section was gated off to discourage the curious, those inclined to vandalism or thievery. But she didn't see it would be much of a problem to bypass. Just as she imagined those who could afford to dock – moor – whatever it was – their spiffy boat in this location had security measures on the spiffy boat.

'That's Violet Holmes.' Peabody lifted her chin toward the woman walking toward the gate.

She wore a crisp red jacket, jeans embellished at the pocket with thin gold braid, and a striped red shirt. The floral scarf looped around her neck trailed behind her in the breeze.

A jaunty navy cap perched over her short, silver hair.

'Detective Peabody. And you're Lieutenant Dallas.' Violet had a firm, no-nonsense handshake. 'I feel I know you after reading the Icove book, and of course, following the reports on K.T.'

'You knew her?' Eve asked.

'Only slightly. I consider New York home now, and only get to the Coast occasionally. It's interesting to meet you both, but I don't understand your interest in *Simone*.'

'The boat,' Peabody explained to Eve.

'Named for my signature role. You're both too young, but

Simone launched my career. The boat's ten now, and one of my greatest pleasures.'

'Speaking of that, your professional beginnings. Can you tell me if it's usual for Joel Steinburger to give a rookie actress twenty thousand dollars?'

'I'm sorry?'

'It's just one of those old details that popped up in routine investigation. Twenty thousand, transferred into your account – a brand-new account – on July eighteen, 'twenty-nine. Was that a usual practice?'

'No, not at all. Which is what makes Joel so unusual, and special. I remember it very well, as it deals, again, with Simone. The role. I wanted it desperately, and my readings went well. I worked on them for days.'

She laughed a little, looking back. 'I ate, slept, breathed Simone. But while Joel wanted me for the part, the rest of the suits were holding out. I wasn't beautiful enough, sophisticated enough. I wasn't sultry, I wasn't sexual. And so on.'

'Okay. Twenty thousand changed that?'

'You'd be surprised. Joel gave me the money out of his own pocket, took that risk. He had me hire one of the top consultants at the time – for fashion, hair, enhancements, attitude.' She laughed again. 'God, it was exhilarating. And with this entirely new look and the 'tude that went with it, I went back in for another reading. And I got Simone. I owe Joel for that, and a good deal for everything that came after.'

'Were you lovers?'

367

'Not then. We were later, for a time. These are odd questions.'

'I know it seems that way. I have another. Since you remember the incident so well, you should remember what Joel asked you for in return.'

'To get the part.'

'A little favor, something he asked for at or near the same time.'

'I just don't understand what this has to do with my boat.'

'There are all sorts of details we have to nail down.'

'Well, I do remember, as it was a particularly exciting time for me. It's simple, really, and sweet, though I never really equated it with an exchange, as you're saying. Not a favor for money.'

'What do you remember?'

'Joel was planning a surprise for his wife, they'd just found out she was expecting their first child. He wanted to take a quick trip down to their villa in Mexico, check on the preparations. He just asked me to say, if asked, that he was with me and the consultant at our first meeting that evening. Which he was, actually, for the first couple hours. Then he had to leave for the flight. Is that what you mean?'

'Yeah, that clears it up, thanks. I guess when the police asked you, you stuck to the story.'

'Oh.' Violet laid a hand on her heart. 'Angelica Caulfield's overdose. Yes, I see the police connection now. What a tragedy, what a waste of a life and talent.'

'The police questioned you?'

368

'They'd spoken to Joel. There were rumors he'd been having an affair with Angelica. Honestly, I can't count the number of affairs I've had, according to rumor, with people I've never even met. It's part of the business.'

'When they talked to you, you told them he'd been with you and the consultant.'

'Well, yes, I did tell them he'd been with us. Germaine, the consultant, was there when the police made the inquiry. Just routine, again. And he automatically confirmed Joel had been with us. So I did, too. It seemed easier.'

She paused a moment, let out a breath. 'I haven't thought of that in years, but I guess it would've been better if we hadn't. Joel certainly would have had his flight records and so on, but the media would have been all over the trip to Mexico, and spoiled the surprise. And Lana was wonderfully surprised when he threw the most amazing party for her at their villa. My first real bash,' Violet said with a smile.

'Now that surprise isn't a factor, would you mind clearing up the discrepancy for the record – for the files,' Eve said.

'Oh. All right, sure. If it's really necessary.'

'Just cleaner,' Eve said casually. 'We'll take care of it later. Would you mind if we took a look at *Simone*?'

'Not at all.' At the gate, Violet swiped a card, entered a code. 'She's in six. My lucky number.'

'Have you been out on it – her – lately?' Eve asked.

'Not in a couple weeks. I've been in Baltimore, on a location shoot for a new series. I only got back to New York yesterday afternoon.'

'Does anyone else have access to the boat?'

'Phillip – Phillip Decater. We've been cohabbing for the last couple years. But he hasn't taken her out. He was with me in Baltimore, and he's a shaky sailor. His only flaw,' she said with a smile as she gestured to a pretty white boat, with shining brass and gleaming wood.

'You take friends out for rides, I imagine.'

'Yes, friends, family. When we can arrange it. What is this about?'

'It may be nothing. Is there a way for you to tell if the boat was taken out during your absence?'

'If you're thinking somebody took her out for a joyride, I don't see how. They'd have to get through the gate, then get through the security in the wheelhouse, *then* access the start code. If you went through all that successfully, why not keep sailing and sell the boat up in Nova Scotia?'

'Good point. But, if someone did, can you tell?'

'I can check the digi-log. It would have a record of the last use, the coordinates, the time elapsed.'

'Really?'

'A new toy,' Violet admitted with a grin. 'Phillip got it for me for my birthday last month. Hardly something I need on a pleasure boat, but he knows I love *Simone*, and I enjoy gadgets.'

'Can we check your gadget?'

'Why not? Come on board. The galley's always stocked,' Violet said as she stepped nimbly from the dock to the boat. 'Can I offer you anything?'

'We're fine, thanks.'

'Gosh, it's beautiful.' Peabody brushed her fingers over the trim. 'I don't really know much about boats, but I know wood. This is really gorgeous.'

'Reclaimed teak. We do a lot of entertaining on her in the summer. She'll sleep eight if we want to make a weekend of it with friends.'

She climbed up a narrow flight of stairs, entered another code at a glass-fronted door.

Though the room looked like a command center, it held an old-fashioned ship's wheel – the helm, Eve supposed.

And a view out the wide ribbon of glass of the harbor.

Eve tried not to think about the way the floor swayed, gently, under her feet.

'Here now.' Violet moved to the right. 'Gadgets. Sonar, which is fun for tracking schools of fish, or whales if we take her out far enough. Various global weather stations. And this is the digi-log.' She opened a counter screen, spoke her name, the name of the boat. 'Phillip had this voice-activated, for fun.

'Display full log,' she ordered. 'You'll see,' she said to Eve, 'we haven't been able to take her out much since … This doesn't make sense.'

It did to Eve. 'Am I reading this right? The boat was taken out yesterday morning zero-one-sixteen and returned to dock just over an hour later at zero-two-twenty-two. For a total of two-point-six miles. And this is the average speed?'

'Yes, the knots.' Violet pulled off her cap, raked her fingers through her hair. 'This is very upsetting.'

'And these numbers, the coordinates? That's where the boat was taken, how it got there.'

'Yes, yes. Damn it. I'm going to be speaking to marina security about this. If someone on staff decided they could help themselves to *Simone*, they're going to find out differently.'

'Maybe you want to check the boat,' Peabody suggested. 'Just to make sure nothing's been disturbed, or nothing's been taken.'

'God. Yes, of course. Damn it!' As she strode out, she dragged out her 'link. Eve heard her say, 'Phillip, someone's been at *Simone*. No, no, she's fine. I have the police right here.'

'He didn't know about the gadget,' Eve said. 'It's new. I bet he knew she was in Baltimore, knew the boat would be here. Knew how to get through the gate, through the door, and start her up.'

'They used to be lovers,' Peabody whispered. 'She lied for him once that we know of, in an official inquiry.'

'Because – my read – she was young, grateful, naive. And whether she knew it or can admit it, felt obligated because he gave her the money for the consultant – was supporting her for the role she wanted. She told us about it too easily – no worries, no evasions.'

'Yeah.' Peabody glanced toward the wheelhouse door. 'He'd have had no reason to give her a warning about it. She wouldn't have expected to be asked after all this time. She looked surprised, but not scared.'

'She's probably changed security measures since they had any sexual deal going. She's cohabbed for a couple years with this Phillip guy. But Steinburger would have been on board since. He's a friend, and he has a boat of his own.'

Eve went out and down, then down again when she heard rummaging belowdecks.

'Everything seems to be as it should be.' Violet stood in an organized galley kitchen, mixing a drink. 'I'm having a Bloody Mary. I'm so mad! Phillip's on his way. He's a man you can count on.'

'You said only the two of you had access, but what about emergencies? Marina security.'

'Yes, yes, I didn't think. They have emergency bypass access.'

'And you said you often entertain on board. Maybe some of your friends and family know the codes.'

'Maybe, maybe.' She took a quick drink. 'But they're friends. They're family. If any of them wanted to use the boat, they'd ask. They'd hardly skulk around the marina in the middle of the night when they'd only have to contact me to get clearance.'

'Have you entertained any of the cast and crew on the Icove vid on board?'

Violet lowered her glass. 'You think this incident is somehow related to the murder? That's . . . I want some air.'

She moved past Eve and Peabody and went up on deck.

Eve gave her a minute, then followed. 'Did you have a party on board for some of the cast and crew?'

'Connie and I are friends. I adore Roundtree. Andi and I have gotten friendly, as well, now that we don't compete for the same roles with regularity as we once did.'

She sat, sipping at her drink. 'I'd met Julian before, and found him just adorable. And Joel and I were, as you know, very friendly once upon a time. We've remained friends. Phillip and I hosted a harbor party on *Simone* at the end of August. They were all here, and K.T., Marlo Durn, Matthew Zank – several others. We did an overnight for a smaller group. Connie and Roundtree, Joel, Andi – we all have boats, you see. We're all sailors. I don't see how this applies to a murder.'

'It's a detail we need to follow up on. Have any of them been on board since that party?'

'Ah.' She rubbed her forehead. 'There's rarely time for too many parties when you're in the middle of shooting a project. Connie and I had lunch on deck one afternoon last month, I think. We didn't take her out. Just had a fancy ladies' lunch catered, here in the marina. And, oh, I lent her to Joel a few weeks ago. He wanted to take some of the money people out, and was looking at renting a boat. I told him not to be silly, he could use *Simone*.'

'You had to give him the codes.'

'Yes, I suppose I did. I meant to change them, just a matter of course. But I've been busy with the new series, and it slipped my mind. Besides, as I said, Joel – none of them – would have any reason to sneak in here and take her out in the middle of the night.'

'Just a detail,' Eve said easily. 'We appreciate your time, and your cooperation. Before we go, I'd like to make a copy of your digi-log.'

'Please do. Shouldn't you look for fingerprints?'

Eve smiled. 'I think the log copy will be enough. Since we're here, why don't we just get that correction for the record.'

'Thirty years ago,' Violet began. 'Really, is it necessary?'

'Just to keep the record clean. Peabody, why don't you go make that copy while I take care of this.'

Once done, they left Violet brooding over her Bloody Mary.

'Peabody.'

'I know, get the log data to the water cops, coordinate with them about pinning the dump location, sending divers down.'

'Make it their priority,' Eve added. 'We got the first sliver, sliver and more with her recanting his alibi for the night of Caulfield's death.'

'He planned all that in advance. Set it up, lavishing the attention, the consultant – who, yeah, I'll track down – the clothes, and dangling a big part in front of a young, hungry actress.'

'Who was probably half in love with him,' Eve added. 'Reo's going to like it. And locating the dumped electronics would be a really nice boost. We'll get the search warrant.'

'It was just luck she had that digi-log deal.'

'Steinburger's had luck his way long enough. Without the log deal, there'd have been something else. Fuel consumption, something. I want a couple of cops to canvass the marina, see if anybody saw Steinburger – saw anything. And I want EDD to check out the gate security. She needed to swipe as well as code to get us in there. Let's see how he pulled that off.'

'On it. Here comes Nadine.'

'I see her.'

'This better be good.' Nadine clipped up to them. 'It better be mega. I'm up to my ass in work putting this special together. I barely got three hours of sleep last night, and I ate two sticky buns for breakfast because they were there. Now I'm all the way the hell out here when I should be putting together my questions for that fucker McQueen.'

'It sounds like you could use a nice walk in the park. Peabody, take care of those items, will you? You can catch up to us.'

'I don't have time for a goddamn walk in the park,' Nadine began, but Eve just strolled away.

'Oh. If I didn't know she could kick my ass, I'd seriously try kicking hers.'

'Trust me,' Peabody told her. 'It's going to be worth the walk.'

20

If you had to be out in nature, Eve figured a city park did the job in a civilized manner. The wildlife ran to squirrels, pigeons, muggers, and the inevitable end-of-the-world-as-we-know-it prognosticator who invariably looked rattier than the squirrels.

She liked the flowers well enough. Someone actually planted them rather than them just sneaking up out of the ground when nobody was looking. And in addition to the weird chirp of a bird or buzz of some bloodsucking insect, came the comforting grumble of traffic.

'I'm not tromping all over Battery Park in these heels.'

Eve glanced down at the towering pumps in glossy tones of rust picked out in gold. 'Why do you wear them if you can't walk in them?'

'I can walk in them just fine, thanks. But I'll be damned if I'll hike in them.' Nadine plopped down on a bench, crossed the legs that ended in the no-hiking shoes, folded her arms. 'What's this about and why the hell couldn't we deal with it on the 'link? My schedule's blown to bits now.'

'You're going to want to add something to the bits.'

Nadine simply gave her the steely eye. 'Do you have any

idea what goes into setting up a multipart special like this? The scheduling, the travel, the writing, the conceptualizing, wardrobe? Added to it, I'm *doing* the interviews, writing the questions, the setups, the narration. And I'm the christing executive producer. So—'

'Speaking of producers,' Eve said mildly as she dropped down on the bench, 'I need you to get Steinburger to agree to an interview. You can dig into his thoughts of Harris's murder, how it feels to be a suspect, how he and the others are handling her death while they continue to produce the vid. Like that.'

'Now you're telling me how to do my job?' Temper spiked up over stress. 'I swear to *God*, I may just try to kick your ass after all.'

'In those shoes?' Eve snorted. 'Your ankles would snap like twigs.'

'Listen, Dallas, the media's jammed with this already, and Steinburger, like the rest, is toeing the company line. Shock, upset, sorrow, and the show must go on. I've already talked to all of them, on record. If you've got something new, an angle I can work with, fine. Otherwise, it's just reprise until you feed us more info. Unless you're going to tell me Steinburger strolled up to the roof and killed Harris.'

'Off the record.'

Nadine's eyes narrowed, flashed. 'Oh, to borrow from you, Dallas, *bite me*. You drag me all the way downtown, lay out a tease like you suspect one of the most respected, successful, and revered producers in the business might have killed one of his most bankable if difficult actors? And you expect me to go off the record.'

'Off the record, or you take a hike in those ankle-killers, and I take one in my new, comfortable boots.'

'God! You piss me off.' Nadine studied Eve's boots and sulked. 'They're nice boots.'

Eve shot out her legs, gave her boots a study in turn. 'I guess they go with the coat.'

'I'm not even discussing the coat because it should be mine. I'd appreciate its soft, leathery goodness and superior lines a lot more than you.'

'I like it.' She waited a beat. 'So do you want to sit here and talk about our clothes, or are we off-record?'

'Damn it. I—'

'Hold that thought.' Eve rose, strode over, and grabbed a skinny guy in a baggy jacket and camo pants by the arm. 'Look, you and I both know that woman's an idiot for carrying her purse that way.'

'What's your deal?' He shoved at her, tried to yank free. Eve just shifted and tightened her grip.

'She's an idiot, and so's the woman with her. But they're probably from Wisconsin or somewhere. So snatching their bags in the park is just bad public relations for the city.'

He sneered, fisted his free hand in warning. 'Get outta my face, lady, or I'm calling the cops.'

'Okay, so you're an idiot, too. I am a cop, moron. I'm sitting right over there, and I'm watching you scope your mark. It's insulting.'

379

'I don't know what the fuck you're talking about.' But his fisted hand fell back to his side, and his voice took on a whine. 'I'm walking here. I'm just walking here.'

'Do us both a favor. Just walk somewhere else. Now.'

When she let him go he didn't walk. He ran like a rabbit away from the two women, possibly from Wisconsin, who strolled with their handbags dangling from careless fingers.

Eve walked back, sat on the bench. 'Sorry for the interruption. Now where were we?'

'How did you know he was a purse snatcher?'

'He's been stalking those two women for the last few minutes, keeping pace, eyeing the bags. Trying to gauge if he could do a double-snatch or just go for the one. I think he was going for the double. Anyway. If you want to know what I know, say the magic words.'

'Goddamn it.'

'Those aren't the magic words.'

'All right, but it damn well better be good. It better be gold. We're off the record.'

'Steinburger not only killed Harris and A. A. Asner, he's killed at least seven other people. I think it's more, but we're sticking with the nine total right now. He's been killing people for forty years.'

Nadine blinked once, slowly. 'Joel Steinburger. Academy Award–winning, Kennedy Center–honoring, Big Bang Productions–founding Joel Steinburger, a killer, for four decades?'

'Starting with one of his housemates in college, and ending, if I have anything to do with it, with Asner.'

'Fuck me sideways.'

'Thanks, but you're just not my type.'

'You're sure.'

'I'm sure men are my type, but if I went for women, I'd do you.'

Nadine gave Eve a punch on the shoulder with the heel of her hand. 'About Steinburger. Of course you're sure. You wouldn't tell me if you weren't sure. Jesus. Jesus. I actually have to hike.' She pushed up, strode along the path, back and forth in her crazy high, glossy shoes. 'This is huge. It's bigger than huge. It's a monster story. It's Godzilla. And a book, oh yeah, the follow-up bestseller with a guaranteed vid to follow with the Hollywood scandal connection.'

'And only nine people, give or take, had to die.'

'Just give me a minute, would you? I'm restraining myself from doing the mambo over this, and that's taking some work. *Joel Steinburger: Producer in Death*.'

'Maybe you can brainstorm your titles after we put him away.'

Nadine sat again. 'All right, I'm finished with the glee portion of my reaction. It probably wouldn't have been quite so gleeful except I don't like him. I expected to, wanted to. The man's producing my book in a major screen event. I admire his work, a lot. But I found him pushy and petulant, and a little on the grabby side. He's an ass-patter,' Nadine explained. 'Tries to make it come off avuncular, but that didn't wash for me so I've kept my ass at a distance.'

'Sex and money are big elements of his makeup, and the

need to exert power. Ass-patting women is just a way to show he's the one at the wheel.'

'You tracked him back to his housemate's death? In college?'

'The working hypothesis is the housemate did his papers, or sold him papers at a fee – or found out Steinburger was buying his grades to keep from getting the boot. Steinburger pushed him down the stairs at their off-campus place. Or, possibly, it was an accident, then covered up. But when you dig in, there have been a lot of accidents resulting in death connected to him over the years. Too many.

'And I just got a recant, on record, from his alibi on the night Angelica Caulfield OD'd.'

'Angelica Caulfield. Oh God, fuck me inside out and sideways. Mind-mamboing. You think he killed Angelica fucking Caulfield.'

'I know he did. Just have to prove it. And there are more.'

Eve ran them through quickly as Peabody came to the bench with a jumbo sleeve of popcorn. Absently, she tossed some to a squirrel.

He was immediately joined by a swarm of his buddies.

'Jesus, Peabody.' Eve drew her legs back in.

'He looked hungry.'

'Now he's an army, and here comes the frigging air force.'

Pigeons swooped so squirrel and bird gave each other the beady eye as they jostled for position.

'Get that out of here,' Eve ordered, 'before they mount the attack. I think that one's got a weapon.'

Looking aggrieved, and a little frightened, Peabody waded through the massing squirrels and pigeons and made a dash away with her sleeve.

'It's the Free-Ager in her,' Eve muttered.

'There's been speculation over Caulfield's death and the paternity of the fetus for years. All the while . . . You can't prove any of this. Yet. Or you wouldn't be talking to me.'

'Peabody contacted the water cops before she decided to play fairy godmother to the wildlife. They'll send divers down. We're going to find the electronics, some of them anyway. We've got him connected to the boat – and the owner of the boat, his alibi for Caulfield, recanted with a detailed explanation of why she initially lied. I can and will bury him in circumstantial up to his neck. There's the partially open dome and his aversion to smoke.'

'I can confirm that. Marlo and I had a couple of herbals in her trailer one day when we were going over a scene. He came by an hour later. You'd have thought we'd burned hazardous waste in there.'

'We'll be tracking down wits from all the murders. I should have the case file and the electronics on the Buster Pearlman suicide by the time I get back to Central. This afternoon we'll hold a media conference, and I'll announce that we're investigating new information, new evidence, and believe we're close to making an arrest.'

'Trying to smoke him out?'

'He'll worry about it, try to backtrack his steps, figure out if he made a mistake. Off-balance, he's more likely to make one now. Mira's worried, and I think she has cause, that he may go as far as offing one of the others to throw suspicion onto them. He's done it before.'

'With the business partner. So you want me to add to the pressure, give him more of a nudge by pushing for an interview.'

'If you get one you go in wired.'

'Wait a minute—'

'For your own protection, Nadine. He may decide you're the one to off.'

'Oh, bull. Why would he target me? We barely brushed by each other. I only went to the set a handful of times, to another handful of table readings or meetings.'

'She pressured you to expand her part, to change some of the scenes, to twist the actual facts of the case to suit her desire for more screen time.'

'I wouldn't say pressured, but—'

'She pushed for it – went to Roundtree, to Steinburger – who would probably be happy now to detail an argument he umped between you – once both of you are dead and unable to say it never happened, or not that way. She claimed your work was inferior, that you were, after all, just a reporter. Not Hollywood, not someone who really understood how to translate the story onto the screen.'

'She never . . . not exactly. Besides she wasn't going to get it.'

'But she went at you the night of the party. Drunk, obnoxious, insulting. Maybe she gave you a little physical push. You responded. You didn't mean to kill her, but things got out of hand.'

'Hey!'

'Now you're riddled with guilt. Trying to cope with it by throwing yourself into another project. But it's eating at you. You know, even though we're friends, I'm sniffing it out, and I'll do my job. You can't face that. The scandal, the pressure, the threat of doing time. So, you take the easy way out and kill yourself.'

'I do not. You know damn well I'd never kill myself, and you'd vow to avenge my death, should it happen, while fighting tears over my beautiful, stylish corpse.'

'I wouldn't go that far. The point is, he doesn't know either of us well enough to know I'd never buy that you offed yourself. You could be, for him, a very convenient, beautiful, and stylish corpse.'

'I get your point. I still think there are more convenient corpses.'

'So do I, but since I don't want to have to spend my time avenging your death and fighting tears, why take chances? You go wired.'

'I'll get the interview, and I'll go wired – on the condition I get an exclusive one-on-one with you, and a full hour with you on *Now*.'

For form, Eve scowled. 'This isn't about media scoops and ratings, Nadine. It's about stopping a killer who's not only slipped the law for forty years, but profited from it.'

'If it wasn't about the media, you wouldn't be talking to me, or asking for my help. You need the media on this. You need me, and I'll play it your way. You just have to play the aftermath mine.'

'Maybe I should let him off you.'

'You like me too much. Plus there's that whole protect-and-serve thing.' She dug her notebook out of her bag, made a few quick notes. 'I'm also going to need your cooperation with the book I'll be writing on this, and for that I'll be putting my considerable resource skills into those other murders. And I'll share.'

She slid the book back in her bag, closed it. Gave Eve her cat smile.

'You know and I know it's going to take research, resources, and manpower to put together the evidence to build all those cases.'

Eve frowned down at the toe of her boots, as if reluctant. 'All right. Deal. But it has to be today. Right after the media conference.'

'Done. We were both going to agree to all this anyway, but it was a nice break in the park.' Nadine got to her feet. 'I'll be at the conference, and I'll let you know as soon as I've set up the interview with Steinburger.'

Eve watched her walk away on her impractical shoes, then got up to find Peabody and make sure she hadn't been eaten by squirrels.

*

Back at Central, she issued a request – through two uniforms she sent to the studio – for Valerie to come into Central, answer a few more questions.

'We'll go to her if she balks,' Eve told Peabody, 'but I'd rather do it here. Make it formal, a little disturbing – and before the media conference. We'll let her know we're making an announcement shortly.'

'And she'll spread that word at the studio.'

'I wouldn't want Steinburger to miss it. I want someone on him. We can't trail him at the studio, but when he leaves, someone's on him. We need to know if he approaches any of the others. He doesn't get a chance to add to his kill score.'

'Baxter and Trueheart?'

'Yeah, if they're not on something hot. Soft clothes. Fill them in. I'll alert Feeney and EDD about Nadine's wire, and update the commander.' She checked the time. 'And let's keep on top of the water cops and the divers.'

It didn't take long. She added a check-and-confirm with Kyung, began to skim the case file, delivered efficiently from California, then smiled at Peabody's text re Valerie. The publicist was in the house.

A few props never hurt, Eve decided, and gathered some files, tucked them under her arm. She walked out to the bullpen.

'Where did we put her?'

'Interview A,' Peabody told her.

'Let's do this. Brisk and formal,' she added as they headed toward Interview. 'Clarifying. We have this media thing shortly, want to make sure we have all the correct information. And when I go in on her, feel free to look somewhat distressed on her behalf.'

'It'll be good acting practice for my cameo. Preston just sent me a message. I have a line: "It's the police." I could say it like that – like a statement. Or maybe like I'm alarmed. "It's the police!" Or maybe sort of like a question. "It's the police?"'

'Yeah, that's a puzzler.'

'Well, I want to do a good job. Maybe with a little hesitation. "It's . . . the police!" My family's completely juiced about this. They're going to let McNab do it with me, like we're standing together, and I say it to him. We're going to be a couple.'

'Of what?'

Eve pushed open the interview room door.

'Ms. Xaviar.' Eve gave Valerie a nod as she called for record on, then read in the particulars. 'Thank you for coming in,' she began, then continued before Valerie could respond. 'You've already been read your rights on this matter. Do you require me to read them to you again?'

'No, but I'm not sure why you asked me to come.'

Eve sat, laid down her files. 'Unlike on-screen, actual murder investigations involve a lot of repetition and routine. I want to confirm a few points from your previous statements and make sure we have an accurate record of your version of events.'

'My version?'

'Five people see the same event. Every one of them is going to report it with variations. Nobody sees the same thing the same way, do they?'

'So you're asking everyone to come in again?'

Eve said nothing, only glanced down as she opened a file.

'Would you like something before we start, Valerie?' Peabody offered a smile in contrast to Eve's chilly formality.

'No. No. I'd like to get this done. We're very busy right now.'

'We're a little busy around here, too.' Eve's tone could have frozen a fiery pool in hell. 'What with investigating a couple of murders, and dealing with the media you and your associates are so fond of.'

'We're doing another media conference today.' Peabody oozed enthusiasm and naïveté. 'We get to announce we have new information and expect an early arrest.'

'Peabody.'

'Sorry, Lieutenant. But Valerie's in the media business, so she knows how it works. Dallas doesn't like to show our hand,' Peabody told Valerie, 'but the brass wants the buzz.'

'Of course. You're going to arrest someone? You know who killed K.T.?'

'We're—'

'Peabody!' This time Eve snapped it out. 'We're not here to discuss confidential and official details of the investigation, nor will those details be given to the media. Whatever buzz the brass wants.'

'I might be able to help. It is my field, and I'd—'

'We're covered.' Eve took a slim tablet out of the file, swiped it on. 'You stated you were seated here during the screen show in Roundtree's theater on the night of K.T. Harris's murder. Is this correct?'

'Ah . . .' Valerie leaned forward, studied the seating chart Eve had created. 'Yes. I think so. I was seated toward the back and to the right.'

'To the best of your recollection is the rest of this chart accurate?'

'I really didn't pay that much attention, but I do remember Marlo and Matthew moved over to this corner, where you have them, and Roundtree was in the front, near you and your husband. Joel was behind me as was Julian. So it looks correct there.'

'And in your statement given the night of the murder you said you didn't notice anyone leaving the theater during the show.'

'I didn't.'

'You were seated toward the back, and to the right. Now the area outside the doors had the lights on low, but there were lights on out there. And when the doors opened – as we know they did more than once during the screen show as it is fact that the victim, the killer, Nadine Furst, and Connie Burkette exited the theater – the light from the opening door would angle over your seat. Those doors opened several times, but you didn't notice?'

'I was, as I said before, doing a little work, which is why

I sat in that area. And I may have been a seat over. It's hard to remember exactly.'

'Which was it? Here?' Eve tapped the screen. 'Or here? Or maybe here?'

'I'm not sure.'

'Now you're not sure.' Eve sat back, eyes cool, nodded. 'Yet you seemed sure when you gave your initial statement.'

'I didn't know the exact seat would be so important.'

'You didn't know where you were seated, *if* you were seated, if you saw someone leave, if you left yourself, would be important to a murder investigation?'

'I never left that theater.' A trace of panic threaded through her voice. 'Julian or Joel would have seen me if I had. They were behind me.'

'You're sure of that?'

'Yes.'

'But not of where you were seated. You know where two other people and – from previous statements – where the vic sat, but you can't quite remember where you were.'

'I was here.' Agitated, Valerie slapped her finger on the tablet.

'Now you're sure?'

'Yes.'

'You were seated here, but never noticed the light from the opening door.'

'No, I didn't.'

'It's funny, because I ran a reconstruction and putting myself in this seat – the seat you're now sure you used – I sure as hell noticed the brief wash of light from the door.'

'Obviously you're more observant than I, or more sensitive to a change in light.'

'That must be it. It couldn't be that you're lying.'

Valerie tried for insulted, but that panic slipped through again. 'I don't have any reason to lie.'

'You have your career. I bet it's important to you. Moving on, you've also stated that you were at Joel Steinburger's New York residence at the time of A. A. Asner's murder. Are you sure about that?'

'Of course.'

'Just checking. Neither you nor Mr Steinburger left the residence at any time that evening, that night, and through to the morning?'

'No.'

'You're sure because you spent every minute of that time together.'

'We worked late, until after midnight – nearly one A.M., trying to get ahead of the story, anticipate the angles. I stayed in the guest quarters as it was so late when we finished, and we agreed to put in some time in the morning.'

'How much do you get paid for that kind of overtime?'

'Excuse me?'

'I wonder what you get for putting in all that time.'

'My job requires flexibility and often entails long and odd hours. I don't see how that's relevant.'

'Cops are nosy. I'm nosy, so I wonder if the time you put in explains the fifty thousand Mr Steinburger transferred to your account yesterday morning.'

Agitation switched to shock – covered fairly well, Eve thought, with sputtering outrage. 'You looked into my personal finances? What right do you have to—'

'Every. This is murder. What did you do for fifty large, Valerie?'

'My job! Joel values exceptional work, which I provide. Handling the fallout from K.T.'s death has involved a lot of extra time, extra hours, and some innovation. He gave me a bonus.'

'But you said your job requires flexibility and often entails long hours.'

'It does.'

'And how often are you given a fifty-thousand-dollar bonus for doing your job? Because unless it was in cash, and went unreported, which would mean you didn't pay taxes on it, I didn't see anything comparable in the last two years.'

'I can only speculate Joel felt these circumstances, and my handling of them, warranted the bonus.' She looked away, and her throat worked. 'You'd have to ask him.'

'Yeah, I'll do that. Are you sleeping with him again, Valerie?'

'I am not! I don't have to sleep with an employer to advance my career.'

'But you had sex with him before.'

'It had nothing to do with career advancement. It was just a momentary weakness on both our parts. We started and ended it before we came to the New York studios.'

'Good for you. Speaking of advances, I just got this wild hair and checked with the hotel. You've moved up to a VIP suite. That's a major upgrade from a standard room.'

'I needed the extra space, and the upgrade for the work.'

'And the – what do they call it – maître d'étage service, the personal gym and private elevator.'

'I needed a larger work space,' Valerie said stubbornly now. 'The studio approved it.'

'You know what fancy digs and a fistful of cash says to me, Peabody?'

'Well . . .'

'It says bribe. Cops are suspicious and cynical as well as nosy.'

'I haven't done anything but my job. I came in here voluntarily, but I don't have to stay and be insulted.'

'I wonder what it's like running media interference for people who make, what? Easily ten times what you do, more for some of them. For people who get all the perks as a matter of course, get all the attention, while you labor away behind the scenes, scrambling to show them all off in the best light. Then have to spin or cover up their fuckups, their stupidity, their indulgences. Their sins, their crimes.'

'I do what I do, and I'm good at it. I work for one of the most successful and prestigious studios in the industry. I have a staff of six who report to *me*, and I report directly to one of the icons of our business.'

'Did the icon ask you to lie for him, Valerie? Or for someone else?'

'I've given you my statement. I don't have anything else to say.'

'That's a "no comment"? You're free to go, but I think we're going to talk again. Really soon. Right now I have a media conference to prep for. Any advice?'

'Sarcastic bitchiness doesn't go over well on camera.'

Eve smiled to herself as Valerie swept out of the room. 'Interview end. I'm a sarcastic bitch.'

'No comment,' Peabody replied.

'And she's a scared liar who doesn't know whether to shit or spin. She'll be dumping this on Steinburger asap. In fact, I'll wager EDD's going to get an earful before she gets all the way out of the building.'

'We may have put her head on the block, Dallas.'

'If he kills her, the upgrade and money only look more suspicious. We'd push at him for accessory, push the compensation as a bribe or payoff. He's smarter to keep her alive, back up her version of the bonus and the need for bigger digs. But we'll keep an eye on her.'

'How?'

Eve pulled out her 'link. 'Dallas,' she said when Connie answered. 'I need you to do something.'

'What do you need?'

'Contact Valerie, and tell her to meet you. I don't care where, but I need you to keep her busy and with you or your husband for the rest of the day.'

'All right. Can I ask why?'

'You can ask, but I'm not going to tell you.'

'That's annoying, but I could actually use some help this afternoon. The studio heads decree I should speak at K.T.'s memorial – and Mason should give the main eulogy. Between that and – well, I could use the help. When do you want me to send for her?'

'Now.'

'Now?'

'Now. And don't tell anyone we spoke about this. I'll be in touch later.'

'But—'

Eve clicked off, the better to avoid questions. 'Valerie can't say no to Connie – the vid star, the director's wife. The memorial's a lucky addition.'

'You trust her? Connie?'

'Trust is a strong word,' Eve considered, 'but since she didn't kill either of our vics, it'll do for the moment.' She checked the time again. 'Let's go drop our bombshell on the unsuspecting public.'

She pulled out her communicator when it signaled. 'Dallas.'

'Steinburger just took a tag from Xaviar,' Feeney told her. 'She sounded a little out of sorts.'

'Is that so?'

'And she had uncomplimentary observations about you.'

'My feelings are hurt.'

'I'll send a copy of the transmission to your files.'

'Thanks. For now, just give me the gist.'

'About you being really rude and offensive? Or the part about you being a bully with bad hair?'

'How about the part where she tells Steinburger I'm looking at her new job benefits.'

'Oh, that part. You had some nerve looking at her personal financial data, and questioning her hotel accommodations, trying to scare her. My take? You didn't try, you succeeded. Steinburger grilled her on it. Wanted chapter and verse, which I'll skip over since you were there. He told her she didn't have a thing to worry about. Stroked and petted, said how she did just right, and the studio – and he personally – was grateful for her discretion and loyalty. He grilled her again when she told him you were making a new statement to the media on further info and an upcoming arrest. Then he told her to hold on, he had an incoming. He didn't.'

'Needed some time to pull it together.'

'That's my take. Left her holding for seventy-three seconds. Had himself cool and collected when he came back on. Told her not to worry. Both of them were only doing what was best for the project and the studio, and when everything settled down again, he'd show her his appreciation.'

'She buy that?'

'She thanked him, then said she was going back to the hotel to work. That she'd watch the media conference from there, and work out an official studio response.'

'She's going to be busy for the next several hours, and out of his reach. Let me know what else you get. We're going into the media deal in a few minutes.'

'Better you than me,' Feeney said and broke transmission.

Eve glanced over, saw that Peabody had stopped, and stood

with her own communicator. A wide grin spread over her face as she put it away.

'Divers are bringing up some electronics from the coordinates we gave them. They'll run the serial numbers when they get them in. But one of them reports he got lucky and found a 'link – a red 'link engraved with the initials K.T.H.'

'We got his ass, Peabody. Contact Reo, fill her in. Tell her she's got her goddamn sliver and to get us the search warrants.'

21

She played the media by the book. It wasn't hard to look mildly disgruntled or show flashes of impatience. She felt more than mildly disgruntled giving the same answer – *We can't give specific details on the investigation at this time* – over and over again. She wanted to talk to the water cops, to Reo, to get her warrants and completely ruin Steinburger's day.

Along with the rest of his miserable life.

She could only hope her statement at least gave him indigestion.

'I'll say again, while I can't comment on specific details, the investigation is moving forward. And with new information that has come to our attention, we believe we're close to making an arrest. But close isn't good enough, so as I've said all I'm free to say, my partner and I are going back to work.'

She stepped away from the podium, glanced briefly in Nadine's direction.

While a number of other reporters continued to shout out questions – hope sprang, Eve supposed – Nadine rose, gave Eve the most subtle of nods.

Even as she walked to the door, Nadine pulled out her pocket 'link.

'She's putting the arm on Steinburger now,' Eve told Peabody. 'We'll want to confirm where she meets him for the interview. When the warrants come through we'll start wherever he's not. No point in tipping him to the search until we have to.'

'He could tell Nadine no interview, or put her off.'

'She won't take no. She won't be put off. She's like a ferret. And he won't have Valerie for cover,' Eve added. 'He'd look weak and stupid if he tried to haul her in away from Connie. He can't look weak or stupid.'

'I think he's both. But there's somebody who isn't. Ever.'

Eve watched Roarke approach. 'He can be stupid. Keep on the water cops, Peabody. Maybe another sliver will move Reo's ass on the goddamn warrant.'

'Lieutenant, Detective. You both looked somber, official, and attractive for the media. Nice boots, Peabody.'

'Don't encourage her. I knew pink was a mistake.'

'On the contrary. They look charming.'

Unable to stop herself, Peabody did a little runway turn. 'I love them.'

'Use your pink boots to walk, Peabody. Water cops.'

'Love them,' Peabody said again with a quick grin for Roarke before she used the boots.

'Charming,' Eve muttered. 'Charm isn't cop, and she's threatened to wear them every day. She *has* worn them every day this week.'

'It's nice to know a gift's appreciated. I made some time as I feel a personal interest in this investigation.'

'That old excuse.'

He smiled at her. 'I thought Feeney might have something interesting for me to do.'

'He's tapped into Steinburger's comms, and we're going to be monitoring Nadine when she boxes Steinburger into an interview. But better, we've got Pearlman's electronics. I'm hoping EDD can track back, using the buried account you found, link the embezzlement to Steinburger.'

'See? Enough fun for all. I'd like finishing out the financials. And you?'

'Waiting for Reo to get me search warrants. Then I'm going to turn the bastard's residence, vehicle, and office inside out until I find something to put his murdering ass away for several lifetimes.'

'Even more fun. I'd enjoy poking and peering into someone's private belongings.'

'You've got plenty of experience.' She considered. 'You could be useful.'

'My mission in life.'

'It would spare Feeney an e-man if I had my own geek along to deal with Steinburger's electronics. That's your favorite poke and peek area anyway.'

'You know me so well.'

'Once done, you could dig into the Pearlman angle.'

'He's bound to have data on the B.B. Joel account on his comp. A man must monitor his money, after all.'

'I guess he must.'

She caught him up on the morning's work as she led him to the conference room instead of her office. Then just stood with him, studying the board.

'That's both efficient and disturbing.'

'It needs updating. We found the boat he used.'

As she added to the board, she brought Roarke up to date.

'And still not enough for an arrest,' Roarke commented.

'I can't prove he used the boat. I can only show he had the means, knew the codes. I can't prove he bribed Valerie. I can only show the money.'

'And it shows pattern. It begins to add up.'

'Piece by piece.' Eve tucked her thumbs into her pockets. 'And Valerie? I can break her. A couple more shots and she'll crack. Right now she's protecting herself, thinking it through. What's best for Valerie. I get a little more on him, push it in her face, bring up accessory to murder, she'll roll on him like an LC on a john.'

'Do you think he plans to eliminate her?'

'Oh yeah. But not now. Too many questions for him if he gets rid of her now. Down the road she'll have a terrible accident, or OD. Whatever suits best. He can't try to implicate her as she'd turn on him like a rabid dog. So I figure she's safe enough, but Connie's a good buffer in the event he panics.'

'Who will he implicate? Or allude to?'

'I'm wondering about that. Connie works. The scene at dinner, the private talk after. And she admitted to leaving the theater, so that gives her opportunity. He doesn't know about the dome, and the fact is that's not going to stand very steady in court without a whole lot more. But it's a detail. And he'd figure we could leapfrog to Connie killing Asner because Harris hired him, and he had something on her or on Roundtree. She knows the boat owner.

'She'd do,' Eve concluded. 'The same in general fits for Andrea, and we know there was the issue with the godson. He'd know that, too. Marlo and Matthew, very unlikely as he'd have to implicate both of them. That gets tricky and sticky. But Julian would work.'

'I wondered if you'd get to him.'

'Drunk, embarrassed, the issue of the underaged banging. Finds out Asner has the goods, too. Pissed. Kills Harris, cleans up with Asner. The thing is the guy doesn't have killing in him, not the Asner kind anyway. Not the planned-out, follow-through, beat-the-living-shit-out-of-somebody kind. And he's just not smart enough to have pulled off two murders in two days.'

'I feel mildly insulted.'

'He'd have screwed up, and he'd bury himself in guilt and fear.' Amused, she gave Roarke a sidelong look. 'He ain't you, Ace.'

'And still, mildly insulted.' Roarke laid a hand on her shoulder, rubbed. 'You need all of them. You need to take him down for all of them. You could bring him in on what you have now, and sweat him. You could break Valerie, add to that sweat. You'd have a good chance of closing it down on Harris and Asner.'

'Pretty good.' And she'd thought of it, weighed it in. 'Yeah, pretty good. Not a sure thing, and not anything but circumstantial, coincidence, speculation at this point on seven others. Even the recant by Holmes doesn't equal proof, just adds suspicion. More if we can dig back thirty years and prove he didn't go to Mexico that night.'

'We can manage that,' Roarke promised her. 'But that doesn't equal proof he killed Caulfield either.'

'It would add more weight. Enough weight, joints and muscles start giving way. Maybe I won't get them all. Odds are slim.'

'You have to try.'

'I can't turn away from those faces.' The young, the old, the famous, the ordinary. 'It may be that all I'll be able to do is let him know I know. Let him know I'll keep digging until I bury him. But before I settle for that, I'm going to try for a grand fucking slam.'

She snatched out her 'link. 'Dallas.'

'Warrants coming through,' Reo told her. 'And believe me, even with your slivers it was a job. How the hell was I supposed to know the judge I tapped is a major vid buff, with great admiration for Joel Steinburger? Jesus.'

'Maybe he'll make more vids from his cage. I'll get back to you when we find something.'

She clicked off, smiled fiercely at Roarke. 'Batter up.'

Nadine settled into the club chair in Steinburger's office, flashed her best camera-ready smile at him and crossed her legs. The man, she thought, wasn't thrilled with the situation, but he covered it well. He sat across from her, a small table with pretty flowers between them, and one of his Oscars on display in the background.

He sat back, hands on the wide arms of the chair, the picture of a man in charge under difficult circumstances.

'I appreciate this, Joel. I know how busy you are, especially now. But because of especially now, it's important – I'm sure you agree – to talk about what's going on, how you feel, how you're handling it. As head of the studio, everyone looks to you.'

He lifted a hand off the arm of the chair in a what-can-you-do gesture. 'We can't put up walls between ourselves and the public.'

'Exactly. Are you ready?'

'Anytime.'

'Good.' She glanced at her camera, gave him the nod.

'And we're rolling.'

'This is Nadine Furst. I'm with acclaimed producer Joel Steinburger in his office at Big Bang Studios, New York. Joel, thank you so much for agreeing to talk to me today.'

'It's always a pleasure, Nadine, even under these circumstances.'

'I know the murder of K.T. Harris has shaken to the core the industry, and the cast and crew of what will tragically be her last vid. Joel, you're well-known for your hands-on, involved approach to projects like *The Icove Agenda*, and I know you and K.T. worked closely together on her role. How are you holding up?'

'It's a raw wound, Nadine. A raw wound. To know that this talented actress, this fascinating, layered woman, this friend is gone, cut off from us in such a needless and tragic way. It's incomprehensible.'

He leaned forward then, eyes slightly damp but intense, and she wondered why he'd never tried his hand on the other side of the cameras.

'K.T. was so invested in this role, the reality of it, the complexities of the character. She worked tirelessly to perfect her performance, to bring out the very best in the rest of the cast. I can't begin to measure how much she'll be missed.'

'And the production continues.'

'Of course. K.T. would have accepted no less. She was a consummate professional.'

'With a reputation for being difficult.'

He smiled now, with a hint of sorrow. 'So many of the greatest stars earn that label because, in my opinion, they settle for no less than perfection. Yes, it can make for some fireworks on the set, but that light, that energy is what *makes* brilliance.'

'Would you share one of your memories of her with us?'

She let him go on, honestly believing he was making up the amusing anecdote as he went. But it served her purpose, relaxing him, lulling him. She'd soft-balled him, let him find that easy rhythm.

'Your insight into her,' Nadine continued when he wound down, 'as an actor, as a woman, is a tribute.'

'It's important, from my perspective, to understand all sides of the people I work with. We become, for a time, a family – and that means intimacy, conflict, jokes, frustrations. I think of myself as the father figure – one who sets the tone, guides the wheel. I have to anticipate and understand the needs of my family in order to draw out the best in them.

'We've lost one of our family now, suddenly and shockingly. We all feel it keenly.'

'You've dealt with loss before. As that father figure, it must help you, and the others. The fact that you endured, survived, and coped. The tragic death of Sherri Wendall. You and she had been a Hollywood power couple during your marriage, and both dealt with the media microscope during your tumultuous divorce. You were no longer together when she died, but the loss must have been devastating nonetheless.'

'Sherri was one of the most intriguing women I've ever known – and loved. And talent, again?' He shook his head. 'Who knows what she would have accomplished had she lived.'

'You were in Cannes – both of you – when she drowned. Had you and she made peace before her death?'

He shifted, just an instant's discomfort. 'Oh, I think we had. Great love often equals great conflict. We had both.'

'The accident, again, senseless, tragic. A slip, a fall, and a drowning death. It, in some ways, mirrors K.T.'s death. That must resonate with you.'

'I ... One an accident, the other murder. But yes, both brilliant stars, gone too soon.'

'Another brilliant star you lost – we all lost, but a personal

407

loss for you again. Angelica Caulfield. You were close, friends and colleagues. Some claim more than friends.'

Nadine saw the way his fingers tightened on the arms of the chair, the sudden, rigid set of his jaw. The camera would see it, too.

'Angelica was a dear friend. A troubled woman. Too fragile, I fear, to hold all the talent, to survive the needs of that talent, and the appetite of the public.'

'There remains endless speculation as to whether her death was suicide or accident, and of course over the paternity of the child she carried at the time of her death. You were close, as you said. Were you aware of her state of mind? Had she confided in you about the pregnancy?'

'No.' He said it sharply, too sharply, then regrouped. 'I was, I fear, too involved in my own life. My wife was expecting our first child. I've always wondered if I'd been more . . . in tune, less wrapped up in my own world, might I have seen or felt something . . . I wish she'd felt able to confide in me, had turned to me as a friend. If she'd contacted me . . . '

'But she did come to see you, according to the reports at the time, just a few days before her death. At the studio.'

'Yes. Yes, she did. In hindsight . . . I have to ask myself, and have, did she seem troubled? Should I have noticed her rising despair? I only know I didn't. She hid it well. She was an actress to the end.'

'Then you believe it was suicide.'

'As I said, she was a fragile, troubled woman.'

'I only ask because, again, according to reports and

statements you've made in the past, you were adamant about her death being the result of an accidental overdose.'

He was sweating now, lightly but visibly.

'I have to say that with time, with healing, comes more clarity. Still, I can only say, with certainty, her death was a terrible loss. Now, Nadine—'

'If I could just circle this back. Three women – talented women, celebrated women – all part of your life in some way. An accident, an apparent suicide, and a murder. Yet another suicide with your partner and longtime friend Buster Pearlman.'

He tensed at that, visibly, and Nadine kept her eyes trained on his.

'You've had more than your share, Joel, of tragedy and personal loss. Even going back to the accidental death of a friend and college housemate, and of course the tragic accident that took the life of your mentor, the great Marlin Dressler. Does it weigh on you?'

His silence held a beat, then two. 'Life is to be lived. I consider myself fortunate to have known them, fortunate to be in a position, to have work I love that allows me to know so many talented people. I suppose when a man has worked over half his life in an industry peopled with so much talent – along with the egos, the fragilities, the pressures – loss is inevitable.'

'Loss, yes. But murder? Let's hope murder isn't an inevitability.'

'I certainly didn't mean to imply it was, but it is, unfortunately, a reality in our society – in our world.'

'And fodder for our entertainment, as K.T.'s role as then Officer Peabody in the screen adaptation of the infamous Icove case is what brought her, and you, to New York at this time. Lieutenant Eve Dallas, along with Peabody and the resources of the NYPSD, broke that case. Dallas is also heading the investigation into K.T.'s murder. Today she announced they've uncovered new information. She claims she believes they're close to making an arrest. What do you think about that?'

'I hope it's not theater.'

'Theater?'

'I understand the pressure, from her superiors and the media, has been intense. I hope the investigators are, indeed, close to learning who killed K.T. It will never make up for the loss, but it may give us all a sense of closure.'

'And relief?' Nadine said with a hint of a smile. 'As one of the select group in attendance at the Roundtree/Burkette home that night, you're a suspect.'

'As are you,' he shot back.

'Not guilty,' Nadine said, raising her right hand. 'I know I'll be relieved when Lieutenant Dallas makes an arrest. It's disconcerting, don't you find, Joel, to be under suspicion – and to have friends and colleagues on that same list?'

'I can't and won't believe any of us killed K.T. – our sister, our daughter, our friend. I suspect this "*new information*" deals with an outsider.'

'An outsider?'

'Someone who gained entry by posing as catering staff, or valet, or what have you. A disturbed fan, perhaps. So, yes, I'll

410

be relieved when this is cleared up, the questions answered, and our lives returned to normal. I understand Lieutenant Dallas is doing her job, but to focus on us? Absurd. After all, we were all gathered together in one place at the time K.T. was killed. You were there yourself. I have to believe some-one else followed K.T. up to the roof, and tragedy followed that. If – off the record.'

Nadine eased back, nodded to her camera. But said nothing as she knew the wire she wore would keep things very much on the record.

'I'm not going to cast suspicion or aspersions on my friends and colleagues on-screen.'

'I understand.'

'It's bad for business,' he said flatly. 'I'm sticking to it being an outsider – on the record. But I'm worried, I'm very worried something happened that night between K.T. and ... one of us.'

'You suspect someone.' Nadine widened her eyes. 'Joel!'

'I'm not going to discuss that, even off the record. It's probably just the nerves of dealing with all this. The fact is, if she hadn't gone up to indulge in the filthy habit of smoking, she might still be alive.'

'They do say even the herbals are bad for our health.'

'Worse yet when it's one after the other mixed in with sense-dulling illegals like zoner.' He waved a hand in front of his face. 'The combination reeks. I'm sorry. I'm upset – tired. I don't want to speak ill of the dead and you don't want that either. It's bad for business as well.'

411

'Joel, I was there, too.' To enhance that connection, she leaned forward to lay a hand over his. Solidarity.

'I'm part of this. If you have reason to believe . . . If you think you know who killed her, tell me. I won't go public.'

'I don't feel right about it. Give me a day or two.' He turned his hand over, gave hers a pat and squeeze. 'I need to think it through. I'm probably making too much of things. Now, Nadine, I really need you to wrap this up. It's been a very long day.'

'Of course.' She settled back, signaled the camera again. She lobbed a couple of easy ones, to reset the tone, put him at ease.

And decided straight interview or undercover, it was going to play very well.

'Again, thank you so much for doing this. I know it's a terrible time for everyone.'

'Life – and work – go on. I'll walk you out.'

'You don't need to bother.'

'I'm heading out myself. As I said, long day.'

When he opened the door, Julian stopped pacing outside, hurried to him.

'Joel. Sorry, Nadine, I need to talk to Joel.'

'No problem. Julian.' Struck, she lifted a hand to his cheek. 'You look so tired.'

'Everything feels off. I can't work like this. I can't handle all this. Joel—'

'Come on into my office. We'll sit down, talk this out.

Good night, Nadine.' As he turned, he sent her a long, sorrowful look over his shoulder.

'What the hell was that?' she muttered when Joel closed the office door. 'What the hell?'

Inside, Julian began to pace again.

'Sit down, for Christ's sake, Julian. You're wearing me out.'

'I can't sit. I can't work. I can't *think* or sleep. I'm one tangled nerve, Joel. Did you see Dallas, hear what she said? She's going to make an arrest. What am I going to do? I should go talk to her, go talk to her and explain—'

'You'll do no such thing. Pull yourself together! I told you I'd take care of things, didn't I? It was an accident, and there's no reason for you to pay any price for an accident. Will it bring her back?'

'No, but—'

'Do you want to risk going to prison, Julian?'

'No, God, no, but—'

'And ending your career, giving up everything you have, can have? For what?'

'I don't *know*!' Julian pushed at his hair, clamped his hands on his temples as he paced and prowled. 'It's all so confusing. It keeps playing back in my head, but it doesn't make sense.'

'You were drunk, Julian. You can't be expected to remember clearly. Drunk, then in shock. My boy,' Steinburger said with such sympathy that Julian stopped, let out a long breath. 'Listen now. It's not your fault. You said you'd do as I said. You said you'd trust me.'

'I do. I do trust you. I don't know what I'd do without your help, your support.'

'Then do what I tell you. Go back to your hotel. Pour yourself a glass or two of that very nice wine we had a bit of last night.'

'You said not to drink anymore.'

'That was last night.' Joel gave Julian a bracing pat on the back. 'You're not on the call sheet tomorrow. Indulge yourself. A nice glass of wine, while relaxing in your whirlpool. I know this has been a terrible strain on you. Put all this out of your mind for a while.'

'It's all so mixed up, Joel.'

'I know. Follow my advice. Wine and whirlpool.'

'Wine and whirlpool,' Julian sighed, then repeated it with a nod when Steinburger stared at him. 'Yes, I will. Wine and whirlpool.'

'You'll see. It's exactly the right solution. Tomorrow, everything will be fine. Just fine again.'

'It doesn't feel like it ever can be.' Grief, guilt, sorrow swam in Julian's eyes. 'Joel, I've never hurt anyone before. I've never—'

'She hurt herself,' Steinburger said flatly. 'You remember that. Tell you what. I'll give you a lift. My driver's ready for me. I'll drop you at your hotel.'

'Okay. Maybe you could come up for a while. I hate being alone.'

'Best thing for you – we agreed, didn't we? You follow Doctor Joel's prescription tonight. Tomorrow, we'll have

414

dinner, and we'll talk it all through. If you're not feeling your-self again, we'll talk about alternatives.'

'All right. Yes. Alternatives. Thanks, Joel.'

'What are friends for?'

Eve stood in the master bedroom of Steinburger's apartment. She listened to Feeney's roundup of Nadine's interview while Roarke searched the dressing area.

Together with the search team, they'd already picked their way over the living area, the dining area, office, kitchen, even the terrace.

She had higher hopes for the second floor, but so far they'd scored a fat zero.

'Okay. Keep me in it,' she told him, then stuck her com-municator back in her pocket.

'He told Nadine he was heading home – tired, long day – but he tagged a friend – some other producer, talked him into drinks and dinner out.'

'So we've more time before he gets here and expresses his outrage.'

'Yeah. Could be he wanted company. Could be he wanted an alibi. Nadine did a number on him, according to Feeney. Tied the dead ex-wife, the pregnant lover into it – even the business partner, college pal, and first wife's great-grandfather. Made him sweat.'

Roarke glanced over as she came in. 'Which you'll enjoy watching, but that's not what's got that glint in your eye.'

'He asked her to go off-record. All keyed up. She's smart,

she had her camera turned off, but didn't voice an agreement. Lawyers might quibble about the wire, but we had a warrant for it. Anyway, he tried to play her, how he might know something, how he's worried he knows something, but can't say. Won't cast stones at his friends, and so on.'

'You think he's picked his patsy.'

'I think he's got to move on it pretty soon, yeah. I shook him with the imminent arrest, then Nadine piles it on. But better yet, he slipped. Trying to cover for this alleged friend, he said Harris would still be alive if she hadn't gone up to the roof to smoke.'

Roarke paused, lifted a shoulder. 'That's true enough and a matter of record.'

'But the zoner isn't a matter of record. And he brought it in. How the combination of herbal and zoner reeks – his term.'

'Foolish to let his abhorrence of the habit slip him up. Still, not to put a damper on that glint, if it was common knowledge she mixed in illegals, it's not particularly damning.'

'It keeps adding up. One after another, he said, too. If he wasn't up there, how does he know she went through multiple, laced herbals inside the dome? She tripped him up some on the pregnant lover, too. Little trips. They add up to a fall.'

She turned, walked back to the bedroom. 'He's organized – in how he thinks, how he lives, how he works. How he kills. Not obsessively so, but careful. Still, there are little things. Too many sex enhancements and toys.'

'Can there be too many?'

'From his supply, he's never met one he didn't like. Sex is power. He's got his awards and kudos in every single room. He has to see them wherever he goes in here. He's got files of what appears to be every article, blurb, mention, photo with his name or face in it throughout his career. We've got his B.B. Joel account on his comps here, just as you predicted.'

'Which should help making the embezzlement connection, when I get my fingers into it again. Until then, it's simply a secondary account – taxes meticulously paid.'

Damned if he wasn't dulling her glint. But she pushed on. 'And there's the file you found, with background checks, deep bio on everyone involved in this project – right down to the last gofer – that's power-tripping again.'

'But not illegal.'

'No, not illegal.'

'But this might be.'

'What have you got?' She pounced, nearly bowled him over as he turned.

'Easy, darling. False bottom in this cabinet, and beneath that a small safe drawer. Which I've handily opened. And in that—'

'Codes. Pass codes, swipe cards, keys – all nicely labeled. Here's the code for the marina gate, for the boat security. Oh, baby. Codes for Roundtree's home, studio office, his vehicle.'

'You may have found your patsy.'

'Can't use Roundtree but his wife's a strong possible. Still,

417

there's a lot of other people in here. That's the pal he called tonight.' She gestured. 'That's his home's pass code, swipe card for the guy's country club locker. Codes for all the trailers, as far as I can tell, being used on this production.'

'Nosy bastard, isn't he?'

'He has to control it all. Won't be shut out. Has to have access and the power it gives him. Plus, useful for setting someone up to take a fall.'

'It appears Steinburger has some explaining to do.'

'Big-time. This proves he had access to the boat. And see this here?'

'Not labeled.'

'3APIS2C. Triple A – A. A. Asner, Private Investigation, Suite 2-C. I'm betting that's the code for Asner's vehicle. Maybe he tossed it in here just in case, or wanted it to remind himself of what he pulled off. But that's more explaining to do.'

She went back to the bedroom for an evidence bag. 'I dump these on him, add in the zoner, the list of murders, the boat. I'll break him down.'

She sealed the evidence, labeled it. 'I'm going to let the team handle the vehicle. We'll go swing by the studio office. Then we'll pay a visit to Ce Soir.'

He thought she looked like a warrior, coolly prepared for battle. 'I can get us a good table. I happen to know the owner.'

'You happen to be the owner, but we're not eating. We're going to interrupt Steinburger's meal and ruin his fucking night.'

'Sounds promising.'

'We can get something from Vending while he sweats in Interview.'

'Sounds disgusting.'

'It's not that bad. Hold on.' She pulled out her 'link. 'Dallas.'

'Listen, Dallas—'

'Nadine, even though we established you're not my type, I may do you after all. You killed that interview.'

'I'm aquiver. You've seen it already?'

'No, but Feeney summed it up. I could get him to do you, too.'

'Aw, you're too good to me. What about Roarke?'

'No.'

'But not good enough. Listen, Dallas, I was nearly to the station, but I hopped out of the van, grabbed a cab. I'm heading back downtown, to the hotel – Julian's hotel. I've got this nagging feeling.'

'About what?'

'Did Feeney tell you how Steinburger hinted around – off the record – about being afraid something happened between one of them and K.T., how he was worried?'

'Yeah, yeah. You think he meant Julian?'

'Julian was waiting outside the office. He looked terrible, which isn't easy when you're that gorgeous. Tired, upset, strung out. Scared – once I started thinking, I think scared. And Joel took him into his office – but as he did, Joel sent me this look. And, it's nagging me. I think he was setting it up,

Dallas. Giving me a look that said this is who I'm worried about, trying to protect. And if I'm right—'

'Then he's planning for Julian to have an accident or off himself due to guilt. We'll check it out.'

'Where are you?'

'Steinburger's place, and we found a few interesting items.'

'It'll take you longer to get there than me. But will you come? Even if I'm wrong, I think Julian knows something, and I think he's vulnerable enough to spill it.'

'Leaving now. Do me a favor, get hotel security to go up with you. Make something up, but don't go up there alone.'

'Julian wouldn't hurt me – or anyone. But all right.'

'I trust her instincts,' Roarke said when Eve frowned at the blank screen.

'So do I. We'll skip the office for now, go straight to Julian's hotel room. I'll let Peabody know the status.'

As she contacted her partner, Eve wondered just how the hell Steinburger could kill – or induce a man to suicide – while he himself enjoyed a fancy dinner with a friend on the other side of town.

22

In the back of the cab, Nadine tried Julian's 'link again. Stupid, she told herself, as she knew it would go straight to message – as it had the other three times she'd tried it. And he'd set the room 'links on DO NOT DISTURB.

Why hadn't she followed up sooner? she asked herself. Why hadn't she listened to that niggling concern and gone straight back to Steinburger's office, or at least grabbed a cab blocks earlier and headed to the hotel?

Because she'd wanted to get into the studio, review and edit the interview. To lick her chops. Do her victory boogie.

'Goddamn it, goddamn it,' she muttered as guilt drove the niggling toward full-blown fear.

The way they were snagged in traffic, Steinburger could kill Julian, have a drink, plan the memorial, and write the fricking eulogy before she got there.

Stupid, she thought again. It was probably nothing. Just nerves, which had shifted from the good, on-your-mark type for the interview to sweaty-palms stress during this excuse for a cab ride.

'Can't you get through this?' she demanded.

The cab driver continued to dance his fingers over the

wheel in time with the hideous music blasting through the speakers.

'Sure, lady. Just let me activate the transport beam and we'll shoot through the wormhole and pop out clear.'

'Goddamn it,' she repeated, swiped her card for payment. 'I'll walk from here.'

She bolted out of the cab, squeezed through bumpers and scrambled to the sidewalk where the pedestrian traffic surged like a sea.

She dodged, weaved, cursed the gorgeous heels that made running a death wish, and which she was no doubt trashing. She cursed New York traffic, cursed tourists who didn't know *how to get out of the damn way!*, cursed what she tried to convince herself was her overblown imagination.

But she kept running.

Inside his hotel room Julian ignored the 'link he'd tossed on the table. He didn't have the energy to get up, power it down. He didn't think he had the energy for that whirlpool either, not when it felt so good to just sit there, sprawled in the chair, drinking some wine, letting everything go. Just go.

Joel had been right, of course. You could count on Joel.

He counted on Joel, now more than ever. Somebody smart, steady, good in a crisis. Somebody who could tell him what to do.

It didn't seem so horrible – not after two glasses of wine, and with another going down so smooth.

Still, maybe he should talk to Eve. Just explain everything –

well, not everything because everything was so mixed up he couldn't actually explain it to himself.

But just talk to her, tell her what happened, what he remembered, anyway.

She'd understand. He knew she would. He knew her.

She was fair, and brave, and just – and sexy.

Joel was wrong about her, Julian thought as he sipped, as his not-quite-Roarke blue eyes drooped. She wouldn't do whatever it took to put him in prison. It wasn't just about the arrest, about the – what was it? The collar. No, not for his Eve, he thought as his mind and vision blurred.

It was about justice.

But Joel was smart. If he was right . . .

He couldn't think about it now. His brain was so tired. And he needed to start the whirlpool. Hadn't he promised? Had he?

Funny, he couldn't remember exactly.

Too much to drink. He needed to stop drinking so much. But he was so upset, so unhappy, and a little bit scared.

No more wine, he ordered himself. A nice, hot, relaxing tub, and some music. Then maybe he'd tag Andi, or Marlo, or Connie. He didn't like being alone. He wanted a woman to talk to.

Women always listened.

He tried to get up, intending to put the wine aside, go start the tub. Drunk, he thought, disgusted with himself.

Determined, he shoved to his feet, managed one staggering step.

The glass flew out of his hand, shattering against the table as he went down.

Winded, reasonably sure her feet were bleeding, Nadine made a beeline for the front desk.

'Nadine Furst. I need your head of security.'

The woman on the desk smiled pleasantly. 'Good evening, Ms Furst, and welcome back. May I ask what you require security for?'

'Listen, you know I'm on the cleared list for ... Mr Birmingham's suite.' She used the alias Julian used to protect his privacy.

'Yes, Ms Furst, you're on Mr Birmingham's approved visitors list.'

'I need security to go up to his suite with me.'

'Is there a problem?'

'There will be if you don't get security, now.'

'Just one moment, Ms Furst. I'll get the manager.'

'I don't want the manager. Hell with it. You send security up, or you, Marree,' she said, reading the name tag, 'and this hotel are going to be the subject of a scathing exposé on *Now*.'

She turned, loped toward the elevators.

He was probably there, cozied up with his *femme du jour*, she thought as she jumped on the elevator. And she was about to make a fool of herself. He'd be amused, she decided, and very likely invite her to join the party – and he wouldn't really be kidding.

They'd have a quick laugh over it. Please. She closed her eyes, struggling to find her usual cool. Please, let him be with a woman, let them have a quick laugh, let his horrible sense of dread and panic be the product of working too long on the crime beat, seeing potential murders everywhere.

She bolted out of the elevator, raced on feet now thankfully numb to the end of the corridor. Ignoring the DO NOT DISTURB light, she punched the buzzer, added several hard knocks.

'Julian! Open the door. It's important. It's Nadine.'

He couldn't hear her, of course, unless he engaged the intercom, but she continued to call out as she buzzed and banged.

And with every second the panic and dread swelled.

'Ms. Furst!' The manager strode down the hall with a big, dark-suited man at her side. 'Please. You're disturbing our guests.'

'They'll be a lot more disturbed if you don't open this door.'

'Ms. Furst, Mr Birmingham has requested not to be disturbed. If you'd like to leave him a message, I'll—'

'Open the damn door.'

'I'm going to have to have you removed. If you and Mr Birmingham have had a tiff, this is no way to—'

Nadine braced on her numb feet, slitted her eyes in dire warning. 'Try to have me removed and you won't be able to get a job managing a dog kennel. Julian's in trouble, and it may already be too late. The police are on their way. Open

425

the goddamn door. If there's nothing wrong you can have me arrested. If I'm right, and something happens to Julian because you won't open the door, I'll do everything I can to persuade Lieutenant Dallas to arrest you for accessory to murder.'

Either murder or Eve's name had the manager stiffening.

'I don't appreciate the threats. And you can be assured we will press charges.' She nodded to Security. 'Open it. I'm sure Mr *Birmingham* will wish to press charges as well.'

'Just hurry. Hurry.'

'I'm going to ask you to step back, ma'am.' The security chief swiped his master, eased the door open slightly. 'Security,' he called out.

Nadine ducked under his arm, shoved through.

'Julian.' She rushed across the room, dropped to the floor beside him. 'Call an ambulance!' She turned him from his side to his back as the security man crouched beside her. But even as he felt for a pulse, Julian stirred.

'Julian! Wake up. Talk to me. Julian.'

'Tired.' He slurred it out. 'Too tired.'

'Julian, what did you take?' She saw the wine bottle, the broken glass. 'What did you put in the wine?'

'Wine. Sleep.'

'No. Stay awake.'

'Let's prop him up.'

Nadine shook her head, reared back, and cracked her palm across Julian's face. 'Stay awake!' She slapped him again.

'Go 'way. Tired. Sick. Didn't mean t'do it.'

'Don't touch that,' Nadine snapped at the manager as she crossed toward the broken glass. 'Don't touch anything. This is a crime scene.'

'That's my line.' Eve strode in, laid a hand on Nadine's shoulder as she checked Julian's pulse, then peeled up an eyelid to check his pupils.

'OD'ing. Keep him talking, get him on his feet, try to make him walk. Roarke, start looking for the drugs. They'll be somewhere we can find them without too much trouble. He's got a better chance if we can tell them what he took. You were right to get the field kit. Saves a trip back down. You—' She pointed at the white-faced manager. 'Go down, get the medics up here quick and fast – and don't come back.'

She shoved the woman out the door.

'Sleeping pills – in with the wine bottles. Empty. K.T. Harris's prescription.' Roarke glanced back as Eve bagged the wine bottle. 'He didn't miss a trick.'

She brought over an evidence bag. 'Seal up if you're going to touch stuff.'

'How bad is it?' Roarke murmured as Nadine and Security dragged a nearly unconscious Julian around the room.

'His pulse is weak, barely there, and his pupils are the size of Pluto. It's pretty damn bad, but it would be over if Nadine hadn't tuned in. Where the hell are the MTs?'

Determined, she marched back to Julian, shoved her face into his. 'Walk, goddamn it. Don't you fucking die on me. Where did you get the pills? Where did you get the wine?'

His head fell forward; Eve shoved it back. 'Stay awake,' she ordered as Roarke stepped over to take Julian's weight from Nadine.

'Sleeping pills.' She glanced at Roarke. 'Somnipoton.' She considered options, went with instinct. And plowed her fist into Julian's belly.

'Dallas!'

'I'm not sticking my fingers down his throat unless I have to.'

He coughed, gagged, slumped. She hit him again. And nipped back to save her new boots when he doubled over. He vomited heroically.

'Lovely,' Roarke muttered.

'It's one way to pump a stomach. Keep him walking.'

He moaned now, staggered a bit, as she took a sample of puke into evidence.

'The MTs are coming,' Nadine called out.

'About damn time. Walk him into the bedroom – and Roarke, stay with him. They can work on him in there, keep clear of my crime scene.'

She pulled out her communicator. Time to call in the team. As the medics rushed in, she pointed to the bedroom door, shook her head at Nadine.

'You don't want to be in there. It's not going to be pretty and I don't want him talking to you yet, if he starts to talk. Roarke? Stay with him.'

'Do you think he's going to make it? I thought he was dead when I finally got that tight-assed *bitch* to open the door.'

'I think he's going to make it. I know if you'd gotten here a half hour later he'd have been dead. You saved his life.'

Nadine swiped at her damp eyes. 'I didn't make him puke.'

'I have that effect on people.'

Sniffling, Nadine found a seat, peeled off her ruined shoes. 'Do you think I can get a drink – a real drink? From room service.'

'Fine with me. Just don't drink anything from in here.'

Nadine limped over to the 'link. 'Yes. I want a vodka martini, dry as the Sahara, three olives. And I want it pronto.'

She sat again. 'How did Steinburger get him to take the pills?'

'Let's hope Julian's able to tell us. Got some blisters working there,' Eve noted.

Nadine winced, continued to rub her feet. 'Shut up.'

'Since you earned them in the line, let's see if the MTs have something for them.' Even as Eve spoke, one of the medics stepped out of the bedroom.

'Status.'

'Cleaned him out good. He's conscious, feeling like serious crap, and stabilizing. We got him hooked up to an IV, get some fluids back in him. He doesn't want to go to the hospital.'

Eve glanced over as Peabody and two uniforms came in. She gestured toward Nadine, turned back to the MT. 'Does he need to?'

'Guy downs a buncha downers with his Cabernet or

whatever, he needs some help. That's auto into Psych for eval and observation. Twenty-four hours.'

'It wasn't attempted suicide.' She tapped her badge. 'It was attempted homicide.'

The MT looked dubious, but shrugged. 'You say so.'

'I say so. Is he recovered enough, physically, to stay here?'

'Guy hadn't barfed most of it up before we got here, you wouldn't be asking. He needs to have somebody with him to monitor, but he's stable enough. Pretty fried, but stable.'

'Somebody will stay with him, and I'll have a doctor examine him.'

The MT looked around, glanced over to where Peabody took Nadine's official statement. 'Guess that's it then.'

'Thanks for your help.' Eve stepped into the bedroom. Roarke sat on the edge of the bed with Julian propped up on a mountain of pillows. His face remained nearly as white as the linens as they carried on a halting, murmured conversation.

'You can tell her,' Roarke said. 'She'll help you.' Roarke rose. 'The MT said clear liquids would be fine, for now. I'm going to go order him something up.'

'All right.' She moved over to the bed, looked down at Julian.

'Record's on. Do you need me to read you your rights again, Julian?'

'No.' His voice rasped out, and he winced as he swallowed. 'Throat's sore.'

'I bet. Where did you get the pills?'

'I swear to God, I didn't take any pills. I just had a couple glasses of wine.'

'Where did you get the wine?'

'Joel brought it over last night. He knew I was … upset. We only had one glass each. I've been drinking too much since … you know. I drink too much, I guess, when I'm upset.'

'So Joel brought you the bottle of wine, but you didn't finish it last night.'

'Just one glass each. And it was fine. Just fine. I don't know why it made me so sick tonight. I guess, maybe, I caught a bug or something.'

'You nearly caught an OD. The wine was full of Somnipoton.'

'Sleeping pills? No, I didn't take any pills. I told the MTs. I didn't take any medication.' Agitated, he tried to sit up straighter. 'I have some of my own sleeping pills – Delorix – but I didn't take any. I don't think.'

He rubbed a hand up and down his throat, closed his shadowed eyes. 'I don't think I did,' he repeated. 'I don't remember taking any. Things get mixed up when I drink too much.'

'The sleeping pills were K.T. Harris's prescription. The empty bottle was in with the other wine bottles.'

His brow furrowed in a combination of puzzlement and pain. 'That doesn't make any sense. I didn't take her pills … did I? Why is this happening?'

'You talked to Joel tonight before you came back here. What did you talk about?'

431

He looked away. 'I was upset. I've been upset, and I can't think straight when I'm upset. He said I should come back, have some of the wine he gave me, take a whirlpool. Relax.'

'He said, specifically? For you to drink the wine *he* gave you?'

'Yes. It's a nice wine, and I promised him I'd have a couple of glasses. I'd have a glass of wine while I relaxed in the tub, but I just didn't have the energy for the tub, so—'

'If you had, you'd have drowned just like K.T.'

'I don't understand, not any of this. I guess I'm being punished.' He let out a shaky breath. 'I told Roarke.'

'What did you tell Roarke?'

'That I killed K.T.'

'Julian, are you confessing to the murder of K.T. Harris?'

'I didn't murder her. I didn't, but . . .' He let out a breath again, but this time it was an exhalation of relief. 'I killed her.'

'How?'

He stared at Eve with red-rimmed eyes dull against the gray cast of his skin. 'I'm not sure.'

'You're not sure? How do you know you killed her?'

'Because I knocked her down. I didn't mean to, but she pushed me, and I pushed her. Not hard, but I shouldn't have. I *never* put my hands on a woman in violence. Never. Never.'

He had to stop, squeeze his eyes shut a moment while he calmed his breathing. 'There's no excuse. I know that. Drinking's not an excuse, being upset isn't an excuse. But she was screaming at me, and she shoved me, and without thinking, I pushed her back. She slipped, and she fell back and hit her head.'

'Back up a little, okay? You went up to the roof with K.T. Harris on the night of her death?'

'Yes. I should have told you, but Joel . . .'

'Joel Steinburger told you not to tell the police. You told him what happened, and he advised you to lie to the police.'

'He was just trying to help me. Protect me. It was an accident. I got drunk – after dinner. It was such an ugly thing she said. And she got me aside after. I told you about those two girls, from the club. I didn't know they were underage. She said she was going public with all of it if I didn't . . .'

'What?'

'She said to meet her up on the roof, and she'd tell me what I had to do. I shouldn't have gone up. I wish I hadn't, but I was goddamn sick of her threatening me. Everyone. So I did.'

'Was the dome to the pool open or closed?'

'What? Ah, closed. I remember that. I can remember that because she was smoking – a lot, and it was too warm under the dome. I thought about having a toke, to tell you the truth. But all I had to do was stand there and breathe.'

'Why didn't you open the dome, get some air?'

'I . . . I didn't think of it, but I don't know how anyway. I was so pissed off. She said I had to get Marlo in my trailer. I was supposed to give her a drink, and it would have some Rabbit in it so she'd want to have sex with me. I said I wouldn't. I'd never do that to Marlo – to anyone. But Marlo, she trusts me. We're friends. Jesus, Jesus.'

He passed a shaky hand over his face. 'I'd never slip any woman Rabbit, but especially a friend. It just made me so mad when she said that's what I had to do. How could she want anybody to do that?'

'You told her no.'

'I told her to go to hell. I think. It's all mixed up, but I know we yelled at each other. I think I said some really hard things to her, and she slapped me, then she shoved me. I shoved her back, and she fell. The strap of her shoe, I think the strap of her shoe broke and she fell. There was blood, and I couldn't wake her up. I got so scared. I was going to run down and get help, call an ambulance, or something.'

'Is that what you did?'

'I started to, then Joel said . . .' He rubbed at his face, hard this time, as if to scrub the memories to the surface. 'It's all mixed up. He said not to worry. It would be fine, but then he said she must've gotten up, or tried, and fell into the pool. And she drowned. He said it wasn't my fault, but you'd say it was, because busting a celebrity for killing a celebrity made *you* a celebrity. And I'd go to prison, even though it was an accident. I'd lose everything and go to prison forever.'

'Listen to me. Look at me.'

He met her eyes, pressed his lips together. 'Am I under arrest?'

'I could arrest you right now, starting with obstruction of

434

justice. K.T. didn't get up and fall into the pool. She was dragged in while she was unconscious.'

'I didn't do that.' His breath began to hitch and tear. 'No. I didn't do that. I couldn't have. I know I was mad, and I was drunk, but . . . I couldn't have done that. I don't remember. I was going to get help.'

'You got Joel.'

'I don't know. Did I? No. That's what's so mixed up because I didn't go get him. He was there, and he said he'd take care of it. Then you said she was dead. I didn't drown her. I couldn't have done that to her. I never hurt women. I shouldn't have pushed her. I'd never have pushed her if I hadn't been drinking, if she hadn't said those things about Marlo. But I'd never have put her in the water. It was an accident.'

'No, it was murder. But you didn't kill her, Julian. Joel did.'

'That's crazy. Please, it had to be an accident.'

'It was murder. And if Nadine hadn't come, he'd have killed you tonight, setting you up to take the fall for him.'

'Not Joel. You're wrong.'

'I'm right. Tell me, was he ever alone last night, out there? Did he ask you to get him something out of another part of the suite? After you both poured that one glass of wine.'

'He wanted to see the pages for the scene we were doing today. I keep them in the bedroom. I always read the pages one more time, last thing.'

'And that gave him the time to add the pills to the wine, plant the bottle, even put the bottle away so you wouldn't be tempted to have more until he had a solid alibi.'

'He made me promise not to drink any more last night. But . . . no.'

But she saw it begin to sink in.

'It all got tangled. What I thought happened, pieces I remembered, what he said happened. It didn't fit right, but he said . . . He was just there, when I ran out of the dome, to the lounge. I told him what happened. He said . . . he'd take care of it. Not to tell anyone. Not to spoil the evening for the others. He killed her. He was going to kill me. Why? Why?'

'It's kind of his hobby.' She looked over as Nadine opened the door.

'Can he have a break? Some food?'

'Yeah. We're done for now.'

'Joel,' Julian said quietly, staring hard at his own hands. 'Joel. He's almost like a dad. He let me think I killed K.T. He let me think I did that. And it made me sick to think I had. Am I going to be arrested?'

'No. But don't lie to me again.' She walked over to Nadine. 'First, contact the house doctor – or if you want to call in a favor, tag Louise. He should have a doctor look him over.'

'I already tagged Louise.'

'Okay. Second. He's going to talk to you, and you're going to get fodder for that book you're thinking about. Keep it under wraps while I go nail this fucker closed. But you can leak – in, say, thirty minutes – that Joel Steinburger's been arrested.'

Eve walked out. 'Peabody, with me. You, too,' she said to Roarke, 'if you want to.'

'Always.'

'I bet Steinburger's having brandy and dessert about now. Let's go spoil his after-dinner liqueur.'

Since Roarke owned the place, with all its raw brick, deep wood paneling, and dark red leather, Eve knew she didn't have to badge her way in.

She just wanted to. Wanted to cause the sort of scene that drew an audience and tipped tags to the media. She glanced at her wrist unit. Nadine had a five-minute head start.

She'd earned it.

'Sir.' Spotting Roarke, the maître d' sprang to attention. 'I'll have a table ready in just a moment.'

'Joel Steinburger.' Eve held up her badge.

'Of course. Mr Steinburger and Mr Delacora are enjoying dessert. I'll show you to their booth.'

Eve had already spotted him – a rear corner, facing out. See and be seen, she thought. He swirled brandy, an important and satisfied look on his face as he spoke with his wiry, wild-maned companion.

'I see him.' Ignoring the maître d', she crossed the restaurant.

Steinburger's expression changed when he saw her approach. The furrowed brow, she thought, a mix of annoyance and concern. Then the polite resignation as he set down the brandy, started to rise.

'Lieutenant. Nick, this is the genuine article. Lieutenant Eve Dallas, Nicholas Delacora.'

'A pleasure,' Delacora began.

'It's probably not going to be. Sorry to interrupt.'

'Has there been an arrest?' Steinburger asked.

'Funny you should ask. Joel Steinburger, you're under arrest for the murder of K.T. Harris, for the murder of A. A. Asner,' she continued, spinning him around, yanking his hands behind his back as he blustered. 'And the attempted murder of Julian Cross. He didn't die,' she added.

Dishes clattered; the murmur of conversation turned to a buzz.

'You've lost your mind.'

'Oh, and we've got more.' She cuffed him. 'A lot more. Hope you ate hearty, Joel, because you won't be dining in style for the rest of your life. You have the right to remain silent,' she began, and reeled off the Revised Miranda while diners gaped. 'Officers.'

The uniforms she'd called in took Steinburger by both arms. 'Book him, Peabody. Additional charges to come.'

'My pleasure, sir.'

'I'll be along shortly.'

She enjoyed, a great deal, watching the cops perp-walk Steinburger out.

'Sorry about dessert,' she said to Delacora. 'It looks good, too.'

'Is this a joke?' he demanded.

'No. It really does look good.' She frowned when she saw

Roarke talking to the maître d', walked to him. 'Look, I'm sorry if arresting a murderer puts people off their dinner, but—'

'On the contrary, I think it stirred some appetites. Including mine. I'm hungry and I'm not risking food poisoning from Central's vending machines.'

'I don't have time to sit down to a fancy dinner.'

'We're getting it delivered.'

'Oh.' She angled her head. 'Good idea.'

23

Naturally he ordered enough for everybody, but Eve couldn't complain since she was stuffing rosemary chicken in her mouth while she stood in Observation.

'I can't believe he didn't lawyer up yet.' Peabody scooped up a fingerling potato.

'He's too pissed for a lawyer – yet. And he needs to prove he's in power. He's Joel fucking Steinburger. He's still thinking of spin, too, I bet. Let's take Valerie first, let him soak in it a little longer.'

'She's scared,' Peabody told Eve. 'The uniforms said she shook all the way here when they picked her up on Accessory. And cried all the way through booking.'

'Then we've primed the pump.'

Tears began to trickle down Valerie's cheeks the minute Eve and Peabody walked into the interview room.

'Please, you've made a terrible mistake. This could ruin my career.'

'Gee, I bet K.T. felt the same way when you and Steinburger killed her.'

'What are you talking about! We did no such thing. I'm getting a lawyer.'

'Okay.' Shrugging, Eve rose again. 'That's going to take a few hours, given the time. Peabody, take Valerie back to a holding cell.'

'No! No!' As if to anchor herself in place, Valerie gripped the table. 'Don't put me in there again.'

'That's where you wait until your lawyer clears. Meanwhile we'll be talking to Steinburger. I'm sure he'll have fascinating things to say about you.'

'This is crazy! I haven't done *anything*.'

'Sorry, we can't talk to you once you've requested a lawyer until your lawyer is present. Peabody.'

'No! I'm not going back in that cell. I'll talk to you now.'

'You are waiving your right to a lawyer?'

'Yes. Yes. Let's just get this straightened out.'

'Who left the theater on the night of K.T. Harris's death?'

'K.T.' Valerie hunched her shoulders, gripped her forearms. 'I saw her go out as soon as the houselights dimmed. Julian went out a few minutes later. I'm not sure how long, but a few minutes. And then, well, a few minutes later, Joel went out.'

'Anyone else?'

'Yes. Connie went out the side door. I only noticed because I was going to move over to her, ask her some questions about the buffet, for a story. But she slipped out even before K.T. And – and Nadine Furst, she went out. That was after everyone else.'

'Now try reverse. Who came back?'

'Connie, but close to the end of the show. And Nadine. I

441

don't think she was gone long. Ten or fifteen minutes, maybe. I wasn't paying *attention*.'

'Keep going.'

'K.T. and Julian didn't come back, but Joel did. He was only gone a little while. Fifteen minutes, maybe. Not much longer than that. But I'm not sure. Honestly, I was getting some work done. That's the truth.'

'Why didn't you give us this information before?'

'Joel asked me not to. He said Julian and K.T. had argued, and she'd had an accident.'

'When did he tell you this?'

'That night, the night it happened. We were working on a statement for the media, and I said something about seeing people going in and out. I asked if he'd dealt with Julian, and how he wanted to handle it if he leaked he'd passed out drunk. And I was upset – anyone would be – and I wondered if the police were going to push at Julian because he'd left and hadn't come back. That's why I wanted to know if Joel had been with him.'

'And, Joel said?'

'He said we all had to do what was best now for each other, for the project. We had to protect each other, and then he told me what had happened. That it had been an accident, one she'd brought on herself but one Julian would pay for if the police knew he'd gone out after her. He said he'd take care of everything, and all I had to do was say I hadn't seen anyone leave.'

'So you covered up a murder.'

'He said it was an accident. He said you'd twist it into a murder because you'd get more play out of it, with all the stars involved, you'd ride on it for months. Besides, K.T. was a hideous excuse for a human being, all right? I worked my *ass* off to keep the worst of her out of the media, and she never had a good word to say to or about me. Julian's a sweetheart. So when Joel Steinburger asks me to keep quiet to keep Julian's head off the block, I keep quiet.'

'For a price.'

Her mouth thinned. 'He offered the bonus. Yes, I understood it was a bribe. I would've done as he asked without it, but I wasn't going to turn down the money.'

'So you lied for him again, the very next day.'

'I was at his place. I was working, but . . . he did go out, at least for a while. He said he had a date, and he wanted my discretion. He and his wife are estranged, but he's still married. It's perfectly understandable he didn't want anyone to know he was seeing someone. He's entitled to a private life.'

'What time did he come back?'

'I don't know. I swear.'

She covered her face with her hands. 'God, how did this get to be such a mess.'

'Lying and covering up will do that.'

'I was just trying to do my job. That night I went to bed about midnight, and I checked, but the lights were still on in the foyer. The next day, before you talked to us about the detective, Joel called me into his office. He pointed out it would be easier, less complicated, if both of us had an alibi for the night before. As it was, neither of us did, and that would mean we'd stay under suspicion for the death of this man neither of us even knew. He said he knew he could count on me, and he said he'd arranged for the VIP suite, since I'd be so busy – and that my creativity and loyalty would be rewarded.

'He makes and breaks careers. He was making mine.'

'And because you lied, Julian Cross almost died tonight.'

Shock radiated as her voice pitched in panic. 'What are you talking about? What happened? Is he all right?'

'Think about it. Think about how many lives your career's worth.'

Eve walked out, leaving Valerie weeping.

'Are we going to stick her with Accessory After the Fact?' Peabody asked.

'We'll leave it to Reo and her boss. Ready for the main feature?'

'Oh yeah. There's crème brûlée. I hid some so it wouldn't get scarfed down. I'm counting on this interview to work enough calories off for me to eat mine.'

'Then you take the first shot at him.'

'Hot dog! Bad cop?'

'No, Peabody.'

'Damn it.' Peabody's face fell. 'You want me to soften him up so you can come in for the kill.'

'Let's stick to our strengths and nail this bastard.'

'Then crème brûlée.'

'Then crème brûlée.'

*

Peabody went in first, alone. She worked on looking slightly intimidated as she read the data into the record.

'Lieutenant Dallas will be here in a few minutes. Can I get you something to drink, Mr Steinburger?'

'I don't want anything but an explanation for this outrage. I'll be speaking not only to your commander, but the chief of police and the mayor.'

'Yes, sir. I should let you know that, well, there have been some discrepancies in your statements. I realize the lieutenant may have ... I realize this may seem like jumping in with both feet, but there are those discrepancies.'

'What are you talking about?' He slapped a hand on the table. 'Be specific.'

'Well, specifically, we've spoken with Valerie Xaviar. She now states she saw Julian, and you, leave the theater for a time after the victim exited same – and she further states you told her the victim had an accident. Prior to the discovery of the body. So ...'

'And you take her word over mine?'

'I'm sorry, sir, but she was pretty, well, specific. And then there's the fifty thousand you transferred to her account. And the fact that you had an account under an assumed name. Um ...' Peabody looked through the files as if searching for the name. 'B.B. Joel.'

'I do that for privacy, and Valerie had earned a bonus. Though I'm rethinking that matter now.'

'Yes, sir. She also mentioned that you went out on the night A. A. Asner was killed.'

'She's mistaken.'

'She was reluctant to give us that information. The lieutenant believes her. Especially with the incident tonight involving Julian Cross.'

'*What* incident? Be specific.' This time he pounded his fist on the table. 'I was having dinner with a friend tonight, as you very well know. I haven't seen Julian since I left the studio late this afternoon.'

'But you went to see him last night.' When Steinburger hesitated, Peabody pressed, gently. 'You'd be on hotel security. You took him a bottle of wine.'

'He wanted company. He didn't want to spend the evening alone. So I took over a bottle of wine. And I limited it to one glass, as he's been drinking more than he should. He ... hasn't been himself.'

Playing me, Peabody thought, and felt those calories burn. 'He ingested two or more glasses of that same wine tonight, along with an as yet unknown amount of Somnipoton.'

'Oh my God. Is he all right? Is he in the hospital? I should have known, should have known he might ...'

'You were afraid he might try to harm himself?'

Steinburger shook his head, looked away.

In Observation, Roarke sipped from his own glass of wine.

'You're not supposed to drink alcohol in here,' Eve told him.

'Arrest me. But let me finish this first. Aren't you going in?'

'She's playing him like a flute. He thinks he's manipulating her, running the show, setting it up so – dead or alive – Julian

446

takes the fall. But she's calling the tune. She's doing a damn good job.'

'Wine?' Roarke said, lifting the bottle.

'No. Jesus.' Then she took his glass, and a minute sip. 'Pretty good stuff. I'm going to let her string him a little longer. So, want to open another bottle when we get home, and have half-drunk sex?'

'I think of nothing else every waking moment.'

He dropped an arm around her shoulders as they watched Peabody work.

'Sir,' Peabody said, honesty shining from her eyes, 'I've got to be straight with you. You're in some trouble here. The conflicting statements, the money, and – well. What I want to say is if you know something, now's the time to tell us. Me. The lieutenant's running hot.'

'Then she should cool off! You expect me to turn on a friend? On someone who counts on my support?'

'Maybe that friend needs help. Maybe he needs to get that help if he – he may not make it, Mr Steinburger. It doesn't look good. Julian's in a coma, and the doctors say he may not come out of it.'

'God. Oh God.'

'Let me do what I can here. While I have the chance.'

'Julian.' He covered his mouth with his hand. 'Poor Julian. I shouldn't have left him alone tonight. He said he would be fine, that he wanted time to rest. He's been so – he's been torn up about K.T. It wasn't his fault, Detective Peabody. You have to understand, it was an accident.'

'What was?'

'Let me explain.' He drew in a breath. 'Let me explain what happened. When Julian didn't come back to the theater, I got concerned. I knew he and K.T. were at odds, and both had been drinking. I went up to the roof.'

'Why the roof?'

'It's where K.T. went to smoke those damn herbals she's addicted to. When I got there . . . It was too late.' He reached across the table. 'She was floating, facedown, and Julian was in shock. He was washing blood off the pool skirt, and barely able to speak.'

'She was in the pool, facedown, when you got to the roof?'

'Yes. Yes.'

'And you didn't attempt to pull her out?'

'It was too late. She was dead.'

'How do you know?'

'Julian said. He said she'd fallen. They'd argued and struggled, and she'd fallen. And when he'd tried to get her up, he passed out. He thought he'd blacked out, you see, and when he came back to himself, she was dead in the pool. I'm afraid that while he was in shock, under the influence, he – he dragged her into the pool. He tried to cover it up. He couldn't clearly remember, you see.'

'What did you do then?'

'I took him downstairs. He was in no shape to talk to anyone. He all but passed out on the sofa.'

'You didn't go for help.'

'It was my help that was needed, Detective. I wanted to

protect Julian. He needed my protection. It was too late for K.T. It was an accident, Detective Peabody.'

'Let me get the details straight, so we can lay this out for Dallas. You followed Julian up to the roof, where he'd met K.T. In the pool area – under the dome, right?'

'Yes, yes.'

'The dome was closed.'

'Yes, of course. It's October. The entire area reeked of K.T.'s herbals. It was sickening.'

'I guess you didn't think to open the dome.'

'Connie prefers it closed in the fall and winter. She swims every morning.'

'See, that's another discrepancy. The dome had been opened, then closed again. But the thing is, the mechanism's faulty. It doesn't close all the way. It wasn't closed all the way after the body was discovered. And, there wasn't any scent of smoke in the dome. It had been aired out.'

'Maybe I opened it. I was in shock myself, you understand.'

'Sure. So did you open the dome?'

'Now that I think about it, yes, I did. The smell was horrible. I needed fresh air.'

'When did you open it? Before you dragged K.T. Harris's unconscious body into the lap pool, or after?'

'Oh, snap it.' Eve slapped a fist into her palm. 'That's my cue.'

Eve walked out of Observation, into Interview.

'Dallas, Lieutenant Eve, entering Interview. You should've choked down the smoke, Joel, and you should have lifted

Harris up rather than dragging her. You shouldn't have said Harris was already floating facedown when you got there.'

Eve set a box on the table, pinned Steinburger with a look. 'One, it looks really bad you made no attempt to get her out, to revive her. Second, it throws your timing off. If you'd come out after Julian allegedly dragged her in, went to get the bar rag, came back, started washing up the blood as you stated, she wouldn't have been floating. The body would have sunk first when the lungs filled up with water. They're like sponges. And it takes some time for the gases to expel and all that nasty stuff before the body floats up again.

'Added,' she said and dropped a recording on the table. 'You should have destroyed this rather than tucking it into your safe. You took that out of her bag after you killed her. I guess you wanted to keep it out of the media, yeah, but you wanted to watch it. Perv.'

She dropped K.T.'s 'link on the table. 'And you took this, which you subsequently dumped, along with a variety of electronics from Asner's place – which you took after you killed him. We know the boat you "borrowed," the time, the coordinates. The divers expect they'll pull up more tomorrow. You're keeping the water cops busy.'

'I have no idea what you're talking about. I see what you're trying to do, believe me. You're desperately throwing everything you can think of against the wall, hoping something, anything will stick.'

'Oh, it's stuck, Joel. You also lifted Harris's sleeping-aid prescription, using one of your handy pass keys. You kept the vehicle code you lifted off Asner's dead body. We've got you, Joel. There's no explaining all this.'

She dumped the entire bag of codes and swipe cards on the table.

'And last night you sent Julian out of the room, added the pills to the wine you'd so considerately brought him, corked it, put it away. So that tonight, he'd be a good boy and follow your orders. Have himself a couple glasses of wine in his whirlpool tub. The irony of him drowning would be good media, and add to your frame job. He killed himself out of guilt for killing her.'

Steinburger continued to stare at the pile of codes and cards. An angry flush worked up from his throat to his hairline. 'You went through my home.'

'Yeah. Home, office, car – and the California cops are doing the same back there. You had access to the boat, to the trailers, to homes, to offices.'

'Of course I have access. I'm entitled to go where I need to go. Do you understand who I am?'

'Perfectly. You're a murderer. Oh, but you didn't add to the tote board tonight. Julian's doing a lot better than Peabody indicated.'

'I did exaggerate his condition a little.'

'He told us everything. So did Valerie.'

'Julian would say anything to cover up what he did, and Valerie's lying for him. She's in love with him.'

'I don't think so. No, Valerie lied for you, because she's ambitious and a little greedy. Julian did what you told him to

451

do because he trusts you like he'd trust a father. And you, Joel, murder's just second nature to you. Julian would only have been the last in a long line that started with Bryson Kane, your college housemate.'

She walked behind him, leaned down close to his ear. 'And we're going to take you down for every one of them. Hand to God.'

'You have nothing.'

'Kane got tired of you buying your way through college. And because he'd had enough, wouldn't cooperate anymore, he got a trip down the stairs and a broken neck.' She pulled out the crime scene photo of Kane's body, tossed it on the table.

'Marlin Dressler, old, rich, and breathing, stands in the way of money and power you want – and maybe wasn't as keen on having you marry his great-granddaughter as he should've been.'

She tossed Dressler's photo in turn. 'A push off a cliff takes care of that.

'Angelica Caulfield, pregnant, won't let go, threatens to tell your wealthy, also pregnant wife.' Eve added Caulfield's photo to the others. 'She gets what we'll call the Julian Cross treatment – only it worked with her.

'I can keep going, right down the line. The media's going to crucify you. And I'm going to pass them the hammer and spikes while my partner and I lock you in a cage for every life you ended.'

'Who do you think they'll believe? I'm the most powerful man in the industry. You're just a cop who married money.'

'You're right. I'm just a cop.'

'I tried to help you,' Peabody said, sorrow in her eyes now. 'We have a witness who saw you entering Asner's office on the night he was murdered.'

'You're lying. No one saw me.'

Peabody nodded. 'Sometimes people work late.'

'If you think anyone will take some cheap lawyer's or sleazy bail bondsman's word over mine, you're mistaken.'

'How do you know who has the other offices on Asner's floor?' Eve asked him. 'Oops! You were there, Joel. On that floor because you contacted Asner and arranged to meet him at his office. He happened to be with someone when you contacted him. I have her statement, too. You contacted him, arranged for the meet, then you killed him.'

'That's absurd. I . . . went to speak with him because K.T. told me she'd hired him. I only went to speak with him, to buy back any data he might have gathered.'

'Was he already dead, too?'

'No. Yes. Yes.'

'No? Yes? It's hard to think under pressure, isn't it? Hard to think when it's all coming down on you. You usually have more time, more space. You get to plan things out better. You didn't wipe the bird off as thoroughly as you thought.'

One lie, Eve thought, deserved another. Why not add a phantom print to Peabody's phantom wit?

'He attacked me. It was self-defense. I only protected myself when he came at me.'

'Beating his brains out when he was on the ground? I

don't think so. Neither will the jury. You beat him to death,' Eve said, leaning in. 'Then you took his files, his electronics, his 'link – and that contact you made to it will be there. It's amazing what EDD can do. And you stole your friend's boat, took it out, dumped it all. Your friend, Violet? She recanted, on the record, her alibi for you on the night of Caulfield's death – and stated you asked her to do so.'

'That's ridiculous. Vi's simply angry with me since she's only been able to get home-screen roles. I can hardly prop up the career of every washed-up actress I've known.'

'She didn't sound angry, did she, Peabody?'

'Just the opposite. She's really fond of you, Mr Steinburger. She was really grateful for the break you gave her way back, paying her so she could hire that mag consultant. She really thought it was sweet of you to want to surprise your wife with a big party. I mean to say she really believed that's why you asked her to cover for you so she was glad to lie about you being with her and the consultant – on the night you killed Angelica Caulfield.'

'Your alibis are tumbling down, Joel. Violet's, Valerie's. With the fifty thousand in bribe money also on record now. Electronics are coming up from the river. Oh, and also from the Coast. We've got Pearlman's comps in our EDD now. Technology's advanced since you framed him, staged his suicide. We're tracking the skimmed funds back to that private account of yours.'

'Angelica was a neurotic, unhappy woman with a taste for drugs and alcohol. Pearlman was weak and greedy.'

'All that may be true, but neither of them self-terminated. You got rid of them, like you got rid of a nosy paparazzo, and a young assistant who got too clingy, an ex-wife who maybe pushed the wrong buttons. I've got nine on your scoreboard, Joel, and I'll be looking for more. If they're there, I'll find them.'

'You'll find nothing.' He reached up, loosened his tie slightly. 'There's nothing to find.'

'Maybe, maybe not. But you're done. You're over.'

'I've been in this business longer than you've been alive! I have more power, more influence than you can dream of. I'll crush you.'

'You're done,' she repeated, watching his color rise again. 'You're over. Unexpected wits, sloppy murder weapon wiping, a botched kill tonight, with Julian alive to spill everything.'

Eve let out a half laugh, eased a hip on the table – disrespect and light contempt in every gesture.

'And you just had to bitch to Nadine. She was wearing a wire, by the way, about the stench zoner added to Harris's herbals. When that was one of those little details we kept back.

'You got cocky. Getting away with murder for so long, you got overconfident. Trying for two in two days, then following it up with a third? Hey, nobody could expect some slick Hollywood type to pull that off.'

'You'll never prove it.'

'I will. All of it.' She held up the bag of pass codes. 'This? Stupid. We're smarter than you, Joel. I didn't know how much smarter until this.'

He shoved up, started to lunge at her. She was on her feet in a finger snap.

'Come on,' she invited. 'Take a shot. We'll add Assaulting an Officer to the mix. I don't mind a bit.'

'I would have made you.' He trembled – not from fear, Eve saw. From rage. 'I would have made you with this production. You'd have been one of the most famous women on or off planet. The most admired police woman in their history.'

'Thanks. But I'm just a cop, and that's good enough. It felt good to kill Asner, didn't it? You don't get to go that physical nearly often enough, do you? The pounding, the blood, the *release* of it. The power of it.'

'No one says no to me.' He swiped a hand through the air, balled it into a fist, rapped it on the table. 'I told him to give me everything he'd gathered on Marlo and Matthew, on me. And he refused. A sudden conscience, going to take it all to the police?'

The fist slammed again, again. 'Who did he think he was dealing with? Did he think he could blackmail me for more money? Stupid? *He* was stupid. He was the stupid one.'

'So you beat him to death.'

'I protected myself. My reputation. It's the same as defending my life.'

'K.T. had to go, too. Same reason.'

'I *made* her. She had no loyalty, no gratitude, no respect. I did what had to be done, and that's the end of it.'

'Not the end. You set up Julian to take the fall.'

'He's a fool. Talented, but a fool. And weak. He'd have gone to you eventually. He wouldn't have been able to stay strong. He'd have ruined himself, and me. He'd be better off dead.'

'So you were doing him a favor.'

Disgust surfaced, smeared his voice. 'He couldn't even die without being told how. I protected myself, my investment, my reputation. One I've built for more than half my life. I had every right.'

'No, you didn't. And that's the end of it.'

'Power has responsibility and privilege. You married a man who'd know that.'

'I married a man who knows more about real power than you ever will.'

'I have nothing more to say to you. My lawyers will deal with you from now on.'

'Fine with me.' She began putting the evidence bags back in the box she'd brought in. 'Be sure to tell those lawyers you're charged with multiple counts of murder, first and second degrees, and get ready for the media roasting.'

Eve smiled now. 'You're going to be a whole new kind of celebrity now – but your new status won't get you into the VIP lounge.

'Go ahead and arrange for him to contact his lawyers, Peabody, then put him in a cell for the night and go get your crème brûlée.'

'That's a big yes, sir.'

Eve walked out, passed the box to the officer waiting to

take it back to Evidence. She smiled as Roarke strolled down to meet her.

'I didn't think he'd actually confess.'

'He couldn't help himself. All those names, the data, the evidence, came at him too fast. It scared him, and he can't be scared. And I made him look stupid and weak, another unacceptable condition. Murder makes him feel powerful. He needed to feel powerful.'

'I'd say he's about to suffer a major power outage.'

'Oh yeah. You know what?' They walked to her office where she retrieved her coat. 'We closed two murders, and one attempted, and are well on the way to closing seven other murder cases. And nobody tried to punch me in the face, stab me, stun me, or blow me up. I think it's a record.'

'It looked dicey for a minute in there.'

She made a *pfft* sound as they headed out. 'He wouldn't have gotten a shot in. Plus I avoided getting puke or blood on my boots for an entire day.'

'Obviously we need to celebrate.' Roarke trailed a hand down her back as they walked. 'Half-drunk sex?'

'Works for me.'

On the way toward home and half-drunk sex, Eve contacted Nadine to give her the rest of the story.

It seemed only fair.

EXCLUSIVE EXTRACT

Read an extract from

DELUSION IN DEATH

The new J.D. Robb thriller

Available in September 2012

After a killer day at the office, nothing smoothed those raw edges like Happy Hour. On The Rocks, on Manhattan's Lower West Side, catered to white collar working stiffs who wanted half-price drinks and some cheesy rice balls while they bitched about their bosses or hit on a co-worker.

Or the execs who wanted a couple of quick belts close to the office before their commute to the 'burbs.

From four-thirty to six, the long bar, the hightops and lowtops bulged with lower-rung execs, admins, assistants and secretaries who flooded out of the cubes, pools and tiny offices. Some washed up like shipwreck survivors. Others waded ashore ready to bask in the buzz. A few wanted nothing more than to huddle alone on their small square of claimed territory and drink the day away.

By five, the bar hummed like a hive while bartenders and wait staff rushed and scurried to serve those whose work day was behind them. The second of those half-price drinks tended to improve moods so the laughter, amiable chatter and pre-mating rituals punctuated the hum.

Files, accounts, slights, unanswered messages were forgotten in the warm gold light, the clink of glasses and complimentary beer nuts.

Now and again the door opened to welcome another survivor of New York's vicious business day. Cool fall air whisked in along with a blast of street noise. Then it was warm again, gold again, a humming hive again.

Midway through that happiest of hours (ninety minutes in bar time), some headed back out. Responsibilities, families, a hot date pulled them out the door to subways, airtrams, maxibuses, cabs. Those who remained settled back for one more, a little more time with friends and co-workers, a little more of that warm gold light before the bright or the dark.

Macie Snyder crowded at a plate-sized hightop with her boyfriend of three months and twelve days Travis, her best work pal CiCi, and Travis's friend Bren. Macie had wheedled and finagled for weeks to set CiCi up with Bren with the long view to double dates and shared boy talk. They made a happy, chattering group, with Macie perhaps the happiest of all.

CiCi and Bren had definitely *connected* – she could see it in the body language, the eye contact – and since CiCi texted her a couple times under the table, she had it verified.

By the time they ordered the second round, plans began to evolve to extend the evening with dinner.

After a quick signal to CiCi, Macie grabbed her purse. 'We'll be right back.'

She wound her way through tables, muttered when

someone at the bar stood up and shoulder bumped her. 'Make a hole,' she called out cheerfully, and took CiCi's hand as they scurried down the narrow steps and queued up for the thankfully short line in the rest room.

'Told ya!'

'I know, I know. You said he was adorable, and you showed me his picture, but he's *so* much cuter in person. And so funny! Blind dates are usually so lame, but this is just mag.'

'Here's what we'll do. We'll talk them into going to Nino's. That way, after dinner, we'll go one way, and you'll have to go the other to get home. It'll give Bren a chance to walk you home – and you can ask him up.'

'I don't know.' Always second-guessing with dates – which was why she didn't have a boyfriend of three months and twelve days – CiCi chewed at her bottom lip. 'I don't want to rush it.'

'You don't have to sleep with him.' Macie rolled her round blue eyes. 'Just offer him coffee, or, you know, a nightcap. Maybe fool around a little.'

She dashed into the next open stall. She *really* had to pee. 'Then text me after he leaves and tell me *everything*. Full deets.'

Making a bee-line for the adjoining stall, CiCi peed in solidarity. 'Maybe. Let's see how dinner goes. Maybe he won't want to walk me home.'

'He will. He's a total sweetie. I wouldn't hook you up with a jerkhead, CiCi.' She walked to the sink, sniffed at the peachy-scented foam soap, then beamed a grin at her friend when CiCi joined her. 'If it works out, it'll be so much fun. We can double-date.'

'I really like him. I get a little nervous when I really like a guy.'

'He really likes you.'

'Are you sure?'

'Abso-poso,' Macie assured her, brushing her short curve of sunny blond hair while CiCi added some shine to her lip dye. Jesus, she thought, suddenly annoyed. Did she have to stroke and soothe all damn night?

'You're pretty and smart and fun.' I don't hang with jerk-heads, Macie thought. 'Why wouldn't he like you? God, CiCi, loosen up and stop whining. Stop playing the nervous freaking virgin.'

'I'm not—'

'You want to get laid or not?' Macie snapped and had CiCi gaping. 'I went to a lot of trouble to set this up, now you're going to blow it.'

'I just—'

'Shit.' Macie rubbed at her temple. 'Now I'm getting a headache.'

A bad one, CiCi assumed. Macie never said mean things. And, well, maybe she was playing the nervous virgin. A little. 'Bren's got the nicest smile.' CiCi's eyes, a luminous green against her caramel skin, met Macie's in the narrow mirror. 'If he walks me home, I'll ask him up.'

'Now you're talking.'

They walked back. It seemed louder than it had, Macie thought. All the voices, the clattering dishes, the scraping chairs ground against her headache.

She told herself, with some bitterness, to ease off the next drink.

Someone blocked her path, just for a moment, as they passed the bar. Annoyed, she rounded, shoved at him, but he was already murmuring an apology and moving toward the door.

'Asshole,' she muttered, and at least had the chance to snarl as he glanced back, smiled at her before he stepped outside.

'What's wrong?'

'Nothing – just a jerkhead.'

'Are you okay? I probably have a blocker if your head really hurts. I've got a little headache, too.'

'Always about you,' Macie muttered, then tried to take a calming breath. Good friends, she reminded herself. Good times.

As she sat again, Travis took her hand the way he did, gave her a wink.

'We want to go to Nino's,' she announced.

'We were just talking about going to Tortilla Flats. We'd need a reservation at Nino's,' Travis reminded her.

'We don't want Mexican crap. We want to go somewhere nice. Jesus, we'll split the bill if the tab's a BFD.'

Travis's eyebrows drew together, digging a thin line between them, the way they did when she said something stupid. She *hated* when he did that.

'Nino's is twelve blocks away. The Mexican place is practically around the corner.'

So angry her hands began to shake, she shoved her face toward his. 'Are you in a fucking hurry? Why can't we do something *I* want for a change?'

'We're doing something you wanted right now.'

Their voices rose to shouts, clanging with the sharp voices all around them. As her head began to throb, CiCi glanced toward Bren.

He sat, teeth bared in a snarl, staring into his glass, muttering, muttering.

He wasn't adorable. He was horrible, just like Travis. Ugly, ugly. He only wanted to fuck her. He'd rape her if she said no. He'd beat her, rape her, first chance. Macie knew. She *knew* and she'd laugh about it.

'Screw both of you,' CiCi said under her breath. 'Screw all of you.'

'Stop looking at me like that,' Macie shouted. 'You freak.'

Travis slammed his fist on the table. 'Shut your fucking mouth.'

'I said stop!' Grabbing a fork from the table, Macie peeled off a scream. And stabbed the prongs through Travis's eye.

He howled, the sound tearing through CiCi's brain as he leaped up, fell on her friend.

And the bloodbath began.

Have you read them all?

J.D. Robb's new thriller
Delusion in Death
is available in September 2012